Rinkmates
NOVA BANKS

The Mates Series Book One

Trigger Warnings

This story contains explicit sexual content, profanity, mild violence, and topics that may be sensitive to some readers. For a detailed list, click here or scan the code below.

Reviews are crucial for indie authors

Thank you so much for reading and taking a chance on this series. Reviews are crucial for indie authors. If you could take a moment to share your thoughts on Amazon and/or Goodreads, or just leave a rating, it would mean the world to me! Thank you immensely!

Love,
  Nova

Playlist

For a deeper dive into the story, check out these songs that I listened to while writing Rinkmates. Each track adds a little extra layer to my characters. You can find the playlist on Spotify or scan the code below to access it directly.

1. Bois Lie - Avril Lavigne feat. Machine Gun Kelly
2. I Will Wait - Mumford and Sons
3. Face Down - The Red Jumpsuit Apparatus
4. The Bad Touch - Bloodhound Gang
5. I'm a Mess - Avril Lavigne feat. YUNGBLUD
6. Meddle About - Chase Atlantic
7. Rumors - Sabrina Claudio feat. ZAYN
8. But Daddy I Love Him - Taylor Swift
9. this is me trying - Taylor Swift
10. Love To Lose - Sandro Cavazza feat. Georgia Ku
11. Sweet Disposition - The Temper Trap
12. I Think I'm OKAY - MGK, YUNGBLUD
13. Avalanche - Avril Lavigne
14. I Was Made For Lovin' You - YUNGBLUD
15. King - Florence + The Machine

Playlist

16. Sex on Fire - Kings of Leon
17. Time to Pretend - MGMT
18. Hide and Seek - Imogen Heap
19. Hello Sunshine - Super Furry Animals
20. California (the OC theme) - Phantom Planet

To everyone who thinks their invisible scars don't matter: they are unseen memories etched on our souls, and they do matter.
You matter.

One

RILEY

"We need to talk," Ethan says firmly.

"Are you breaking up with me?" I say, but my publicist doesn't think I'm funny.

On the contrary, his facial expression worsens as he throws his phone in my face.

"Shut up and read."

Swallowing hard, I take his smartphone and read the headline of *The New York Times* Sports section and—oh damn. I'm so glad we're sitting on this bench right now.

Hockey game in New York leads to further fisticuffs. Huntington is on the hunt for drinks and a ton of trouble again. Is this the end of the star player's career?

Ethan theatrically throws his hands up, as if pleading with the universe to comprehend the monumental headache of handling my shit.

In any other circumstance, I would have another witty comeback ready, something along the lines of *They call me Deadshot for a reason. My shots come like a hammer, just like my fists,* but…well, not today.

Because right now, we're far from the rink.

We're sitting in a fucking police station, watching the harsh fluorescent lights cast shadows on the worn linoleum floor beneath my shaky feet while my assistant, Nina, works her magic nearby. She's trying to salvage my tattered reputation after I lost my cool again and gave a rival player a lesson in bar breaking. Great for viral videos, not so great for my image, which has gotten worse and worse over the past few years.

I've had numerous discussions with my coach, and the only thing keeping me from losing my contract is my status as the top scorer in the league. But despite leading in scores, my coach made it clear that the lawsuits—*yes, plural*—and negative media coverage were tarnishing the league's reputation, and if I don't improve my behavior, I'd be let go.

And yet, here I am, tucked away in a quiet corner of the NYPD station's rear office with an alcohol-drenched shirt and someone else's blood on my jeans.

Classic.

My career's over.

Ethan lets out another dramatic sigh and snatches his phone back. If I didn't already feel like a mess, his judgmental gaze would do the trick. So, I glance away, trying to ignore headline after headline spreading across his smartphone while I run my free hand through my jet-black hair. *Fuck. I fucked up.*

Since I don't know what else to do, I try to focus on Nina.

She's standing across the office, separated by a large window, with her back to us. Her tight coils of black hair bounce with each fervent gesture as she argues in my defense, desperately trying to talk me out of it. When they brought me here, I felt as though I was a child again, being ushered into the back room and warned to stay silent while they worked to get me out again.

But alas, even with Nina's efforts, all I can see are three stone-faced police guards and a disgruntled PR manager, pointing at me, clearly blaming me for *everything*. But how could they not? I can't even be mad at them. The Boston Bears are missing their center for tomorrow's game.

I practically smashed Houston with my fists.

My gaze locks with his agent and I offer him a smile.

I refuse to show any remorse in front of him. I don't regret socking the fool, he deserved it, but I do feel bad for Nina having to clean up my mess. For my coach since I'll be blocked for the next game for sure.

Oh, my fucking mess of a life.

It's as if some deep-seated, self-destructive desire has been fulfilled, and at the same time, it's eating away at me.

Damn me and my left hook.

Ethan scoffs. "'Does Riley Huntington need timber? Because he chops down the bar!' 'Watch Riley Huntington taking down the Bears and defending better than their own defender.' 'Riley Huntington mistaking hockey for rugby.' 'Riley and his tantrums—a timeframe?'"

Ethan slams his phone on the bench and slumps over, his fingers raking through his usually perfectly styled golden hair.

I wish I knew what to say, but all I do is stare at the ugly floor again.

What the heck was there to say, anyway? It's not the first time I get my ass booted because of my "rink aggression." I'm an idiot. Always have been. Maybe it's time to just accept it. But there we have my next problem. I just can't. If only I could understand why this anger is consuming me from within, refusing to be swallowed down.

Away from the ice rink, I'm pretty chill; maybe a bit cocky sometimes, but mostly I like to think things through. But when it's hockey time, my brain just goes haywire.

All I see is winning.

I don't see players—I see rivals.

I see red.

After getting trounced by the Bears, that ass Houston wasted no time rubbing salt in the wound.

I know we have a code of conduct, and incidents of violence or misconduct can result in disciplinary actions. But the other teams are also aware of the code. It was a planned move, and I walked right into their trap. If I'm lucky, I'll only be benched for one game.

Despite my best friend's efforts to get me out before anything could happen, it was already too late. In just sixty seconds, Houston said the one thing that would always set me off. Jayce had no chance to talk me out of it. Even with all the anger management techniques I've learned, there was no stopping me.

And within mere seconds, my ears felt like they were getting pounded by a sledgehammer, my vision faded to black, and before I knew it, I was spitting blood.

And Houston? He was out cold.

"I thought we talked about this. I thought you learned from the past." Ethan shakes his head, and I notice his black tie lying abandoned, a crumpled heap on the floor. His light blue shirt hangs loosely on his shoulders, collar splayed open in defiance of its usual pristine state.

This is a side of him I have never witnessed before.

I used to tease him about having a broomstick up his ass because of how impeccably put together he always is, but today, that image shatters like glass around me. "I'm constantly defending you to the league, Ri. You're always on edge, and it's becoming a real problem." I open my mouth to respond, but he cuts me off. "I already told you, everyone is fed up with you. You get triggered so easily. Boy, you need help."

"We tried therap—"

"No," Ethan says, and for the first time, I feel like he's on the brink of losing it too. My gaze snaps to the tension in his jaw, the way the muscles bulge and twitch. "*You* let *me* talk now.

Keep flappin' your mouth and you'll be out on your ass faster than you can say 'waivers.' And with your reputation for brawling on and off the ice, no other team in their right mind would touch you. Everyone knows if there's a headache on the team, it's probably coming from you. We're at a breaking point here. Either you get you need to change, or I'll quit."

My throat tightens and I struggle to breathe.

So he *is* breaking up with me. Almost.

I try to swallow down what Ethan just said.

His words strike me harder than any physical blow I've ever received.

As the saying goes, the truth can be painful, and right now, it feels like my entire world is collapsing around me.

My fingers drum impatiently on my denim-clad thigh, trying not to rip them apart. How can I possibly leave the Falcons? They're more than just a team, they're my family, and our journey to the top is just beginning. Without hockey, what am I?

Nothing. Absolutely nothing.

I can't help it and stupidly blurt out, "But I'm leading in goals this season. They wouldn't—"

"Sure, but rumor has it you're a hotheaded dick making hockey look bad. Not only are you disappointing the kids who idolize you, but you're also giving everyone fodder to label hockey as the epitome of toxic behavior. Congratulations, you're turning the NHL into a laughingstock faster than you can lace up your skates. And hey, who needs critics when you're doing such a great job making hockey look like a daycare for misbehaving toddlers?"

His voice rose until he shouted the last part, and I just blink. And blink again. Wow. He's never screamed at me before.

"God, it's okay, man," I say, trying to breathe against the ringing in my ear.

"No, it's not. And all those girls swooning over you won't save your spot when your antics turn your career into something like figure skating." He takes both of my shoulders in his hands and shakes me. "Wake! Up!"

"Okay, fine. I'll take care of it," I yell back, pulling myself out of his grip.

"You've said it over and over again. I'm done."

A bitter laugh escapes my lips, almost sounding like a grunt. I'm at a loss for words, feeling incredibly uncomfortable in this situation. Laughing seems to be the only way to mask my inner turmoil right now.

"I got it, Ethan," I repeat and glance at Nina again, but the expressions on the police officers' faces tell me a lawsuit is bound to happen. "And I'll take care of the damages at the bar."

"Of course, you will, but this won't fix everything. Houston has a nasty concussion and *needs* to play. You better pray for a speedy recovery. His coach is furious, and so is the team. No parties for you until the end of the season, do you understand? They'll rip you apart."

I want to make a snarky remark about how another head injury wouldn't make much of a difference when it came to Houston, but I keep my mouth shut. After all, what good would it do? Praying seemed like the only viable option at this point. But, well, the big man upstairs has better things to do than listen to my petty requests. He must've used up all his divine spark crafting my life of luxury in the lap of a rich-ass family. All I ended up with was a trust fund the size of a small nation's GDP and a family hating my every being. So, in my case, money does squat to bring me joy.

"Look," Ethan says, dragging his hand through his hair once more. "Nina and I have been talking. We both agreed you've got incredible potential. You could go all the way to being the number one player in history. But you won't get there if you can't keep your temper in check. In fact, you're so close to losing it all, and the sooner you understand, the better. I'll be honest with you, I'm not sure you'll be a player after this season, whether we win the Stanley Cup or not."

My stomach knots as the truth hits me.

The worst part?

I knew it.

The moment Houston started provoking me, I knew it was a trap to get me off my game. I knew if I lost, it could be my last hit.

And yet, I did it anyway.

My foot taps nervously against the floor. "I'll do whatever it takes," I whisper, but as the words leave my mouth, I can feel doubt creeping in. Maybe Houston was right about me all along—just a spoiled nepo baby who doesn't deserve to be on this team. My family's influence and wealth had gotten me drafted while players like him had earned their spots. And just like that, the demons in my mind come to life again, whispering I am not worthy enough and all my success is because of my father's achievements.

Because, well, it is.

My parents were the ones who molded and manipulated me into this career, paying for everything until they saw their desired outcome of a successful hockey player son. The bitterness rises in my throat as I contemplate the fact that money can solve everything according to my parents. Everything but my damaged self.

Ethan claps me on the shoulder. "Yes, you will because there's no other choice. Houston's just as loaded as you, and I've got a hunch we'll need to go all in when we hit the courtroom. Let's hope it's just a concussion and nothing more."

The door creaks open, and out strides Houston's agent, a bald man in a tailored gray suit screaming corporate power. My stomach plummets at the sight of him, but then I notice

Nina trailing behind, her bright smile a stark contrast to his imposing presence. I make a conscious effort to reign in my emotions. After all, Nina wouldn't be beaming if it were truly the end of the world for me.

I observe as Houston's agent saunters toward the entrance, completely disregarding my existence. He swings open the front door, and we're hit with a wave of chaos from eager reporters and flashing cameras.

I cringe.

Of course, the whole circus has gathered out there to hear my side of the story after being hauled away by the cops again just three hours ago. It's only seven in the morning, but these journalists never take a break.

Nina clears her throat, and when I finally look up, my sweet assistant is giving me the evil eye. And honestly, I can't even blame her. She was thrilled to land this job. I am a star player, but, just as my dear old dad loves to say, I'm also the only mistake he's ever made. Maybe Nina is starting to think so too.

"Good or bad news first?" she says, standing there like the little shy girl she's always been.

The first time Ethan brought her along, I didn't think she'd cut it, because she looked like she was twelve. She's always flaunting her pink lip gloss, sporting merch from pop stars, and gulping down three hot cocoas daily. But here she is, outshining Ethan and me in handling lawsuits with finesse. She's a maestro with numbers and a pro at connecting the dots, and when it's time to call out my shit, I'd rather it come from her than Ethan. I bet those policemen were pleased to chat with her and not us. Ethan is the grumpiest guy I've ever met and I'm me. She's dazzling. Her flawless brown skin and infectious smile could thaw the iciest of hearts. Despite our rocky start, she's become something akin to my little sister.

"Bad," I mutter, ignoring the disapproving look Ethan is giving me. I guess every word I say is bound to be off today.

"They won't drop the case, so it's going to court," Nina says.

I rake my hand through my hair in frustration. Damn it. Mercer, my coach, will kill me. The team will. Dad will.

"But," Nina interjects, wagging a finger at us, "they're leaving the statement up to us and won't use any footage against us, so we can control the narrative."

Ethan lets out a sigh. "The *narrative*. You mean him being an idiot?"

"Absolutely not," she exclaims, feigning shock, as if I haven't acted like a complete fool—which we all know is the case. "We'll make it seem…less foolish, but yeah, okay, it's clear we need to change things."

She looks at me and I don't say anything, so she raises her eyebrows and I nod. "Yeah." Yes, we do have to change something.

And that something is me.

News alert. I've been struggling with myself since birth.

"Oh, and…" Her voice falters, and I sense her struggle to speak.

"What else?" I ask.

"Well…" She hesitates, her gaze dropping to the floor, biting on her lower lip.

"Out with it." Ethan gestures impatiently, urging her to speak faster with a wave of his hand.

"You won't like it, but your father posted bail, so we're free to leave," she adds reluctantly.

I lean back, my head banging against the wall. Of course he did.

"He called me and said you didn't pick up and—"

"Nina," I groan, cutting her off midsentence. "I didn't respond for no reason. I wanted to shut him down."

"Oh," Nina murmurs, her gaze flickering.

"It's okay, he always finds a way to use his money on me.

Thank you, though. Thanks for pulling all the strings in there, you're an angel," I chime in, offering her a strained smile as I push myself off the bench, feeling the ache in my muscles from colliding with several tables.

"Wait." Ethan's voice stops me in my tracks.

I turn around, my tall frame towering over Nina now. I notice her swallowing nervously as Ethan speaks again.

"I hate to repeat myself, but Riley...this is it," Ethan says sternly, his green eyes locking with mine. "You need to pull yourself together and remember it's not just your job at stake here. Ours is too."

I slump my shoulders in defeat, cursing my inability to separate work and personal matters. But before I can utter another pathetic excuse, Ethan interjects, "So, let's make sure we don't waste your talent. We have an idea about how to pull you out of this, but we'll discuss it later—when you're sober. For now, trust that Nina has everything under control." Ethan turns to face her. "You have everything under control, right?"

Nina straightens up. Her gaze locking onto him, her dark eyes suddenly wide as saucers. "Y-yes!" she says, sounding almost on the verge of adding a formal *sir, yes, sir*. "I had an idea to fix it all," she adds, looking up at me. "But we'll need to make some changes. Okay, a lot of changes."

"I'm aware..."

"Ri, all you have to do is cooperate. Understand?" Ethan says.

I shift my gaze between them and suddenly get the sense that they're up to something big. I want to ask for details, but Ethan interrupts me with his trademark scowl. "Go home, freshen up, and do something non-hockey related. Clear your head and, um, no girls. We'll come visit you later."

"Something non-hockey related that doesn't involve girls?" I say with a smirk playing on my lips. "It might be a challenge."

"You'll figure it out," Ethan grumbles as Nina chuckles

until she catches his icy glare, prompting her to clear her throat and straighten up once more.

"Thank you, guys," I say, meaning it and wanting to finally get out of here, but Nina points to a back door, urging me to use it instead.

"You don't have to confront them, Ri," she says gently.

I shake my head. "I chose to punch the guy, so I have to face the consequences."

"You just want to give your TikTok girlies something to obsess over again," Ethan says, sighing.

"That's what you said," I say.

Nina rolls her eyes but hands me my sunglasses. "Just remember to keep your shades on this time, your eye looks… unwell. We don't need a repeat of last month's headlines."

I take the glasses and want to ask where she got them, but I drop it because Nina always has everything I need at hand. She's like my fairy godmother, ten times faster than everyone.

I slide on my black sunglasses and run my fingers through my hair, attempting to tame the unruly tangles. But despite my efforts, some stubborn black strands still hang in front of my face, brushing against my cheekbones. My shaggy haircut has grown out a bit too much for my liking.

"Yeah, we have enough to do with the ones this week," I hear Ethan grunt once more as I push open the front door, mentally readying my best PR smile. I may have ruined a lot tonight, but thank God I negotiated for a hefty cut of the merch sales. After all, if my antics are going viral, I might as well cash in.

Two

LIORA

According to my mom, God places strangers in our lives to get us to higher places.

What if, in my case, the stranger will get me in a basement? Killed?

I may be dramatic, but those are exactly the kind of thoughts I have while mentally slapping myself right and left for agreeing to rent a place through Instagram. Who does this?

It's dangerous.

Stupidly dangerous.

I haven't been online in like five fucking years, but since I couldn't find a place I could afford in New York, I posted on my story asking if anyone knew of a shoe box I could live in. Stupid, I know. And just like someone unscrewed my lightbulb, I agreed to meet with the first person who seemed halfway nice and real.

Desperate times and all...

My hand clenches around the old luggage next to me. It reaches up to my hip. It seems big but it's actually all I have and I'm not even exaggerating. My suitcase contains my entire life within its twenty-seven-to-thirty-two-inch confines.

Yes, I'm so broke that I'm still standing right where the airport shuttle bus spit me out, waiting for someone I've only FaceTimed with once.

A girl named Nina.

What if this Nina doesn't even exist?

What if someone catfished me and I'm meeting with a Sven. Or a Brutus. Or—

"Hey, Liora!" a voice rings out and I jerk up. "Liiiiiiiooooora!"

My attention is drawn to the noisy source, and I see Nina, full of bubbly energy, breaking through my panic dream like a ray of sunshine.

I glance around again, fully aware everyone at this busy train station now knows my name. *Hi, New York. This is me. Liora James. The girl who quit the Olympics even though she was running for gold.*

With each click of her heels on the pavement, Nina sprints toward me, evading the pedestrians as if she were the police chasing a burglar. Oh my.

Her face lights up with an apologetic smile, holding a frappuccino that looks like it has been through a hurricane. The trail of evidence behind her is a sticky brown disaster zone. "Oh my goodness," she gasps between breaths as she comes to a halt.

Her frame casts a shadow over mine by a solid three inches. "I'm so sorry for being late, hon. You know how New York can be."

I blink at her but muster up a grin. No, I don't know how New York can be, but I see a lot of cars and busy traffic, so I imagine it's easy to get late.

"Are you ready to see the apartment?" Nina's excitement bubbles over, her smile lighting up the gray space around us. I try to mirror it, but my stomach churns with nerves. The TV show I'm auditioning for today could be a life changer, but now that it's actually happening, I'm terrified. Nina has been nothing but supportive since I explained why I needed to move to New York, which is why I agreed to stay with her for six months. Her spare room is a godsend.

And she's definitely no Sven or Brutus.

"Sure. Thanks for picking me up again, I'm a total country bumpkin." Not gonna lie, all these people and the constant car honking and the noise are already getting to me.

"No problem, I'm your personal city ranger!"

We head toward the subway, and I relax a little. I'm relieved to find she's just as warm and genuine in person as she is through the screen.

Nina slurps her frappuccino and chats about the habits of true New Yorkers all the way to the subway station. She even had a MetroCard ready for me, and I think it might be easy to be friends with Nina. She seems like the type of person everyone likes. I'm not. Back home in Orlando, I don't have many friends aside from my mom and good ol' Dan. Our eighty-year-old neighbor.

"How was the flight?"

"Good, I mostly slept through it." I had to wake up so early, I felt like a complete zombie. On top of that, I haven't flown in years, which just added to my jittery nerves. With the casting happening today, I'm basically running on autopilot.

"I'm sooo jelly of your skills, girl," Nina says as we perch on the subway seats, my luggage wedged between my legs. "I once tried figure skating, but my legs aren't cut out for it. My feet always twist, and then my ligaments tear. Don't even ask."

"Oh, I'm so sorry."

"It's okay. I started working as an assistant for hockey players, so it all worked out. I still get to skate for free on my days off."

My eyes practically pop out of my head. "No rink fee?" I'm

floored. Typically, a single public skate session can cost up to twenty-five dollars per day.

"The apartment is near Chelsea Piers. It's just a five-minute walk and we've got some free tickets to spare from the team, so you can practice as much as you want! That's the perk of working for a hockey player." She winks at me.

I remind myself I'm human and need to breathe. This just seems too good to be true. An apartment with an actual roof and...a rink? "Which team do you work for?"

She looks at me as if I should know this. "Um, the Falcons?"

Damn. I suppose I should have remembered, but with my hectic work schedule, things tend to slip my mind. Plus, I have a bad habit of quickly scanning through messages without fully absorbing the information. I guess that happens to your brain when you work three jobs. "Oh, my bad. I think I mixed something up from our messages."

"It's okay. Not everyone is into hockey or knows all the players."

My face splits into a wide grin as I realize she works for one of the most famous hockey teams in the damn league. Like, seriously?

It's then I notice posters of their star players plastered all over the train. I resist the urge to roll my eyes and focus on one player in particular. The one with chin-length black hair and the fucking perfect, toothpaste smile. I know him from somewhere. I guess he came up on my For You Page a few times, punching around like a little kid who didn't get his candy. He's flanked by two other handsome players. Buzz Cut and Maroon Man Bun. They're all probably just as cocky and douchey as they look. I mean, have you ever met a humble hockey player?

Nina nervously fidgets with her fingers, her voice quivering as she asks, "You...you don't like hockey?"

"Not really. I mean, I used to watch some games back in

the day, but men who trash bars on a regular basis aren't exactly my type." No thank you.

Her lips twist into a grimace, but she regains her composure in a matter of seconds.

"Oh, let's see if we can make this work then," she says.

I mentally kick myself for my thoughtless comment about her favorite sport. Shit. She's going to be my roommate. I should be nice. What is wrong with me? It's clear I have lost touch with polite interactions after years of dealing with my trailer park boys and cranky customers while working bars and restaurants. I make a mental note to work on my social skills.

"Sorry," I add quickly. "My last experience wasn't the best. You know, sharing the rink and all." I let out an uncomfortable chuckle, and she responds with a similar awkward smile.

The train jolts and screeches as we sit side by side, avoiding the topic of skating or hockey entirely. On the way to her apartment, we talk about our favorite food and we actually have something in common. We both love sushi, so that's something, right? I think rooming with her could work. Food connects after all.

Eventually, Nina leads me to a luxurious complex I immediately try to pass by. But she stops me with a pointed cough and gestures excitedly to the building.

I'm not sure what she expects from me, especially since she knows I don't have much time for sightseeing. I need to be ready in an hour.

"This is it!" she exclaims, throwing her arms up in the air. "Home sweet home!"

My heart does a nervous pirouette. What the actual— "This is...the...*apartment*?"

Nina nods, smiling brightly.

I take another look, and my eyes keep going up. The building basically looms over me, all sleek and modern, with massive floor-to-ceiling windows showing off nothing but wealth. My internal warning sirens blare again.

"Um, I don't think I fit in here." I pull the white cardigan over my blue leggings, suddenly feeling all too self-aware. It looks perfect, too perfect for someone like me with a budget stretched thinner than ice in spring.

"No, it's okay. Believe me." Nina takes me by the arm, nudging me to the entrance.

I stumble after her, as if she's going to throw me in a beehive. But she can't be serious. She told me she'd have a wonderful, totally affordable apartment for me. Apparently less than seven hundred dollars per month. I should have known this was gonna be a scam. This isn't a cheap-ass apartment, it's the kind with a fancy doorman and gleaming golden initials above the entrance.

I stop in my tracks.

"Nina," I protest. "These apartments must cost a fortune… I can't afford to live here." My heart sinks at the thought of having to search for something else. I thought I was all set. Sure, I've got three other places lined up because I'm not dumb enough to come here without backup plans B, C, and D, but I was really hoping—praying, even—that this would be the one. Just for once, I wanted to turn those thousands of lemons into lemonade.

She comes to a halt in front of the revolving door. "Liora, it's fine. Money isn't an issue at all. Trust me. Just check it out, and if it really isn't for you, I'll let you go, okay?"

I blink at her. And blink again. My gut says don't trust her. It actually screams at me to run. How could I trust her? An apartment in this area? For me? No way.

"It will be *fine*," she repeats, dragging out the *fine*. "Look, we even have a doorman here, he'd never say yes to trouble, right, Attie? We're all nice people here."

She beams at the red-haired porter. His face lights up like a

Christmas tree covered in freckles. The blazing sun seems to have a vendetta against him, turning his ginger locks into a beacon of light and giving him the complexion of a tomato. But I guess he couldn't care less, because he's flashing a grin that makes my alarm bells snooze away a little. "I ensure that only decent individuals are allowed inside this place. Anyone who shouldn't be here won't get past me. I promise, Miss."

"Perfect, thank you, Attie. This is Liora James, by the way. She's joining us. Maybe."

Attie smiles and nods at me. "We'd be thrilled to have you, Miss James."

What. The. Actual. Fuck.

I just stand there, staring as if I've forgotten how to speak.

Their eyes are fixed on me, probably already sensing that something's off. I want to speak, to say anything, but I'm completely stunned. And when you're stunned, you're speechless—or at least, I am.

"Um, th-thank you?" is all I manage to say. Nina has a doorman. Holy shit.

As we enter, I strain my neck trying to take in the opulent ceiling of the fancy building.

The walls are covered with Italian Renaissance–esque paintings.

Shit. Shit. Shit.

This can't be real, but Attie is just like a security man, so if Nina planned to sell me to a mafia boss and ship me across the world, he wouldn't play along, would he? Oh boy. I should stop reading mafia romance novels. I'm getting delusional.

"Come on, you look like you're going to faint," Nina says and motions to an elevator. "You'll love it."

We enter, and she takes me right up to the top with a… secret key. I swallow. She has a secret penthouse key. And I think I'm actually fainting. Or puking. Something along those lines. I thought she was taking me to a ramshackle house. I never thought she'd bring me...here. I had braced myself for a filthy rug and creaky floors. Maybe even a cat to add to the expected musty smell.

"A-a...penthouse?"

"Well, Riley loves to be alone most of the time."

"Um...okay." I recall that she talked about another friend living there. But she's busy and away most of the time, or something like that.

When Nina unlocks the door to reveal a spacious living area bathed in the soft glow of afternoon sunlight, I actually gasp. I'm 100 percent sure she's going to introduce me to a Russian don now and this is my last day. Fuck me. I should know better than to trust random people over the internet. Just because it's a woman, doesn't mean I'm safe. Women can be snakes. This is my last day on Earth, and—

"Riley? Where are you?" Nina sighs and curses, as if mentioning any ordinary roommate. But anyone living in this kind of space couldn't be ordinary. Why would anyone who lives in such a place be in need of a roommate? Nina and Riley must be rich as fuck. They don't need me.

Nina slams the keys onto a white cupboard, causing my jaw to drop once more or possibly just remain hanging open—I am not aware of its current position. I just—I'm downright shocked. This apartment is the most beautiful thing I've ever seen.

I wander around in a daze.

The floor-to-ceiling windows flood the space with natural light, illuminating the sleek, contemporary decor around me. It's an open-concept layout with the living area seamlessly flowing into the dining space and kitchen. It's all white, black, and gray. I practically stumble over nothing to the expansive views of the city skyline, feeling humbled by the towering skyscrapers and the vastness of the urban landscape below. I think a little screech left my lips. At least, I hope it was little.

This is insane. The kitchen itself is bigger than my trailer…

I'm struck by the attention to detail, from the elegant artwork adorning the walls to the luxurious finishes throughout the apartment. And then I spot various hockey trophies and some pictures of…and more pictures of…I gulp.

Hell no.

My heart drops into my pants.

What's his name again…

Oh no. There's this really funny feeling in the pit of my stomach now.

This can't be true.

"Um, Nina? Riley is a *girl*, right?" I ask, trying to keep my voice level as I turn to face her.

"Who says I am?" a dark voice rises behind me.

I jerk around.

First I see the shadow, and then I look up and up and up and see him. *Him*.

Not just anyone, but Riley fucking Huntington—*the* Riley Huntington. The sexiest hockey player alive, whose face graces billboards and magazine covers.

I think TikTok wouldn't have much content without him. Even the damn subway we just rode was practically covered in his face.

Now he stands right before me and his presence fills the room like a storm cloud rolling in, and just like that, the air feels oh so charged. I don't smell cats. No. I smell sandalwood. Amber. Musk. All kinds of alluring smells.

I swear I can't breathe anymore.

This is it. I'm done.

Thank you for all the months I was granted to live on this planet. But rest in peace, Liora.

"You're suddenly mute?" Riley says.

I stupidly shake my head, trying to ground myself as I stare at him like a guppy.

Nina wants me to room with *him*?

She said it would be a piece of cake.

But there's nothing easy about being around him. I mean, he's got a nasty lawsuit on his hands, and that's just the tip of the iceberg. Nothing simple about that situation.

But as he just stands there, I'm starting to think Nina meant he's like a cake. A total eye-candy cake. A towering six feet, three inches of pure sexiness in gray sweatpants and a black shirt with a bold NY Falcons logo—there's no mistaking him. I'm definitely in Riley Huntington's penthouse.

My eyes can't help but drop to his chiseled pecs, which seem to be making a guest appearance through his hoodie.

I find myself gripping the couch's backrest like it's the only thing keeping me from falling over.

Swallowing, my gaze flicks up to his tousled black hair, framing his handsome face as his intense eyes lock onto mine.

My pulse stumbles like it's drunk.

A strange feeling passes between us as our eyes lock, almost like an electric shock. It's fleeting, but in that moment I see a hint of...well, what was it? Hatred? As quickly as it came, it disappears and he reverts back to his stoic demeanor, but I can't help but wonder what sparked that quick flash.

Yes, he's breathtaking. And intimidating. So intimidating.

I know hundreds of girls will hate me for it, but I can't do this. I can't. I need to get out of here.

"Ri, this is Liora." Nina tries to save the situation, but I can barely hear her over the sound of my heart crashing against my ribs. We still stare at each other, and it seems like we're running out of time. Of what time though? I just met him. This is a bad sign.

"No," I say, and his eyes darken.

I notice that his sleeves are rolled up and my eyes are drawn to his forearms. There are scars. And muscles. And tattoos. Lots of muscles. And tattoos. "No," I repeat.

"No? No to what?" His head turns to Nina, who nervously bites her lips.

"We talked about things that need to change, so..." Nina taps her feet on the white marble floor. "Ethan and I had an idea, Liora is going to participate in a TV show and needs a place to crash, and you...well, you need a chaperone. So we thought she could move in for free and help us out!"

I blink at her. Um, what?

"Wait, actually, I think there's been a mistake," I blurt out, the words spilling out of me like a clumsy stumble. The sudden urge to fucking run hits me like a slap shot to the chest. "I thought you had a friend, a girl, who wanted me to move in with you." I point at Nina so that it's clear I mean her. "To take her room or whatever and, well, pay for it? You mentioned someone named Riley, but I thought it was a girl. Not... not...*him*," I say, my voice tinged with disbelief. I thought this was going to be a straightforward housing arrangement. Something that normal people would do.

Nina's lips stretch into an awkward smile, her cheeks flushed. "Yeah, I might have left some things out...there's a bit more to it. I thought I'd explain it to you two once you see each other. I thought you might say no otherwise?"

I scoff and notice Riley looking at my hand still clutching his couch. "You left out everything, Nina. I think that's a rather nonsensical idea and I'm not a charity case." I totally am a charity case.

"Wait, this isn't a joke? You're actually wanting Liora James to move in with me to play my fucking babysitter?" Riley interjects, his tone dripping with sarcasm. I have no idea why, but the sound of my name on his lips struck me like an arrow to the chest.

"Look, Liora," Nina continues, cutting off Riley's protests with a raised hand. I'm surprised his assistant would do something like this without him even knowing. "It's a win-win situation for both of you. You won't have to pay a cent—"

"Excuse me," Riley tries again, but Nina barrels on, her words tumbling out in a rush, forcing him to shut his mouth once more.

"You get to live here, train on the rink whenever you like, and all you have to do is keep an eye on him," she finishes, her voice laced with a hint of desperation, as if I'm her last hope. It's ridiculous.

"'Keep an eye on him?'" Riley and I say as if from one mouth.

"What does that even mean?" I demand, struggling to process.

"You know Riley's reputation," Nina says. "This could be the perfect PR coup. Everyone loved you back in the day, and once you're on *Grace on Ice*, you need publicity to—"

Riley scoffs. "You shit on the Olympics for a reality show? Are you kidding?"

I glare at him, my nerves giving way to a surge of anger. I know him from social media, and I've always hated him, with his cocky attitude and his belief that he's invincible on and off the ice. The way he flashes his stupid, handsome grin every time a camera is on him. It's just gross. I learned the hard way to stay clear of pretty boys.

"No, I'm sorry, Nina," I interject, my voice firm. "I appreciate the offer, but I can't live with someone like him. Money isn't everything in life." I'll sleep in a car. Whatever. But not here.

Without waiting for a response, I turn and practically sprint out the door. Nina calls after me, but I shake off her attempts to stop me. This was a mistake.

Riley Huntington is a violent prick. I can't live with someone like him. If I wanted to live with an ass, I could go find my father. Or my ex-coach.

Just as I slam the door shut, Nina swings it back open again. I frantically jab at the elevator buttons, contemplating the merits of taking the fire stairs for a quicker exit. I just can't believe my life.

"Nina, I—"

"Listen, I know this sounds crazy. But we *really* need you. He's on the verge of ruining his career, and he needs someone to keep an eye on him when we're not around, and you're perfect for it."

"That's what therapists are for," I mutter under my breath, silently urging the elevator to move faster. How tall is this damn building?

"It's more complicated than that, and this arrangement could benefit you too. We'll make sure you have everything you need. Is there something missing here, Liora?"

"Yes, a half-decent roommate. I can't live with someone who's prone to violent outbursts. I'd like to wake up in one piece tomorrow, thank you very much."

"No, he's not violent, I swear. I wouldn't offer you this opportunity if he were. He just struggles with anger issues on the ice, but there's so much more to him. He's actually one of the most genuine people I know, and deep down, he's really sweet. I promise! I wouldn't let you run into anything dangerous. Have you ever heard of fake relationships? It's just pretend and he's barely at home—" The elevator chimes and I step inside, but Nina holds the door open, her expression pleading. "Look, it's New York. Finding a safe and affordable place to stay at such short notice is nearly impossible. You could be waiting months, even years, to find something decent."

"I'll figure it out, thank you but no," I reply tersely. Sleeping in a car isn't ideal, but it beats risking getting beaten up over a trivial disagreement, like looking at him the wrong way or whatever sets off this giant man-child.

As the elevator doors start to close, Nina jams them open

again, cursing under her breath. "I swear, he's helped me through so much. He's genuinely kind and decent. Just give him a chance. Google him if you don't believe me.

He just loses it on the ice when rival players provoke him. It's a guy thing."

"Just. Yeah," I say. "I'm sorry, Nina, but I'm the wrong girl for you." This whole situation is absurd. I can't blame her for not mentioning it before, as any person with an ounce of common sense would have declined her offer.

"Liora, please. Let's get in there and talk. Get to know each other?"

"Thank you for considering me. I wish you all the best."

Nina pushes the doors open one final time. "You've got my number. Call me anytime, day or night. I'll be there to pick you up, okay? The offer still stands."

I scoff as the elevator doors finally close. Play chaperone for Riley Huntington. A fake relationship. Sure, they'll probably ask me to sleep with him for money next. Yeah, not a chance.

Three

RILEY

Nina shuts the door, the sound louder than it should be.

"Careful there," I say, sitting on my couch and googling Liora James.

There she was, standing in my living room like a forgotten relic from my past.

I never thought I'd see her again after she disappeared from the public eye years ago. It's like she was erased from existence. She used to dominate the headlines as a US figure skating princess, poised to bring home all the medals. And just like that, she vanished in the middle of the Olympics.

"Of course, you messed it all up again. I should have come with Ethan," she grunts. "But here I am trying to solve things alone. Great idea."

"Look, I didn't agree to any of this," I say, halting in front of a familiar photograph that still sets my pulse racing. After all these years and women that made me forget my name at times, it's still her that makes my stomach flip. There she is, sitting casually on a bench at the rink, a sly grin on her lips, almost daring me to unravel the mystery behind those blue eyes. Her hands are folded neatly between her thighs, that snug purple dress accentuating every curve just right. With her blonde locks and that angelic face, she's always been a vision of temptation for me.

My father forced me to watch several sports championships, including the US figure skating nationals. He has a thing for sports bets, and I guess it was an attempt to get me onto it, too, but I was eighteen when I saw her. I didn't care a bit about my father's bets on her. I'm not exactly proud of it, but her face was the reason I started to beat the meat on a daily basis.

From that day on, I watched every championship she competed in. I even had a nickname ready for her. Lia. I was one crazy teenager.

And today, that girl almost moved in with me.

I could never tell Nina why I didn't think this would work, but fuck—it wasn't for lack of words. It was more about the fact that Liora was too tempting. I would be desperate to fuck her at some point, and besides my father, there's only one other thing that could get me to run: the thought of binding myself to someone. To lose myself. It wouldn't work. It never did, and especially not when she still looked the same, maybe even more captivating now. That ass in leggings. Shit.

Nina interjects before the silence can stretch into discomfort, "Riley, I'm afraid you don't have much choice here. Your image needs serious rehab if you want to stay in the league and I thought Ethan made it clear that you have to cooperate. No matter what."

"Your heroine ran away from me and now you're blaming me for it?"

Nina gives me that *you know what you did* look, but I shrug it off. "If she can't stomach a little remark, it's not a good idea to move in with me anyway."

"You mocked her job, Ri…"

"You know, just like I do, that a reality show isn't a place for someone like her. She's been a legend. I never saw someone as talented as her on the ice."

Nina narrows her eyes. "Since when do you watch figure skating?"

I snort. "Everyone who reads the sports section knows her. I'm just saying she should try to compete again."

"Well, it's also common knowledge that it's over at her age. She's too old."

"Please. She's twenty-four."

Nina dramatically flails her arms in front of her face. "Hold up! Why on earth do you know her age?"

I clear my throat, feeling a bit caught. "Just a casual google search. I mean, you wanted her to move in with me, I had to check on her." She's three years younger than me. I even know her birthday. It's September 18.

Nina shoots me a suspicious glance.

"Anyway, it's a moot point because she's not keen on moving in with me."

"Oh, she will be."

"What was your grand plan, anyway? Her moving in and playing bouncer while she takes me hostage in between games?"

Nina grins. "Yeah, pretty much. Ethan and I thought you two could fake a relationship. Just until the season wraps. It boosts your PR, and she gets a nice roof over her head and maybe some more calls to keep her in the show. Win-win."

My heart pounds like a bass drum at a rock concert.

Liora James pretending to be *my* girlfriend? Nina must have gone mad.

"Absolutely not," I protest, shaking my head vigorously. The mere thought sends a shiver down my spine, though not entirely unwelcome.

"We said all you have to do is play along!" Nina's

frustration is palpable, her expression teetering and close to a full-blown tantrum. "Is *this* playing along?"

"You failed to mention I'd be sacrificing my personal space to live with someone." To *live* with *her*. "How would you feel if I dropped a random stranger into your apartment?"

She snorts. "Please, you're used to having random girls over every night."

"Yeah, but they leave in the mornings."

Rolling her eyes, she lets out an exasperated huff. "You may be right, maybe I should have warned you, but I was afraid you'd say no and vanish. Listen, you've got more rooms in this place than I have plushy socks. And trust me, that's saying a lot. We'll turn that empty room into something special just for her, make it so she'll never want to leave! Plus, with your crazy schedules, you'll hardly ever see each other. We'll just have to take some staged photos every now and then to keep up appearances. The media will eat it up—they'll think you're a reformed playboy, all thanks to the power of love. And when the season is over, and her show is done, you both can separate again, and during season break, you'll finally have time to work on your anger management at that posh facility down the street."

Her monologue is over, but all I can do is stare at her. "Please tell me you're kidding."

"I'm not."

"Fuck. This sounds like you're going crazy, you do know that, right? Do you want me to call that posh facility for you now?" I stand up and pretend to check her temperature on her forehead. "Yup. High fever. I need to get you to the doctor, nugget."

"Idiot," she says and slams away my hand. "Just imagine it. You'll be the bad boy turning over a new leaf with the help of Liora, who plays the sweet little fixer-upper for you. You'll have the perfect excuse to skip those tedious parties, fewer brawls to deal with, and on top of it all, we can work on your anger management. It's an amazing deal. And let's not forget the publicity she'll bring once she announces her comeback. You remember the media frenzy she stirred up five years ago?"

She grins, knowing that she's right. "It's almost too good to be true!" she adds.

"Because it isn't true. Plus, there really was a huge uproar when she withdrew from the Olympics. The haters gave it their all," I say, recalling all the comments I'd read, and maybe a few punches I threw for defending her honor whenever someone bad-mouthed her. Maybe.

"People are idiots. I'm sure she had a damn good reason," Nina says, her tone resolute.

"And what if she's secretly a serial killer? Or did something really messed up that got her booted from the Olympics?" I tease, knowing it'll get under Nina's skin.

Nina grunts in frustration. "I swear, one comment like this to her and I quit."

"Ah, look at my little girl revealing her inner beast."

She emits another grunt, and I half expect her to growl next. "It's her or no one, Ri. I think she's practically in dire straits financially."

"Be honest with me, you think we'll actually benefit from this?"

"It'll definitely shift the focus away from your mess. And no one will question why you're laying low until the end of the season, because you're busy loving that wonderful girl, understand? We've got to give it a shot. You know it," Nina insists.

I squeeze her in a hug. "This is an insane plan, nugget."

"But aren't those the best kind?"

"I hate publicity stunts…"

"You'll love it," she says with a wink.

There's something in the way she said *you'll love it* that pricks at my heart, a strange sensation I can't quite pinpoint.

Just the idea of Liora moving in here makes me...uneasy? No, it's something else. But regardless, I don't think Nina's plan will actually happen. She was basically killing me with her glance. *I can't live with someone like him.* She hates me.

"Helping each other out is what friends are for, right? Either way, you still owe me that pizza. Stress eating is the only way I can cope with your drama."

"Ah, yes, the pizza debt," I reply with mock seriousness. "But what about your friend out there? Should we save her a slice or two, because I don't think she'll show up here again."

Nina shrugs, settling into the couch like she owns my damn place. "We wait. She needs a place to crash, and I have a feeling New York's charm will work its magic for us. She'll be back soon enough. Trust me. You may be a challenge, but your apartment is drop-dead gorgeous."

Four

LIORA

Everything comes down to the next three minutes.

Relaxing? Not a chance.

"Quiet on set!" The command blasts out, jolting me upright as I step onto the ice. Seriously, these TV people and their constant shouting. While I was waiting, they yelled at everyone and everything.

"Just skate to the middle, right where the white *X* is and wait," a woman dressed in all black tells me and rushes to the back.

I glide across the ice, my worn skates leaving precise cuts in its smooth surface, and I do as she says.

The rink I'm standing on is oval shaped and behind me is a backdrop of large, high-definition LED screens showing some vibrant graphics in blue and yellow. Surrounding it all are the audience seats. Hundreds of them.

Who would have thought that I'd land here one day?

Reality shows were not part of my plan—ever. But here I am, trying to snag a spot in one. Talk about a plot twist.

I'm not entirely sure what I'm waiting for. But the sound of my music has always been my cue to start. I just try to maintain my posture and wait for the crew to start the song I chose.

I look confident. At least I hope I do.

But deep inside, I am so jittery that I'm questioning my choice of drinking four cups of coffee on the way here. No one should drink this much coffee in an hour.

My heart pounds like a runaway train, thudding against my chest as I take in the figure skaters standing behind the rink, waiting for their shot. The arena is filled with top-level skaters, all dressed in colorful and attention-grabbing outfits.

I stare back, practically hearing them gossiping and nodding at me like I'm some kind of spectacle. It's like they're not even here to perform. They're here for the drama—to find out about all the thousands of mistakes that landed me here.

"One minute, we need to get the cameras right," a booming voice rears up again.

"Okay!" I say to wherever that voice came from.

Fidgeting with the thin, see-through fabric of my cheap Craigslist dress, my heart sinks as I notice missing pearls on the neckline and fraying edges along the hem. Oh for crying out loud. Everyone else in the room seems to be dripping in designer gowns and sparkling jewelry, making me feel so out of place.

What if they know that I lived in a trailer for the past few years? What if it shows that I ate nothing but cheap food, what if— No. I shake the thoughts off and remind myself why I'm here.

It's my shot at a fresh start. *He* needs me to be strong for the both of us, and I am.

I try not to think about how I've scrimped and saved these last few months, scraping together enough to get some practice time in. Rink fees aren't kind to the wallet of a waitress who used to compete on the world stage.

I lift my arm over my head and stretch. I've got this under control.

I'm no stranger to skating. This shouldn't be difficult for me. Yet, this audition feels like the most challenging thing in the world. I take a deep breath and force a smile onto my face, straining to see the judges through the bright lights on the stage across from me.

"Music starts in three," another faceless voice behind the glare of several studio lights calls out.

My eyes adjust to the lights and land on Grace Holland, the mastermind behind this TV show that bears her name: *Grace on Ice*. She was a former US pairs figure skating champion. She and her partner, Maxwell, were *the* figure skaters in the United States. No one has won as many medals as them to this day. She was my idol and now she holds my fate in her hands. If she says no, I can't take part in her show. And it's my only chance at a normal life again.

"Sixty seconds!"

Letting go of the hem of my skirt, I force myself to get into my starting position, flashing an even bigger smile for Grace as her cold eyes follow my every step. Her once fiery red hair is now tucked into a sleek, gray bun. Her piercing blue eyes hold an intense stare. The chairs on either side of her are empty, leaving me alone to face her judgment. My heart races as I try to maintain my composure, but her presence alone makes me feel small and insignificant. Memories flood my mind—she was a judge at the US figure skating nationals where I won in my category. But that was five years ago, and when it comes to skating, five years is a lifetime.

I raise my hands over my head.

When another voice counts down from ten, I close my eyes and take a deep breath.

I feel the hot light on me.

Five. Four. Three.

I open my eyes.

Two.

I position my foot to push me off.

One.

The music starts and muscle memory kicks in.

Gliding onto the ice, I carve deep arcs with each stroke of my blades, the cold surface whispering beneath me. As I build speed, my body tenses with anticipation, ready to execute the intricate dance of jumps and spins that have defined my life. With a powerful push, I take off from a backward edge, jump, and rotate in the air before landing it perfectly. When the music amps up, I kick it into high gear, riding the wave, and when it calms down, I gracefully move my hands in fluid motions, allowing them to follow the beat as if they have a mind of their own while I swirl and jump.

The melody switches, getting more desperate, and I lose myself in the choreography.

Spin, leap, glide—each element a testament to a resilience borne of necessity.

The final note of the music echoes through the rink, and I come to a stop. My chest heaves from both exertion and nerves as I hold my ending position. I raise my arms up toward the sky, feeling my spine curve as I attempt to force another smile on my face, desperately searching for any hint of approval from Grace.

I squint, trying to see through the blinding spotlight shining into my eyes.

It feels like being attacked by a pack of aggressive fireflies.

But was it enough? Was I enough?

Silence stretches out and my thoughts start to spiral once more.

My technique wasn't exactly flawless.

With limited time and funds for proper rehearsal, or well-fitting skates, it's been hard. I didn't skate for five years. Yet, the familiar burn in my muscles reminded me that I still had it in me. Should be enough, right? It's just a dance show, after all. Yet, this wasn't your ordinary skate by any means.

If they pick me, it means I'll have to skate two more times just to get onto the TV show, and then I'll be paired with a famous celebrity. They haven't announced who's joining yet, but once we're paired up, we'll compete for a *million* dollars. And that's exactly why I'm here. The fast money. My one-way ticket out of hell.

And boy, did I need it.

I quickly glance at Grace, who's jotting something down in her notebook.

I pray that the blue dress I had chosen would be enough. I spent extra time doing my makeup and curling my long blonde hair—because, in figure skating, looks are just as important as talent, no matter what anyone says. The pressure on your body in this sport is unreal.

I hope the curves I got over the years are a good thing.

"Thank you, Miss James." Grace's voice finally breaks the silence. "We'll take a moment and then give our feedback."

"Thank you." I skate off slowly, my breath catching up to me.

I AM GENTLY ESCORTED out by a crew member, my blade guards sinking into the plush foam boards that cover the whole floor as I make my way toward the backstage area.

I'm greeted by a makeshift room in no time with plain white walls and a cardboard floor. Along the sides, benches full of white ice skates and bags belonging to other professionals line the walls. A simple buffet is set up on one wall, while my huge suitcase waits for me on the opposite side, serving as a reminder of my living situation.

I'm practically homeless.

Plan B was a bust too. I was running like hell after that horrific encounter with Nina and Riley, frantically calling plan B landlord, only to find out that room was gone faster than a bag of chips at a party. But well that room wasn't my favorite anyway because it had the toilet outside of the apartment. Imagine having to pee at night and leave the apartment. I'd die.

I find a spot on the bench to sit down, untying my skates. As I look around, I notice the girl sitting next to me staring in my direction. I'm well known in the world of figure skating, so I'm used to attracting attention, but her intense gaze catches me a bit off guard. In response, I lock eyes with her and find myself captivated by her beautiful features—her sun-kissed skin and that shining black hair.

We share a smile and continue removing our skates side by side.

"How'd it go?" she asks at some point, thankfully skipping the whole *why are you back* nonsense.

"Okay. I think," I reply. I've never been one for grand displays. "How about you?"

"Oh, I have no idea. I hope I did well. Grace is so intimidating. She looked like I was pissing her off." She rolls her eyes and a warm smile lights up her face, revealing a set of perfectly straight white teeth. "I'm Priya Patel, by the way." She greets me with a firm handshake, her perfectly manicured nails matching a bold red lipstick.

Memories rush in of seeing her before I took the stage. My nerves had me all jumbled up then, but her routine on the ice was something else. With her red dress and the black hair swaying in the wind, she looked like a fire bolt.

"Your routine was beautiful," I tell her, and she beams. "And don't worry. Grace has a resting bitch face."

"Thank you. Coming from you, that means a lot. I'm surprised they didn't let you in automatically, to be honest."

I fake another smile. "Grace isn't one to play favorites. I think it's good we all have to prove ourselves first." I slip my feet into the worn, gray sneakers that used to be white. They are scuffed and frayed at the edges but still comfortable. I hurriedly stuff my skates in my bag and drape my white cardigan over my shoulders, trying to hide my shabby dress from curious looks around me. From the glances I get, I think word has spread that I'm back.

But instead of constantly wishing I could disappear, I gotta toughen up. I signed on the dotted line for this TV gig, after all. If they pick me, they're bound to grill me about it. There will be interviews, media coverage…it's time to buckle down and get ready for the interrogation.

I sigh. Oh, if only things were that simple.

"I heard she's tough, that's all I needed to know to make me stand there like a deer in headlights," Priya says.

"She is," I admit. "But she appreciates hard work. Um… are you hungry too?" I ask, making my way to the buffet, wishing she'll join me. I haven't eaten in a while.

I hope she won't judge me for rushing to the buffet as soon as I have the chance. I don't want to admit that I'm desperate for any free food. But I am.

She bobs her head up and down, hopping off the bench. "Oh, thank you for asking! I'm, like, super famished right now. Where are you crashing? Oops, never mind, I can be a little busybody," she apologizes with a nervous giggle.

I can't help but break into a real smile. I think she's the first figure skater I actually like.

I was taught to see everyone as a rival—basically, anyone who's in my way of winning medals. My coach was all about that mindset. He always said there are no friends in competitions, just distractions. But I don't want to buy into that anymore. Nope, I'm done listening to his dumb advice.

I need to open up and I will.

It's time to change patterns.

"Don't worry, it's fine. And to answer your question, I'm still figuring that out," I say as we make our way toward the array of muffins, cakes, and chips.

When I submitted my application for the show, it stated in the fine print that we're responsible for covering our own expenses. And that's what's nearly breaking me—having no money, only debts, and my mom unable to help. We're both just trying to get by in our little trailer in Orlando.

My stomach grumbles in protest and I eagerly grab a large muffin with blue icing that matches the show's theme. Oh my, it's good. Each bite is like a mini party in my mouth, a buttery disco ball of blueberry flavor.

"What do you mean you're not sure where you are staying?" Priya goes for the chocolate cake as more skaters filter into the room, each one feeling like a member of a shy troupe.

We all know that even if I make friends today, our time together will be brief since only twelve figure skaters will be chosen. The daunting reality sinks in as I realize there are three initial casting groups with thirty contestants each. Only a select few will move on to the next round...but I saw her skating. They'd be stupid to not cast her.

"I had a loose promise and it turned out it wasn't for me, so I'm back to looking for a place to stay." I pick up the lost thread between bites. "But I'm checking out some more apartments later. How about you?"

Priya reaches for the bowl of chips, her long, slender fingers delicately picking up a few before dropping them into her mouth. "I live in this tiny apartment around the corner," she says between bites. "My parents wanted me to live as close to the studio as possible, since I'm alone here. They're very angsty people. But it's filled with models and influen*zas*, can you believe it? I've been here since last week and I already feel so out of place next to them. I can't even."

She shakes her head with such disgust that I can't help but laugh at how she pronounces *influencers.*

Priya stops mid-bite, gazing at the chips as if they've suddenly sprouted heads. "Oh no. Maybe they put out these tempting snacks to test our willpower and weed out the weak!"

She drops the chip, sending it on a downward spiral toward the bowl. I chuckle, unable to contain myself as her eyes balloon to cartoonish proportions.

I offer her the bowl of chips. "Come on. Eat. Don't worry, I bet they'll replace these with celery sticks soon enough. Plus, you look amazing. These chips won't do any harm."

She sighs heavily but takes more from the bowl. "Thanks, but I swear, if I gain an ounce, my room will declare war on me. It's so tiny. New York's price tags are off the charts—like, seriously."

I nod.

Yep, Grace chose one of the most expensive cities to produce her show. I wasn't joking when I said I was considering renting a cheap car and sleeping in it.

"Oh hey there, *Liora James.*"

The sudden voice startles both of us. Priya's chip crumbles in her hand like a sandcastle, leaving her sparkly dress covered in crumbs.

We turn to see a girl in a glitzy dress adorned with pearls. Shiny brown curls cascade down her perfectly made-up face, framing her sharp features.

I notice the initials of Vera Wang on her hip and almost gasp. I remember Wang designing figure skating dresses for Michelle Kwan, but now it seems she dresses Stacey Saab too. I know her from the US figure skating nationals; she was so mean to all the other girls that it was my mission to beat her, and when I did, she bawled her eyes out—didn't even manage a congrats.

I heard she got injured and had to retire from competing in major competitions.

"Long time no see. What brings *you* back?" Stacey's question makes my stomach drop and I suddenly feel sick, but I force myself to breathe through it. Of course people would ask why I returned after disappearing for so long. I'm a gold medalist, and was on my way to win gold for the second time in Beijing.

It's natural for people to want to know the whys.

And it's foolish to believe the TV producers won't exploit my story.

Like, what did I even think?

A small voice inside me insists they'll only cast me for ratings and publicity anyway. Liora James. The mystery of Team USA. I sigh, reminding myself that I'm more than just that. More than a question mark. I can do this, because I deserve it. My talent is not defined by what happened to me years ago. But just thinking about the Olympics makes me want to cry, run, vomit.

But I won't, because I'm here to fix things.

I can fix it. I will. I have some white lies ready.

And that's why I resist the urge to snap at her and channel my inner fake smile again. Oh, I'm so good at it it's actually sad.

"Stacey, it's great to see you again," I reply smoothly. "I got curious and just wanted to check out what Grace has planned for this event. What about you? You look lovely!" She does.

"Well, it's interesting to see you again for sure. You look...nice."

Stacey takes a long sip of her water bottle, her eyes narrowing as she notices the half-eaten blueberry muffin in my hand. She then casts a disapproving glance at the overflowing buffet table.

And just like that, Priya steps away from the buffet and there's a knot tightening in my stomach. It feels like a flashback, and I'm thrown back to the dark side of figure skating, where every tiny bit of fat is scrutinized under tight-fitting dresses. We are all beautiful in our own way, but body dysmorphia is a constant struggle. How do you tell the girl who is constantly judged for having curves—boobs and an ass—that less is considered more in this line of work?

Of course being back in these dresses triggers old habits within me and, apparently, Priya too. The pressure to be thin never truly leaves you in this business. But I'm disappointed in myself for reacting this way, rather than being upset with Stacey. She's consumed by the unrealistic standards portrayed by the media, while I thought I had moved on from that mindset. I told myself not to worry about it anymore, but one offhand comment and I'm back to criticizing myself. It's ridiculous, yet so easy for our minds to get caught up in. Why oh why do women tend to tear each other down?

We should be supporting and lifting up one another instead.

Smiling at Stacey, I reach for a chocolate heart, stuffing it into my mouth and trying to convince myself that I am fine. That we are all fine the way we are, because we fucking are.

"You know," Stacey's high-pitched voice fills the silence, staring at my mouth, "we've all been wondering why you, well, dropped out of the Olympics. Everyone fought so hard and you just…gave it all away."

I grip the desk next to me, my nails digging into the flimsy paper tablecloth, creating small tears.

I gave everything *away*?

I never willingly gave up anything.

If I could, I'd still compete.

And then another thought creeps up. Shit.

What if my return was actually too early?

If she of all people can get under my skin so easily, how will I handle the pressure if I get chosen? How will I speak to my followers or make a statement? Give interviews? The uncertainty of it all churns in my stomach like acid and I struggle to answer. What should I say? The truth?

No. I can't.

I just can't—

"Oh, Liora." Priya's voice cuts through my thoughts. "I think your phone is buzzing! I bet it's your aunt finally calling back!"

I blink. I don't have an aunt.

Priya's hand grabs mine and she pulls me away from Stacey.

My head spins as I try to say goodbye, but all I can muster up is a feeble wave. Look at me, getting jostled around like a human punching bag and still attempting to cling to the etiquette rule book. Priya positions herself in front of me, creating a barrier between me and Stacey's curious stare as we walk toward our bags. I quickly sit on the bench, burying my head in my lap.

I take a deep breath and just don't care if Priya sees me like this. I need a moment. Or two. Or three.

Shit. Shit. Shit.

I thought I'd prepared for this. The minute I filled out the email application I tried to mentally prepare myself for any kind of interrogation. I played it through over and over again but yeah, I guess it's time to admit that it's just more complex in real life.

It's so hard to speak about the most challenging period of one's life, and those who have never experienced true pain will never comprehend its depths.

But there's no way around it.

I need to stick to my script.

I can't turn to ice every time someone speaks of my past.

"You don't have to talk if you don't want to," Priya says softly, her hand gently rubbing my back.

I look up at her, and her warm brown eyes give such a softness that I actually relax. She smiles at me, and damn, it's surprising, but I feel like I've known her for much longer than just twenty minutes.

"She's horrible. When I arrived, she was already making another girl cry. She told her she wasn't good enough to compete," Priya says.

I swallow hard against the lump forming in my throat and manage to breathe freely again.

"Thank you," I say, squeezing her hand. "I'm so grateful to have met you."

She returns my smile with a warm one of her own. "It's okay. I just saw you needed some help and couldn't resist lending a hand."

Her eyes flick to my hand, then back down to Stacey. As she glances away, I feel a sharp sting in my palm. I slowly open my fist to see a small drop of blood pooling on my skin. The pressure of my nails digging into my palm must have caused it.

My heart races.

I didn't feel a thing.

With a soft smile, Priya reaches into her jacket pocket and pulls out a tissue, offering it to me like a lifeline. I take it.

"Thank you. Again. I'm a mess, sorry."

"No. Please. Don't worry about it even for a second," Priya says. "I've always had a sense that something big must've happened to you. But, look. I'm sure you'll make it onto the show, and you know how they are…" She hesitates, and her glance turns from kind to worried. "They'll pry. And I hate to say this, but I bet they're itching to use your story for clickbait." She pauses, as if debating whether to say more, and I jerk a little when I see my sad reflection in her dark eyes. "You gotta be prepared for when they come sniffing around, Liora."

I swallow. "Yeah, I know."

"I know we just met, but I'm here for you," she offers, and I just have this feeling that she means it.

Something must have happened.

Oh yes. It fucking did.

"Thank you, it means a lot to me," I say.

And just when Priya opens her mouth to say something else, the door bursts open and a crew member comes in. The tall, middle-aged man with a shiny bald head grips a wooden board in his hands and scans each of us. Priya takes my hand and all the skaters stare at him as if he's going to tell us right away if we've won the million dollars. But we are just the contestants from the first round of skaters auditioning. They'll select up to twelve contestants across three rounds.

"Ladies and gentlemen, please welcome the following contestants to the next round...Patricia, Priya, Liora, Molly, Tony, Stacey, and Rhett! Congrats to our lucky seven. And to the rest of you, better luck next time."

Priya's joy is infectious as she jumps up and down in front of me, but I feel like I'm watching from a distance. I've made it into round two!

I'm doing this.

I can do this.

And now I have all the power in the world to hunt down a cheap-ass apartment!

Five

LIORA

"*Köszönöm, anya,*" I say into the phone, the familiar words slipping effortlessly from my lips as I talk with my mother in Hungarian.

She's called me five times already, all worried about where I am and if everything's okay. Well, it's not, but there's no way I'm telling Eszter James that. My mom would totally freak out—she can't afford to come here and help in person, and I don't want her doing anything drastic. So, I've been telling her I'm fine.

But honestly, I'm not.

Even though I felt like a superhero with all the belief and power in the world after they told me I'd made it to the next casting round, I couldn't find a cheap-ass apartment.

After a relentless search through the city, dodging yet another unsettling run-in with a dubious landlord, I now sit perched in Priya's cramped kitchen. I'm so glad she gave me her number because even renting a car was too much for my savings. She lives in a cozy place where sunlight spills through rainbow lace curtains. Pictures and postcards cover the walls, each telling its own story about her five roommates, who seem to have vanished for the day.

Despite its modest size, there's an undeniable coziness to her apartment, with enough room for everyone to gather around the small table in the middle of the room. Each chair has a different shape and color.

"Of course, I'll keep you updated," I promise Mom. "Bye, *Szeretlek*."

Ending the call, I turn to Priya with a grateful smile. "My mom is pleased I've found a place to stay for tonight, even if it's just temporary. Seriously, thank you so much for letting me stay with you, even though we only met today."

Priya waves off my concerns with genuine kindness shining in her eyes. "Hey, I'm alone in this city too. I'm happy to finally talk with another skater. We've got to help each other out, right?" She cringes at the small kitchen and the tiny bathroom around the corner. "I know my apartment isn't much, just a mattress, and I guess my roommates will go to war with us at some point, but we'll make it work for some time. We can cuddle if needed."

"It's more than I could have hoped for, Priya, I swear I'll return the favor somehow." I plaster a smile on my face, but inside, I feel like I'm drowning.

It's been a fucking rough day, starting with an early wake-up call, a three-hour flight from Orlando to NY, and a frantic rush to get to the TV set after that shitshow with Nina. And now, on top of it all, I was faced with the harsh reality of finding a place to stay in fucking New York overnight without any money. All my funds were tied up in rink fees and basic necessities.

This wasn't at all how I envisioned my big move to the city.

All the apartments I had lined up to check out were the worst, and one was even more frightening than the thought of living with Riley Huntington.

After cooking noodles for dinner, I tell Priya all about the absurd run-in with Riley and his assistant. Priya's reaction is priceless. She sinks into the chair across from me, mouth agape. "You're kidding. Are we talking about *the* Riley Huntington?"

"Yup," I confirm, taking a mouthful of noodles.

"I say again: you're kidding."

"Nope."

Priya quickly grabs her phone and proudly displays her lock screen, revealing a shirtless Riley. "Oh. My. Gawd. Look! I'm obsessed with him."

I snicker at the sight. "That guy is so in love with himself. Gross."

"No! Don't you ever use gross and him in one breath again! He's my baby, and he offered you to live with him! I think I might die right here and now. And you turned it down? Girl, I can't believe you!"

"Well, technically speaking, it was his assistant who offered it, and I'm not an asset. I don't want to be his babysitter or whatever. What am I, his mother?"

I shake my head, but Priya just stares back at me incredulously, blinking several times. "I don't understand you."

"I did speak English, right?"

She kicks me under the table and I cry out, "Ouch, hey."

"You're insane. Can I go instead of you?"

I laugh at her enthusiasm. "Sure, I can text Nina if you like. I'd be happy to live here instead."

She shakes her head, blushing slightly. "No, my parents would kill me. I'm not allowed to live with a man before I'm married. Pretty conservative, you know."

"Sorry to crush your dream."

"But you can live it for the both of us. Go to Riley, girl. I'll even bring you to him, as selfless as I am." She wiggles her eyebrows and I break out in a laugh.

Guilt suddenly swoons over me. She probably would

love to sleep alone in a bed she's paying for. Shoot. "I promise I'll find another place soon. I've been looking everywhere, but everything is either too expensive or in sketchy areas. Even car rentals are ridiculously pricey here, and—"

Priya's face softens. Her hand stretches out across the table and envelops mine. "Liora, I didn't mean it like that. You can stay as long as you need."

I sigh in relief. "I honestly don't know how to thank you enough, but I will find a solution to this, I promise."

A mischievous glint sparkles in Priya's eyes as she makes a playful suggestion. "I have an idea. You could tell me all about how Riley is living. And I mean all of it. That's totally enough for me."

My phone buzzes and it's Nina. I sigh.

It's a photo of Riley's bathroom.

> Nina: You could be bathing in here.

I sigh again and put the phone away.

PRIYA and I have been sleeping on a tiny mattress for two days, and my guilty conscience is eating away at me.

I wanted to split her rent, but she wouldn't take any money from me, so I bought food and cooked for the both of us after we practiced at a tiny rink around the corner. Mom sent me her killer recipes, so I tried to cook them for Priya. Naturally, Mom's version was way better but Priya loved it anyway. Her roommates are understandably unhappy—okay, that's understated, they absolutely hate it that we are now a group of seven people sharing the little space. I feel terrible about the situation.

When we first went to the rink, I gasped out loud at the cost. Twenty dollars per day, and only if I go at off-peak times. I tried to search for other ice rinks, but the ones that cost less are not in the city and the subway cost would add up, so it equals the same. Damn it. If I'm unlucky and the producers don't cast me for *Grace on Ice*, I can't even afford to fly back to Orlando because I'm that broke.

But I can't put my head in the sand just now, so I paid the rink fee and tried to come up with a decent routine for the next casting round while listening to my playlist. I tried to do a double axel and fell numerous times. I just need to train more, but once my time was up, I always had someone telling me to leave ASAP, and I started to think about Nina. That stupid arrangement would come with a nice apartment AND a rink.

As I browse the grocery store, getting some spaghetti for Priya and me, Nina sends me another picture. How does she always seem to know when I'm thinking about her?

Sighing deeply, I look at Riley, teaching hockey to a group of kids. He looks genuinely happy, with a kid hanging off his shoulders and a big grin on his face. Seeing this, I feel a knot in my stomach. He just loves being in the spotlight—this is nothing more than a PR stunt. Sure, it might look like giving back to the community, but it's all part of Nina's job.

> Nina: He teaches pro bono once a month, and let's not forget all his donations to children's hospitals and hockey programs!

Yeah, she's trying hard to influence me, but I'm not buying it.

> Liora: Nice try, but it's not working.

I text back and slip my phone into my jeans pocket.

When I get back to Priya's apartment, she tells me we've got an email. They've postponed our second casting round because the third group had so many strong contestants. Apparently, they need another round to narrow them down first. Great. That means I have to wait another five days, which means more daily expenses with no payday in sight. This is going to be rough.

"Come on, it will be all right, let's eat and go back to searching for some apartments," Priya says and I nod. She's right. It will be all right.

"UNBELIEVABLE. Two hundred dollars per night, a crappy room on Airbnb," I say. "How much do you pay for this room?"

"Two thousand dollars," she says, and I look at the mattress we're sitting on. There's not much space next to it. She's got a tiny bookshelf stuffed with nothing but monster romance novels, and a nightstand that is her closet. That's it. The room really is a shoe box.

"Wild," I say.

"And I had to book it *months* prior. My parents have a friend who knows a friend who owns it. Since it's in such a good neighborhood, we just said yes."

Shit. What if I can't find an apartment? "I think I need to vomit."

My phone buzzes next to me and another message from Nina pops up. It shows a picture of Riley playing hockey with kids again. A girl with red locks is hugging his foot while he smiles at her.

"What is it?" Priya asks. "Why are you frowning this hard?"

"Nina is a PR girl through and through. Look." I give her the phone and Priya swoons in less than two seconds, she's only missing the drool pooling out of her mouth.

"This man is so hot."

> Nina: Did you find a place to live yet?

"She can't be serious. She knows I didn't," I say, stopping myself from pulling at my hair.

"Girl," Priya says. "I think you should consider it."

I wince, burying my face in my hands. "No."

Priya takes my phone, reading all the messages Nina has sent me over the past few days. She totally outdid herself, texting me more than Mom ever does. And that's practically a miracle, because I swear Mom has a PhD in texting.

Priya squeals. "Jeez! You'll get your own furniture! His PR firm is paying for everything you want, girl. Why don't you just say yes? You'll live your dream, and I can crash at your place when my shoe box is killing me."

"I can't."

"Why?"

I give her a wary glance. "He's, he's…he's awful."

"He's not."

"Did we watch the same videos about him?"

"Probably not."

"He's got problems."

"He's a hockey player, Liora. They all fight. It's hot."

"It's not."

Priya nudges me. "Come on, give him a chance. I'll be your backup plan. You can call me anytime, and I'll come get you, or call the police if needed."

I roll my eyes. "You don't know him. You just have a celeb crush."

"Yes, that might be true," Priya admits with a slight blush, "but just think about the offer. Did you see his apartment? It's in a safe neighborhood, unlike the areas we've been looking at. I think it's your safest option to live with him."

"No, I don't have the time to do whatever his PR people want me to do. I need to focus on the show, Priya."

"Okay, okay," she says. "I'm just not sure if we can find something in this short time, but I'll do everything I can."

"Thank you."

"Always."

I scroll through a terrible one-room listing on Craigslist. One thousand dollars a month for a room shared with another guy, located over an hour away from set. Yep. Not gonna happen.

I'm on the verge of launching into a tirade when Priya's doorbell rings.

She jumps up. "Oh, I think that's the new dress I ordered for the next casting round. Yay!"

My stomach drops. I can't afford a new dress. They'll get what I can afford. My old dress. I just hope it won't fall off.

As I scroll through various Facebook groups, I hear a sharp gasp from Priya.

My body tenses in response.

"What's wrong?" I yell, but she doesn't respond.

Panic rising, I grab the closest object within reach—a long, metal shoehorn—and sprint out of the room, my heart pounding in my ears.

When I reach the living room, I freeze at the sight before me: Priya is standing motionless in front of...Riley.

She's as still as a statue, not even flinching until she lets out an ear-splitting shriek and covers her mouth. And then he looks at me like I'm the one causing all the commotion.

I can feel the tension in my body loosening, but my grip on the shoehorn remains tight as I watch him. Every inch of his muscular form fills the door frame, making it seem like we're living in a dollhouse. His black hair is pulled back with a blue sweatband and his hands casually rest in his gray sweatpants, which match perfectly with his Falcons hoodie.

I lift my chin with defiance, refusing to let him unravel me completely.

He nods to the shoehorn. "Is this a threat or are you flirting with me?"

When he flashes a smirk that could charm the socks off a sloth, I swear I hear Priya swoon, clinging to the wall next to her like it's the last lifeboat on the Titanic.

I lower the shoehorn and stride toward him. "It's definitely a threat. Believe me, if I was flirting with you, you'd know it." He lifts a black brow in amusement, and I quickly add, "For a second there, I thought we were getting robbed. So, what's up with you?"

He scoffs. "You really think a shoehorn would have made a difference?"

Shrugging, I twirl the curved end of the horn between my fingers. "Oh, trust me. In the right hands, this little beauty can work magic."

"The right hands, huh?" His voice trails off as he leans casually against the door frame. "Those hands of yours are pretty small."

"Small hands, maybe. But I've got a talent for making the most of what I've got. Want me to show you?"

He grins, and I'd never admit it out loud, but that look he's giving me makes my heart jump in a very funny way.

But I'm not the only one in the room with this problem, because Priya squeals again, shattering the strange tension between us.

"I can't believe it's you," she says.

The good friend I am, I rush to her and pull her behind me. She's going to hate herself for being so embarrassingly starstruck. I guess it's like being drunk. You don't know what you say until you're sober again.

"What do you want?" I try to sound as casual as I can.

Priya does another funny sound behind my back and Riley nods to the hallway. "Can we, um, can we speak outside? Alone?"

I narrow my eyes. Why would he want to speak to me alone? Anything he wants to say, he can say in front of Priya. "Depends on why you're here?"

"Because."

My eyebrow shoots up to my forehead. "Because?" That's all he has to say?

Has he taken one too many hits to the head?

He straightens his posture and slides both hands into the pockets of his sweatpants again. When he bites his lip nervously, I resist the urge to roll my eyes. If this is his usual seduction tactic, he's barking up the wrong tree.

Riley signals for me to follow him, but I fold my arms and shoot him a defiant look. I'm no dog to be ordered around just because he thinks he's some kind of ice prince.

A sharp poke on my shoulder causes me to spin around and I face a furious Priya. She's silently mouthing every swear word known to mankind, her eyes nearly popping out of their sockets as she emphatically gestures toward him, insisting that I talk to him.

I dramatically roll my eyes and make wild hand gestures back, signaling that he's completely bonkers, entitled, and I have zero intention of following him just because he's famous.

Priya looks confused, but before I can continue my silent protest, she wrenches me around and shoves me toward him.

Thanks for the backup, Priya.

I come to an abrupt halt, narrowly avoiding a collision with this massive mountain of a man. I regain my balance and quickly smooth out my hair.

I look up, and his eyes catch the light, revealing a mesmerizing shade of whiskey.

Damn. Those eyes could drown a girl. Drown me.

No, not me. Never.

He grins, obviously enjoying my reaction, and I grind my teeth. I can't hide how I stared at him—he's infuriatingly irresistible. But it's just looks.

I narrow my eyes, trying to mask the unwanted attraction, but he grins like he just won sexiest man alive.

"Don't get any ideas," I snap, trying to ignore the way my heart flutters.

He leans in a little closer. "You mean because you checked me out?"

"Hardly. I was just wondering how someone so infuriating can also be so…"

"Charming?"

"I was going to say insufferable."

"Well, lucky for you, I'm both."

I roll my eyes. "Okay. Fine. Just let's get this over with." I nod behind him.

He smiles, a flicker of something more serious passing through his eyes. "Perfect."

Six

RILEY

My hand rests lightly on the worn wooden door frame as I watch Liora closing the door behind her.

She's so fucking tiny, standing there and frowning up at me. And all I can think about is how easy I could lift her up and throw her around in my bedroom to make her shut up and—

The door closes with a loud thud. "How in the world did you manage to track down my address?"

Damn. She looks at me like she's the one towering over me. Her piercing blue eyes are full of defiance, making it clear she's not someone you can just *throw around*. She's a wild one, and it drives me nuts.

I clear my throat, feeling the cool hallway air mix with the leftover warmth from her friend's small place. "Um, well." Shit. So how do you politely tell a girl that your assistant stalked her? "Nina found you. She's crazy good at stuff like this."

"Doesn't sound legal."

"I don't think it was."

She narrows her eyes at me and I steady myself for what I

have to do. Fuck. I've never begged before. I feel like a complete idiot asking her to move in with me. The irony isn't lost on me—considering how much I love my single life. My single apartment. My single nights. Just thinking my man cave is going to be full of things smelling like strawberries soon gives me the ick.

"Listen, I know I screwed up and I'm sorry. You got the wrong impression of me last time." I clear my throat again. Damn it. What's up with me? "I didn't mean to come off as rude. My team never mentioned their PR strategy to me either."

"That's what really turned me off, to be honest. Your own team doesn't even inform you when you have to move in with someone."

I don't tell her I want to turn her on, not off. Instead, I just say, "I suppose they were concerned that I might reject it and we'd all lose out on this chance."

And now I even cough awkwardly. Shit, I wish I'd brought some water. I probably sound like a castrated cat. This should be easy. Apologize, ask her to move in, take her home, done. Okay, good, she can't hear my thoughts because I sound like a total creep. It's not like I can't just snag her and—

"What?" she snaps, and I realize I must have looked at her like I just stepped out of reality and into the Twilight Zone.

I sigh, running a hand through my hair. "This isn't easy for me."

"To apologize? You must be very comfortable up on your high horse, huh?"

I bite my lip. What a little brat. "I am sorry."

"For what?"

Is she serious? I bite back a snarl. "For mocking your current...job."

"And?"

"And being an ass," I grunt out.

She grins, and that beauty of a smile might have knocked me out if I didn't lean against her crappy door. I quickly add, "I think Ethan and Nina had a good idea and that we should take it into consideration and go along with their plan. Let's keep it casual. You move in with me, we ignore each other but pretend to have a relationship when needed, and profit from it?"

She looks like she's contemplating it, so I keep pushing it. "Once we step out holding hands, the news will eat that shit up. You need some publicity to keep up the voting in the show, and I need everyone to think I'm settling down." I pause, hoping she'll see the practicality of it too. "It's simple."

"You think living with *you* will be simple?"

I ignore that knife coming at me and continue, "Like I said, I won't be around often. Ethan and Nina will set the terms for us later. So, what do you say? Want to move in with me?"

I flash my best smile, the one that usually melts hearts, but it seems to bounce off her like a rubber ball hitting a brick wall.

Teenage Riley would be heartbroken right now.

"Let me guess, you're always this eager?" she says, leaning against the other side of the door frame, looking up at me.

The light bounces off her little nose and there's a loud jingle in my mind, telling me that I need to keep my dick in my pants in case she says yes. Liora is my last chance. I can't afford to fuck it up. To fuck her. But she doesn't have to know what her face does to me.

"Only when the prize is worth it," I reply smoothly.

She adds a sweet eye roll for good measure. "You must've been a c-section because there's no way your mother could've pushed both you and your ego out naturally."

Ouch. I can't help but laugh out loud. "Okay, okay, you're out for blood, I see."

If she only could understand that this is my last resort.

Even Mercer got in on the act, pulling me aside after practice to sell me on the idea of a fake relationship for the sake of *our* reputation. It's not only for me. This is for the whole team. The league.

She sighs and finally speaks up. "Okay, let's assume…" I grin widely, and she continues, louder this time, "*Assuming* I say yes. How do we pull this off? Fake a relationship? It just sounds ridiculous."

"Nina suggested a minimal effort sort of relationship—me attending some of your shows, you tagging along to some games, no need for any actual conversation. Some photos here, some photos there, and we'll leave."

Her piercing blue eyes narrow, dissecting my words as if she's cutting up a frog in biology class, analyzing each condition. Then, in a split second, her gaze snaps up, and I'm left hanging, waiting for her verdict. Leaning closer, her eyes catch the light and sparkle like a cold January sky full of stars. Damn it. She makes me feel like she could see right through me. It's both electrifying and eerie.

All I want is for her to say yes, and I'm terrified. As if a *no* from this little stranger could give me the final blow.

Gathering my courage, I try again. "Look, I'll be gone on a string of away games starting tomorrow…Come on, you can't hate me this much. You don't even know me, and I'm not that hard on the eyes."

She scoffs. "So you think I should say yes just because you're hot?"

Oh, there you go. She thinks I'm hot. "No, because fame is the ticket to your victory. People will be buzzing about us and you'll stay fresh in their minds when it's time for nominations. You need me as much as I need you."

She bites her lips and I'm getting impatient. Why is this so hard?

No word is coming out of this fucking plush mouth. Every time I try to open up, she shuts down.

I let out an exasperated sigh. "I'm here trying, Liora. What are you afraid of?"

"A lot," she says.

"I'm pouring my heart out, damn it. What else do you want me to say?"

"Fine." She throws up her hands. "My biggest fear is that you'll continue hurting others, that you use me like your sidekick and then the media will turn against me as well. I can't take that risk."

My stomach drops. She truly believes I'm the worst piece of shit around. But that's the reputation I've earned with those who didn't fall for my looks online. "Okay. Fine. If you're that convinced I'm the worst, let's just scrap the whole thing then."

She repeats, "Fine," once more, spinning around as if relieved to be finally rid of me. I'm left breathless at her abrupt dismissal.

I never had a problem persuading a girl to stay at my place before. What the fuck is happening right now?

A surge of desperation floods my body, and I touch her on the arm to stop her. She's not running from me like that. Hell no.

She halts, glancing at my hand on her arm, and I reluctantly release my grip, realizing I've held on longer than intended. I slide my hands into my pockets. "Look. This started off totally wrong and I— You know what? What about we start over?"

I carefully reach my hand out. She just looks at it. Damn, I'm not sure if she's going to hit me again or laugh at me. I say it anyway, "Hi, my name is Riley Huntington, I'm a hockey player and have a spare room for you. Scouts honor, I'm a nice guy."

She doesn't take my hand and I just stupidly leave it there for her to shake. The seconds stretch and I'm so close to just storming off. For real this time. But her frown changes into a smile that could kill me. Fuck, she's so beautiful.

And then, she finally takes my hand and I can't help but sigh in relief. I shake it and there's this sizzling spark shooting from my fingertips up to my spine, and I do everything in my willpower not to say something stupid like *woah*.

"I'm Liora James, a figure skater who turns homeless soon if she doesn't agree to this stupid idea," she says.

I let out a nervous laugh. She doesn't join in.

"So, you're up for grabbing a bite and getting to know each other before sharing rooms?" I ask, flashing a smile.

She averts her gaze. "I can't really afford eating out."

"No worries, I've got it."

Her frown deepens once more and I have absolutely no clue what I did wrong this time.

"Riley, if we're doing this, I won't be your charity case. I mean it," she says. "We need clear rules, a contract, both of us laying out what we expect."

So much for getting to know each other. But she's right, we're talking business here. "Got it, you want to keep this as professional as possible."

She nods. "No distractions. I need to win this show, there's no other option for me. We'll think about a strategy that makes us both win, and nothing else. And I want a key to my own room."

I halt for two seconds, wondering what she must have gone through if she trusts people so little. "Sure. So, are you in then?"

She nibbles her lip but nods eventually. "I hate feeling like a burden on my friend in there, and we've been on the hunt for a decent apartment nonstop. Yours is…okay. So, yeah, I'll give it a shot."

"Okay? It's fantastic."

"Don't need another girl boosting your ego."

I laugh. This is going to be a catastrophe. "Okay, okay. I got it. Then let's grab your stuff and head to my 'okay' apartment."

Seven

LIORA

When Riley drove up with his black, shiny Aston Martin, I couldn't help but marvel at the sleek lines. I've never been in a car that cost this much.

Just as I'm about to ask where to put my stuff—feeling embarrassed about my worn suitcase I bought when I was fourteen—he snatches my bag from me and puts it in the trunk. Apparently, there's no arguing with him when it comes to loading his car. He then holds the car door open for me, and I behave for once and slip in. But I can't ignore that my hand brushed slightly against his when I do. It's awkward. We're both adults and should know how to act around each other, but instead, it feels like we're seeing someone attractive for the first time.

I give Priya a wink and a thumbs-up. I giggle. She's practically glued to the window, and so gone for him. He even snapped a selfie with her, causing her to die a little inside.

It's strange the effect he has on women. I'm not immune to his looks either, but every time a girl just looks at him, she seems to momentarily lose her train of thought. Okay, I do, too, but it's amusing. It's like he's the kind of guy everyone finds attractive, the point where all threads meet.

Priya said that Brea, her influencer roommate, only dated hot guys, but even she pranced past us with a look of sheer astonishment, and I think her soul had momentarily escaped from her body the minute she saw Riley. And the worst is, he just knows he can have them all. I googled him the other night...

He grew up in the Hamptons, with a silver spoon practically welded to his mouth. His family owns multiple hotels in New York, a legacy spanning decades, and his mom sells mansions to pop stars. If girls didn't swoon because he looks like Michelangelo's *David* come to life, they'd swoon because he can probably buy anything he wants. It makes me hate my situation even more, feeling like a stray he's taken in. I need to make it clear this is a job.

The car ride to his apartment is filled with tense silence.

After a while, unable to bear the heavy silence any longer, I clear my throat and muster up the courage to speak. "So, um—"

"Are you—"

We both speak simultaneously and burst into laughter.

"Sorry, I couldn't stand the silence. You go first," he says.

I feel my cheeks heat up. "No, same. You go."

He shakes his head, smiling. "I just wanted to know if you're ready. The minute we step out of this car together, it's real. There's no backing out. I can drive you back now, but once we're out, we're linked together."

I swallow, not entirely sure what he means but replying anyway. "Yeah, I'm sure. I'm all in."

"You know my life can be crazy. People know me out there, and it's possible you might get photographed in situations you don't like. It's better to always be prepared. I have shades with me in case I feel like my eyes look like shit. People make the dumbest assumptions when you have rings under your eyes."

"Do I have rings under my eyes?" I pull the mirror down and look. It seems normal.

"What? No. Damn. I didn't mean—you're beautiful. Um." He swallows his lips as if he needs to stop himself from talking.

I look away, shutting the mirror. My cheeks are hot, glowing. He thinks I'm pretty? "Thank you," I say, but it comes out in a shy whisper.

The minute we arrive at the apartment complex, Riley practically leaps out of the car to grab my luggage. I want to protest—being a woman doesn't mean I'm incapable of handling my own things—but he's already there, his grip firm yet gentle on the handle.

Standing next to him, I stare up at him. His cheeks have a rosy hue. Is Riley blushing? Because he just called me beautiful?

No. It can't be.

He has at least five women on each arm. He must have called a dozen of women beautiful. This can't make him blush. No.

I open my mouth to say something, but as he shuts the trunk, I catch sight of a group of teenage girls huddled together, their smartphones out, recording our every move.

I freeze.

Did they wait in front of his home to get pictures of him? Panic floods my system, and my heart races as I squeeze myself between Riley and his car—using all of him as my shield. This is why he asked me if I was ready. I had no idea how famous he is.

He tilts his head down and raises one brow in surprise.

"O-over there," I say and nod behind him.

With a sly glance over his shoulder, he probably notices their love-struck gazes and winks playfully at them.

My face burns with embarrassment, but Riley stands tall and unbothered in front of me. He's so used to this.

"Um, is this normal?" I whisper, hoping to blend into his broad chest and disappear forever.

He places a finger under my chin, softly guiding my gaze to meet his. "Listen. You need to get used to this. I have some crazy-ass followers, and while it's nothing compared to those movie stars, you'll encounter things like this on a daily basis from now on. I'm here. Always. They won't get near you. They'd have to go through me first, okay?" I'm still frozen. "Okay?" he repeats, so I nod. "Just to be clear, they will take photos and might even follow you."

I want to glance behind him, but his grip holds me captive. Suddenly, my pulse seems to beat for a whole other reason. But he's right. And just in this very second, I realize that I need this fake relationship more than he knows. It's better for people to talk about our romance than to wonder why I vanished for years.

"I won't back out," I say firmly. "I want this, Riley."

"Good girl," he says, his grip on my chin tightening ever so slightly. "I'm going to pull you in now."

I pause, as if he'd just thrown a can of ice water down my back. "What. Why?"

"We need to give them something to talk about. So, are you okay with me pulling you close?"

I remain still but nod nonetheless.

I've agreed to this. I can do this.

He straightens to his full height, his touch both gentle and possessive as he cradles my face now, drawing me closer until our breaths mingle. There's a jolt shooting through me. My stomach wobbles. Is he going to kiss me?

My skin tingles and my heart gives an impatient twang, but instead of closing the distance between our lips, he touches my earlobe with his lips. I shiver slightly at the sensation of his warm breath and the low, husky timbre of his voice. "I think we need to practice this," he continues softly, the tip of his nose brushing against my ear like a caress.

There's a playful edge to his words, and his touch shifts from my face to the small of my back, sending another wave of unwanted sparks of heat through my skin. I'm torn between the urge to lean into his embrace and the nervous flutter in my sternum. But this is ridiculous. I don't even know him, and this is just proof that if you think someone is attractive, you go delulu. This is all about looks. But my heart bounces as if it needs to get out of his grip or—stay there. Stop it. We should be in love with a soul, not a face.

"Chill. You're acting as if I'm about to kidnap you."

I swallow, mustering up some strength to keep speaking even though he's making my brain go haywire. "Well, depending on whatever romance novel you've been reading, that could be the start of a bestseller."

He leans back a fraction just enough that I can see his smile, and suddenly, I'm eye to eye with him, captivated by the subtle hues in his irises—neither quite brown nor orange, but a warm whiskey color with a hint of golden amber that's utterly mesmerizing. I've never seen eyes like his before.

I hold his gaze, feeling a playful glint dance from his eyes to my lips. Without thinking, I moisten them with a flick of my tongue.

"You read?" he asks.

I clear my throat. "Hm?"

"I asked if you read."

"I do," I reply softly, feeling his touch grow stronger against my back.

"What kind of books?"

Our hips brush against each other. That feeling. It's like my whole body knows he's there.

"Anything I stumble upon at the thrift store," I say.

"If you could only read one genre for the rest of your life, what would it be?"

"I have a weakness for romance novels," I confess, meeting his smile with a shy tilt of my head.

His smile widens, and his nose brushes against mine. "Then take some inspiration from them and touch me like you mean it. I don't need a TikTok video of me squeezing a girl to death against a car."

"Touch you? How?" I ask, feeling a sudden surge of awkwardness. Can one man really render me this speechless?

"Are you a virgin?"

"No. Why?"

"You act like it."

"Better a virgin than a manwhore," I shoot back, trying to regain my composure.

"There's that fire. Touch me on my back."

I reach out tentatively, my fingers brushing against his back. He presses his body against mine, and I let out an involuntary sound. Am I this needy? It's been quite a while since I last had sex, but it's not like it helps me or anything. I don't get off having sex. I need my fingers or my vibrator. Why am I this thirsty now?

"Excited already?"

My throat tightens as I reach out, my fingers trembling as they make contact with his taut back, layered with muscles upon muscles. Jesus. All of him is hard. I wish I had longer nails so I could scratch him—hurt him. Just as I start to get lost in the moment, he interrupts with a playful tone, reminding me that this may not be as thrilling for him as it is for me. "Mm-hm, keep going like that, baby," he teases.

I release my hold on him. "Okay, I think we've played enough. Let me go."

His grin widens, infuriatingly charming. But he steps back,

grabs my luggage, and nods to the doorman by way of greeting. "Come on."

Once we reach Attie, Riley tosses him the keys and they fly through the air. "Thank you, man."

And we're in, away from all of his fangirls.

"So, you're even too lazy to park your own car?" I say as we enter the elevator.

I can still feel the heat in my cheeks, but I try to shrug it off and act as calm as possible.

"He likes to drive my cars, so actually, I'm doing him a favor and he can use it whenever I'm away. Paint me the villain you think I am, but don't be disappointed when you realize I'm not the bad guy you thought I was."

Inside the elevator, the space feels impossibly small.

My heart races as Riley's cologne, a heady mix of woodsy smells and fresh laundry, wafts toward me once more. I try to keep my eyes ahead, but I couldn't help sneaking a glance at his strong jawline and these impossibly broad shoulders.

He must have sensed my gaze, because he turns to catch me staring. "Like what you see?" he says. Oh, that stupid teasing glint in his eyes.

"There's leftovers from your breakfast right above your jaw. I thought I'd tell you, so that you don't end up embarrassed."

"What? Where?" He rushes to the mirror, but of course he won't find anything because his damn face is perfect and I just wanted to say something—anything. I feel bad about it, but I can understand these girls out there. This man is so handsome I feel like an ogre next to him. He's way out of my league, and I have no idea how they can believe that I could be his girlfriend. I live in a trailer. He lives in this rich penthouse. He looks like a Calvin Klein model, my hair hasn't seen a hairdresser in years. My face is plastered with makeup that's worth ten dollars in total, and my nails are short, broken, and not even worth mentioning. I look down at my feet, suddenly feeling absurd for saying yes to this clownery.

People will laugh at us. At me.

"You're seeing things, girl," he says, and we enter his minimalistic, oh-so-manly apartment.

"Sorry," I say with a mischievous grin.

He catches my smile and his own grin widens. "You're quite the trickster. Got me good."

I chuckle, feeling a bit more at ease. "So, where's my room?"

MY ROOM IS TUCKED AWAY at the end of the hallway, three doors down from his.

Once a guest room, it now hosts a jumble of my belongings, a mix of cheap finds strewn across the floor. My room oozes luxury with its silk-draped canopy bed, nestled amid a sea of plush velvet pillows and golden-threaded linens. Sunlight dances through floor-to-ceiling windows, illuminating polished mahogany furnishings.

Leaning against the devastatingly beautiful closet, I ponder where to begin unpacking while talking to my mom on the phone.

"Unpacking is supposed to make me feel better, to solve my problems," I tell her in Hungarian. "But it's killing me. I thought I'd be moving in with a girl. With someone nice like Priya. Mom, I packed my silly pajamas. Can you even believe it?"

"I'm sure it's not that bad, honey," she replies, barely containing her laughter.

It's clear she's amused by the whole idea of me living with

Riley. Apparently, my mom isn't any more discerning than Priya. Unbelievable.

"Mom. My shower gel and shampoo were chosen for price, not scent. All I have is that bottle of *PAW Patrol* shampoo."

In my defense, I did get three bottles for the price of one, and they are massive. It will probably last forever.

"It's going to be okay. You'll see," Mom says, and I wish she could see me roll my eyes.

Slumping amid all my stuff, which mirrors the chaos of my life, I sigh deeply. Among the mess are my worn, gray ice skates, my flimsy dress, and a black box in the center. At the sight of it, my heart grows heavy.

Mom rambles on about how good ol' Dan's trying to convince her to cook for him, now that I'm not around. Even though I miss them both, her story fades into the background as I carefully place a blue teddy bear on the shelf behind me.

"Are you still there, honey?" she asks.

"Yeah," I reply, touching the little blue bear. I squeeze it, and even though she can't see me, I hear her sighing as deeply as I do. "It's going to be all right. I just know it. You'll be amazing and he'll be so proud of you."

The teddy bear feels like a lifeline. It is. I'm not doing this for fun. I have to make things work with Riley. This is my only chance to make things right.

I pat the bear one more time. I can do it. I will do it. "Thanks, Mom. I already feel better. I just miss you both so much."

"I miss you too. But look, it's only six months. It'll be over before you know it."

A knock on the door makes me jump. I hurry to open it.

"How's it going?" Riley asks, and my eyes drift to his tattooed arm. Of course, his entire right arm is covered in tattoos, and of course, I've always found tattoos incredibly hot.

"Um, good," I lie and tell my mom that I'll call her back.

Riley glances over my shoulder, his brow furrowing as he takes in the chaos of the room that was perfectly organized just half an hour ago.

"*All right.* Looks like it. Need any help?"

"Nope. Thanks," I say and stuff my phone into my pants' pocket. I need a lot but definitely don't need a man's help with unpacking.

"Well, Ethan and Nina are here to discuss the contract."

"The contract?"

"I thought you wanted one?"

Oh. "Right."

He glances around the room once more before nodding toward the living room. "Come on then."

I give a small nod, and just when I want to get out, I catch sight of my black bathroom and around twenty packs of tampons.

"Riley…" I say, stopping in between the doorway.

"What?" He looks at me with big eyes.

"Do you think I'm dying each month?"

The way he looks at me makes me think he can't keep up with my train of thought, but before I can say more, he follows my gaze to the tampons and scratches the back of his head.

"Um, well…you're a woman, so I figured you'd need them."

I burst out laughing. "Well, thank you, I'll have tampons until the menopause hits me. Did you buy these all by yourself?"

"Yep. Used to do it for my sister all the time. And I got you some other stuff too. What's wrong?"

I must have given him a weird look, so I quickly say, "Sorry, it's just…unexpected. In a good way, I mean."

He shrugs nonchalantly. "Just wanted to make sure you were covered."

Twice in one day he's made me blush.

Trying not to look at him too much, I quickly close the door behind me and follow him into the massive hallway.

His penthouse is crazy vast, and having it all to myself for the next few days feels like a dream. I'm relieved that I have my own bathroom too—sharing one with him would be…well, too much. Just thinking about accidentally walking in on him half naked in there makes my cheeks flush.

I follow him, unable to tear my gaze away from the way his defined muscles shift beneath his tight T-shirt as he walks. The way his tattooed arm makes me feel things. I shake my head in disbelief at how something as simple as walking can be so attractive. So much for getting my shit together.

"Liora! I'm so happy you decided to move in!" I hear Nina's voice and try to glance behind Riley to find her. When I do, I'm greeted with a rosy smile that stretches from ear to ear.

Nina sits on the white, plush couch beside a man in a perfectly tailored gray suit. His dark blond hair slicks back, and he focuses intently on a stack of papers spread across the coffee table, with a contract and pen waiting to be signed.

"We need you both to sign on the dotted lines," the man says by way of greeting.

I come to a sudden stop and glance up at Riley.

"Sorry about him," Riley says, shooting a scowl at him. "This is Ethan, my agent and publicist. He's a bit on edge right now and it's my fault." Riley's gaze shifts back to Ethan, his tone turning firm. "How about you start with saying hello, or did you forget your manners?"

Ethan spins around, his expression curt as he gives me a quick once-over. All I get in return is a nod, which prompts me to cross my arms and nod back. Typical New York, full of jerks.

He slides the weighty paperwork toward me, and it stops right before falling off the edge of the table. "This contract outlines your roles and responsibilities as a couple, including no PDA in private, no dating anyone else, and maintaining the charade in public at all times." He says it like there's no possibility to ask or add things. Then he takes the pen and hands it toward me. "On the dotted lines, please."

I raise an eyebrow, unimpressed. "It might be shocking to you, but I'd like to actually read this before I sign my life away."

"Do you need me to read it out loud for you?"

I walk up to him and snatch the document from the table. "I can read just fine, thank you."

There's an uncomfortable silence, and I notice Riley arguing with him with his hands next to me, but I don't pay attention to it. I'm used to people like Ethan, judging me based on my tax bracket. There's a shift and a sudden sweet scent fills my nose. When I look up, Nina is next to me and touches my shoulder. "Sorry. Come on, let's sit at the counter. Ethan is... well, Ethan. Grumpy."

"He's a jerk," I mutter and move to sit at the marble kitchen counter.

"Help her with the legal jargon, will you?" I hear Ethan growling at us.

I turn around. "Oh, how about you worry about your manners rather than me understanding your damn contract. I did a year in law school. Terms like *fiduciary duty* and *force majeure* aren't exactly foreign to me. But thanks for the offer."

I shoot him a pointed look before sitting down on a bar stool and diving into the contract, determined to make sure I know exactly what I'm getting into.

I'm not sure, but I think I catch Riley smiling proudly.

Eight

RILEY

I sit next to Ethan, watching Liora work through each line of the contract with surgical precision, crossing out words and rephrasing clauses. Nina types away on her laptop, fixing five typos that I couldn't help but smirk at every time she found one. With each correction, Ethan's ego deflates like a popped balloon, making him sink further into the couch next to me. Oh, and he's such an angry grumbler.

"Look at you, getting your ass handed to you," I tease, raising my beer in a mock salute.

Ethan grunts, clearly not in the mood for my jokes. He takes a long sip from his beer. "I've had a long day. All I want is to go home."

"To your cats?"

"Purrcasso and Moire need me," he replies defensively.

"Sure they do," I say, winking. This guy seriously needs a hobby. All he has is me and his cats, and I'm a full-time headache. I think he even said I'm his human migraine once.

"We need to add several things," Liora says.

I've never bothered to read the contract, but Liora's got it handled. I wonder why she stopped pursuing law; she's a natural.

"Are you guys finished or what?" Ethan says, slumping even further into the couch.

I nudge him with my elbow. "Cut it, man."

"Look at you, suddenly caring for someone."

"Hey, this is my chance of a lifetime, remember?"

"It is…"

Liora stands up, the bar stool screeching as she turns. She saunters over, sitting on the chair opposite from me and Ethan, with Nina grinning proudly behind her.

"We changed a few things," Liora announces. "I found some issues."

"Which are?" Ethan asks, his piercing blue eyes locked in a fierce stare down with Liora. I wish I had popcorn.

"Well, I changed some wording, but the legal framework remains intact. Do you need me to read it aloud for you?" she offers, a hint of a challenge in her voice.

Nina and I both suppress a chuckle.

"No. Thank you," Ethan grunts out.

"Good," Liora continues. "Let's review the added rules. Both parties agree to no nudity in the apartment."

I cough at her wording. "No what? I hate shirts."

"No nudity," she repeats. "We need to wear at least a shirt and shorts. This is a professional environment, nothing sketchy."

"Afraid of my muscles?" I lean in, teasing.

"No," she retorts, meeting my gaze head-on. "But I want this to be a professional setting."

"Fine. What's next?"

"No bringing people over. It could harm our image."

"Agreed," I say, though the thought of a sex drought is painful. Guess it'll just be me and my right hand for a while.

"I clarified the PDA in private part as well. There's no physical contact in private," she continues.

"At all?"

"At all. Including private kisses."

I recline, resting my hands behind my head as I gaze at her. I notice my shirt rising up, and she glances at the skin revealed above my sweatpants before quickly glancing away again.

"But we need to practice," I say. "Does that count as breaking the rule?"

Her cheeks go pink. She's so cute.

"No. But anything that could mess with one party's emotional attachment does."

"Got it. No messing with emotions." What if she's already messing around with mine?

"Right."

"What else?"

"This contract lasts six months. Once the show is done, I can move out without any further costs."

"Agreed."

"And…"

"And?"

The top of her cheeks are still flushed and she won't meet my eyes.

"No sex," she says.

I huff out a laugh. "You already mentioned that. Worried I'm going to host sex parties or something?"

"No." The way her nostrils flare. "I mean between you and me."

Oh. "Sex, between you and me?" I sit up straight again and adjust myself as secretly as I can. Shit. Just the thought of it.

"Yeah, no sex."

Fuck. Did I give myself away? Did I ogle her too obviously? "What makes you think I'd want that?"

Her eyes flicker, as if I said something unexpected. "I just want to be clear. No sex between us."

"And what if you want to? Can't have you going to jail for lusting after me."

She grunts, and I hear Ethan muttering something about why he had to end up with me as a client.

Liora's eyes narrow to slits. "No. Sex."

Oh, she's firm. "Okay, okay."

"Can we *please* wrap this up?" Ethan sighs, raking a hand through his hair.

"I think it's getting interesting," Nina jokes, watching Liora and me closely.

"We have to talk about what happens if we mess with the rules," Liora says.

"Isn't it stated in the contract that if one party messes it up, the charade is over?" I say.

Liora nods.

"Okay." I point at Nina. "Please add that if that happens, I want to make sure she has a place to stay until her show finishes."

"Oh yeah," Nina says and starts typing away on her laptop.

"No, that is not necessary—"

"It is." I don't want her having to go back to that tiny apartment, or landing somewhere worse.

"Is it over now?" Ethan says.

"Thank you." Liora's cheeks all heated again. "And yeah, I think I got it all covered now. Let's sign so he can feed his cats," Liora says, earning a giggle from Nina.

Nina prints out the revised contracts and hands one to Liora and one to me, along with pens. I sign mine quickly, but Liora reads through hers again, making Ethan groan about having the worst job in the world.

Nine

RILEY

The air smells like a mix of jet fuel and that sweet Southern breeze as we fires up at Raleigh-Durham International Airport. I slump into my seat, totally beat from the two-hour flight from JFK and that fucking game we lost. I still had to sit on the bench, and we all know this one's on me. Coach didn't speak a word to me. His name might be Mercer, but he knows no mercy.

I knew he was counting on me to step up and really change my ways this time. But it was hard, knowing that my team needed me but also knowing that my reckless behavior could cost us everything. I need to prove myself, to make a difference in the game. That's why I agreed to start early with therapy. I have to get my shit together. I have weekly phone calls scheduled with my therapist and in-person meetings whenever I'm at home.

My eyes are heavy with exhaustion as I glance sideways at Max, our regular bus driver, who seems like he was born behind the wheel. Seriously, I don't think there's anything else in his life than our team. He's always there, ready to drive us wherever we need to be. He sports a round beer belly, has the kindest smile there is, and glasses the size of small tires. Patient as ever, he waits until all of our gear is stuffed into the bus and each player takes their seat.

Even though it's a routine we all know well, like the crisscrossing streets we roll through in every city, midseason is the hardest, and everyone who argues differently doesn't know shit. Being in the NHL means back-to-back games with very little time in between. We played against the Buffalo Bears at 7 p.m., and shortly after, Max and our staff picked us up and we flew to North Carolina.

Since I turn into a robot that only focuses on winning on game day, I didn't have a lot of time to mull over Liora being back at my apartment all by herself. But now, as I sink into my seat and shut my eyes, she's all I can think about. I still can't believe I agreed to this. There's a *girl* living in my apartment. A fucking beautiful one.

I can't help but wonder what she's been doing for the past few days. We swapped phone numbers and I saved her as Bladezilla after she saved me as Puckster.

I hope she got along with the smart home features.

But she would have texted if anything—

"Man, I'm beat," Jayce mutters, dropping into the seat beside me.

"Tell me about it, I feel old these days," I reply with a tired grin.

Jayce looks as rough as I feel, his wild maroon curls poking out from under his headband, dark circles under his usually bright blue eyes. We're boosting hard through the play-off push, trying to secure our spot. I touch his shoulder, giving him some support. At least we're not alone in this insanity. My team is my family.

And I know why the bus is full of groaning guys right now. Across such a long season, our lives inevitably meet unexpected disruptions.

There are aching muscles, swelling bruises, engine malfunctions, blown tires, stiff mattresses—those are the routine challenges. NBA teams may average more back-to-backs, and MLB teams play a dense schedule, but hockey's physical demands, spanning a vast geographic range and contending with factors like border crossings and weather delays, make NHL back-to-backs arguably the most challenging in professional sports. But let's face it, most people don't see this side of hockey—and maybe that's what makes it so exciting.

"Ri, man," I hear our youngest rookie, Shane Martinez, who we call Shiny, pipe up from the seat across the aisle.

I raise my eyebrows at him. Is he insane?

There are house rules when it comes to the bus or plane. The captains, coaching staff, and veterans usually claim the front seats. It's our time to discuss our team's play while our rookies get the seats near the lavatory. We've all been there.

A few seats behind them, there are rows of players in comfortable leather seats. Some of us passed out still wearing their headphones. Others watch a movie. Some play cards but everyone knows their place. Expect Shane.

"Ohhh, Shiny, ready to meet your maker?" Derek calls from the back, and everyone cocks their head, ready for some fun to interrupt our dense day. We may be like family on this bus, but that means we fight like brothers too. And it's been a few rough weeks since my lawsuit.

"Just wanted to chat about that viral video," Shane says and refuses to move an inch. Instead, he wriggles his eyebrows at me.

"What viral video."

"The one with that hot blonde."

"What's your point?" I mutter.

"You know, I was just wondering if she's as good as she looks." His tone is dripping with innuendo.

"You better shut your mouth," I say, and I notice Jayce already gripping my arm.

A dark shadow looms over Shane's body. "Move."

Within seconds, the corners of Shane's mouth, which were once turned up in that stupid smile of his, droop into a frown. He startles, realizing whose seat he's been occupying. When his eyes meet with Colton King's silver gaze, Shane jumps up to his feet.

There's nothing amusing about King staring at you like that.

Standing at a towering six feet, five inches, and covered in so many tattoos that it looks like a tribal coloring book had exploded on him.

We often joke about him being our Russian assassin with that buzz cut and his actual name being Koltun Kirillov. We wanted to name him Killer but since his surname means *lord* or *ruler*—or whatever—in Russian, Mercer prefers we call him King instead. His nickname went so far that it's written on his jersey now.

"Move," Colton says again, his stare boring into Shane.

Shane nods, glancing at me nervously before running back to his seat right next to the toilet. Colton shakes his head in disbelief and slumps down.

"I hate fucking rookies," he mutters, and I can't help but smirk.

We all know if Shane keeps up this attitude, he'll end up locked in the bathroom. But knowing our idiots, someone probably clogged the toilet before.

I hear Malcolm's voice from the rear. "What's up with that girl, Ri? She really moved in with you?"

Other teammates chime in. They howl, and through the smudged bus window, I see their hands gesturing wildly, mimicking hearts and blow jobs.

Jayce, my best friend and captain, gives me a playful punch

on the arm, smiling knowingly. Even Colton's chuckling from the side.

"Yeah, how about you tell us, Ri." Colton smiles, and even though I love the fact this guy only smiles like this when it comes to me and the stupid things I do, I hate Shane for bringing up that topic.

I mutter a sarcastic "Thank you" to Colton and Jayce, causing them to snicker even more. Of course they know the truth. They know about our contract, the promise I made to do better. I trust them with my life. They won't spill the secret, but the rest of the team can't know. It's safer that way.

"Riley, come on. Who's the girl?" Derek leans forward from behind.

Derek Devereaux is our goalie, and even though we get along, it's only because we have to. He's something like my rival, since he loves to point out that he made it in the NHL all by himself and I, well, didn't. A tale as old as time.

"Nobody important," I tell him, trying to appear nonchalant, catching Jayce and Colton exchanging grins.

"Maaaan. So you have a girlfriend and didn't tell us? Don't worry, we won't tell her about all the other girls you sleep with during away games. We promise," Malcolm insists.

"Fuck off, Malcolm," I grunt.

I hear Mercer sigh, and I rub the bridge of my nose. This is going to be my living hell.

"Leave him alone," Colton interrupts. "He'll talk when he's ready."

The shrill sound of whistles pierces the air, and someone's yelling, "Shit, Huntington's really serious about it."

I turn my head to look out the window, watching as the scenery outside becomes a blur. However, my focus is soon interrupted by the growing sounds of laughter from behind me. When I turn back around, I see Derek and Shane sharing videos with the others. My curiosity gets the best of me, so I lean backward and grab Devereaux's phone.

There it is: footage of Liora and me against my car, her fingers clutching my shirt, my lips near her ear.

The angle makes it seem as if we're kissing, her eyes closed, our bodies touching. Then, footage of me carrying her luggage into my home—it gives the impression we're a couple, and my heart sinks. Fuck. She looks so small next to me, and I act like I'm afraid to break her.

The team erupts in laughter, and I flip them off. Fuckers.

"You gonna make it official then?" Devereaux teases and I shove back his phone. "Risky move, man. Risky move. It will break some hearts."

"Maybe he didn't tell you because he doesn't want you idiots gossiping about the girl he *loves*," Shane interjects, earning a glare from me. Love? Woah. I prefer it when he keeps his mouth shut, like he usually does.

Jayce leans in close, making sure only I can hear his words. "Or you don't want them to know she's the one you fantasized about in high school, wanking so hard until your hand ached," he says, causing me to nearly choke on my drink.

I don't know what I did to deserve these two as my best friends. Killer over there isn't talking as usual, and our resident genius here is the epitome of a golden boy with his Sunday mass attendance. But when it comes to me, they turn into bumbling idiots. Must be some sort of cosmic joke.

But. Damn. I forgot Jayce knew about my history with Liora.

We've been friends since college, so of course he knows about my obsession. I spent countless nights daydreaming about her. Just the thought that she moved in with me…it's absurd. Insane. Unbelievable. Way too far-fetched. Okay, I'm out of adjectives to describe the mess of my life. But it's happening. No, it happened.

Past tense. Liora moved in and I'm not even home with her. While she might be lounging on my couch, using my shower…damn, this is all it needs for my fucking dick to twitch, and I practically collapse into my chair faster than I could even say the word *shit*.

"Jesus Christ, that boy's done. I thought this was a joke," Malcolm says, and I can feel all the curious eyes on me.

"Could be good," Devereaux yells from the back again. Always the loudest mouth. "Maybe he finally gets his horns clipped and we actually have a shot at winning."

"Cheers to that!" Mercer chimes in from the front row, and Max honks in agreement. "Now, everyone, rest up and keep the fuck quiet. Tomorrow will be tough enough without having to listen to all this nonsense."

I sink back into my seat with relief as our coach gives me a breather.

Naturally, Ethan discussed the fake dating situation with him first. He was pleased that I found a babysitter. Liora is the perfect cover for me to skip out on social events and steer clear of trouble. My go-to excuse…and I made a promise to her to behave. Look at my five-foot heroine.

Ten

LIORA

"Can you believe they got all these stars for the show?"

Priya takes a deep breath, her eyes shining with excitement as we stand at the back of the busy training room. We gaze at some well-known influencers, as well as actors and singers who used to be popular but haven't been in recent years.

I'm a little starstruck since I listen to Mara Jane's songs on a daily basis and now she's standing close to me, talking to me as if it were normal.

For the past couple of days, Priya and I have been hitting the ice rink hard.

Thankfully, Nina hooked us up with member cards, which got Priya in for free too. Nina's generosity saved us a ton, and I couldn't be more grateful.

The best part?

Riley's been MIA for three whole days with zero communication, giving Priya and me the perfect excuse to have a blast at his penthouse. Of course, I got his go-ahead before inviting her over. Keeping her from rummaging through his things was a real challenge though, but I think I finally have monster Priya under control. We also developed an unhealthy addiction to Riley's fridge, particularly the ice cube function, while binging one romance movie after another on his streaming accounts. There are definitely perks to having money. Is a hot tub and a balcony the size of two trailers necessary? Absolutely not.

But it's incredibly convenient when you want to soak and belt out Spice Girls songs with your friend under the open sky without anyone watching.

"Yeah, I'm curious about who they'll match us up with." I shake out my limbs as I stand in front of the wall-mounted barre.

I firmly grasp the polished wooden handle and lift my foot, stretching out my leg to warm up for my routine. There's this familiar burn in my leg, and I can't wait to show my new routine. Getting back on the ice regularly feels amazing.

"I hope I'm paired with Mason Stone," Priya says, folding her hands as if she's praying to God.

"What's so special about him?" I ask, stretching my other leg on the ballet barre. Stacey catches my eye as she finishes stretching at the other end of the studio. Rumor has it she's already flirting with some stars to make sure she'll get a good partner—apparently, she wants some guy named Aiden.

"Liora! Have you seen him? He's absolutely gorgeous!" Priya brings me back to reality.

"Who?"

She clicks her tongue. "Mason Stone!"

She nods toward the back of the room and I lean over slightly to steal a glance at the blond actor.

He looks like Prince Charming...if he was secretly a villain.

It's like we're divided into two groups. The skaters and the stars.

Grace and her team cast the stars back in October, and now they're looking to narrow down the field and pair us up after today's final casting round.

It's crucial that we get along with our partners because this show is a bit different from the ice dancing shows that are already out there. We don't have coaches to guide us. Each team is responsible for creating their own routines. So, it's not just about ice-skating skills—being a good choreographer is equally important. That's why they're paying such close attention during these initial casting rounds.

Mason saunters over to Stacey, offering her tips on her stretches as if he's the expert. I cringe, but Stacey laughs—not a genuine laugh, but one that seems aimed at getting his attention. They'd make a perfect match. I think he was in a popular soap opera, but after the show ended, he sort of vanished from the spotlight. Maybe he's hoping this reality show will be his big comeback.

"Nah, he's absolutely not my type."

Priya pouts. "You only say that because you have Riley."

"I don't *have* Riley."

"TikTok says something else."

"S-sorry, but did you say Riley?"

Patricia, another skater who seemed rather shy last time, approaches us cautiously. She has bronze skin and a brown ponytail that she nervously twirls around her finger, as if gathering the courage to talk to me took all her strength.

"Is it true that you...live with—with Riley Huntington?"

I swallow.

All this attention because of one stupid video on social media?

This can't be real. The clip is seven seconds long. Seven. Stupid. Seconds. But now, everyone and their dog is asking me if I'm his girlfriend. It happened in the subway. On my way to the rink. When I went grocery shopping.

Are you Huntington's girl? The girl from the video?

It's unbelievable, especially when you consider that only a single second actually shows my face. I scrolled through the clips and had the urge to watch all the different types of videos his fans had made, but it became overwhelming and I had to stop.

But whatever—I've practiced this. I need to be happy they ask about him. It's easier to talk about a guy than my past.

Smile. Be glad. Smile—damn it.

I grin at her and hope I don't look like a serial killer. "Ohh, *yes*, Riley's my *boyfriend*." Ugh. This feels weird.

And just like that, I have four girls swarming me, bombarding me with questions about how it happened and how long it's been going on. I look at Priya and mouth a desperate *Help me*, but she just steps back like a crab, clearly enjoying my misery. She may look like a sweet Disney princess, but oh my friend is evil.

So, I stutter out awkward responses about my hockey boyfriend, who I haven't seen in three days and actually know almost nothing about. But hey, he has a cat now. No. Wait. What the heck did I say? He doesn't have a cat. Shoot. What if he's allergic? My brain must be on vacation in Hawaii without me.

"All right, everyone, Liora James is next!" calls out the casting director, clapping his hands to gather our attention.

I take the opportunity and almost stage dive out of the situation. Even though I was nervous as hell a minute ago, the ice calls to me like a sanctuary now. Why is everyone so interested in a relationship?

I'm starting to think that maybe agreeing to this was way bigger than I thought it would be. I figured we could just tell everyone we're together and that'd be it.

It's not like he's an A-list actor or anything. Well, maybe I should have stalked him on Google before saying yes. I mean, just because I don't care about hockey doesn't mean it's not a big deal to everyone else. Apparently it's life or death for some people here.

"The music is your starting signal," a voice tells me.

I'm scanning the stage, but the blinding lights engulf everything in their radiant glow. It's like trying to find a needle in a haystack made of sunshine. I guess I need to get used to random voices telling me stuff.

I have to write a list of things I have to get used to.

With a deep breath, I step onto the ice, the chill seeping into my bones and I prepare to perform the routine I worked on for the last days. We need to perform a new routine each week and we also have to train someone who isn't used to figure skating at all and make it all look like we're used to pair dance. I'm not. I'm a single skater. But I'll show them that I do this.

I glide into my opening pose.

As the music starts, I let it guide me, every beat syncing with the rhythm of my heart. I chose the song "River Flows in You" by Yiruma and focus on the technical elements first—some mohawks, some paragraph brackets, a lutz jump, each executed with precision. Then, I let the artistic side take over, my body flowing gracefully, interpreting the music with every movement as I go for a single axel and land it cleanly. Oh thank the heavens. I used to land three, but there's no way I can do it now. A triple axel is one of the most challenging jumps in figure skating. I trained like hell to land it.

As the final note rings out, I strike my ending pose, my chest heaving from exertion. Silence fills the room for a heartbeat, and just as I'm about to turn around and leave, there's… applause. From Grace.

I blink, then blink again. The light changes and I look to the podium in front of me. There she is, standing and clapping away.

This is the first time I notice the two other jury members. It's Twain Teller, one of America's top casting show judges, famous for shows like *The Voice*. Next to him stands dancer Idris

Bell, who's mostly been on dancing shows. The way he looks at me, he doesn't seem all too critical—he's clapping with such joy that a small, triumphant smile tugs at my lips.

Out of the corner of my eye, I spot Priya giving me a thumbs-up, and I can't stop smiling.

Sometimes life is so strange.

For so long, the only friend I ever had was my mom, and now it feels like I've known this girl forever. But it's been nothing more than a week. Even though I should be nervous because fucking Grace Holland, an actual ice queen, applauded for me, I'm more nervous because Priya's next.

"Congratulations," Grace says. "You're in the show."

"HEY, GREAT JOB OUT THERE!" a friendly voice makes me jump as I watch Priya fly over the ice in her new orange dress.

I turn to see a tall man with short brown hair extending his hand to me. "Hi, I'm Aiden. Aiden Smith."

"I'm Liora James," I reply, taking his hand.

His grip is firm but gentle. And that's when I recognize him. *Oh, I know him!* Up close, he's even more striking than in his Instagram reels—well built, olive skin, with a nice jawline and deep brown eyes. His athletic build suggests countless hours at the gym.

"Your routine was really impressive," he continues. "I've been trying to learn how to skate for this show, and it's not as easy as you make it look."

"Trust me," I say, "it wasn't always like this. Nerves still get the best of me sometimes, even after all these years, and let's not mention the countless times I fall."

Aiden smiles. "I just hope I can keep up with you guys on the ice. Just look at my knees."

He lifts the hem of his joggers and shows me a ray of purple bruises all over his feet, and I grin. So that's why they cast them months ago. They need even more initial training, of course.

"Oh damn," I say and examine the bruises. "Ouch, that looks like you've fallen quite a lot."

"Well, times one hundred and you've got the number."

I laugh and see Priya jumping through the air.

"Oh wow, she's so good."

"She is." I grin proudly and try to see Grace's face, but I can't tell how she looks. I start to kneed my fingers as she does her last jump. I know she struggled with this part. She takes the leap, I grip the door frame, and…she makes it.

I sigh in relief.

"She stood it well," Aiden says.

"Yes," I say, and I can't wait to take her in my arms. She was amazing. "Do you know what we're doing now?" I ask him.

"From what I know, we'll start with dance classes together. They'll pair us up and test different combinations."

"Dancing?" I say, looking up at him.

"Yeah, we have the chemistry check on the floor, and the second one is on the ice."

"The chemistry check?"

He winks. "If we look good on camera together. If some sparks fly."

I nod. I know how this goes.

I remember what Ethan told me that night. I need to choose the most attractive partner so that people become obsessed with us and the media will cover me and Riley extensively. He said if I can make people believe I'm falling for my skating partner while still being with Riley, the media buzz will boost my chances of winning. But I'm skeptical—people need to like me, not hate me. Still, he might be onto something. There could be two factions: Team Riley and Team Whoever I'm paired with. Whatever happens, we need to play it smart.

But Ethan also said not to fixate on media coverage.

The focus is on the star, not the skater.

We both earn a hefty sum per episode, and if we win, financial worries will be a thing of the past. Even if I don't win, each episode gets me closer to freedom. I just need to do whatever it takes to advance as far as possible.

"There she is," Aiden says as Priya comes running at us.

"I'm in!" she screams and basically runs into my arms.

I hold her tight and we jump up and down together. "Oh shit! Priya, we made it!"

We keep on jumping for quite some time, but since both of us just gave it our all with our routines, we stop before we fall dead to the floor.

IT DOESN'T TAKE LONG before they start announcing the names of who made it and who didn't.

They kick out some skaters I thought had major potential, but in the end, we are down to twenty. With only twelve stars, it means we still have to narrow it down, but Priya and I got into the chemistry stage. That's all I need. Now it's up to us to flirt the crap out of these pop stars.

And just like Aiden said, we start with dancing.

We were told to change into a ballet skirt and a matching leotard, and once we hit the dance room, we were split into two groups—ten skaters and six stars in each.

The setup is like speed dating but with waltzing.

We pair up and dance while being filmed, then switch partners and repeat until we've danced with all the stars.

Stacey practically throws herself at Aiden, desperate for his attention. I can't help but roll my eyes when she ignores the smaller actor and forces Aiden to dance with her for the second time in a row. I catch Aiden's gaze and he makes a face at me. It's satisfying to know that he isn't a fan of Stacey either.

Also, I have no clue why Priya likes this Mason Stone. He was my worst dance partner, constantly standing on my feet and telling me I should let him lead, even though he didn't lead at all. Prick.

By the time we are done, my head is spinning.

I don't even remember getting home.

All I know is I fall headfirst onto the couch and I'm out like a light.

Eleven

RILEY

The apartment was dark, save for the glow of the streetlights filtering through the blinds, casting amber shadows on the walls as I silently close the door behind me. I thud my gear bag to the floor, and peel off my jacket, wincing as my shoulder protests the movement.

Man, the game had been intense.

I was allowed to play, but our rival team, the North Carolina Thunderhawks, had a target on my back. Despite not throwing any punches (thanks to biting down hard enough on my tongue to draw blood), I still ended up in the sin bin more often than I wanted. But I didn't let those assholes get the best of me. They wanted to get me back on the bench. But we won, and I scored, baby. Fuck the shoulder.

My stomach growls, reminding me I'm starving.

Yawning, I shuffle to the kitchen, my eyes set on my cereal like it's the holy grail. It's always been my thing. After a hard day, I earned myself some Fruit Loops. I just hate eating all that perfectly healthy food my dietitian organized for me. So every now and then I deserve my bowl of sugary cereal. But just as I yank open the fridge door, I almost knock myself out with it.

Because right there, sprawled out on *my* couch, sleeps Liora. My eyes inevitably drift to her bare ass, barely covered by a tiny blue ballerina dress that rides up those glorious cheeks. I let out a sigh and bite down on my fist, trying to will away the impulse to stare at her perfect curves as if I haven't seen any before. I've seen them all. But hell, this is different. She's my roommate. And damn, what an ass.

The moonlight streams in through the window, casting a seductive glow on every inch of her body, and I can't help but stare for a moment too long before jerking myself back to reality. *Thou shalt not ogle thy roommate's perfect ass* was probably carved somewhere in that silly contract.

But how am I supposed to resist when it's right there, taunting me? It's like trying to ignore a glowing neon sign that says, *Look at me! Bite me!*

Fuck it, it's just an ass. A really fucking amazing ass. I grind my teeth and turn away. Something must be wrong with me. I've seen plenty asses before. But none have made me bite into my own fist like I want to take a bite out of hers. Shit, this could be a problem.

Trying—and failing—to be quiet, I rummage through the fridge for the milk. I just need to focus on something else. I'm a pro hockey player. I'm a focused person. I can avoid that ass. I can resist staring at a girl. What kind of thought is that, anyway? Like I am so weak-willed that I cannot resist the sight of a stranger's bare skin. It's pathetic and stupid, really.

I pour the milk into a bowl, then grab my cereal, dumping it in. Just as I'm about to turn around and go to my table, I freeze. I won't admit it, ever, but I know that if I turn and see her again, I'll be glued to the spot, unable to tear my eyes away.

Normally, I'm strict about eating at the table, but here I

am, nibbling while standing up, trying to keep my eyes on the fridge. My mind spins with exhaustion from the game and... something else. Something intoxicating, electric, that I can't quite name. It's her. It's always her. I want to stare at her so badly, but I do everything I can not to. I force myself to face the fridge, gripping the bowl, desperately trying to think of anything other than the pull I feel.

I grab my phone and text Jay.

> Riley: I'm an idiot.

> Jay: I know.

> Riley: That's all you say??

> Jay: You've got so many problems, man.

> Riley: I want to fuck my roommate.

> Jay: You're an idiot.

> Riley: I came home and she flashes her ass, sleeping on my couch.

> Jay: It's her couch now too. Stop being a creep and go to your room.

> Riley: Why do you think I'm being a creep? Maybe I am in my room.

> Jay: Go to your room! You can fuck someone else. Not her.

I finish eating as quickly as I can, feeling nauseous from wolfing it down. Just as I'm putting the bowl in the sink, my eyes betray me and I look at her again. My stupid dick stirs. Seriously, fuck. I need to talk to Ethan and Nina. I can't live with a woman without thinking about sex. When Jayce told me I can't have sex with her, my brain wanted her more. Not even going to talk about my dick. That thing wants her all day. I'm going to mess this up. They can't expect me to have her—and that ass—in my apartment and not think about it. It's impossible to resist when they practically handed me my dream woman on a silver platter. I have to stay away from her or risk losing my career for good. Fuck. My. Life.

I quickly sprint to my room, refusing to even glance at the pile of dirty dishes in the sink. But as I'm escaping to safety, I happen to catch a glimpse of her shivering legs and stop. She's freezing. Not my problem, not my problem…but wait, maybe it is my problem. What if she gets sick? I trudge back and grab a blanket. And that, folks, is what we call being a responsible adult.

Yet, as I approach her, I'm paralyzed.

She looks so peaceful, and all I want to do is touch her. No, I need to stop this. I need to get it together. If I could, I'd punch the shit out of me right now.

Her breathing is slow and even, and I can't help but notice how soft her skin looks under the pale moonlight streaming in through the window. My heart starts to race as I reach out to gently push the blanket over her body. My fingers brush against the smooth fabric of her dress. She makes a soft sound in her sleep, mumbling something incoherent, and turns over slightly on the couch. And I think my soul just left my body. My heart is hammering up to my temples and I seriously question my sanity.

Her head tilts to the side, and a strand of blonde hair falls into her face. Acting on instinct, I gently tuck it behind her ear, my fingers grazing against her cheek. I quickly look away, trying to ignore the burn on my cheeks as I realize what I just did.

Enough.

I finally rush back to my room.

In my bedroom, I lie down under my covers, staring at the ceiling fan turning lazily above me.

I try to shift my thoughts away from her velvety skin. Those rosy cheeks. The way I wanted to bite into her ass. I know I need sleep—tomorrow will be a new day and everything will be back to normal. I count sheep.

But those damn lambs just keep transforming into Liora's perfectly sculpted ass, causing me to let out a sigh. Fuck. Sheep-induced arousal is not something I ever thought I'd have to deal with.

Don't fuck your roommate.
Don't fuck this up, Riley.

All kinds of people are yelling in my brain right now, screaming at me for seeing her this way. But I've always wanted to fuck her. And I have several times in my mind before. Why stop now? I run my hands over my face.

My cock throbs against the tight fabric of my underpants.

I've fantasized about her countless times. Her lips pressed against mine, her clothes slipping off under my touch.

My cock is rock hard now, aching for release.

She'll never find out. It's only me and my hand.

I groan again and throw off my blanket in frustration as I slip my hand in my pants. She has no idea what I'm doing. She's sleeping. Nothing will change if I imagine this one more fucking time.

In my mind her curves get closer and closer until they're tangled up with me, until she sits on my face. I fist my cock and it twitches against my hand. Fuck, this feels good.

Without pausing to consider, I firmly grasp my cock and begin stroking it slowly at first, savoring the firm texture against my palm as I envision her hands gliding through my hair and down my chest while we kiss on my couch. In my mind, I didn't return to my room. Instead, I fuck her right there as she lies before me. And she craves it. Enjoys it. Oh, she wants it so much. Wants me.

I just know her pussy would taste sweet like cotton candy.

I know my hands would greedily grab onto her plump ass cheeks.

Something primal escapes my lips.

Yeah. I just know her mouth would be so plush and needy against mine.

And when I come, I come so hard I have to promise myself to forget this naughty image of her. To straight up delete her out of my mental system and remind myself to do everything I can to never see her like this again.

It's going to be six months. Fuck. It's going to be a challenge.

I WATCH the empty cereal box clatter into the trash can, remnants of Fruit Loop dust mocking me. She ate them. She fucking ate my cereal. The one thing I hid from her. She can have anything. Anything but my cereal.

I never thought I'd say it, but living with Liora has been the absolute worst.

I messed up, and she's not giving me an inch of slack ever since. She's even punishing me with emptying my cereal.

Fantasizing about her the other night caused an intense orgasm that left me wanting to shout from the rooftops. And then I couldn't help but snap at her for sleeping on the couch. I know, I know. Major asshole move. But when I met her in the kitchen the next morning, I just panicked, as if she knew what I had been up to.

I thought it'd be better to make it clear she needs to stay in her room, locked away from me because, hell, I can't get obsessed over her again. I just can't. If we fuck, I'll ruin it, and she'll quit. It's better to set boundaries, make it clear this has to be professional, and we both need to stay in our fucking rooms.

It's been three days ever since, and I've managed to avoid her for the sake of my sanity. But now she's crossed a line—not one Loop is left. It's the one thing that keeps me grounded after a long day. I storm down the hall, not bothering to knock before I burst into her room.

"Did you seriously eat all my Fruit Loops? What the hell, Liora?"

She looks up from her laptop, surprise flashing across her face before it's replaced by irritation. I barely register that she's on a video call before she snaps something in Hungarian and shuts the laptop.

She stomps toward me. "First of all, you don't just barge into my room like some crazy maniac! Ever heard of knocking, genius? And second, you said I could have anything in the apartment. Did you forget that or what?"

"I meant furniture and stuff. Not my freaking cereal. I hid it for a reason!"

I throw up my hands, my frustration mounting. But it's not just the cereal; it's everything. It's the way she's always in my head, making my pulse race when she's supposed to just…not.

Her eyes narrow, and there's that dangerous spark again—the one that both infuriates and excites me. "I need that cereal. It keeps me grounded."

"I'm sorry. Will you forgive me, Your Majesty? I had no idea your sacred cereal was off limits. Next time, I'll make sure to consult the almighty Riley Huntington before I dare touch anything in this holy place!"

I try to keep my cool, but it's hard when she's so close. "Like I said. You can have anything. Just not my fucking cereal. It's not that complicated!"

"You're such an ass, you know that? It was the only thing we had left," she says, her voice sharp, but it's the way her eyes lock onto mine that makes my breath catch.

"All right, but if you use something up, make sure to replace it, okay?" I say, but all I can focus on is that anger in her gaze—it's fiery, almost magnetic. Fuck, it's so hot. A heated pull that makes my pulse race.

We're standing so close now that her warmth radiates back from her.

"Fine. You're— It's just—" she stammers, her gaze darting to my lips.

Something in the moment makes her trail off, and I find myself at a loss for words as well. I look at her chest rising and falling with each breath, hoping it's a subtle sign of her own racing heart. The space between us feels so fucking charged and I catch myself leaning in slightly. In just a moment, she flipped me from boiling mad to feeling genuinely sorry. What the actual hell is going on?

Liora tilts her head up, her plump lips parting just enough to make me wonder how it would feel to kiss them. There's a visible struggle on her face, her breath catching as if she's fighting the urge to move closer too. I can't do this. I can't kiss her now. We need to live together for six more months. I can't mess it up now.

Just as I'm about to bridge that damn gap between us, she turns away abruptly, her face flushing. That's when I notice what she's wearing—a white silky top and shorts, no fucking bra underneath. My heart skips a beat, and I quickly turn around, trying to focus on anything other than how soft her skin looks, how close she is, how close we were to fucking kissing. Shit. This is ridiculous. I planned on hating her, not kissing her.

The second I turn she says, "Fine. I won't touch a thing in your apartment anymore, okay?"

She still glares at me, but there's a flicker of something softer in her eyes now, something I'm not sure I can handle.

"Well, that's gonna be tricky considering we're stuck here for the next six months."

For a second, we're just standing there, probably realizing at the same time that we're indeed going to live in this limbo for *months*.

She breaks the tension by flipping her hair and huffing, trying to act like she's not affected. "It'll be fine. Just do me a favor and get over yourself."

"Get over myself?"

"You're throwing a fit over Fruit Loops like it's the end of the world, Riley. Living with you would be a lot easier if you'd stop being such a hothead. I'll replace it and never touch it again, okay?"

I cross my arms, a smile playing at the corners of my lips. "How about you just say sorry? Or is that too much for you?"

"I've already apologized! How many times do you need me to say it?"

"It was sarcastic as hell."

"Fine. Sorry I ate your cereal. Why would you even yell at me like this over fucking cereal?"

"It's not just cereal." This. Woman.

She rolls her eyes. "Then what is it? Tell me. Please."

"Maybe it's because it's the only thing in this apartment that's not driving me up the wall!" I shoot back. "And the way you're always right there, just—" I pause, pointing at her, at the way her boobs are just so fucking perfect "—just making everything so much harder."

"Well, why don't you just kick me out then, huh?" she snaps.

"Maybe I will!" I yell back, but my voice lacks the conviction. The truth is, I couldn't kick her out even if I wanted to. The idea of her leaving makes my chest tighten.

For a moment, we're both silent, breathing hard.

With a defiant glint in her eye, Liora sighs deeply and says, "I'll get you another box. Just…just leave me alone now."

That's the problem—I can't. I open my mouth to apologize once more because yes, I acted like an idiot again, but before I can say anything, she marches over to her speaker and cranks up a Hungarian pop song at full volume.

"Oh, real mature!" I shout over the music.

"Since you're so bad at reading the room, I figured this would make it clear that I'm done talking to you," she yells back.

Unbelievable.

If she wants war, fine. She can have it.

I head back to my room and blast a rock song loud enough to shake the windows. As I relish the way she yells at me, calling me immature, too, a nagging thought won't leave me: I can't help but wonder if we're both just waiting for the day when hating each other isn't enough anymore.

Twelve

LIORA

I found Riley's kryptonite. It's lavender. He hates is. He almost gagged when I brought home a bouquet of lavender, so of course I immediately bought a lavender spray. And I use it. *There you go, jerk.* I spray the entire apartment with it.

On my way to set, I text Nina.

> Liora: Is there a way to keep the Puckster on away games longer?

> Nina: No, but what did he do?

> Liora: Being himself.

> Nina: Oh shoot.

Grace paired me with Aiden while Stacey sulked in the corner. She's paired with a singer named Russel Ro, and I think he's way too nice for her, but who am I to say?

I really like Aiden, though.

He's been nothing but nice. The complete opposite of Riley. I still can't wrap my head around how furious he was when I ate his cereal. He repeatedly assured me that I could feel entirely at home and use anything I needed, and then he practically snapped my head off because I had a few handfuls of Fruit Loops. My mom once said that men can be like kids, but wow, I didn't realize how spot-on she was.

Anyway, each couple gets different training times, so the rink and dance studios are never overcrowded. We start our training in the studio because it's easier to practice lifts on solid ground, especially for those of us who didn't grow up on the ice. I'm really nervous, but Aiden makes it easy. He's so forthcoming and always polite.

The studio is simple, with mirrors on every wall and the faint smell of sweat and rosin in the air. I show Aiden the little dance I came up with over the weekend, and he claps for a whole minute until I beg him to stop because I'm not the best when it comes to praise; I tend to get all shy and awkward.

I've created a routine to Lewis Capaldi's song "Someone You Loved." It may not be the most complex dance, but it needs to impress the judges and audience if we want to make it onto *Grace on Ice* together.

Grace has reminded us that nothing is guaranteed at this point. We have to perform together flawlessly and hope the judges give us a pass. If they do, we'll be part of the final cast for the show. I don't want to get my hopes up, but I have a strong feeling about us. I can't help but think Grace feels the same way. Even though she hasn't come down to talk to us directly, I know she watches us closely, silently observing our every move.

We spent all of Monday in the studio, perfecting each move, every step, and it didn't feel like work at all. It was fun to dance and come up with different moves with Aiden. I was really surprised by how talented he is. If I didn't know any better, he could pass for a dancer.

But training with a constant filming crew rushing around is

a surreal experience. Producers dart back and forth, cameras always rolling, creating a buzz of excitement and nerves in the air. It's nothing like practicing in the quiet solitude of an empty rink—this is pressure on a whole new level.

Laughter echoes from the next room, and I can't help but roll my eyes. Priya is paired with Mason. I'm pretty sure he's just playing her for those pretty doe eyes of hers. And damn it, it's working because their chemistry on stage is off the charts. But I worry for Priya, I think she actually likes this guy. It's written all over her face whenever she talks about Mason, and each time, I want to gag. I just hope he's not going to break her heart. If he does, I'll break his dick. That's a promise.

When I come home, I'm greeted with the mouthwatering aroma of Riley cooking. I don't only mean the scents and spices in the air but seeing him standing there, a headband in his wild mess of black hair, a gray shirt, and his stupid tattooed bicep rolling while he stirs the pot—it makes my knees wobble.

Shit. I looked too long while I untied my shoes.

Not that I'd ever admit it out loud, but if he weren't such an ass, I'd actually enjoy that view. Then again, I shouldn't enjoy it anyway. So, all good. Perfectly good. Be the ass you are, Riley.

"Hi," he says as I walk to the shower.

His eyes drop to my leggings and stay there.

"Hi," I say back, noticing he's making red curry with shrimp. Why does it have to smell this good?

"Thanks for the cereal," he says casually.

"You're welcome," I respond, a little taken aback that we're actually having a civil conversation.

By the time I'm out of the shower, he's finished and slides a bowl my way over the kitchen counter. My stomach drops. No. No. No. Don't start being decent now.

I manage to frown at his nice gesture. "You gonna scream at me if I eat that?" I ask, arms folded.

He sighs, taking his bowl and sitting at the table. "Again. I'm sorry. Fruit Loops is my stress food. Come on, sit down. Give me compliments about my cooking and light up my day."

My stomach growls, and the food looks too amazing to resist, so I take the bowl and sit down. "I bought you two boxes," I grumble, nodding to his cupboard where he hoards his holy grail of sugar.

He looks genuinely surprised. "Oh, thank you. You didn't have to—"

"You transformed into a gorilla. I had to." I take a bite of the curry, and—oh shit. "Wow. Where did you learn to cook like this?"

I take another bite and actually moan, the flavors practically explode in my mouth.

Riley stiffens, his eyes glued to me as I savor his food.

The spoon lingers in front of his slightly parted lips and he looks pained.

"What?" I say, my voice muffled with a full spoon of this red goodness. His gaze flicks to my lips, and he shifts awkwardly in his chair. Is he okay?

"Nothing," he says, finally putting that spoon in his mouth. "I'm just happy you like it." He clears his throat. "Our team had dinner at a Thai restaurant where they cooked in front of the tables, and I talked with the chef and got some recipes from him. It's his gaeng phet but without celery. I'm allergic."

"Funny. I always thought you were the type to have chefs cooking for you at home."

Riley snorts. "Well, my family does. I only learned to cook in college. I don't like to have too many random people at my house. I need someone helping with cleaning since I'm away a lot, and I don't want to spend my weekends dusting everything I haven't touched."

I nod, remembering how surprised I was to see him doing

his own laundry last week. Maybe I pictured rich people wrong.

"But otherwise, I like taking care of my own things."

I smile at him and then take another bite and moan again. Damn, this is good. His cooking stirs something deep inside me that I can't ignore.

Riley clears his throat again. Is he okay?

My trembling hand loses grip of the spoon, causing it to clatter against the bowl with a loud clang. "Sorry," I say and quickly keep on eating. I've never had this before. That a man could make me have all these feelings about him. Just hours ago I fantasized about killing him with lavender, and now. Well now, I want—

Damn it. It's easier when he's not nice to me.

I can focus on hating him. But when he looks at me like that, like he's undressing me with his eyes, I get the feeling he sees nothing but me. My heart races, and I don't want to think about that because he clearly has other women on his mind. I've seen the fan mail he gets—hundreds of women begging for his attention. If it wasn't for our contract, he could just text whoever he wants, like he's browsing a catalog for hookups. The thought sends a pang of jealousy through me.

"Why are you looking at me like that?" I ask, his gaze still focused on me, making my skin tingle.

There's that smile again. Damn it. I hate this smile so much I know it's all I'll think about later. It's infuriating how much power he has over me with just a look.

"I think I like cooking for you, James. Those little sounds you make. Be careful. You might turn me into an addicted man."

I snort, trying to play it cool, but deep down I am swooning. But I don't want to swoon. Shit. "I didn't moan." Oh, I did.

"You did."

"You wish."

"I may."

We stare at each other again. My cheeks are *burning*.

I release a breath and stand up. Are my knees shaking? Shoot. They are. I can't let him see how much this little banter is affecting me. But more importantly, he can't know he's making me wet between my legs.

"Good night, thanks for the curry." I put the bowl in the dishwasher and lock myself in my room, not daring to come out again.

THE DAY STARTED on a different note.

Not only do I finally get to hit the ice with Aiden, but it seems like Riley genuinely feels sorry for flipping out over the cereal. He got me a romance novel and acted like it was no big deal, but I'm surprised he remembered I mentioned liking romance books. I didn't think he'd be the type to remember details like that. The blurb sounds so fun, and I'm looking forward to diving into it during our breaks or downtime between training sessions. It's been years since I bought myself a paperback.

After the warm-up off the ice, Aiden and I glide hand in hand, using the whole rink. We begin with some basic duet spins, and it's clear Aiden must have had exceptional training beforehand to pick up the steps so smoothly. Then we move into mirrored crossovers.

"Hey." I grin and guide him to the right. "You're doing great!"

"Thanks. I'm a bit nervous about the lift, though."

"We'll manage," I say and slow him down. "Let's try some

small steps first."

Private conversations are scarce between training sessions, always wary of the cameras that could flare to life at any moment. It's hard to open up when you know your words could be edited into a neatly packaged clip for TV. So we stick to small talk, like reminiscing about my cat, Kittie—who isn't actually a purebred but a scrappy stray I couldn't resist taking in. Aiden shares about his golden retriever back home in LA, gushing with love for her and telling tales of their hiking adventures while I show him some moves on the ice.

I demonstrate an advanced crossover step, the movement fluid from years of practice. Aiden watches intently, absorbing every detail. He stands at the end of the rink, wearing black trousers and a shirt while I wear one of the two pair of training leggings I own and a fitted training jacket.

"You try."

When he tries it himself, his first attempts are shaky, his balance wavering on the thin edge of the blade.

"Relax," I encourage, skating over to him. "Let the edges do the work. It's all about finding that balance."

He tries again, and this time, he manages the step just well enough. It's a start, but I see the frustration in his expression.

We spend the rest of the session refining his technique and transitions. Once he's steady enough, I suggest we try the dance we practiced in the studio, this time on ice.

The song starts with Aiden alone on the ice, he sits in the middle of the rink and slowly stands up when the music starts. He then takes a turn and a little jump. He lands it nicely and I grin proudly. Yes! It looks great.

Then it's my turn and I glide into the picture, spinning around him until we move into a spin together. We glide some rounds over the ice, and I make sure we're perfectly in sync, even as we spin faster and faster.

Next up, we hit this footwork sequence. We're weaving in

and out and glide in big waves around the edges of the rink. As we transition into a synchronized twizzle, every muscle in my body tenses. It is a delicate balance of timing and precision.

He takes my hand and then comes the lift. Just a small one, but still, it's a risk.

I position his hands on my hips. "Just like we did in the studio, Aiden."

Nodding, he lifts me, and for a moment, I'm airborne, the world a blur of ice and lights and music. I tap his shoulders. We're not gliding while he lifts me yet.

"You're doing amazing."

We try again and again and a couple of minutes later, the lift is solid. It shows that Aiden has spent a lot of his life in the gym. In the end, we're both breathing hard, the music fading around us, but I'm convinced my choreography will work just like I imagined it. "I think we can win this shit, Aiden."

"You think?" He smiles brightly.

"Absolutely. But now back to practice, golden boy," I say and take his hand.

After training for two straight hours, we finally run the whole routine with music for the first time, and damn. It's magical. We move gracefully to the music, every step in harmony now. When the music swells to its core, he twirls me around and pulls me close. And with one final, graceful movement, he lifts me up in the air, our eyes locking in a moment of pure joy. He twirls with me, I bend my back, and we soar together over the ice. We move into the final pose, with him wrapping his arms around me from behind. We hold the position until the music fades away.

I turn around, grinning like a Cheshire cat, but as soon as I glance up at Aiden my smile drops. His usually cheerful expression is replaced with one of deep sadness and he can barely look at me.

"I'm sorry," he chokes out, his voice barely a whisper. He

quickly turns and skates away, leaving me standing there.

I'm frozen in the middle of the rink, unsure of what to do. Did I do something wrong? I watch him skate to the end of the rink, stumbling out until he crashes against the wall and sinks onto the floor, crying.

My stomach drops and I skate after him.

"HEY," I say softly, my hand closing around his in a reassuring grip as I kneel down in front of him. He's curled himself into a ball, his hands trembling in his lap. I'm not sure what to say since we don't really know each other, but I still care about him. I just hold his hand, trying to offer support even if it might not make a difference for him.

He nods through his tears but doesn't meet my gaze.

I gently stroke his shoulder, unsure if it's been seconds or minutes. The music must have triggered this. That's the thing about art: when you pour your soul into something, you risk getting lost in it. Dancing, singing—it's all about emotions. When you're performing, the audience needs to connect with you, but it also means you risk connecting too deeply with your own feelings. I've been there. Several times. Whenever a song hit too close to home, I'd find myself crying on the ice. Alone.

"It's okay. I'm here. You're not alone."

He cries harder at this, his sobs wracking his body. Without a second thought, I reach up to hug him tightly and he clings back, holding on.

Time seems to stretch as we stay locked in that embrace, the music around us fading into the background. His crying gradually softens into quiet sniffles, and finally, he sighs—a deep, heavy sigh that carries the weight of his own baggage.

"I'm so sorry," he whispers, wiping away the tears in his eyes as he smiles nervously.

"Don't be," I say. "We hurt ourselves when we keep it in."

"You must think I'm a joke."

"No, of course not."

He lets out a desperate laugh, his head falling back to rest against the wall.

It's the first time I truly see his face. His brown eyes are rimmed with red. In that fleeting instant our gazes lock and I feel the weight of my unspoken struggles pressing against my own heart. "Never feel sorry for showing how you feel, Aiden. Not with me."

"But what if I feel like dying inside." He lets out a desperate laugh.

Without a moment's hesitation, I reach out and gently clasp his. "Then I'll tell you that I've been there too. I know we don't know each other well, but I'm here for you, Aiden. If you want to talk. I'm here."

"I don't know what I'm doing." He lets out a long, long sigh. "I'm trying to get more known through this show and get better deals for acting…I feel like, I'm just not good enough."

"You were amazing out there. The audience will love you."

"Not me. The idea of me."

I pause, uncertain of what to say next. "Aiden?" I finally muster, my voice tentative. "What is this about?"

He takes a shaky breath, and to my surprise, he starts to speak. "You can't tell this to anyone."

There's a knot inside me. Why would I push him into telling me anything? I can't tell him about the contract with Riley or my past. I don't have the right to ask him about anything. "Aiden, I'm sorry. You don't have to tell—"

"Ah, you know. Never mind. I can ignore it. Get going again…" His voice trails off, and he takes another deep breath and I feel bad.

"No. Aiden, please. If you want to tell me, please do. I won't tell anyone. I just don't want you to feel pressured to talk, but I'm here to listen. You matter to me, Aiden."

"I don't want to be here all whiny, I totally understand if you'd like to get back to training…"

"We have enough time. I'd love to hear your story."

He looks up, his eyes welling with unshed tears. "I'm famous for my shirtless videos, I'm just a body to most people on Instagram, and a few pictures on Pinterest made me famous because an author used my profile pic for one of her characters. I've become a popular male model ever since, and I landed an acting deal for a new TV series, it's promised to be a huge hit."

I remain silent.

He takes a moment, as if reliving something painful. "But then the casting director saw my phone screen. It was me, kissing my ex."

He pauses, expecting me to understand, but I'm at a loss. "And that idiot got jealous because you're a catch?" I try, but he doesn't smile.

His expression, caught between a crooked smile and a sob, tugs at my heartstrings. "What did he say, Aiden?"

"I kissed a man. He wasn't jealous, he realized I'm gay. He told me to get rid of my boyfriend and that there was no career in this show for a gay actor. I was just a body for girls to obsess over. My role was never intended to be more than showing off my abs."

It's like something kicks me in the stomach. "But this can't be. It's the twenty-first century, we're working toward—"

"Well, showbiz is still a shitshow. We may have Pride Month, rainbow flags, and emojis, but there are still plenty of assholes out there treating us like shit. You might have a sense of how it is in the sports world—how people reacted when a famous soccer player came out. I don't want to sugarcoat it; it's still hard to come out in the spotlight. It might be easier, but it depends on who you want to work with in the industry. I'm a nobody when it comes to acting, so building a career as a gay actor from scratch isn't exactly easy."

I nod. People can be terrible. I want to believe in a better world, but all the things that have happened to me—and now Aiden's story—remind me again that despite living in a modern world, despite wishing that we are able to change, some people just haven't learned from our past. And I wish they would. I wish people would learn and grow together. But some never will and even though I knew this all along, it's just a thought I don't like. It's reality and it makes me feel nauseous.

"And you still want to work with those guys?"

"That's the thing. I don't know what to do with my life. I feel there's nothing I can really do. My Instagram account is all I have. My body. The way I look. The way I present myself, but it's just…well, a mask. I know I need to build myself a second option. Still, I lost my boyfriend because I hesitated."

I wince. Shit.

Aiden's shoulders tremble as he fights to breathe. "I still miss him."

This was about more than success—it was about proving his worth.

I rest my hand on his arm. "So you told your boyfriend about what happened to you and he just left?"

"Well, he knew I was considering it. I thought about breaking up with him just to get that shitty role. I didn't say it out loud, of course, but just thinking about ending our six-year relationship over my career was enough for him. He packed his things and never looked back. I didn't get the role in the series, and my agent thought this show would be a way to get back into things. I've felt like shit ever since. It was my biggest mistake, and yeah…the music—it just hit."

"I'm sorry, we can change it. What music would you—"

"No, no," he says, suddenly breathing easier. "It's good if I can channel these feelings. We need this. We need to go far. Maybe I'll get better roles if people in the industry recognize me from the show. And if not, maybe I can build something meaningful with the money."

"If they cast me alongside you."

It's then that his eyes sparkle. "Oh, I'm sorry, I thought I told you. I asked them to pair us together, and they said yes. So we're already kind of a fixed pair."

"Really?" I laugh and nudge him with my elbow. "Well, thanks for asking if I wanted to skate with you!"

He laughs too. "Miss James, do you want to skate with me until we win this damn thing?"

"Well, you're the worst when it comes to lifts, but do you know what? I've never seen anyone pick up a camel spin that fast." I give him a reassuring squeeze. "No, seriously. I'd love to skate with you. We're going to nail this routine, I know it."

With a shaky nod, Aiden dries his eyes with his sleeve. "Thanks. I...I needed to hear that."

"Anytime. I'm here if you need me. We're in this together," I say, patting his leg. "Now, how about we try it again? We still have time to polish it up before tomorrow, right? Also, you need to watch your hands while spinning."

Aiden manages a small smile, a ghost of his usual grin. "You know it, James. Let's show this rink who's boss."

"That's the spirit, Aiden."

He stands up, pulling me up with him. "Huntington can be really proud of you. You're an amazing human being."

I want to ask why on earth he should be proud, but then I remember and almost gasp. Oops. Of course. I smile awkwardly. "Oh, yeah, he's obsessed with me," I joke. It's so surreal that a guy like Riley could ever be obsessed with me that I can't help but laugh. As if.

Thirteen

RILEY

The roar of the crowd still echoes in my ears as I step into my apartment, the thrill of another win buzzing through my veins.

We scored 8–2 against the Bristol Leaves. Mercer has never been so happy with me, and I start to believe that I can actually do this. I can change for the better. Maybe it's because my mind is so occupied with Liora living with me and what her moans did to me when she ate my food that I simply had no time to get angry at silly remarks from rival players.

I remember that my dad always told me to not waste my time on women. That keeping my head in the game was everything I needed. But stepping away from it seems to be just what I was missing. I was on the phone with my therapist for almost two hours, and one particular sentence keeps echoing in my mind: *Being dedicated to your work can be a positive quality, but it's important to recognize when it's becoming detrimental to your well-being.*

He's right.

I need to stop focusing on my career so much and enjoy the process again. I toss my keys on the black kitchen counter and my eyes settle on a stack of photos—Liora's photos. Oh, what has she done now? Commercial shots, by the look of them. I know I probably shouldn't check on them because the five-foot monster will rip my head off if she sees me, but against my better judgment, I check the apartment. I hear the shower running and just as I "accidentally" knock over the stack of photos and they conveniently fan out, one specific picture catches my attention.

Oh, just my luck.

"She's going to be the death of me," I mutter and snatch the damn photo up for a closer look. Yeah. I'm a dead man walking.

My heart races and I study every detail of her.

That fucking ass, perfectly round and barely covered by a lacy skirt. The way she stands with her back to the camera, her head turned just enough to look directly at me—or rather the fucker who snapped her like this—it makes my skin prickle from head to toe. She's giving me that look like *You know you want this.* And just like that, my little soldier betrays me and stands at attention.

It's official. That ass is my weak point, but as soon as I see the hulking man standing next to her, my dick takes a nosedive.

There's another figure skater, one arm wrapped around her, grinning like he's the luckiest man alive. And I think he is.

Jealousy rips through me, hot and sharp.

What the hell? Who is this guy? I need to talk to her about making our relationship public, posting something on my Instagram together, and she's showcasing my ass with another man.

Suddenly a shriek pierces the air—Liora's voice, coming from the bathroom. Startled, I stuff the photo into my hoodie's pocket and ran down the hall to her room.

"Lia? You okay in there?" I blurt out, knocking on the door.

Damn it. I didn't mean to call her that. It's that stupid nickname I made up when I was a teenager. Whatever. Now I have to stick with it and pretend it means nothing.

"No, and never call me Lia again, but shit, everything's ruined!" There's a pause and I hear water streaming. "Come in! Hurry!"

I jiggle the handle of the door, but it's locked. Of course it is.

Worry claws at my chest.

I need to get to her, now. "Why do you always lock your door?"

"Because I want to keep your nosy self out!" Or rather her secret werewolf self in.

"Well look where this gets you. Just tell me you have clothes on. Please."

"Riley! The shower it's—"

"Lia?"

Since I can't hear her anymore, my mind races, a sick feeling rising in my gut. She's clearly in trouble. I need to man up and get to her, busted door be damned.

I take a step back, steel my resolve, and prepare to bust my way in, praying she's all right…I slam my shoulder against the door once, twice, until the latch gives way with a splintering crack. Stumbling into the bathroom, I'm met with a scene of utter chaos.

The shower head lies in pieces on the tiled floor, water gushing out of it like a broken dam. Below lies the shattered faucet handle, and I have no idea what the fuck had happened. The once-clean tiles are now slippery with inches of water, making it dangerous to walk across. And there, in the midst of the chaos, stands Liora—a slender frame shrouded in nothing but a damp towel, her hair plastered against her face as she desperately tries to stop the broken pipe from spewing more water. And I know I should be frantic about the water damaging my apartment, but all I can think of is that she'll ruin me if that flimsy towel loses its grip where she tucked the ends in.

"Riley! Help me!" she yells, her fingers grasping onto the valve as if trying to hold back a raging river. "The shower just —exploded!"

"Jesus," I say and finally wade through the toe-high flood toward the main valve under the sink. The damage is already done as water seeps out of the bathroom and into her bedroom, creating a chaotic mess.

Shit. Shit. Shit.

I manage to shut off the water supply and turn back to Liora, my heart clenching at how small and vulnerable she looks, shivering in her tiny towel. Water drips from her lashes as she blinks up at me. "I'm so sorry. I don't know what I've done. I just took a shower and then, well, the shower head exploded, and that thing went off and my shower is different and I didn't know where—"

I get up again and walk over to her. My heart flutters at the sight of that scared look on her face, making me want to touch her shoulders. But she's all wet, and I'm basically dumbstruck already, so I force my hand to slide into my jeans pockets and stay the fuck there.

"Calm down. It's okay. There must be something with the pipes. Don't worry, I'll get a plumber and it's done before you can say *tide*."

And there's that little signature frown of hers again and I'm back to feeling comfortable. I can't cope with scared Liora, but angry Liora I know.

"I just damaged your entire bathroom, Ri." It's the first time she's used that nickname, and my heart rate picks up. I've never liked my name—Riley. It always sounded too nice and fluffy for someone as broken as I am. "I should help clean up and pay for the repairs and—"

"Don't start with that. I'm your landlord, aren't I? So if there's a broken shower, I'll handle it. Now, come on, let's get you out of here." I guide her by the elbow, careful to avoid any more slips. But as we step into the hallway, I mutter a curse under my breath.

The water soaked the carpet of her bedroom. Fuck. She can't sleep in here tonight. I quickly pull the door shut, stemming the spread onto my hardwood floors in the hallway.

"My clothes," Liora says, trying to grip the door handle, but I hold her back.

"Hey, hey, we don't want any water in the hallway," I say. "You can borrow something of mine for now. We'll fix it. Don't worry."

"I-I'm so sorry. I don't know what to say. I—"

"It's nothing. You can't afford to catch a cold, so we're going to get you dressed. ASAP." I'd love to tell her that I worry more about her seductive body than the flood she caused, but hell, I would never say that out loud.

"How can you be okay with it? Just thinking about the cost, it's—" She drives both her hands through her wet hair, and just from the corner of my eyes, I see it coming. My death sentence. Luckily, my reflexes are sharp, like a hockey player's, or I wouldn't have managed to catch that godforsaken towel in time. With trembling fingers, I clutch the cloth with all my might. But just as I keep it up, I realize how much of an idiot I am.

"Um," she mutters, suddenly not seeming to panic at all anymore.

We just stand there.

I blink. She blinks.

And here I am, with my hands on her towel.

I cough nervously and nod to my hands. "Um, would you please?"

Her plush mouth forms a little *O* and she grabs her towel. Her cheeks are as red as beets, and I'm pretty sure mine look the same. It's then that I realize we're so damn close. In my bedroom. She stands there, rooted to the ground. Damn, it's the first time a girl is half naked in here and not mine.

Our feet touch, her gaze flicks up to my mouth, and as if that tiny reaction alone would earn me a twenty-year sentence, I retreat and search for something she can wear. Fuck. Fucking shit. I need to fuck someone. My hand just isn't enough anymore. This is embarrassing. I've never felt anything like this. Her living in my apartment and not fucking me must be wrecking my brain.

With the first shirt I could find, I turn around and find her staring at my room, so I try to say something. Anything. Just to get rid of that silence.

"Not what you expected?"

She turns around. Her knuckles white from clasping the towel against the swell of her breasts. "What?"

"My room."

She grins. I take a deep breath.

"You have more books than I thought."

I blink, surprised. She's the first person to notice the massive bookshelf next to my bed. Most girls usually comment on the array of trophies lined up above it. The truth is, I just don't know where else to put them. Since I didn't want them cluttering the living room, I ended up stashing all the medals and trophies in here.

"Ah, because hockey players don't read, huh?"

"I didn't think *you* read."

Ouch.

There's that challenging grin of hers, and if I didn't know she hates the guts out of me, I'd think she's flirting.

My mind drifts back to the photo burning a hole in my pocket.

Liora in another man's arms.

I stretch out the shirt in my hands and notice it's one of my jerseys.

Oh. I quickly add a few pairs of boxers for her to wear, hoping she doesn't realize how much giving her one of my jerseys means to me. It's a sensitive thing. Seeing her wear my name feels almost primal, like a possessive urge.

"You can keep it, it's yours," I say rougher than I want and drop it on my bed.

"Thanks," she says, still staring at my bookshelf as if she's dying to know which books I've got in there. I know that feeling. Each time I find a bookshelf I need to know what the owner reads.

"I mostly read thrillers or mysteries. Dan Brown. Gillian Flynn. Stieg Larsson. You name it," I say. "I do enjoy some fantasy, too, a story that takes me somewhere that's anything but my life."

A knot twists in my gut and she looks up to me as if to ask why on earth I would be anyone but me. "It's not all gold that shines," I simply say, and she nods as if she understands. Or at least tries to.

But then she shifts and I stare at the rivulets of water still trailing down her bare legs. But yeah, I notice. I swallow. The towel ends just inches below her pussy. And the way she presses those thighs against each other. Damn it.

That image will be seared in my memory forever.

I need to go.

"You wanna watch?"

It takes me a second that she wants me to leave and *not* watch her undress. Because—well—yes, ma'am, I'd like to watch.

"Of course not! I'll call the plumber," I say, my cheeks turning a bright shade of beet red.

Fuck, that sounded like something out of a porn I'd watch.

As I step out to give her privacy and make the call, I grit my teeth, this bathroom situation is going to be a headache. *One problem at a time, Huntington.*

THE PLUMBER FINALLY ARRIVED, but Liora is still in my bathroom. The first thing she did was call her mom to share what had just happened, and I think it's really sweet how her mom is always her first call. It's clear that her mom acts as an anchor for her. When I think about my own mom, I don't feel any sense of calm.

Next she started blow-drying her hair.

I don't think I've ever seen someone take so long to dry their hair. It's like she's hiking Mount Everest in there. And while I wait for her to finish, I can't help but laugh at the thought of her barricading herself in there to avoid me. But can I blame her? Nope. Not after that stupid towel attack.

The plumber's eyes widen as he takes in the state of Liora's bathroom and lets out a low whistle. "You're gonna need to replace all the pipes in here," he says, shaking his head. "And the bedroom carpet is a lost cause."

I run a hand through my hair, frustration mounting. "How long will it take?"

"The carpet? At least a week." He shrugs apologetically. "The bathroom? A month, considering the expensive tiles."

Liora steps out of the bedroom wearing nothing but my oversized jersey and the boxer shorts. The plumber, who's crouched down trying to sop up water from the flooded bedroom, does a double take when he sees her, his eyes lingering far too long on her bare legs.

I wish I could say I didn't gulp at the sight of her in my jersey. With my number on her. That big fat *Huntington* on her back. By now I'm used to fighting against my obsession and manage to bark at the plumber, "Hey, eyes up here."

Then I turn to her and take her hand in mine like it's the most natural thing to do. "Are you feeling all right, baby?"

Fourteen

LIORA

My jaw drops. I can't believe Riley just called me baby.

Or, let's say, I can't believe what it did to me.

I never considered myself a *baby* kind of person, but I guess now I am, because the minute he says it—my heart does a somersault.

His eyes meet mine, a playful glint in them, and I can't help but smile. The way he says it, so effortlessly, so naturally, makes me feel a familiar warmth pulsing between my legs. It's like he's peeling back another layer of the walls I've built even though I'm trying so hard to keep them.

He must have sensed I liked it, because his whiskey eyes narrow down on me and he grins that lopsided, charming grin that always gets to me. "I'm just glad you're okay," he adds in a serious tone before leaning in for what I think is a kiss. But at the last second, he hovers just above my lips and mutters, "Play along."

And then it clicks. Riley, my boyfriend. And the plumber.
Shit. Shit. Shit.

I am terrible at spur-of-the-moment situations and I... awkwardly pat his shoulder.

He raises an eyebrow and stifles a laugh. "Did you just, pat me? Have you ever seen people who love each other do this?" His voice is soft, only for me to hear.

"Did you just call me baby?" It's still all I can think about.

"Yeah. You got a problem with that?"

"What if I say yes?"

He tucks a loose strand of hair behind my ear. "You're out of luck then. Because I kind of like saying it." He takes my hand, and his lips brush against the back of it. His gaze then falls on the delicate tattoo etched beneath my wrist—a fading reminder of two dates that caused me unimaginable happiness and pain. I had them permanently marked on my skin, a cathartic release from my heartache. May 28 and May 30.

I take my hand back, ignoring the questions on his face. "Please don't ask."

He winces slightly, kisses my cheek, and turns back to the plumber, asking with a straight face, "So what's the damage?"

Why is he's so damn good at this? I've never seen anyone flirt like him, and it's all fake. How must it be if he's really interested in a girl? He smiles, and my knees already turn to jelly.

I make my way to the living room and sink down on the plush couch, my mind reeling. Living with him is such a mess. He called me his girlfriend so easily, even though the very idea of seeing me naked seemed to disgust him. Why else would he swan dive out of the way to avoid glimpsing me in just a towel?

My stomach twists as I replay the scene—the flash of horror in his eyes, the way he couldn't get away from me fast enough. He clearly hated the thought of me that way. But it's okay. We're business partners anyway. He doesn't need to be attracted to me just because I am attracted to him. For whatever reason.

I text Priya.

> **Liora:** I totally destroyed Riley's bathroom. A pipe burst while I was showering. I'm MORTIFIED.

Her reply dings a moment later.

> **Priya:** Don't even worry about it, girl. That smoking hot jerk treats you like crap anyway. Serves him right! Burst anything you can!

I frown at the screen. The thing is, Riley doesn't treat me badly, not really. He's not a jerk. He just…doesn't seem to like me very much. And in return, I don't particularly like him either. I mean, what was there to like? His smoldering eyes? That crooked, knee-weakening smile? The way his hair always looked effortlessly tousled, like he'd just skated off the ice? That huge bookshelf I wanted to live in once I saw it? His stupidly good humor that I secretly adore but pretend to hate? The stupidly good curry? Yeah. I hate Riley Huntington.

And I refuse to be one of his vapid, puck bunnies.

My phone buzzes again.

> **Priya:** But how do you break a shower?

SIGHING, I TEXT BACK.

> **Liora:** The plumber said it wasn't my fault. Old pipes or something.

> **Priya:** You know what this means, right?

> **Liora:** No?

> **Priya:** There's only one bathroom. GIRL. I'm dying!

My stomach drops. Shit.

Just then, I hear Riley's footsteps approaching, and I brace myself.

He swaggers toward me, a frown creasing his face, clearly stressed out by the situation. He halts in front of me, concern flickering in his eyes. "You okay?" he asks.

I force a smile. He's worried about me? He should be worrying about his apartment. "All good, just having the worst guilty conscience."

He sits down beside me, closer than necessary, and I can feel the heat radiating from his body. "I'll say it one last time. We'll get it sorted. Don't worry. We just have to"—I watch his Adam's apple work down a swallow, as if he, too, notices our thighs are touching by now—"share a bathroom for some time. Easy as that."

I nod. Yeah. Just a room. We can share it. "You're away anyway…right?"

"That's the thing. I'm not."

A knot tightens in my chest. He's…not?

What the heck does he mean he's not going away? He needs to!

He must see the panic in my eyes because he quickly adds, "We made it to the play-offs and have a little time off now."

"Oh." That's all I can say. "Congrats?"

I have to share a bathroom with him?

Is God making fun of me?

We nearly throttled each other last week, even though we only saw each other for two days. I can't imagine living with him for a whole week. One of us isn't going to make it out alive.

"Yep," he says, and then he draws a long breath. "And there's more."

"More?"

"We need to make it official. Nina reminded me it's time we make a hard launch. On social media, I mean."

I arch an eyebrow. "A post? Now?" I'm not sure I'm ready for this. I've already gotten so many texts and calls from magazines asking if it's true that we're a thing.

He shrugs. "It's the next step. The rumors are out there already, but we need to sell this relationship, make it believable."

I can't argue with that. "Fine, let's post a pic. Perfect timing since I'm wearing your jersey."

He winces like something pains him. "Exactly."

"What if we take a quick selfie? One of those sickeningly sweet ones where we gaze at each other and write something about twin flames finding each other?"

Riley snorts. "You mean like those perfect couples on Instagram who probably fight like cats and dogs behind closed doors? Yeah, that sounds like us."

"Yep."

He considers it for a moment, then nods. "All right, but you'd need to touch me for it." He raises an eyebrow mockingly.

"I don't have a problem touching you."

"No? Every time we do, you look like you want to vomit."

"Maybe I do, but that doesn't mean I can't push through and touch you." I smile like it's my war paint and place a hand on his chest, pretending it doesn't make my stomach flip. "See?"

"Yeah, and if you keep touching me like that, people will think I'm your brother."

"Ew." I make a face. "How do you want it then, genius?"

He yanks me closer, his hands firmly on my waist, and I crash into his chest with a squeaky, unplanned yelp. For a second, I swear he leans in and— Wait, did he just sniff my hair?

Is he sniffing me? What the—

"Do you like how I smell?" I ask, half joking, half creeped out.

"Hmm, you smell like daddy issues," he replies, looking way too pleased with himself, like he just solved a riddle only he cares about.

Jerk. "Yeah, well, that's because I used your shower gel."

I pull away, just enough to catch a glimpse of his face—grinning like he's the first guy to ever tell a joke.

"Come on," he teases, "I was just trying to loosen you up a bit. Now, quit frowning and look at me like I'm the center of your universe."

I roll my eyes. Where on earth is he coming up with these lines? I frown at him, barely stifling a scoff.

"More like a solar eclipse. Briefly interesting, but mostly blinding and probably bad for my health," I say.

"Oh yeah, I feel that love. It's burning hot."

I sigh and he positions his phone in front of us, the camera showing him grinning and me giving him a death glare. He snaps a photo. "We should post this. It reflects our personalities. Me, Prince Charming, and you, the dragon I need to fight."

I smack him, and he takes another photo.

WE SPEND the next half hour attempting to pose like a head-over-heels couple for a selfie while the plumber works his magic in the bathroom. To say the least, it's not going well. Either Riley is the worst photographer there is or neither of us can pretend we're a couple. As if the idea of us having romantic feelings for each other is some kind of cosmic impossibility.

"Come on, just act like you like me," he says when another pic looks crap. "It looks forced."

"Because it is?" I roll my eyes. "You're not making it easy, Mr. Hockey Star. You're all stiff when you touch me."

"Well, if you would lean in a little, it wouldn't be so hard."

I look up at him, ready to fire back a retort but he's faster.

"Okay, this won't lead us anywhere. How about we try a kiss on the cheek?"

Huh. That might be a good idea. Perhaps if we avoid direct eye contact with the camera, it will turn out better. "That's actually a great idea."

He grins, and my traitorous heart skips another beat. "See? I'm not just a pretty face."

"Okay, hotshot, let's try it your way."

Riley adjusts his grip, his fingers brushing against the small of my back. "Ready?"

Nope, but I nod anyway, trying to steady my breath. It's just a peck. Relax, girl.

He pulls me closer, and I lean into him, planting a soft kiss on his cheek. His scent—clean soap with a hint of something uniquely Riley—makes my hair stand on end.

"Perfect, just like that," he murmurs, snapping away. "Attack that cheek, baby."

I let out a guttural growl and sink my teeth into his cheek instead. He chuckles, and I can't help but giggle too. And then his hand moves, sliding down my back, dangerously close to my butt. His touch sends a jolt through me, igniting a fire I didn't know existed, and somehow—from one second to the other—it's not a tease anymore.

I falter and reach my hand out only to accidentally grab onto his muscular thigh, my fingers way too close to his…dick.

I freeze, mortified. His face is only inches away from mine.

He raises an eyebrow, trying to suppress a grin. "Wrong target there or can I get excited?"

I jerk my hand back like I've been burned. "Sorry! I was aiming for stability, not your...um..."

There's amusement dancing in his eyes. "Sure. Next time, just aim a little higher or lower, depending on your intentions."

"I swear, I didn't mean to grab you like that. I would never—"

"Let's blame it on gravity. But you know," he murmurs, his voice husky, "I think we're getting pretty good at this." His hand still burns on my hip.

"I don't know. Maybe we should practice more," my voice drops to a whisper, too, barely recognizing the flirty tone in my own voice.

His gaze flicks down to my lips. "Maybe we should."

Time seems to stand still as we lock eyes, and it's bizarre because I know it's not normal to stare like this, yet I can't seem to look away.

"This one would be a great pic," he says, his whiskey eyes gleaming in this light.

I lick my lips and notice his grip getting lower even. "Then take it."

His nose brushes mine softly, tentative and sweet.

My heart skips a beat, and then another, and he takes the picture.

"Maybe we..." he starts. "Maybe we should try an actual kiss, just in case we need to—"

"Kiss?" My heart races up to my temple, and I feel so dizzy. "But the contract. We said—"

He pulls me in, and my breast touches his chest. "We agreed practice kisses are fine. We need to kiss when you visit my game next week. We can't mess it up."

I wrap my hands around his neck. "We can't."

"As long as we both agree, we're not breaching the contract, right?"

"Right..."

Our eyes burn into each other for another intense second, and then he looks at my mouth like it's the only thing that could keep him alive. I can't hold back any longer and lean in toward him. His lips crash against mine with a fierce intensity I never experienced before, and I can't help but think that practice kisses might be the only kind I ever want again.

His lips move urgently, like he can't get enough of me, and I press myself fully against him. His hand grabs my butt possessively, and I know this is just to show me how it can be, but just when I gasp, he deepens the kiss, sliding his tongue slowly inside my mouth. It's sweet and minty and I can't help but grip his shirt in response, pulling him closer until I don't know where his space starts and mine ends.

He sighs softly into the kiss, as if we've found home after a long search, hungry for each other's touches and tastes. His tongue moves fast, so slick and hot. I can't believe it, but I think this is the best kiss I've ever had and it's a fake one. I don't want to stop.

I slide my hands up his chest, feeling the hard muscles rippling beneath the fabric of his hoodie, and damn, he feels so good. I squeeze and a sigh escapes me. In return, his tongue slides against mine and my skin tingles from head to toe. Riley cups my face tenderly for better access to explore my mouth even further with his tongue, and my treacherous mind explodes with desire as my body moves on its own accord.

I can't take it anymore and practically jump onto his lap, straddling him as if he's my ship and I'm the pirate ready to plunder it. Unable to resist the intoxicating scent of him, I basically attack his mouth. This is too good. Why the hell is it this good? It's just a kiss and then—no—it's not.

"Fuck," he moans into my mouth, and it's like he's ignited a fire within me. I'm suddenly ravenous, craving more. This is nowhere near enough.

His fingers hungrily roam beneath my shirt. The intensity

of his touch has me on the brink of surrender, not caring about the consequences. That is, until the unmistakable sound of a smartphone camera snapping a photo pierces the air—and we both just stop.

I open my eyes to see Riley's shocked face.

At first, I'm stunned by what just happened, by how that fucking kiss felt—my heart stumbles as if I actually…as if I *like* him, even though I'm not supposed to feel anything at all. And then the crushing realization hits: someone photographed us.

Riley's hands are tucked under the seam of my—his—boxers, so there's no way he could take a picture. We scramble apart as if our bodies are suddenly toxic, only to find the plumber sneaking photos of us. He curses, calling himself an idiot for leaving the sound on, and dashes away.

"Fucking asshole," Riley grunts and dashes after him. I struggle to keep up and sprint to the door. When I reach the scene, Riley's cursing and pounding against the closing elevator doors.

"Shit!" he yells, looking at me and probably realizing at the same time that the clip is out in the world already because there's no way we can get to the plumber in time now. That's the downside of living in a high-story penthouse. It takes forever to take the stairs.

There's a cough and we turn to see Riley's neighbor—a middle-aged man who looks like a Chadwick Bumpleton in a polo shirt—stepped out to investigate.

When his eyes land on me, on my naked thighs, Riley's jaw tics.

He turns to me, his gaze icy.

"Get. In," he commands.

I hesitate for a moment. It's clear he's angry, but beneath that, I see a flicker of something else—a protectiveness that surprises me.

That single grunt is all it takes for the neighbor to quickly shut the door and for me to get in. I hurriedly retreat to where I came from while Riley tries to beat the odds and runs down the stairs.

Fifteen

RILEY

Even though my name is Huntington, I lost the hunt against the plumber.

By the time I made it downstairs, he had vanished into thin air. But that didn't stop me from making sure he faced the consequences of his actions—I called his firm right away and gave them a piece of my mind.

That fucker took an unauthorized photo of us. The nerve. I want him fired immediately.

Of course that scumbag is going to sell the photo and make a fortune, while those magazines spin some sensational tabloid story. But Liora…If it shows her skin. I want to be the only one who gets to see her like this.

I have no idea how much I've revealed since my hands were all over her, and I can't even guess how far we might have gone if he hadn't interrupted. I completely forgot he was even there.

My fists clench. I should've caught him, should've slammed his head.

Wait—no.

I force my hands to relax. This is exactly why I started anger management therapy. Shit. I thought I was better, that I could manage my temper. But clearly, my control is still tenuous at best. I don't know what I would have done to him if he hadn't run for his life. Just the thought of it scares me.

I need to keep my distance from Liora. Lock myself in my room until I get a grip on myself. But as I enter the living room, I hesitate. She's curled up on the couch, blonde hair spilling over her face. The lost, frightened look in her blue eyes twists my heart. And it's like all this suffocating hatred inside of me just vanishes. As if all I've thought about seconds ago is erased. All I see is her. That look on her face.

"Lia..." I sink down beside her with a heavy sigh. "I'm so sorry. I tried to catch him, but he got away."

She meets my gaze, vulnerability tempered with steely resolve. "It's okay. What's up with that nickname by the way?"

"I like how it sounds." Lia. It's short and beautiful. I think it fits her perfectly and the way she blushes right now just tells me she likes it too. "Sorry. I feel like shit."

"You did your best."

"No. I should've done more. Him invading your privacy like that..." I swallow hard. "It makes me want to track him down and teach him a lesson he won't forget."

"Hey." She lays a comforting hand on my arm. "You can't solve everything with your fists, no matter how justified it feels. You've come so far. Don't let one jerk ruin that progress."

I run a hand through my hair, probably a tangled mess by now. "It's just...when something triggers me, like that guy taking a photo of you, my mind goes into overdrive. I don't know how I can fix it." Fix me.

Sometimes it feels like I'm watching myself from the outside, punching and punching, like a ghost standing next to me, completely lost in the hurt and anxiety of losing something. Something I can't even identify.

She's silent for a moment, and I wonder if I've said too much. Usually, people don't want the real me.

They want Deadshot, not a whiny nepo baby who struggles with his emotions. Oh, that poor rich guy. Look at his problems.

"I appreciate you standing up for me, Ri. But you need healthier ways to handle this," she says and then brushes away some strands of hair. It's a simple gesture, but it makes my heart flutter in a different kind of way. "You can do it. You're more than that."

I look at her. I'd love to believe her. But what did my therapist say? I know how to love but not how to be loved.

"You know," I look down at my hands in my lap, "hockey used to be my outlet for that aggression, but…" I sigh, feeling the weight of my shortcomings. "I guess I never really learned how to manage it."

"Change needs time, Ri," she begins softly. Her lips are still swollen from our kiss, but somehow we manage to pretend it was nothing. Just a practice kiss—but what if it's not even pretend at all? Maybe it was nothing for her. Just the way she kisses any guy. But I don't kiss girls like that. I never have. "I always thought you were a hotheaded guy. I like being honest, and I don't like that side of you, but you know what? I like the side you're showing me right now."

I have no idea how to respond to that, so I chuckle nervously and keep talking, not wanting to reveal how deeply her words affect me. How much I need someone I care about to say something like this. "Yeah, I have that reputation, and moments like today show why I need you—our fake relationship, I mean. These blackouts aren't something I'm proud of. When you grow up with hockey and all those expectations…it's easy to let it define you. It defined me."

She shifts closer, her eyes never leaving mine. "I get it. It's hard to break free from what people expect of you. But you're more than just a wall of steel for your team."

Her words hang between us. Great. She's devastatingly

beautiful and smart but I can't have her. I can't because all that I touch turns to shit. "Thanks."

"Can I ask you something?"

"Anything."

"Don't answer if this touches something you're not ready to talk about. But I've been wondering why men are triggering you so hard? You seem so nice to women. I just saw you carrying bags for the old lady downstairs, even though you seem to hate the guy next door."

"Look at you, Sherlock," I say, hesitating. Usually, I clam up whenever someone asks me a deep question. I deflect with sarcasm or change the subject. But when I look at her, I want to tell her everything. I don't want her to think I'm a bad person. I want her to understand me. But what if I don't even understand myself?

"I think it's about my father. I really am the one with the daddy issues, I guess." I finally admit. And dang this feels good.

"Isn't your father a hockey player, too, Henry Huntington, right?" she asks.

"He was, yes. He's big in finance now. He did everything to get me up the ranks, but at some point, he became my rival. At first, when he was still better than me, he loved showing me how to play. But when I got faster, better than him in general, he started playing it down. He did everything to get me where I am now, but he always told me that I'm nothing without him. He still loves to remind me of that. The only time I got any sort of affection from him was when I beat others up." She narrows her eyes, processing my words. It's the first time I say this out loud, and I just keep talking. "I felt like his pit bull, and I guess I was. Eventually, I ignored him, moved away from home, and now I only visit my parents a few times a year. I thought if I stopped acting how he wants me to, stopped listening to him and waiting for that praise, I could change, but I still can't. It just takes one snarky comment and I snap."

"It's because you never healed, Ri." She looks down on her knees and there's something telling me that she knows what she's talking about. "Ignoring your father is just like running away from it and we can't shake off a feeling that's buried inside of us. We first have to find it and release it."

"It's not that easy."

"No, it's not."

And just like that, there's a flicker of understanding between us. Maybe she sees more than just the hockey player with a temper. Maybe she sees someone who's trying to do better, someone with vulnerabilities and scars. Because fuck, that's what I am.

"So, what picture do we post?" she asks, changing the subject lightly, and I'm glad she did.

"I think my ex-plumber just decided what our 'grand reveal' looks like. How about we wait until his photo hits the gossip rags, then post the one with you kissing my cheek? Unless you want me to go after him and get the pic deleted."

I look at her with pure honesty. I would do anything she asks me.

"No. It will be good PR wise. Any press about us is good press, right? And I like the one where you're looking at me like you're in *love*," she teases gently, dragging out the word *love*.

I snort. "That's not love. That's called 'tolerating your antics.'"

She chuckles softly. "Tomato, tomahto. But I'd definitely pick that one."

I prepare the Instagram post and use that photo as my phone's background. Next, I call my therapist. I need to talk to him about Liora. The situation is getting out of hand.

OF COURSE, that slippery skunk sold the pic.

Ethan called me the minute *US Life* published it.

The caption was *TikTok Hottie Riley Huntington Spotted in Steamy PDA with rumored Olympic Athlete Girlfriend!*

Ethan asked if my fake girlfriend had turned into a real one and reminded me of the contract. I told him it was staged. But was it? Liora and I keep pretending it is—or rather, we pretend it never happened—and I'm fine with it. Turns out, if I can't have someone I want, I immediately turn into a jerk and channel all that pent-up energy into being annoyed by practically everything she does.

My therapist said it's a tactic to keep me from shouting my feelings at her. I told him I definitely don't have any feelings for her, and his chuckle on the phone made me want to hang up. But I didn't because I'm trying to change. Still, it's driving me insane.

I'm starting to think I should just sleep with her because maybe I'm pushing her away due to my mood swings rather than risking breaking her heart since I don't do girlfriends. It's like choosing between pests or cholera while I try to relax in the tub. The practice for the play-offs was intense and all my muscles are sore, so my physician suggested a bath with some kind of herbs.

My phone buzzes on the table next to my tub.

> Bladezilla: Come out of that damn bathroom!

I check the door. She's banging on it, and I realize the music was so loud I didn't hear her. My bad.

> Riley: Nope. Living my spa prince dream right now. Bubbly bath and cucumber mask and all that shit. I learned from you, baby.

AND ALL THOSE HOURS OF BLOW-DRYING THAT HAIR.

Bladezilla: You've got ten seconds to open that door! I need to get to set for our costume fittings.

Riley: Or what?

Bladezilla: Or I'll donate your PS5.

MY HEART DROPS IN MY PANTS. SHE WOULDN'T. I'D LOSE ALL MY TROPHIES.

Riley: Does your mom know she gave birth to the devil?

Bladezilla: I'll contact Nina, I bet she'd love to donate it for us.

I run to the door and yank it open so that she's satisfied. But I do it naked. *Here you go, princess.* "Pleased?"

Her eyes widen, moving from the tattoos on my arm downstairs and looking at my shampooed abs, my dick, my balls, and even though I don't have any problems with that, since I'm packed and I know it, she seems to have the shock of her life. And fuck, I turn around and grab a towel because I can't have her know she can give me a boner just looking at my cock.

"Is this the first time you've seen a proper dick?" I ask, trying to hide the way I blush.

"No," she grunts. "No, please get out of here. I really need to get ready, Ri."

"Okay, okay." I wink at her. "Don't get off on the thought of showering in the same spot as I do."

"I won't," she says, pushing me out and slamming the door behind me.

Well, I do. Thinking about her showering is a tantalizing turn-on. Especially after that kiss.

I spend the rest of the day watching cooking shows and posting that adorable pic of us. My followers gobble it up, gushing about how perfectly we fit together. I can't help but laugh at it—if they knew we were at each other's throats daily, they'd think otherwise. But they're doing exactly what I hoped for. They're taking my ex-plumber's videos and mixing them with the photos I posted, creating new clips. In no time, there are hundreds of videos of us circulating on the web, and my bar brawls are nowhere to be seen. They're all buzzing about *Grace on Ice*, hyping it up, and I'm thrilled because Liora's finally getting the attention she deserves.

I'm a happy man, until Liora comes back home with a plant. A dead one. Bigger than her. And she calls it Oscar. Who gives their plants names?

She got it from the production crew, who forgot to water it, and I learn that she loves all plants and apparently takes great joy in trying to rescue them. The downside: that plant looks like a mess, and I'm left to watch Oscar die. It's a brown stick with actual black leaves and moldy points, sitting in the middle of my living room, slowly withering away.

I couldn't resist her puppy-eyed look, especially since she's been sleeping on the couch while we wait for the technicians to fix her bedroom. They've removed all the carpets and the damaged furniture. I count down the hours until she moves back into her room because once night falls, I find myself unable to leave mine. It seems like she has cast a spell on me after all.

Sixteen

LIORA

If I hear the words *quad* and *salchow* together in a sentence one more time, it might be the thing that finally tips me over the edge. I've been on the edge since I woke up this morning with a knot of nerves in my stomach. After another grueling training session, all I wanted was a few minutes of peace under the hot spray of the shower. But just as I begin to unwind, I hear them: Stacey, Patricia, and Molly. Their voices bounce off the tiled walls.

"Did you see how Liora stumble today?" Stacey's voice is like nails on a chalkboard. "It's a wonder she hasn't broken an ankle yet."

"Yeah," Molly chimes in, her tone dripping with mock sympathy. "Maybe she should stick to something safer, like knitting."

I clench my jaw, feeling a wave of anger washing over me.

It's like being back in those cutthroat competitions where every skater was both a competitor and a potential enemy. Priya had to leave early today for dinner with her dad, and without her calming presence, the studio feels even more toxic.

I chose to use the bathroom here, hoping to avoid another awkward encounter with Riley at home. Now, I'm regretting it.

I finish my shower quickly, keeping my movements as quiet as possible, but when I hear Stacey and her squad laughing and something that sounds a lot like running away, I wrap a towel around myself and step out into the changing area, only to find—nothing. My clothes are gone. Every single item has vanished from the bench where I left them.

Panic tightens my chest as I scan the empty room.

Stacey.

Shit. Fucking shit.

I run out of the shower, but she's gone.

It's all closed up—everyone else has left.

My stomach turns into a storm of nausea.

Ever since our first day, Stacey has had it in for me. Her obsession with pushing me out intensified when Grace commended Aiden and me for our routine last time. In this studio, compliments are ammunition, and jealousy is the battleground. Stacey must have seen this as her chance to take a shot at me. It's clear she is dead set on bullying me away from my place here. But I won't go. She's messing with the wrong one. What I've learned is that karma will pay back. She'll get what she deserves. Stupid bitch.

I'm grateful that she didn't take my skates and didn't steal my clothes during the first week. It would have been a disaster. Now, I receive dresses from the set crew and can finally buy new clothes for myself.

Wrapping the towel tightly around myself, I hurry to my locker to grab my phone. I should have stored my clothes there, too, but it never occurred to me that someone might be childish enough to steal them. Holding my phone, I realize there's no way I can risk taking the subway or calling an Uber in just a towel. Heat of humiliation floods my cheeks as I just stare at the screen.

It's a frustrating situation, but with neither Priya nor Nina owning a car and Aiden already on a date, there's only one person I can turn to. The thought causes my heart to race for a completely different reason.

The second Riley picks up the phone his voice comes through, all tense and concerned. "Lia? What's wrong?"

Well, I have never called him before, so I can't be surprised he assumes I need something from him. I do. I take a deep breath and push aside my pride to ask for his help. I considered asking him to just bring me clothes, but the thought of him rummaging through my stuff—and potentially finding things like my little teddy bear and asking about it—made me hesitate. I just couldn't do that. Instead, I ask, "Hey, can you please come get me? Maybe?"

The line goes quiet for a few seconds, and I worry he might say no.

"Yeah, of course. Where are you?"

Wow. His quick agreement surprises me; he doesn't even ask why I need him. This is...kinda sweet?

"At the studio. Everything's closed, and...I don't have my clothes."

"Wait—what? Why don't you have your clothes?"

"Long story. Just—please hurry. I owe you big time, okay?"

"I'm in New Jersey right now, giving the kids free skating sessions. It'll take a bit to get to you. Are you all right to wait?"

"Wait, you weren't just making that up to impress me?" I say, my heart warming at the thought of him working with kids in need.

"Nope, it's my monthly altruistic deed," he replies, sounding rushed, as if he's getting all of his things ready to leave. "You know, I could send Ethan to pick you up. He might be faster—"

"No way, I'll wait." The thought of cranky Ethan escorting me in my semi-naked state makes me shudder.

"Okay then, what's in it for me?" I hear a car door open, his voice dripping with cocky amusement.

"Anything you want," I blurt out, immediately regretting my hasty offer.

"That's a dangerous promise to make."

"Is it? Maybe I'm just feeling generous today." I reply, trying to sound nonchalant despite the nervous flutter in my chest.

"Generous, huh? I might hold you to that."

"Just get here before I freeze."

"On my way," he replies, a hint of amusement in his voice.

"Lia?" Riley's voice calls out in the studio's parking lot.

I step out from behind the large concrete pillar where I've been hiding, my towel barely covering me.

His eyes widen as he takes in the sight, and he visibly swallows hard, his breath catching. His gaze roams, and he clears his throat. If I didn't know any better, I'd think he's making an effort to focus on anything but the fact that I'm standing there wrapped in just a towel.

However, he quickly pulls himself together and reaches for the black hoodie draped over his shoulders. With a quick shrug, he pulls it off and hands it to me. I slip in, grateful for its length as it reaches past my knees.

He opens the car door and practically urges me inside.

"I swear," he says, sitting in the driver's seat. "Press those thighs together for the life of you."

"Um, okay?" I say, catching a whiff of his scent.

His hoodie smells like fresh laundry and a hint of musky cologne.

Damn, he smells so good.

The ride home is awkward.

Riley keeps glancing at me out of the corner of his eye, a frown tugging at his lips. He looks like he's in pain, and for a moment, I wonder if it's because of me.

At some point he finally breaks the silence and asks, "Who would do something like that?" I notice his tight grip on the wheel. "Steal your clothes, I mean. Is bullying common on set?"

"Not really," I lie, my fingers tightening around the hem of his sweater. "It's complicated." Something in his voice makes me hesitant to mention that Stacey and her squad have been badmouthing Priya and me for a while now, or that one comment about my cheeky ass made me stick to salad for lunch whenever the girls are around. It might sound silly, but some habits are hard to shake off, especially when you've lived with them for so long. It takes constant effort to change. Even though I try to act confident and tell Priya that all bodies are great, which they are, my mind still quickly reverts to old insecurities.

"Why wouldn't you just shower at home?" he presses.

I can feel his gaze on me, searching for answers.

"Because…" I trail off, not wanting to admit that it's partly because of him. Not partly—it's 100 percent because of him. "You know it's not a big deal. It doesn't matter. I'll get it sorted."

"Doesn't matter?" He scoffs. "I wouldn't shower on set again. Find out who did this. It's bullying."

I know who did it.

Fucking Stacey Saab.

But I keep quiet and nod instead.

I just need to be more careful.

Grace on Ice has been toxic from the start, but what do you expect when there's a million-dollar prize at stake? It's a life-changing amount, and Stacey has always been deceptive—even when there's no prize involved other than a medal.

She used to bully others instead of relying on her skills.

We pull up to the apartment building, and Riley shuts off

the engine, turning to face me. "Liora, promise me you'll be careful."

"I promise," I whisper, my cheeks burning. "Thank you for the ride."

He rakes a hand through his hair. "Always. Now, let's get you inside before I track down whoever did this."

I QUICKLY CHANGE AND, as I step out of Riley's bathroom, I find him sprawled on the couch, lying on his stomach.

"You're invading my bedroom," I tease, glancing at the TV with the paused show. Ever since they renovated my bedroom and I started sleeping here, he's been watching his shows in his own room.

"Well, you wrecked my evening plans, so I thought I could watch my show on the big screen for once."

My throat tightens. He's so kind, and I feel a pang of guilt. He probably had other plans tonight than driving me around town. "I'm sorry. Did you miss anything because of me?"

"No, no. I was planning to read. It's all good. I just wanted to check on you and there's this new series that got me hooked...so..."

"I'm good, thank you," I say, sinking down next to his feet.

He tries to get up but winces, collapsing back onto the couch.

My stomach drops. "What's wrong?"

"Nothing. Just—fuck. My back. I must have strained a muscle with the kids today. I love them, but they use me as their personal playground. So yeah, maybe I wanted to check in with you and noticed I couldn't get up again. But just wait a bit, it will be all fine—God, this hurts."

I can't even blame the kids for wanting to use him as their play tower. I want to too. But in a different way that's absolutely not okay to think about right now. "Oh god, I'm sorry," I say, blurting out without thinking, "want me to massage you? Maybe I can find the spot."

He blinks. I blink back, my mind racing.

What is wrong with me? Massage him? Am I really this eager to touch him? I glance at the way his muscles strain against his shirt. Yep. I am.

"No. You don't have to," he says.

I notice his flushed cheeks and the way he stays still. He's in pain.

"I know, but I owe you…"

"You don't owe me anything. You needed my help, that's fine. Forget it. I'll just lie here for a few minutes, and when I can get up, I'll let you rest."

"No," I insist, realizing this might actually help him out. "It's really not a big deal. Let me take a look."

"Liora."

"Stop being such a stubborn hothead and let me help."

I push aside my fluttering thoughts about his sexy body and move to straddle him. What's a little massage, right? I position myself over his hips, hovering slightly as if the touch might set me ablaze. I press my hands into his back, feeling the warmth of his body seep through his shirt.

Damn, he's ripped. This was a terrible idea.

"You're going to have to sit on my ass if you want to do this properly," he murmurs, his voice muffled by the cushion.

"Bossy much?" I tease, shifting my weight and lowering myself onto him. The moment I sit down, I feel a shiver run through him.

"What's that you're watching?" I ask, trying to sound casual while my entire body tingles.

"New mystery series on Netflix," he replies, swallowing hard. "Thought I'd give it a try."

My fingers tremble.

Damn it, why I'm suddenly this nervous? It's just a massage…

"Want to watch?" he asks.

"Sure," I say.

He presses Play and I start to knead the muscles in his shoulders, eliciting a deep murmur from Riley. At the sound of it, everything tingles between my legs.

Oh no. I'm in hell. A sexy hell.

"Jesus Christ, this feels good," he says, relaxing under my touch.

I start to wonder if he sounds like this when he fucks—wait. Stop. I don't wonder. No. I never *wonder* about things like that.

I chuckle nervously, working my fingers deeper into his tense muscles.

Each knot I unravel brings another appreciative sound from him, making my heart race a little faster. He's so fine, it's not even funny.

I take a breath. And then another.

I'm not sure how, but I manage to keep it together and look professional, sort of. And when I finally get to the spot that's been bothering him so much, I do my best to knead it out, just like the physiotherapist always did when I had a pinched muscle. Eventually, Riley sighs in relief, his whole body relaxing beneath my hands.

"Wow. That's it. I can actually move now. You're amazing," he says, his voice still a little strained. "Maybe you missed your true calling."

"Ha, yeah, right," I laugh, trying to play it cool.

My hands continue to glide over his back, even though he

said I'd already fixed it. I don't want to stop. Instead of pulling away, my touch softens, becoming gentler, more…intimate. I can't help but trace the lines of his muscles, savoring the moment.

Just like that, I skim through daydreams I'd never let myself fully acknowledge.

Every caress feels like a confession, each touch a tiny secret I hadn't meant to share. The closeness makes my heart race, and a stupid grin spreads across my face. Touching him feels like the warm rays of sunshine on a summer day.

Why does his body feel so fucking good?

He sighs.

I sigh.

And then I realize what I'm doing.

My jaw is on the floor.

I'm groping Riley Huntington!

"Okay, I think you've paid your debt," Riley says suddenly, his voice hoarse.

"Um, yeah, okay." I quickly scramble off him, cheeks burning.

He sits up gingerly, adjusting himself and clearing his throat while I scoot to the far end of the couch.

His cheeks are faintly pink, and he avoids my gaze while I do my best to hide my own blushing. In a swift move, he snags a blanket and wraps it around himself. It's hot like a sauna in here, why would he need—oh. *Oh.*

We both turn our attention to the TV.

He didn't just get a boner because I massaged him, right? Right?

I swallow.

Just the thought gives me a drumbeat pulse between my legs.

Don't think about Riley's dick. Don't.

"Thank you," he says, and this time it's me clearing my throat. "That was one amazing massage."

I smile awkwardly. *It would have been if I didn't get off on groping your fucking muscles.*

"Thanks for rescuing me," I whisper, keeping my eyes on the TV.

"Anytime," he replies, doing the same.

We don't say much during the show—we're both too caught up in what's happening—but as the second episode wraps up, I turn to face him.

"Do you think it was his brother?"

"Wanna find out?"

I check the clock; we both need to get up early, but the show is so good, I just have to keep watching. "Turn it on."

We watch three more episodes, and by the end of it, I'm sprawled on my belly while he lies next to me as if we're used to watching TV together. We're so close that our limbs touch—something I only now realize. We sneak glances at each other, and I have to admit, I really like the way he looks at me.

It makes me feel beautiful. Desired.

"Oh, I'm jealous about the plants his wife has. Speaking of which, why don't you have any plants in here?" I ask him during a cliffhanger moment when the credits start to roll. I love plants. If I had the money, I'd live in a jungle.

"Plants? Me? Nah," Riley says, shaking his head.

I glance at him, he has his arms draped behind his head and I see the abs pressing through his shirt. I'd love to lie on those. Okay. No. I don't. Absolutely not. They are hard. Hard as fuck. "I could kill a cactus just by looking at it."

"Really?" I laugh. "Cacti are pretty resilient."

"Not resilient enough for me, apparently. Can't share your obsession but it's cute."

"I guess I really am obsessed," I say, feeling a warmth

spread through my body at the memory of all the plants I grow back home. Summer is my favorite—I love trying to grow the veggies and fruits we eat, and more often than not, it works. I'm over the moon whenever I manage to make something grow. "Plants are little pieces of nature you can keep close by and with just a bit of care, they give so much in return. It's calming. Oh, and I think they make the rooms so much prettier and— Shoot. Sorry, I'm totally babbling."

"Don't be sorry. I enjoy listening to you talk about the things you love. You're eyes light up, and it's…well, it's kind of adorable."

I catch myself smiling at him, my heart doing a stupid little flip.

Dangerous. This is definitely dangerous territory.

"You know, you're different than I thought you'd be."

"Different how?" I ask, raising an eyebrow.

"Well, I always saw you as this driven, no-nonsense athlete. But here you are, not wanting me to tear apart the idiot who keeps bullying you, talking about plants like you're a gardener instead of a skater, and spending all night watching TV shows with me," he says with a crooked smile. "You're…softer. And I mean that in a really good way."

"Yeah, I think I'm softer off the ice," I admit, biting my lip. It's because I have to pretend to be hard to keep on going. "But you're not exactly what I expected either. It's really great what you do for those kids, Riley."

"Yeah, I love it," he says, his face softening. "Working with them keeps me grounded, reminds me why I love hockey in the first place."

"See? That's what I mean. You're different too," I say, shifting slightly closer. "In a good way too."

"Glad to hear it," he murmurs.

We watch the next episode, and our conversation starts to

slur. Before I know it, my eyelids grow heavy, and the last thing I remember is Riley's body beside me as I drift off.

WHEN I WAKE up it's early in the morning, the room is dark except for the soft glow from the TV screen. My body feels unusually warm, and I notice a musky scent—sandalwood, maybe? No, definitely musk, and sort of fresh. And I feel a tickling against my neck—something soft yet firm. I glance down and notice a way-too-heavy arm draped across my stomach, pulling me close against his chest. It feels good. His chest.

Wait. *His* chest feels *good?*

That's when I notice we're fucking cuddling! What? We're a tangled mess of limbs! How did this happen?

Riley's breathing is slow and steady, completely at ease. Mine is not. No, I think I'm hyperventilating.

I carefully disentangle myself from his embrace, moving as quietly as possible, like I'm defusing a bomb in a spy movie. One wrong move, and I'll wake him. Green wire or red wire? I go for it, holding my breath the whole time and—I slip free and sit up, gazing at him as he sleeps.

It's strange, I've never accidentally cuddled with someone before.

I study the peaceful rise and fall of his chest, his face softened in slumber, every line and curve relaxed. The way his dark hair falls across his forehead. The sound of his breathing. Cuddling with him felt nice. It shouldn't, though.

I mentally shake myself and scurry back to my room to get ready for set, hoping he didn't notice I craved that cuddling. I need to talk about him to Mom later; she's the only one who will understand why I can't let these feelings in. She knows, as well as I do, that I need to get my life in order first. I make a mental note: No more massages. Ever.

Whatever the reason, I'm dangerously close to becoming addicted to his touch, and that's a risk I can't afford. I'm already struggling to keep my emotions in check—I don't need to add heartbreak to the mix.

Seventeen

RILEY

As Mercer blows the whistle, signaling the start of the drill, I explode into action.

I dart across the ice with lightning speed, our goalie, Derek Devereaux, waits for me in front of the net as we practice for the upcoming game. With a swift flick of my wrist, I send a blistering slap shot toward the net.

The puck hurtles down the ice like a bullet fired from a cannon, leaving a trail of icy mist in its wake. Derek tracks the puck's trajectory with laser focus, but there's little time to react. As the puck approaches, it seems to accelerate, gaining speed with every passing millisecond. Its surface blurs, reflecting the glint of the arena lights like a shooting star streaking across the night sky. I watch Derek bracing himself, positioning his body, ready to make the save. But this shot is different, and I smile because I see it coming. It's not just about velocity. It's about deception. At the last moment, the puck seems to change course, veering off in an unexpected direction. It sails past Derek's outstretched glove and —GOAL!

"Ha!" I yell, doing a little victory dance. "Lucky for you,

you don't have to play against me, huh," I shout in his direction, meeting Derek's enraged gaze.

He remains sprawled on the ice, frustration in every heavy breath he takes. Derek had been all talk since he joined us, boasting about his skills nonstop. Sure, he's good, but not as great as he makes himself out to be, and it's moments like these I relish—proving him wrong during practice.

"Keep it up, Huntington! One more!" Mercer's booming voice echoes from the bench, urging us to keep going. He's an old man by now, his hair white, his glasses stained, but he's still a force to be reckoned with.

I was on the verge of gliding away to give the shot another attempt when the sound of Derek's mocking scoff halts me in my tracks. Pausing, I pivot to face him as he rises to his feet again.

"Must be nice having everything handed to you, eh? First your spot on the Falcons, second an Olympic athlete as a girlfriend." His snide voice cuts through my concentration like a knife. What did he say? "How much did your wealthy parents pay to get you a girlfriend like Liora James?"

I grit my teeth, staring at him while he adjusts his gloves. We had never gotten along. Not really. While my family indeed had used their connections to help me, Derek had clawed his way into the league without any assistance, and he has reminded me ever since.

I get it. I hate the fact my fucking parents paid for my career. But I will make a name for myself, without their help. It's not just my parents who can claim my achievements. I am in control of my own destiny. At least that's what my therapist engrained in my head a couple of days ago. They didn't say Derek would become the best sniper in the league's history. I will.

"Jealousy doesn't look good on you, Devereaux," I snap back, feeling his anger flare up.

Addressing stressors and teaching coping skills to manage stress effectively can reduce the frequency and intensity of anger episodes, my therapist's voice rings in my head.

Coping skill number one: breathe. *I take a deep, deep breath.*

Skill number two: check your surroundings. *I'm on the rink.*

Skill number three: reframe your thoughts. *This is frustrating, but I can find a way around it. His words hurt me, but it doesn't mean they are true.*

He chuckles and I take another deep breath, doing everything I can to force myself to speak past this threatening lump working up my throat. "You know what? I'm sorry, Der, let's drop it. Please. We have to drill, let's keep it up."

"No," he says, skating toward me. "I heard you. Jealousy, you said, huh? Hardly." He smiles as if he finds the situation funny. I startle at this expression—it's like a déjà vu from weeks ago in the bar against Houston. I had fun smashing his head just because he provoked me. I don't want to be that person anymore, but the way Derek stands there, threatening me, brings back old feelings with no place to go.

I try to focus on something else—Liora. I nearly missed my alarm this morning. We ended up falling asleep on the couch, cuddling. It felt amazing. Really amazing. I played it cool, pretending I didn't notice her slip away and practically bolt from the scene.

"I've worked hard for every inch of ice I've skated on, unlike...well, you." He slips out of his gloves and drops them on the ice. "If I were you, I'd wipe that self-satisfied grin off your face after slap shots like that. It's amazing you can score but not everyone has had their game handed to them on a silver platter like you have." Closing the space between us, he pushes me—fuck, he actually pushed me. "Not everyone had the chance to practice with the best players and copy their style."

My jaw clenches as I try to block out the insults.

Somehow, I manage to skate backward.

Breathe, Huntington. Breathe.

He saw a picture of Liora and got jealous—it has to be just that. We're a team.

Skating back to keep the peace, my mind reels. I must focus or risk smashing that puck into his face.

As professional athletes, we're expected to maintain composure and teamwork; disagreements are common under pressure, but fighting within our own team is unacceptable.

Breathing in and out, shaking off his idiocy—I glance toward Mercer, who's already standing by the rink with arms crossed over his beer belly. He watches me with a stern face—counting possibilities silently.

Why isn't he saying anything? If roles were reversed, he would have snarled at me already—fuck, I can't snap now.

I swirl to the opposite end, my feet gliding over the frozen surface. Desperate to think about something other than those fucking words Derek said, I glance toward my other teammates. Some are stretching and warming up at the edge of the rink. Jayce, Colton, and some rookies do a stickhandling warm-up. They stand around a circle with two pucks and, on the whistle, two players start stickhandling around the circle. But Jayce's face is tense, watching me, knowing something is wrong. I avoid making eye contact with him. He must have overheard the comments made earlier. But it's Colton who screams my name.

"Everything all right?" he yells.

I hold an arm up, signaling him with a thumbs-up that I'm fine. I'm not though.

I hate feeling like a child, but I have nobody to blame except myself.

It's understandable that my friends are concerned. I asked them to stop watching over me on the field because it affects their performances. I understand their desire to protect me and keep me on the team, but ultimately it's my decision. If I can't handle it, then I don't deserve my spot on the team. And that's probably why Mercer paired me with Derek today—to toughen me up.

I get ready for the next shot, expecting Derek to come back to his spot, but he's still fuming, refusing to take his position. "Come on, Huntington, I guess it's time to tell me. How much did your daddy pay to get you on our team?"

The rink goes dead quiet in a heartbeat, like it's turned into some eerie ghost town. All eyes fix on me and Derek.

I hear Jayce swearing and the sharp scrape of blades.

But I'm already in a tunnel.

"What did you say?" I growl and skate toward Derek.

He grins, skating up to me as well, throwing his hands up in mock defense. "Just addressing what everyone thinks."

"Who's everyone?"

Hatred floods in like a rising tide, drowning out any sense of reason or compassion.

"Ri, let it be. I swear. Ri!" Jayce screams after me.

I slow down my pace, cursing under my breath. I think somewhere in the background, Colton swears in Russian, and fuck, I know I can't hit him, no matter how much he deserves it. As their sniper, I am expected to score goals and not engage in physical altercations like defensemen or enforcers. Mercer is right. I can't miss any more games. I'm vital for the team.

"The whole team thinks it," Derek says.

"Stop lying, asshole," Jayce yells, grabbing me and holding me back.

"Shut the fuck up," Colton says somewhere behind me.

"Or what? He'll have his family make me leave the team? They buy you everything, huh? Skill, a girlfriend, and your own team." Derek sneers.

I stiffen up.

"Enough!" Mercer's voice booms through the air, but my

emotions have already spiraled out of control. Blind rage consumes me as I leap at Derek, Jayce and Colton's frantic screams echoing around me. Their voices blend into a chaotic racket as I charge toward my own teammate.

But just as I'm about to reach him, I see Liora behind him. I break.

Fuck. How did I miss her? When did she get here?

I skid to a halt mere inches from Derek, and Liora's eyes meet mine, filled with fear—fear of me.

It pierces through my fury like a knife, slicing it into overwhelming sadness and shame. I freeze, every muscle in my body tensing.

No. She can't look at me like that.

I want her to feel safe.

Time seems to stand still as I grapple with the horrifying realization.

And then, without warning, a sharp impact explodes across my face—and everything fades to black.

Eighteen

LIORA

I can't erase the image of Riley crumpling to the ice, blood smearing across his pale skin. The sound of my own scream still echoes in my ears. In that moment, something primal took over—I shoved that mammoth of a goalie with a strength I didn't know I possessed, not caring about the consequences. All I could focus on was getting to Riley.

Now, as I stand next to him, my hand gripping his like a lifeline, I silently will him to open his eyes. The medical staff bustles around us, their voices a low murmur as they assess his condition. "The punch triggered a vagal response," one of them explains. "The sudden impact can cause a reflex through the vagus nerve, leading to a drop in heart rate and blood pressure. That's why he fainted."

I nod, only half listening as they clean his wounds.

An eternity seems to pass before Riley finally stirs and his eyelids flutter open. Those whiskey-colored eyes find mine, and my name forms on his lips. "Lia…"

"Hey," I whisper, so happy he's awake. He scared the shit out of me. "You forgot your keys. I didn't know if you needed them, since I'm training with Aiden all night. Our show is in three days, and—"

"Thank you," he interrupts, a faint grin tugging at the corners of his mouth. He starts to draw circles on my skin and each trace of his feels like a burning fire while he looks at me like I actually mean the world to him.

I swallow hard, suddenly aware of Colton and Jayce's curious gazes boring into us. Heat creeps up my neck, but I don't let go of Riley's hand. "How are you feeling?"

"Like I got sucker punched by a grizzly bear," he jokes weakly. "But I'll live."

"You better," I threaten, trying to keep my tone light even as my heart constricts. "I didn't just scream my head off in Hungarian for nothing."

He laughs. "You did?"

"Yeah," Jayce and Colton say as if from one mouth.

"I think Devereaux is afraid of her now," Jayce says.

Riley's grin widens, and for a moment, the pain and uncertainty in his eyes fade away. "Guess I owe you one, huh?"

"More than one," I shoot back, a playful smile spreading across my face. "But who's counting?"

"Let's just stick with one because you downgraded my apartment with that hideous plant."

I burst out laughing. "Oscar isn't hideous, and he's already looking better."

"I'm obsessed with—organization," he snaps, but the way his voice wavers makes me pause. There's a flicker in his eyes, a tension that makes it seem like he's holding back something more personal—as if he wanted to say he's obsessed with me, not just his need for order. But that's absurd, right? My thoughts are absurd.

I quickly change the subject, my heart racing as if I've just dodged a bullet. "Do you need anything? Meds?"

The medical staff offers him various meds the second I ask him, but he shakes his head.

"No thanks, I'm fine. Just tell me, is my nose still the prettiest you've ever seen?" And that stupid smile of his makes me forget the worry I just felt because of him.

"Yes."

"Then I'm okay."

The doctor gives him an ice pack, and he holds it against his cheek.

"Shit, is this how you get all those ladies in bed?" Jayce throws his head back and lets out a loud, hearty laugh, and Colton joins in.

I want to laugh, too, but then Riley winces and shifts uncomfortably on the exam table, adjusting the ice pack on his bruised cheek. Jayce and Colton had rushed him to the team doctor after Derek's punch landed square on his eye. The sight of Riley crumpled on the ground had been enough to send a chill through me.

"Derek was just being his usual asshole self, trying to get under my skin," Riley explains with a pained expression.

The doctor takes a look at Riley's eye. "It's definitely going to swell."

"What did Derek say to you?" I ask, feeling an unexpected surge of protectiveness rushing through my core.

"It's okay," Riley tries, but the pain etched in his features tells a different story.

No, Derek said something that cut deeper than any punch ever could. When I entered the arena, I saw them immediately. At first, I thought they were just talking, but then I noticed the yelling and the look on Riley's face. It was as if something inside him shattered. I couldn't stand it, and before I knew it, my feet were moving toward the ice in overdrive.

"No, it's not," I insist.

The doctor interrupts us with a bottle of ointment. "I'll

give you this for now. It should reduce the swelling, and you'll be fine by next week for the play-offs."

Frustration boils in my chest and I let out an exasperated sigh. "This is ridiculous. Who would sabotage their chances of winning by purposely injuring you? What an idiot!"

There's a flicker of amusement in his face. "This isn't funny, Riley. What exactly did he say to you?"

"Baby, it's fine," Riley repeats, wincing as the doctor applies surgical glue to the cut under his eye. "I charged at him first. It was my fault—ouch."

The doctor apologizes but keeps working.

My hand involuntarily grips Riley's arm. "What—"

"He said his dad bought him a spot on the team," Jayce chimes in, glancing at my hand on Riley. The way I hold him.

I quickly let go of him, forcing myself to remain calm. "Anything else?"

"Yeah," Jayce says, standing up straighter. "He said Ri's copying skills from other athletes and that his parents bought his career and, well, you."

"That asshole," I mutter through gritted teeth, earning a surprised look from Jay.

I notice Colton stifling a laugh, and anger flares hot in my chest. How dare Derek treat Riley this way!

I bend down to Riley, our eyes locking with a depth of emotion. "Listen to me. He's wrong. Your father may have helped you, but it's you making those shots. Do you hear me?"

Riley hesitates, then nods slowly.

"I saw countless rich girls trying to match me. But who won the gold? I did. And I didn't have a penny. It's about skill. You can't buy success in sports. Sure, money can help, but in the end, it's you and your team out there. It's you making those decisions. It's you calling the shots out there. Not your father or his money. Don't ever believe a guy like Derek. Believe in yourself, because people will always try to be like you and hate on you at the same time."

His eyes soften, a flicker of gratitude breaking through the pain. "Thanks," he whispers, voice shaky.

"Now, excuse me. I'll be right back."

Before I can second-guess myself, I charge out of the medical room, ignoring everyone's surprised looks as I head to the locker room, and lucky me, I spot Derek lingering in the hallway. His eyes widen when he sees me storming toward him.

"What the hell is wrong with you?" I demand and push him with both of my hands. Just like he did with Riley, but he doesn't move an inch. It's as if a fly collided with him.

Derek holds up his hands defensively. "Woah. Watch out there. You know I'm a giant compared to you, huh?" His mouth is twisted into a sneer as he looks down at me.

"I don't fucking care."

"Look, I'm sorry, okay? Coach asked me to provoke him. I took it too far."

"Damn right you did," I snap. "Hold on. Your coach did what?" Riley's *coach* would mess with his mental health like that?

Derek rakes a hand through his short black hair, his eyes shifting back and forth. "He wanted me to check if Riley's able to control his shit or not."

"That is stupid," I say. "Provoking each other won't help. All that got you is him having a black eye and you risking your game next week. I can't believe you said yes."

"I'm…I'm sorry, but Coach—"

"You have your own mind! Do you even understand what you just did? You deliberately provoked another teammate into hurting you. Whatever your coach said. That's not coaching, that's abuse."

He just stares at me, his mouth agape.

I nod to the locker room at the end of the corridor.

"Everyone in there is pissed at you. You better start thinking of one hell of an apology."

Leaving him sputtering in the hallway, I march toward Mercer's office. I know abusive coaches when I hear about them and this needs to be stopped before it gets worse. Fear claws at my throat but I swallow it down. I'm done being timid.

I burst into John Mercer's office without knocking. He looks up from his desk, startled. I'm a little taken aback since I had imagined him dark haired with a suspicious mustache but, well, I guess my imagination just ran away with me. He looks more like Santa Claus. His beard is shorter but still. Riley's coach is Santa during summer vacation.

"Miss James, how can I help you?"

"What kind of messed-up coaching tactic is having one player assault another?" I say, my voice shaking with fury.

To my utter disbelief, Mercer actually has the nerve to laugh. "Well, well," he says, leaning back in his chair and folding his arms across his chest. "Looks like our resident hothead has found himself a little spitfire."

"This isn't funny," I say. "What you did today was cruel and unnecessary. You know he just started therapy. He was about to knock the shit out of your player and then what? What if he got hurt? You just risked your own game."

"No offense, sweetheart, but I've been coaching longer than you've been alive. I think I know how to handle my players."

"I'm not your sweetheart, and if this is how you handle them," I grind out through clenched teeth, "then you don't deserve to be called a coach."

Something flickers in his expression—a hint of surprise, maybe even a grudging respect. But I won't back down. I'm none of his players, I'm not even Riley's girlfriend, and since he knows of our truce, there's no way he can punish Riley so I just say what's on my mind.

"If I were you, I'd let him heal instead. Mental wounds are

just as real and serious as physical ones. He's already going to therapy once a week, so let the professional handle it. Instead of pushing him to face his fears, be a source of stability in his life." I'm so proud of Riley for facing his fears. Mercer is not going to ruin it for him.

"You've got guts, kid," Mercer acknowledges, tilting his head to the side. "I'll give you that."

"I don't want your praise," I say, straightening up to my full height, which is not much, but I think I'm making my point. "I want your word that you'll never put Riley—or any other player—in that position again. He's healing. Let him."

Mercer regards me for a long moment, his eyes searching my face as if trying to gauge my sincerity. Finally, he nods. "Fair enough, I won't do it again," he says, leaning forward to rest his elbows on the desk. "But let me ask you this: How far are you willing to go to protect him?"

"What do you mean?"

A slow, calculating smile spreads across his face. "I have a proposition for you," he says, steepling his fingers under his chin. "Come to our high-stakes games. Like the one against the Bears. Be there to keep Riley calm when he meets Houston again. I'll even pay you for your time."

I stare at him in disbelief, my mind reeling. "You want me to be his...what? His emotional support cheerleader?"

Mercer shrugs. "Call it what you want. But I think we both know that you have a unique ability to get through to him. And if that means the difference between winning and losing..." He trails off, letting the implication hang in the air.

The nerve this man has. "I'm not interested in your money," I say, almost spitting the words out. "But let me make one thing perfectly clear. If you ever pull a stunt like this again —if you ever put Riley's well-being at risk for the sake of your own ego—you'll have a lot more than a 'little spitfire' to deal with. I can be one hell of a pain in the ass when I want to be."

Mercer's eyes widen almost imperceptibly, and for a split second, I swear I see a flicker of fear in their depths. But then it's gone, replaced by a mask of cool indifference. "What if I tell you that I'm willing to pay you *a lot* of money?"

"Then I tell you again that I don't want your fucking money. I'll be there for him nevertheless, and he'll tell me where and when he needs me."

"Noted," he says, waving at me in dismissal. "Now, if you'll excuse me, I have a team to manage."

I give a curt nod and spin on my heel. Shit. My heart pounds in my throat and my hands shake with adrenaline. I have no idea what I've just gotten myself into, but one thing is clear: I don't like it when Riley gets hurt. But the most startling part is, why would I fight for him like this when I'd never have the guts to do it for myself?

Nineteen

RILEY

I bang on the bathroom door again, desperate. "Lia, come on! Open up, I'm about to burst! I mean it."

"I'm shaving!" she calls back over the pounding water, and for fuck's sake, this one bathroom situation is my nightmare. Having an expensive apartment is great and all, until you need to replace items and find out they take forever to arrive because they're handmade. I considered just buying something from IKEA, but since I've already paid for it, I guess I'm stuck waiting.

"I need to look flawless for our dress rehearsal tonight! Grace is going to kill me otherwise," she yells.

I sigh, hopping from foot to foot. Damn my genius idea of not installing doors that open from the outside. "Woman! It's an emergency!"

"Fine. I'm hurrying up."

"Faster!"

"I. Said. I'm. Hurrying. Up!"

I bang at the door again. "Open it or you'll regret it!" Well, I guess I'll regret it because I'm going to pee in my pants.

All I get in response is an annoyed hiss.

I give the door one last frustrated kick before my eyes land on Oscar in the corner. Desperate times...

I run, open my jeans, and—she's yelling my name, but I don't care anymore, all I care about is making it to the plant in time. In my peripheral vision, I notice the bathroom door flying open, steam billowing out as she stands there in that pink bathrobe I forced her to wear in the bathroom as a safety measure, hair tied up high. And I hold my dick with the biggest smile there is, relieving myself into her hideous plant.

I shrug. "I told you to let me in."

And for the first damn time, Liora James is left speechless and without a clever comeback.

"You're a caveman, Riley Huntington," she says, throwing a towel at my head. "If Oscar dies, you owe me a new plant."

I sigh in relief as my bladder finally empties, then tuck everything back into my jeans, grinning like the cat who got the cream. This was so worth it, if not for saving my bladder, then for that look on her face. "I told you to open the door."

"I swear, if I see your dick ever again—"

"You'll give it a kiss, baby?"

She snorts, muttering something while finally storming off in a huff, blonde ponytail swishing.

I barely have time to toss the towel aside before there's pounding at the front door. Jayce and Derek barge in, our rookie Shane trailing behind them.

"Party time!" Shane bellows, arms full of beer. "Last chance to let loose before the play-offs, boys!"

I watch as they dump the booze on my kitchen counter. Maybe getting trashed is what we need to smooth things over after that fight at practice. Or maybe it's the dumbest idea we ever had.

Derek approaches me as I stock my fridge with some of the beers. "Hey, man, about the other day...sorry, again. I was way out of line. I know you've been through a lot. No hard feelings?"

I almost huff out a laugh. Growing up with ice-cold parents and an obsessive need to be the best—he doesn't know the half of it. But I clap him on the back anyway. "Water under the bridge. Let's just focus on bonding as a team tonight, eh? God knows we'll need it for the postseason games."

As the guys start setting up for the party, I survey my apartment. It's about to get wild in here. I know not everyone from the team is coming—lots of the married guys are spending time off with their families. But our core crew always rounds up some other friends to get rowdy with when we have the chance.

It was Derek's and my idea. He came to me right after Liora scared the living daylights out of him. She somehow got him to apologize, and with everyone on the team still fuming over the whole mess, we all decided it was high time for a party. Derek and I offered to foot the bill. Gotta bond and forget about the crappy months we've had.

That damn lawsuit is still dragging on, causing headaches for everyone. But now, we're facing off against the Boston Bears in our first play-off game, and we all know they'll be coming at us hard, seeking revenge. They almost didn't make it into the play-offs, thanks to me. And with Houston back and fully recovered, it's going to be a bloodbath on that field for sure.

I even shot Coach an invite tonight, but he just snorted. *I spend enough time wrangling you shitheads at the rink. I'll pass on doing it during my downtime too.* He's probably right on that one. We planned on making some chili for the crew and talking things out. I think it's the right thing to do. Derek and I have hated each other since the start, it's time to let those feelings go.

The team is family. Period.

With an air of frustration, Colton barges into the room and

plops down on my dining table, tossing a stack of papers while grumbling in Russian.

"What's with him?" I ask Jayce while he drops the ingredients on my kitchen counter.

Jayce gives me a knowing look, raising his eyebrows and making some wiggly motions. That's all I need to know that he got mail again.

I suck in a sharp breath and Shane is all ears. "What? What's wrong with King?" We all try to casually glance at him, thinking we're being sneaky while looking like a bunch of nosy gossips.

"That crazy bitch," Colton says, his eyebrows furrowed and his jaw clenched as he furiously types on his phone.

"Wowza," I say. "He's aaangry."

"He's been the worst to ride with to your place," Jayce says, and I know what he means.

Colton usually is a man of few or no words, but when he's angry, it's like he forgets English and starts spewing out heavy Russian curses. We'll ask him what's wrong and all we get are snarls in return. So whenever he wakes up on the wrong side of the bed, you can bet your bottom dollar you'll need to learn Russian to get through to him.

"But what's up?" Shane says.

Derek gives me a look, silently pleading for permission to spill the beans. But we all know Colton's current legal mess isn't exactly top secret. If it weren't for our blabbermouth of a younger friend, he'd already have the scoop. But I give in. The sooner Shane shuts up, the better. "Go ahead," I tell Derek.

"Colton's in a legal smackdown," he says. "His ex took their daughter to England, violating their joint custody. He's fighting tooth and nail for full custody now, since she's not mom material and just in it for his money."

"And then there's the lawyer drama," Jayce adds, his knife slicing through onions with surgical precision. "Colton insisted on hiring the top custody attorney in New York, the same girl he used to bully during their senior year of high school. She's agreed to represent him, but only if she can call him names throughout the case. They've been at it for weeks—each time he gets mail, he's like this."

"King bullied a girl?" Shane's jaw drops, and the minced meat nearly slips from his hand. He stares at me, wide eyed and slack jawed, as if I'd just told him the moon was made of cheese.

"I *didn't* bully her," Colton snaps back. "I just moved to the states from Russia, my English was shit. So I didn't stop the goons from picking on her for her red hair, curves, and braces like I probably should have. But now I'm paying through the nose for legal fees. Fucking shit!"

We all exchange stunned glances, shocked that Colton has strung together more than a sentence.

Jayce blinks at me, and I give him a shrug.

Looks like this lawyer's getting under Colton's skin.

"You gonna read us that letter?" I ask with a grin.

Colton slams the paper down on the counter, his expression dark and intense. If I didn't know him as one of my closest friends, I'd be terrified just by the way he's looking at me. He just looks like he's straight out of a mafia movie.

"Oh, absolutely," Shane chimes in.

"Read loud and clear, King," Jayce says with a sheepish smile.

Colton grunts. "I'll only read the first sentences because this woman is crazy. Look at this shit:

'Dearest dickhead,

Congratulations! You've managed to turn what should have been a routine custody battle into a comedy that would make even the *Three Stooges* cringe. I hope you're proud of yourself, because I'm sitting here questioning all my life choices. Let's address the elephant in the room—yes, you are indeed a colossal idiot.'"

King grunts out in frustration. "I don't even know what she meant with 'Stooges' and had to google. I thought I needed to google legal shit, not some American slapstick shit."

I glance at Jayce, who's barely containing his laughter, his eyes wide with amusement. We share a look that speaks volumes: he found his nemesis.

Just as I'm about to catch my breath from laughing, the bathroom door swings open, and Liora walks out like a force of nature. Instantly, the room falls silent. There she stands, looking fierce and drop-dead gorgeous in a costume that leaves little to the imagination. My initial amusement fades, replaced by a surge of protectiveness that catches me off guard.

"No way," I blurt out, trying to sound authoritative but failing miserably. I toss the limes I was holding onto the kitchen counter, not caring where they land. Closing the distance between us, I face her head-on. "You're not taking the subway dressed like that."

Liora arches an eyebrow at me, her expression daring. "Like what?"

I gesture vaguely at her outfit, struggling to find words. "That…barely there thing. You can't just strut around the city in that. This isn't Springfield."

Her frown deepens, and she crosses her arms defiantly. "Watch me."

Before I can protest further, she storms off, and I hear Shane whistle softly, muttering about trouble in paradise. I dash after her. "Liora. I'll come with you if you don't stop."

"If you don't have anything better to do, fine."

She quickens her pace, but I manage to grab her just before she reaches the elevator.

If she thinks she can brush me off like that, she's got another thing coming.

In a flash, I scoop her up and sling her over my shoulder. She huffs and puffs, but I couldn't care less about her protests or the punches she's throwing at my back.

To the amusement of the guys—Colton's scoff included—I carry her into my room.

I set her down and brace myself for the storm that follows.

"Are you insane?"

"Yes. Is that news? What I wanted to say is, you're practically naked and there's no way I'm letting you go out alone. It's getting dark and—"

"You're worried."

"Yes."

"Why?"

"Because."

She laughs, a sharp, sassy sound that makes my skin tingle. "If this is your argument structure, I wonder how your English exams turned out."

"I was a straight-A student, how about you?"

"Same, but I was homeschooled, so I have no idea how it is in the great wild."

"Homeschooled?" I ask, feeling a shift in the air between us.

"Yeah, I competed in figure skating since I was eleven. Started in Hungary, then moved to the US with my coach and mom. No time for high school."

I sigh, unable to stay mad at her cute face. "No prom?"

"No."

From one second to the next this woman makes me feel boiling angry to worried to sad?

And just like that, there's a short scene I remember from prom.

All the boys drank their asses off, thanks to the booze we snuck in.

And then the ultimate thrill—my first threesome. Yep. In high school.

As I think about it now, another tinge of sadness creeps in knowing she didn't get the high school experience like the rest of us. But then again, I'm glad she didn't have a threesome on prom night. It's a fucked-up thought, but I don't want anyone else having their hands on her. Only me.

"Now come on, be a good girl and let my driver take you. He needs the extra cash for his daughter's birthday this month."

Her demeanor softens. "How old is she?"

"Five."

"Oh." She averts her gaze, and I wonder what's going through her mind now. Why does she look so sad when I bring up the topic of kids? "Fine. Call him."

"That's all it took? A kid's birthday?"

She swallows. "It's sweet that he's saving."

"Fine. Let's get you downstairs. He'll be waiting."

"I can walk down myse—"

"Liora, please don't make this harder. Consider yourself lucky I'm not wrapping you in a potato sack right now."

She steps out, and I grin proudly, earning an amused headshake from Jayce.

The doorbell rings, confirming it's my driver. I nod toward the door. "He's here. Good luck tonight. I hope Grace is kind."

"We all do," Liora says, moving toward the door.

I clear my throat. "Baby, don't I get a goodbye kiss?"

She frowns, and I grin. I'm not letting this chance to kiss her slip away—not with an audience here. Even if it's just Derek and Shane, it's enough to keep up appearances.

She struts toward me, rising on her toes to press her lips to mine. I might have pulled her up a bit too eagerly, my hands settling on her waist. Her lips are impossibly soft, and there's a brief hesitation before she leans in further. The kiss is fleeting but charged, a jolt that takes me back to the intensity we shared just days ago. Her breath mingles with mine, a tantalizing blend of defiance and something more that makes my heart flutter. There's no denying it anymore. I want her. So much it hurts.

Her fingers lightly graze my jaw, and just as I'm about to deepen the kiss, she bites at my lower lip. Um, yes. Wanting her hurts.

"Ouch, shit," I whisper-shout, hoping no one else noticed.

She grips my jaw firmly, her voice low and fierce. "Stop playing mother hen, okay?"

"Never."

With a final, fiery kiss that feels more like a punch than a caress, she turns and walks away.

"Maaan, you're over the moon," Derek says. "I couldn't believe the rumors but now that I see it. I wonder where you two got to know each other?"

I shrug, trying to play it cool, but Jayce's smirk tells me he sees right through it.

It's not the first time someone has asked how I met her, but thankfully, Liora and I have our story straight. "We met at a sports gala my parents organized back home," I say smoothly. "I walked up to her, we hit it off, and the rest is history."

My lips still tingle from the kiss, and I can't help but wonder if it's really all just an act anymore. Even though we call each other names and claim we want this to end, there's this undeniable tension between us. Maybe it's because we're both competitive—neither of us wants to lose in this stupid game we're playing. But I'm not ready to confess anything yet. Maybe I just need to kiss someone else, let that steam off, and get that blonde firecracker out of my system and then I'll be good.

"Will she come to the party later?"

I feel the eyes of the whole room on me as I answer gruffly,

"Well, she lives here, so, yes. But let's get something straight—she's off limits, got it? No trying to chat her up or any shit like that. You know what? No talking to her in general."

Jayce grins knowingly. "Afraid we'll embarrass you in front of your lady, loverboy?"

"I just don't need you idiots saying something dumb and pissing her off. It's better for everyone if you steer clear." I give them each a hard stare to drive the point home.

The last thing I need is the boys blabbing about locker-room antics to Liora.

Eager to change the subject, Shane pipes up, "So how about them Boston Bears?" The guys immediately jump on the new topic, arguing about play-off predictions.

Twenty

LIORA

The living room is bursting with people.

I'm still dressed in my rehearsal clothes from earlier and since I didn't want to show up alone, I asked Priya and Aiden if they'd like to join me. A little party never killed anybody, right?

"Holy cow, this apartment is amazing," Aiden says, and I nod away.

"It is. The owner is not." I've come to trust Aiden with my heart, so I told him about our fake dating, and he found it hilarious. I spot many unfamiliar faces mixed with Riley's teammates. There are women fawning over the players, hanging on their every word, and I roll my eyes.

I notice heads turning our way. I hear a younger teammate say, "God, she's beautiful!" before Jayce promptly elbows him in the ribs.

Heat rises to my cheeks at the attention.

Where is he?

I scan the room for Riley, and when I notice Ethan out on the balcony, I assume he's with him but no, he's nowhere to be seen. Then, Derek catches my eye, nodding in greeting as he smoothly introduces himself to Priya, whose face flushes a charming shade of pink at the sight of him. What is it about Priya that attracts the most questionable men in town?

Another teammate approaches Aiden and he's quickly handed a beer and pulled into a conversation. Since I'm basically standing there like the third wheel, watching my friends talking without being looked at once, I weave through the crowd, smiling and greeting people as I go, but the weird thing is, no one seems interested in talking to me.

They grin politely before turning back to their own conversations. I try it again and steer to Jayce and Colton. They stand in the kitchen behind the brewing chili, talking away while drinking beer. Something's up.

"Hi," says Jayce. Colton only nods my way until both revert to talking about whatever they talked about before. I sneer. What is this?

Fine. If they won't talk to me, I'll just have to find someone who will.

I spot the rookie standing alone and make a beeline for him. "Hey, can I ask you something?"

His green eyes widen and he quickly checks on his other teammates. Then I notice it. He's looking for permission to talk to me! He shifts, his face turning red like a tomato, and to top it off, he has the audacity to turn around and leave! But I won't let him get away like this. Oh no. I grab him by the collar, holding him back.

"Hey, what do you think you're doing?"

He sighs and his shoulders slump. Turning around, he says, "Hi, er. What's up?"

I cringe. *What's up?* "Why isn't anyone talking to me? Did I do something wrong?"

He shifts uncomfortably. "No, no, it's just...um, actually, I can't tell you."

My eyebrows shoot to my hairline. "What? Why?"

He sighs again, driving a hand through his hair. "I—you know—I need to. Phew, is it getting hot in here? I think the balcony sounds great—"

"You stay here," I say, my hand latching on his arm. "What is up?"

"I can't tell you."

"Why?"

"He'd kill me."

He. Huh. It could only be a certain black-haired hunk then. "Thank you so much."

"Oh please, no," is all that I hear as I make my way through the apartment.

Since *he*—the ass of all asses—is not out on the balcony, or in the bathroom, because I knocked on it like a lunatic, I head straight for his room.

But once I touch his door handle, I stop.

Wait. What if I find him with another girl in there?

No, he wouldn't. Not at a party where everyone could see them.

But then, why does it bother me?

He's not mine, not really. Our contract forbids him from flaunting anyone else in public, but it's not about the contract —it's the idea of him being with someone else that twists my gut. Damn it, I need to shake these thoughts. He's not mine to worry about. There's no room for a real boyfriend in my life anyway, especially since he'd never wants to be a part of my life once he knows everything about me.

With a deep sigh, I push the door open and relief washes over me when I find him alone, pacing the room.

"Hey," I say, trying to sound casual.

His gaze flicks over my dress, and something tightens in his jaw. "Hey. How was your rehearsal?"

"Excellent. Care to explain why your friends are giving me the cold shoulder?"

Riley stops pacing, a knowing smile playing on his lips. "Because I asked them to."

"You told them to act like total assholes?"

He strides toward me, stopping just a few feet away. "I didn't want them to get the wrong idea."

"What idea would that be, exactly?"

"That you're available. Because you're not. You're mine."

His possessive tone makes my heart skip a beat, and I can't deny a tiny thrill at his words. *Mine.* I'm a feminist through and through, but this little word wakes up something primal in me and I don't like it. "I don't belong to anyone, Ri. You can't just—"

"I know. I'm sorry." Riley steps even closer, his whiskey-colored eyes pleading.

I swallow. His eyes tell me he's had a few beers. "Sorry for what?" I shoot back. "For treating me like an object?"

Riley's gaze flickers, before his voice drops low. "For putting you in an awkward spot with my friends. I didn't mean to complicate things."

"That's all you've been doing since day one, Ri."

He sighs, running a hand through his jet-black hair in frustration, and his biceps bulge as he does it. He's wearing a T-shirt, and all of his tattoos are on full display. Damn it. He looks so hot. I swallow again. "I just wanted them to understand that you're off limits. That this"—he gestured vaguely between us—"isn't a joke for me, and the guys can be idiots, so I wanted to keep you safe."

"I think they'll figure out we're together without you marking me like a dog on the grass."

He took a step back, leaning against his closet. He's still way too close for my liking.

"Because we made a deal, Liora. And this is exactly how I'd act if you were my girlfriend. I'm well aware of my friends and their tendency to become idiots around beautiful women. So I make sure I protect what's mine. Even if it's all pretend."

He said I'm beautiful. Yes, that's all I heard. "So…your solution is to isolate me? What kind of fun would being your girlfriend even be?"

"I never claimed to be a fun boyfriend. I'm a walking red flag, baby. It's clear I'm not boyfriend material at all." He steps toward me. "I'm jealous." Another step forward. "I'm possessive." Another step. "And I couldn't care less what others think, except when Coach calls about my career." He stops right in front of me, and I don't care he's in my space. "I'm trying to keep us on track. That's all."

"Right," I say. "Because we have too much to lose."

He nods, his expression pained. "Exactly."

Riley doesn't respond, and the silence stretches between us, heavy with a ton of unspoken words. I want to believe him—to believe that this was all just part of the act—but something tells me there is more to his actions than meets the eye, but if he's not ready to go there—I'm not either.

He lets out a heavy sigh, as if grappling with words he wants to say but chooses not to. Instead, he casually folds his tattooed arms behind his head, stretching. His white shirt clings to his ridiculously sculpted chest muscles. My eyes involuntarily lower, tracing the faint line of hair disappearing beneath his waistband.

A strange flicker of heat shoots through me, traveling from my chest to the spot between my legs. My body tenses, my fingertips tingle with a sudden urge that catches me off guard. Oh come on. So what if the guy has a physique worth noticing? It doesn't mean I want to throw myself at him like some overeager fan. Suddenly, I remember what he looked like naked in the bathroom, and it's overwhelming. I want to throw myself at him. No honestly, I want to climb that man.

Clearing my throat, I say, "What are you doing in here anyway? All by yourself."

"I'm just on edge about next week's game against Houston," he finally says.

"Are you afraid to meet Houston again?"

He nods and I lift my hand to touch him—just in comfort, of course—but I don't and let my hand fall to my side again. He tracks my action and there's a look of understanding in his eyes.

"Where is your game?" I ask, remembering that his coach said he'd act differently if I was around. I don't want to read too much into it, but I also want to be there for him. Somehow.

"Boston. You coming?" There's something like hope flickering in his eyes.

"If I can bring Priya?"

"Anyone."

"I'll be there," I say.

The tension drains from Riley's broad shoulders. "Thank you, Lia. That means more than you know." He glances back toward the party still in full swing. "We should probably head back out there."

"But we need to act accordingly," I say, and I'm kinda nervous and happy that I can kiss and touch him out there. It's a foolish thought though.

"We'll manage."

I nod, turning to leave, but Riley catches my wrist. "Wait. You might want to change into something a little more... appropriate first."

"Well then, I guess you'd better unzip me," I say, suddenly feeling bold.

I turn around and offer him my back.

Riley's fingers trail along my spine to the top of my zipper. I shiver, mind racing ahead as he slowly lowers it.

How far will he take this?

And, more importantly…how far will I let him?

He touches the lower part of my back and I close my eyes. Too far.

I remember what's waiting for me at home. The trailer. Mom. My life.

It's not this bubbly life Riley knows. I don't fit with someone like him. It's not going to work, whatever scenarios I play in my head.

"T-Thank you," I mutter and practically run into my room to get changed.

I'M REALLY RELIEVED to have my room back.

They replaced all the carpet, and it looks so fresh and clean now. The bathroom is still a construction site, but at least I have a room where I can walk around and lock myself in again.

I stand in front of my mirror and eye the slinky black cocktail dress I chose. It's an old one. I wore it to a party I went to during training camp. It was the most expensive dress I've ever bought and I still love it. It's short and A-lined but narrow on the top. It hugs my curves in all the right places. I'm about to choose my underwear, when there's a knock at the door and I hear Priya's voice.

"Can I come in?"

"Sure," I say, and Priya rushes in with two blue cocktails in her hand.

"Priya, we can't drink."

"It's just one, okay?" she tells me, and I know she already had one.

"Fine," I say and reluctantly clink it against hers. "But after this one, we stop."

"Okay. But girl. What's with the chemistry between you guys!"

I shake my head. "There's no chemistry. Guys like Riley... they have girls throwing themselves at them constantly. He'd never go for someone like me. Besides, with my past, a relationship is the last thing I need right now."

Instead of answering, I drink a big gulp of the cocktail and notice it's way too strong. I wince. "Woah. Who made this?"

"Der," she says, and I arch an eyebrow.

"It's 'Der' now?"

"What." She shrugs. "He's nice."

"He's not. Priya, why do you always fall for the wrong guys?"

"I don't *fall*." She averts her gaze in a way that tells me she has to tell me something.

"What happened?"

She widens her eyes. "Why do you think something happened?"

"During rehearsal you've been looking at me strange, and now too."

She sighs and wobbles on her feet. "Fine. Mason kissed me."

I let out a shriek and stifle it with my free hand. "Shit. Priya. When did this happen?"

"Yesterday after practice," Priya replies, her voice tinged with regret, and I hope it is only because she didn't tell me ASAP. "I didn't mean for it to happen. It just...did."

I reach out to grasp her hand in reassurance. "You deserve someone who respects you. Mason is nothing but trouble. I bet you're not the only one he's fooling around with."

She nods. "I know..."

We both take another gulp and my head already feels dizzy. Well. It's a strong one and I don't really drink. Shit. "Be careful, okay?"

She nods. "I try."

"I just don't want anyone breaking your heart."

"He can be so sweet though, and all the time we spend together. It's just easy to mix it all up. Isn't it intense between you and Aiden?"

Well, it's not like he's interested in me, or women at all, but it's not my place to tell, so I just say, "No, we're not each other's type."

"Because you're falling for your roommate." She grins and wiggles her eyebrows again. She really likes to do this.

"No way. Guys like Riley...they have girls throwing themselves at them constantly. Besides, a relationship is the last thing I need right now."

Priya's expression softens, understanding in her eyes. "I know it's complicated, but that doesn't mean it can't work. Just give it a chance."

I sigh. "I can't."

Priya hugs me. "It will be fine. Just do what your heart wants. Everyone will understand."

What my heart wants? I finish the cocktail and I regret it already. Because right now, my heart tells me I should forego underwear entirely and flirt the shit out of Riley. It tells me to kiss him. It tells me to pull him into my bed.

"Let's join the party again," I say, but before we leave, I let my hair loose, and since it's been in a bun all night, it waves down in big curls now. I even put on my red lipstick.

Twenty-one

RILEY

Everyone's cheeks are red by now as the alcohol finally kicks in.

We're listening to loud music while some people are dancing at the back of my living room. Others are already making out in a corner, while I found myself playing a lively game of naughty trivia.

Of course, Liora's my partner, her thigh pressed against mine as we huddle together on the couch. We're giving the perfect couple in love, and I think everyone is buying it. Priya and Derek are paired up, sitting across from us and exchanging flirtatious glances between questions, while Aiden and Jayce each found their own ladyfolk for the game.

As much as I hate to admit it, Aiden is a genuinely kind person. He told me he was raised on a farm and has only been living in New York for two years. The hustle and bustle of the city can be overwhelming for him, but he's determined to make the most of his time here.

The game of trivia revolves around asking and answering provoking questions. The more creative and unique the answers, the more points you get. However, not answering a question gets you penalty points. One individual poses the questions while the rest of the group provides answers, with the group ultimately deciding which response is the most original and deserving of points.

"'What's your favorite sex position?'" Priya's cheeks flush pink as she reads the card.

I don't hear the others answering and just look to Liora, fully interested. "Sixty-nine," she says.

I grin. I love that one.

"Cowgirl," I say, never leaving her eyes.

Liora leans in close as the rest give their answers, her warm breath tickling my ear as she whispers, "Why cowgirl? I thought you'd come up with something more exotic."

My hand grazes her back as I fight the urge to grab a handful of that ass.

"I like to watch when a girl enjoys riding my dick. The moment she gets lost is the biggest turn-on." Her cheeks turn red and I keep myself from telling her I'd love to be her tool.

As the game progresses, the questions grow more and more interesting and I can't keep my eyes off her anymore—the way they sparkle, the curve of her lips as she smiles, the enticing expanse of her neck as she tosses her head back in laughter. The alcohol buzzing through my system only amplifies my desire, making it harder and harder to resist the magnetic pull between us. But I love these little pretend moments, because I can hold her just the way I want. They way I would if she were mine.

"All right, next question," Aiden announces. My gaze flicks to Jayce, whose arm is slung around a girl whose name I can't remember. "Who was your celebrity crush?"

My heart skips a beat as all eyes in the room turn to me, since I'm first in line. I don't miss Jayce's knowing smile. He's such a bastard sometimes.

"Easy," I say, looking at the girl in my arms. "Liora James."

The words hang in the air between us, a confession years in the making. I watch as her eyes widen, a delicate blush blooming across her cheeks. She seems at a loss for words, her lips parting slightly as if to speak, but no sound comes out.

Say something, I silently plead. My heart hammers against my rib cage. Anything.

But before Liora can respond, the room erupts in a chorus of cheers and catcalls. Our friends whoop and holler, their drunken revelry drowning out any chance for a private moment. I force a smile, trying to play along with their good-natured ribbing, but inside I'm reeling. Had I just made a huge mistake? What if Liora thinks it's creepy? I was a hell of a creepy teenager.

Across from us, Derek leans in to whisper something in Priya's ear, eliciting a coy giggle from Liora's friend. But I barely register their flirtation, because I'm caught up in Liora's hand finding mine under the table, our fingers lacing together. The simple touch sparks a blaze that races along my nerve endings, kindling a hunger I'd never known before.

"Is it true?" she asks as all the other pairs of the game seem to talk to themselves about their celebrity crushes. "I was your celebrity crush?"

My thumb traces delicate circles on her smooth skin. "I remember watching all of your competitions after I found out about you. You were only fifteen, but you were magnificent." I glance over to see Jayce and his girl passionately making out, causing me to look back at her. "I think the reason I get so worked up when I see you in your costume is because it's become a kink for me."

She leans in. "Did you see my routine in Orleans?"

"It lives rent-free in my head." It was Moulin Rouge themed and the sexiest shit I've ever seen.

She sighs, her gaze flicking to my lips.

Some people are saying goodbye—probably Derek—but I

don't care. I pull her in, and do what I've wanted to for weeks now. I kiss her.

"For the show?" she whispers against my lips.

"Mm-hm," I breathe in her mouth just so she wouldn't know how much I actually crave a kiss from her.

The room fades away. I have no idea how many people are here, and I just don't care. Right now, she's all that matters to me. Her lips part, inviting me in, and I respond. My tongue meets hers, which moves against mine, smooth and slick like satin sheets. I can feel the heat of her mouth against mine. It's so hot. Her hands slide up my chest, fingers curling into my shirt as she pulls me closer. The world could end right now, and I wouldn't notice.

Until Shane's scratchy voice echoes from the back of my living room. "Hey, everyone! Our video is finally up and ready to watch!"

The cheers around us barely register. We're still kissing like we're alone.

Suddenly, a sharp bang on my head jolts me back to reality, and I jerk up. "What the fuck?"

Fucking Shiny.

He holds his hands up in surrender. "I swear, I'm sorry. But we need to watch our promo video. You can make out after, okay?"

Liora stares at him.

I stare at him.

Then we stare at each other, completely dazed. Shit, that kiss went a little far...

She scrambles away from me, and I do as Shane says, feeling like a robot. I think that kiss fried my brain.

My remaining teammates are cuddled up on my couch, some around the dining table, as I turn on my huge TV to show our new promo video, which was supposed to launch next week on YouTube but apparently got uploaded earlier. I don't get excited about stuff like this anymore but it's natural for a rookie to be excited.

Liora's still standing in the middle of the room, her lips slightly swollen. So I grab her by the hips and gently guide her to the back of the room, finding a free stool and positioning it so we can still see the video. I sit down and pat my thighs.

She hesitates.

"What? Just sit down."

"But..."

"Come on, it's just a seat," I say, giving her a playful grin.

She rolls her eyes but finally sits on my lap, her back resting against my chest. I wrap my arms around her waist, holding her close, and the room falls silent as the video starts playing. My teammates cheer and laugh, but all I can focus on is the warmth of Liora in my arms.

We start watching the video of our team sleeping on the tour bus and getting ready for a game, discussing our preperformance routines. I can't help but notice Liora squirming nervously every time I appear on screen.

Each time she writhes like this, my dick throbs eagerly.

I feel her goddamn ass press against my bulging dick, causing a low growl to escape my lips. Fuck. Her body melds perfectly with mine and my hand trails down from her hip, teasingly brushing over the silk fabric.

"No," she suddenly says, holding my hands to stop them.

"No to what?"

"Don't go lower. It's—it's against our contract. It's PDA in private. Sort of."

I scoff at her hesitation, that little uncertain edge in her voice only making me want her more.

"You're really bringing up the contract now?" I nuzzle my nose against her neck, breathing in her sweet, intoxicating scent. Fuck, she smells so good. "I'll be honest with you. I'm ready to toss that thing out of the window." I trail soft kisses along her neck and murmur, "If you want, I can tell Ethan I broke it and cover the cost. Just say the word. We can end this, and I'll find you another apartment to move into."

This is dangerous territory. I'm teasing her, but at the same time, I'm fucking afraid she'll tell me that she's done with me. That she never wanted to break our contract. I nibble gently on the tender skin beneath her ear, and the soft moan she releases lets me know she's not concerned about it either. I've already made up my mind anyway.

I'm making her mine tonight. Fuck that contract.

But then she tenses up again and whispers, "Riley, I'm not wearing any underwear." She says it with a mix of embarrassment and vulnerability, and damn, it only makes me more intrigued.

Now I just have to make her mine tonight. "Is this supposed to stop me?"

The video shows our teammates in the locker room and we're without shirts. They zoom in on me and I wink at the camera, my abs on full display.

She squirms again, and I press my hard cock against her perfect ass. "Aren't you a naughty one? Going commando and having a thing for hockey players, huh?" I tease, letting my hands explore her hips.

This time, she doesn't resist, only fueling my fire further.

"Well, can you blame me? You're kind of *hard* to resist." She arches against my boner and I silently curse everyone crowding my living room. Damn it, all I want right now is to fuck her senseless. I've waited for so long. I can't wait any longer. I'm about to burst.

I need her.

I kiss her neck in answer and another tiny gasp escapes from her lips as my free hand traces its way down to her thigh. She feels so good. Everything I'd ever imagined and more at the same time.

"Still want me to stop?" I say.

"No," she breathes and keeps on grinding.

Fuck. She's so hot. I can feel the heat over my jeans radiating from her bare skin, knowing there is only a tiny barrier between us as she rubs her pussy over my throbbing cock.

"I want you," I whisper hoarsely. "I want you so bad."

She tilts her head, looks at me with those piercing blue eyes that always make my heart race, and licks her lip before leaning in for a kiss. This time, we both dive into the kiss, our need for each other so intense that it feels like we're trying to merge into one. Our tongues tangle together as we explore each other's mouths again and again. My other hand moves down to cup her ass cheek, squeezing it gently. Shit. I've wanted this for ages, and it feels so much better than I imagined. So fucking good.

She increases the pressure of her body against mine, desperately seeking more friction.

I fear being caught so I pull away from the kiss.

We are both out of breath and our eyes are fixed on the screen in front of us again. No one has noticed us yet, and I'm grateful that we chose to sit in the back, hidden from view by the seats in front of us. Glad that she keeps rubbing my dick with her ass.

My lips graze over the sensitive skin beneath her collarbone, and she shivers underneath me—a powerful tremor going through both of us like lightning striking twice during a stormy night.

That's when I can't take it anymore and my hand fumbles under her skirt.

She leans back, her head resting on my chest to give me full view of what my fingers are doing. I move to her clit and bite back a groan as she arches her back, pressing hard against my erection. Fuck this is too good to be true.

I need more of her though. This isn't nearly enough.

My fingers move deeper under the fabric, tracing the outline of her body and her hips rise to meet my touch. After sneaking another peek around the room to make sure we're still unwatched, I plunge my finger deep inside her velvety pussy. A faint whimper escapes her lips, only meant for me, and my free hand circles around her neck as I put a second finger in. I watch the muscles in her thighs tensing with pleasure. Fuck yeah.

"Riley," she whispers, grinding against my fingers.

I tighten my grip on her neck, feeling the rapid beat of her pulse beneath my palm.

Leaning down, I whisper, "You feel so good, babygirl. I can't wait to be inside of you."

She shivers again, but much to my surprise, she still tries to push my hand away. Oh no. I won't let her. I stay firm.

"Riley," she whispers more urgently now. "We can't do this here, not now."

"I know," I say, putting my thumb on her clit and pressing on it while I keep on plunging my fingers in and out and in and out. There's another little sigh of pleasure and I think I'm living only for this. "But I can't stop. Tell me stop."

"I can't," she whispers.

And just as she's about to come and I'm close to losing my mind because of it, the video cuts off. My hand hastily moves out from under her skirt.

Within a second, she sits up straight and the light goes on.

"Wow, that was great," Shane yells and others chime in.

"It was," I whisper. "Just too short."

Jayce turns around, and our gaze meets.

I'm not sure if he's aware of what just happened, but when Liora stands up, I quickly grab her by the hips and guide her back. "Don't you dare stand up just now. My boner's the size of a skyscraper."

"Don't flatter yourself."

"Need me to show you how big it is?" My dick twitches again. Fuck. "This banter isn't helping. Tell me something sad."

"I have more sad stories than happy ones. Consider yourself lucky."

While the others start to grab some more drinks, Liora tells me about her father hitting her mom until she finally kicked him out. My boner is gone in a minute, and I want nothing more than to find her father and kick his ass.

"It's okay, don't worry," she says. "He's gone now, and as for us, I think it's safer if we stick to the contract."

I watch her striding to her bedroom, locking it from the inside and I think my heart just broke in two.

Twenty-two

LIORA

Fingertips tremble against my clit, gasping breaths echo in my dark room.

The memory of Riley's touch is burned in my mind.

His fingers filling me, taking me to the chasm, only to leave me aching.

When he knocked, I pretended to be asleep, too overwhelmed to face him and admit that I wanted to stick to the contract because I was afraid I might actually develop feelings. Afraid to tell him that I kind of already have.

Instead, my mind replayed every moment of his touch over and over.

The rumble of his voice.

The hunger in his eyes.

The bold press of his hardness against my ass.

I couldn't fall asleep, and as soon as he was in his own room, my hands instinctively went into my panties.

I imagined his sculpted body, remembering how it looked with water and soap cascading down every defined muscle. My fingers work frantically beneath the covers, chasing the release he'd denied me.

I'm close, so close.

But climax hovers out of reach.

And just when I think I can make it, a muffled groan sounds from the other side of the wall.

The cadence is unmistakable—Riley is pleasuring himself too.

I squeeze my eyes shut, imagining his strong hand fisted around his cock, stroking in time to my fingers rubbing tight circles on my clit. Soft grunts escalate to deep moans of ecstasy. Hearing his pleasure pushes me over the edge. I bite my lip to stifle my cry as I shatter.

I pant and mortification replaces the fleeting bliss.

What was I doing, getting myself off to my roommate? I can't let myself fall for his charm and risk everything I'd worked so hard for.

I roll over and will myself to sleep.

But sleep doesn't come in a while.

I TIPTOE out of the apartment after hiding in my room for hours.

I told my mom what happened—though obviously not the part about the fingering. I just mentioned that we broke the contract by kissing, and she advised me to trust my instincts. But my gut tells me that Riley isn't ready for a serious relationship, which is what I need. We're on different pages in our lives. The sooner I accept that, the easier it will be to realize that if I let this go any further, it's just about sex and nothing more.

My skates bump against my back with every hasty step.

I need to clear my mind before tonight's show. The thought of seeing Riley only adds to the jumbled chaos in my head. After yesterday, I just can't handle the thought of seeing him today. I'm feeling so shy and guilty that I don't even know if I can look him in the eye again. Okay. No, I can't.

I know I have to eventually, but not today.

Yesterday was just too much.

He fingered me. In a crowded living room.

And after the party, we touched ourselves, fully aware of what the other was up to.

It's incredibly embarrassing.

When I make it to set, the dressing room buzzes with nervous energy as stylists wield hairspray and powder brushes with the intensity of soldiers arming for battle. I sit statue-still, barely daring to breathe, as Nora, a severe-looking woman with purple hair, pins my hair into a sleek updo with a crazy amount of glitter.

Priya plops into the chair beside me with an exaggerated sigh. "I think I'm going to puke."

"Why? Are you hungover?"

"No. Please, I only had one cocktail."

"Two."

"Fine. Two. I'm still standing. No, I've never seen so many people out there! The audience room is bursting!"

"You've got this," I reassure her, squeezing her hand. "We've practiced the routine a million times. Just pretend it's only Aiden and me out there watching."

"Easy for you to say," Priya grumbles. "I don't have a hot hockey player waiting to comfort me after."

I roll my eyes, ignoring the flutter in my chest at the mention of *my* hot hockey player. "It's not like that. We're just friends."

"Right," she says. "Friends who eye-fuck each other across the room."

Before I can defend myself, Stacey saunters over, all faux concern and barely concealed glee.

"Aww, I hope you're not too worried about Riley being away. I'm sure he'll behave himself...then again, you know how athletes get on the road."

White-hot jealousy churns in my gut, but I school my features into a mask of calm indifference. "I trust Riley. But thank you for your concern."

Stacey smiles. "If you say so. I just think it's weird you're not more concerned. I mean, he does have quite the reputation as a player, both on and off the ice."

Priya glowers at her. "Don't you have anything better to do than stir up drama, Stacey? Like, I don't know, actually practicing your routine for once?"

She huffs and flounces away, but the damage is done. My mind reels with unwanted images of Riley, shirtless and glistening with sweat, tangled up with a faceless puck bunny. I shake my head to clear it. No, I wouldn't let Stacey's poisonous words infect me. I had to stay focused on my goal. Everything else was just a distraction. And, as long as no one sees it, he can have others.

Our relationship is fake, damn it.

I don't even have the right to feel jealousy.

But maybe, after yesterday, he doesn't want another woman...

"Skaters, two minutes to places!" the director says.

I put on another layer of red lipstick, and we're ready to roll.

Priya grabs my hand, and we dash behind the stage, where Aiden practically crashes into my arms. His fidgeting hands mirror the butterflies swirling in my stomach. Priya waves at me before running to Mason. When he kisses her forehead, I want to gag.

Aiden releases me and I nod toward a crew member

snapping photos of them. "Do you see that? He's only nice to her when someone's watching." I'd be devastated if Riley was the same way. Only showing affection when the camera's on. But then—crap. That's exactly what we agreed on. What is wrong with my brain? We even signed a contract. Damn it.

"Mason is a prick," Aiden says as we plop down on some chairs by the stage entry, watching the show start from a big screen.

I hear Priya laugh, her sweet voice is high pitched as she flirts with Mason. She looks amazing. Actually, any color on her does. Today, it's a bright green with hundreds of rhinestones.

"Will you help me bury him if he hurts, Priya?"

"Where's the shovel?" Aiden jokes, and we settle in as the lights dim and the audience erupts into applause.

Shayleen and Tim, our ever-smiling show hosts, step into the spotlight. I've seen them a couple of times during practice, and exchanged hellos, but they only show up when the cameras are rolling, so I don't know much about them. Tonight, they're dazzling under the lights, Shayleen's glittering hair pinned up, and Tim's brown locks neatly styled. They banter effortlessly, their chemistry popping even from backstage. Both are decked out in shiny blue costumes, skating on the ice. The audience giggles at the short videos showing them learning to skate just for the show, their struggles hilariously endearing.

"Welcome to the premiere of *Grace on Ice*," Shayleen announces, her voice bubbling with excitement as the lights turn pink and yellow. "We have an incredible lineup of talented skaters for you tonight, each vying for a chance at glory—"

"And a hefty cash prize," Tim hollers into the mic. "Wowza! I'm not even joking. We're talking one million dollars!"

The crowd erupts.

Shayleen chuckles. "That's right, Timmy. And let's not

forget our judges, who will be putting these hopefuls through their paces. Speaking of which, let's introduce them now!"

The lights swivel to illuminate the judges' table, where Grace, Twain, and Idris sit, their faces impassive. Grace, in particular, looks like she'd rather be anywhere else, her red lips pursed in a thin line, but when they mention her name, she forces a smile.

"First up, we have the incomparable Grace Holland. She owns more gold medals than most people own toilet paper and is our current ice queen extraordinaire," Tim says, earning a few smiles from Twain and Idris and a death glare from Grace. She didn't even crack a smile. Guess she didn't like the toilet paper joke.

As they introduce Twain Teller and Idris Bell, I lean in to whisper to Aiden. "Is it just me, or does Grace look even more terrifying than usual tonight?"

He grimaces. "She's definitely on the warpath. We'll need to be flawless if we want to impress her."

"Talk about pressure, huh…"

On the screens flanking the stage, a montage of clips featuring the competing pairs starts to play, each set to a pulsing beat. When Aiden and I appear, spinning and leaping in perfect sync, the audience roars their approval. Hearing my own voice on television is always awkward and makes me cringe a bit. During my competitive days, I gave plenty of interviews, but I never watched them back because I spent every spare moment practicing.

Aiden nudges me. "Hear that? They love us. And it's all thanks to Riley and you."

My heart stutters at the mention of his name. "What do you mean?"

"Come on, don't be modest. You know the only reason we have so many fans on social media is because of you and Riley and all his fans. The golden boy of hockey dating a gold medalist figure skater? It's a publicist's dream come true."

"I told you it's f—"

Aiden stops me, as if the walls have ears. "It helps us and I'm happy, thank you. We don't need a charade like Mason does or to be mean like Stacey. It's great that you two work for us, and I just wanted to thank you, that's it."

Aiden smiles. He's just the nicest person there is. I lean into him, well aware of the cameras snapping photos of us now. I sigh. I bet those tabloid magazines will call me a cheater any time soon. Whatever.

As Priya and Mason are announced, I sit up straight in my seat. Dressed in vibrant green and black outfits with intricate designs, they glide onto the stage. The music builds to a crescendo, matching the intensity of their gazes as they take their positions. The singer starts and they burst into motion, their bodies moving in perfect harmony like two green flames dancing.

My jaw drops as I watch Priya glide across the ice. She is stunning. She casually mentioned last time we went for a coffee that she used to compete in pair figure skating but never made it far. I can't help but wonder why. From what I've seen, she's incredibly talented. But then she tells me the heartbreaking story of how her partner ditched her for another girl and she lost all interest in pairs. That is, until she found *Grace on Ice*. She looks like she's enjoying it again and I'm happy for my girl.

Upon striking their final pose, chests rising and faces flushed, a flicker of uncertainty dances in Priya's eyes.

Grace leans forward, her gaze piercing and critical. "Adequate," she says with disdain dripping from her voice. "But hardly exceptional. I demand more from you next time." The other judges echo her sentiments, each critique sharper than the last.

As the scorecards are raised, Priya and Mason's expressions

falter. Twenty-one out of thirty—a commendable score, yet falling short of their true worth. My gaze shifts to Aiden.

"They're out for blood," I say.

"Grace is not called the Ice Lady for nothing."

"'Adequate,'" I mimic her. "They were great." I can't believe it.

As they leave the ice, I run to the exit.

Priya's shoulders are shaking with barely suppressed sobs, but before I can act, Mason pulls her into a tight embrace, murmuring words of comfort against her hairline. I look around and see the camera team filming us and, as if on cue, Mason closes his eyes dramatically and kisses her forehead. I frown at him. This really is just a show for him. My heart aches for Priya. But the night is far from over. There's always the audience's vote, and from what I saw, their romance—even if it's one sided—could really make an impact. People go crazy when they think a couple is in love. Especially with all those rumors about them falling for each other during practice.

"It's going to be okay, you two were amazing," I say, shoving Mason playfully as I pull Priya into a hug. He grumbles something under his breath, but I choose to ignore it.

"Why can't she ever say something nice to me? I think she hates me," Priya says.

"She doesn't," I say. "It's her. She's always been cold like this. When I mastered my thirst triple toe loop at sixteen, she didn't even blink."

The stage manager yells my name and points to the stage.

I give Priya one last squeeze before heading to the ice with Aiden. The lights are dim, but I can still feel the weight of a thousand eyes on me. I know next week will be tough. If we make it to round two, the interviews will start. Questions will come. I need to be ready.

I close my eyes, take a deep breath, and center myself.

As soon as Shayleen and Tim call our names, the lights blaze on, and we begin.

AS THE FINAL notes of the music drift into silence, I strike my last pose, chest heaving, heart pounding like a drum. For a heartbeat, everything is still—then the audience explodes into applause. Some are even on their feet, clapping and cheering like it's the best thing they've ever seen. I can't help but beam as Aiden sweeps me into a hug, his laughter bouncing off the walls. "We did it," he says against my ear, his eyes twinkling with pure joy.

But as we turn to face the judges, my grin starts to falter. Grace's expression is like a stone wall, completely unreadable. She presses her lips into a thin line before leaning into her microphone. "Technically impressive," she says, her tone as cool as ice. "But I'm not feeling the emotion, the connection between you two. It's…adequate."

I start to hate that word. The way she says it. It makes all of my hair stand on one end.

My heart sinks even further as the other judges chime in with equally tepid feedback, their enthusiasm draining away like air from a balloon. By the time they hold up their scorecards, I brace myself for the inevitable blow.

Twenty-five out of thirty.

The same score as Stacey and her partner.

I let out a breath, relief flooding through me. It's not a perfect score, but it's enough to keep us in the running without needing the audience's vote. We're through to round two.

As we leave the ice, Aiden pulls me into another hug. "We

were amazing out there, and we're going to keep getting better. We'll find a way."

We're quickly interviewed by our media staff and give some statements about how we rate our routine, and all the time Aiden is holding me. And honestly, if he hadn't been there, I might have fallen—my knees are shaking uncontrollably. Even though I'm wearing a cardigan, the tremors just won't stop.

Once we're done with all the interviews, I collapse onto the nearest chair. Aiden hands me a water bottle, and I take a long swig, trying to calm my racing heart.

"You were amazing out there," he says, sitting down beside me. "Don't let what the judges said get to you."

I nod, but I can't help feeling a twinge of disappointment. We've worked so hard, and I thought our routine was flawless. But maybe Grace was right. Maybe there was something missing, some spark that we hadn't quite captured. "Our next choreo needs to be more emotional."

My phone buzzes in my cardigan's pocket, and I pull it out, half expecting a message from my mom. But when I see the name on the screen, my heart does a little dance.

> Puckster: Hey, just wanted to say congrats on an amazing performance. The whole team watched, and you were absolutely stunning out there. Can't wait to see what you do next.

I stare at the message, reading it over and over, my cheeks heating up. He'd been watching. Him and his entire hockey team. And he thought I looked stunning.

I type a quick reply, my fingers betraying a slight tremor. "Thanks!" I hover over the send button, contemplating if I should add more. But what else is there to say? Thanks for fingering me, sorry I ran away right after?

But before I can hit Send, Riley sends another message.

> Puckster: How's Oscar doing by the way?

> Liora: If I say he's fine, will you stop texting?

> Puckster: No.

I chuckle, drawing a curious glance from Aiden.

> Liora: He's alive, but if he dies, I might have to strangle you for real this time.

> Puckster: Can you even reach my neck, baby?

> Liora: I've got my methods. Don't underestimate my wrath.

> Puckster: Well, if you're mad, I've got 70 ways to make it up to you. Number one: a hug.

> Liora: Are the others better?

> Puckster: Well, it's 69, so yeah, definitely.

I sigh inwardly, burying my face in my hands. What am I doing?

I can't let myself get distracted by Riley, no matter how charming or attractive or funny he might be. I have to stay focused on the competition, on proving to the judges and everyone else that I deserve to be here. But even as I try to push thoughts of him aside, I can't help but feel a flutter in my stomach when I stare at my phone. He makes everything so much easier. Just seconds ago I was a nervous mess, and now? I'm smiling like an idiot.

> Liora: Goodnight, can't wait to see you score.

Twenty-three

RILEY

I've been on the edge since I woke up this morning, wondering if Liora really is mad at me after what happened in the living room. The memory flashes through my mind as I run on the treadmill—her soft skin under my fingertips, the quiet gasps escaping her lips, the way her body arched into my touch. It's seared into my brain, replaying on a loop.

Next to me, Jayce spots Colton as he grunts through another bench press rep. "Ri, you going to the gala in the Hamptons after play-offs?" Jayce asks.

"Ugh, not sure, man," I say, legs pumping steadily on the treadmill. "Kind of just want to lay low and recharge during the short break. Although my sister's been bugging me to go… and I kinda said yes."

"Oh yeah, Rosie's graduating Julliard next year, right? Damn, they grow up so fast. She still loves dancing?"

"Yep. Bachelor of Fine Arts that one." Pride swells in my chest thinking about her. She's been struggling, too, but I hope she's got it under control. But, well, I'm one to talk.

I slow down and pull out my phone, a new idea forming.

What if Liora didn't just want to be my date for the night? Maybe she'd be up for coming to my parents' with me. God knows I can't go alone—my father drives me up the wall. But a weekend in the Hamptons with her? That actually sounds pretty tempting.

> Riley: Hey, good morning…Wondering if you'd want to go to this bougie Hamptons gala thing with me in a few weeks and stay at my parents? No worries if not, just thought it could be fun…

I hit Send before I can second-guess myself. Within seconds, bubbles appear. My heart hammers in my chest.

> Bladezilla: Hmm, I'll have to check my very busy schedule. But I suppose I could make an appearance as arm candy for NY's star center…

Relief floods me, a dopey grin spreading across my face. I'm typing out a flirty response when Jayce's voice cuts through my trance.

"Damn, you're smiling, Huntington. What are you doing?"

"Ah, nothing, just texting Liora about the gala," I mumble, feeling my cheeks heat up.

"Mm-hmm, sure. You two were looking pretty cozy at the party. When's the wedding?" he teases.

"Ha, funny."

King pushes through one more rep, and Jayce carefully guides the bar back to the rack. King sits up, his face flushed, giving me his signature frown. "You two looked grossly in love."

I roll my eyes. "We didn't."

Jayce and Colton exchange a glance and then, as if rehearsed, they both say, "You did."

I run faster, trying to escape thoughts of that little blonde, but it's impossible.

"Did you see her last interview? They grilled her about her Olympic disaster," Jayce says carefully. "Do you know why she exited?"

I keep running. "No. I didn't ask. I don't want to force her to tell me something she isn't ready to share."

"She kinda told it on camera though," Jayce says, and I stop the treadmill, hopping down.

"What?"

Jayce shrugs. "Well, it was just a thing about time. Everyone wants to know why she left and hid for years."

Can't say I'm not dying to know, though.

I pull out my phone, stop the music playing in my earbuds, and head to YouTube to search for the interview. Liora told me she and Aiden were invited to *The NY Morning Show* today, but I didn't know she'd talk about what happened. I've been dying to know for years, and there's a pang of sadness that she didn't tell me first.

I start the video while Jayce and Colton continue training.

I see her sitting on a yellow couch on a bright TV set, next to Aiden. They talk about their first show and how they scored an impressive twenty-five points to advance to the second round. I've had my fair share of interviews, and I've sat on that yellow couch a couple of times.

They're talking with Rosanne Montgomery. With her short red hair and glasses, she gives off old teacher vibes, bringing back unkind memories of being forced to read aloud in class, ending with the entire class laughing at me. I've hated reading out loud ever since.

Rosanne asks Liora and Aiden about their plans and private lives, and they chat away. Then she asks about me, and Liora's cheeks turn pink as she tells Rosanne what a nice guy I am. Damn. She's so damn cute. I know she has to talk about me like that, but it does something funny to my stomach nonetheless. I wish I could be the nice guy for her.

Then Rosanne turns serious and says she'd like to address the elephant in the room. In an instant, I see Liora tense up, and my fingers tighten around my phone. This is exactly why I hate dealing with media people. They pry and hope you falter because this is where the money lies. They can't just focus on Liora's impressive skating skills. No, they want the clicks.

Aiden's gaze drops to his feet, his hands nervously fiddling with each other. A flicker of emotion crosses his face, leaving me to wonder if she confided in him. Perhaps he asked her.

I didn't.

My heart clenches at the thought of pushing her away with that question. And there's the fear that she'll tell anyone but me. I want to be the one she turns to though. But the thing we have going isn't meant to last, so why should she bother to let me in?

Rosanne leans forward, crossing one leg over the other as if she's about to eat popcorn with her nosy mouth, and asks, "Honey, the internet is buzzing. Everyone's asking why you left in the middle of the Olympics. You were expected to win gold again. Why would you leave and disappear?"

Liora swallows hard. "I-I'd rather not go into detail, since this is a very personal issue, but I was only nineteen at the time, and something happened in Beijing that made me physically and psychologically unable to continue in the Olympics. I understand that you're curious and concerned about what happened, but please know that I'm fine now and more than happy to be back on the ice."

Something happened. What happened?

"Doesn't sound good, huh?" Jayce says, taking over for Colton on the bench press. I can see the worry written all over my friends' faces, and I'm pretty sure mine looks the same. I'm on edge, dying to find out what happened to her.

"No," I say. "It must have been something really big. No athlete gives up a gold medal just like that."

Jayce nods.

Rosanne at least seems to understand that it's something Liora doesn't want to talk about on camera and asks them about their pairing for the show. Aiden says they've become friends and that Liora is the nicest girl he knows. They talk about Grace and their next routine. Liora is handling it like a pro, and I think she practices that response because she acted so calm and professional. I'm proud of her.

I turn my phone off and start running again.

But the question of what the hell happened to her burns in my chest. What could have happened in Beijing? A lot. And she needs money. She lives with her mom in a trailer park. Nothing you'd expect from a family that could afford all the costs of figure skating before. It's a crazy expensive sport.

Maybe a lawsuit?

I just can't wrap my head around it, and hell knows I've tried everything to find anything about her past. It's like she died after Beijing. There's no record of her whatsoever.

But what can I do? I can't force her to tell me anything. Not when we still pretend to hate each other. Maybe it's time to tell her that I don't. That all the snarky things I said were to keep her from getting too close because I'm a fucking scaredy-cat when it comes to any form of relationship. What did my therapist say? *Your fear of bonding is a way your mind is trying to protect you from potential pain or rejection.*

And that man be damned for handing me my issues out cold but fuck, he's right. Just the thought of Liora leaving me after I open up my heart makes me want to run. To forget her. To snarl at her again in the hope she'll never talk to me again.

Hate me before you love me, you know.

Opening up emotionally and being vulnerable feels so fucking threatening. It's so much easier to wear the mask of a cool, unbothered hockey player who doesn't give a fuck about anyone instead of being judged, rejected, or hurt when revealing my true thoughts and feelings. Because once you're honest, people talk about the real you. When I'm fake, their reactions can't hit close because it's not me.

I run as fast as I can.

My life should have come with a manual.

Twenty-four

LIORA

Nina, Priya, and I sit in Aiden's sleek silver Volkswagen Polo. The cool leather seeps through my shorts as we head to Boston to see the Falcons play. Nina sits next to me, and in the front seats, Priya and Aiden are chatting about our routines and the upcoming show.

Boston, here we come.

It's about time we took a break from our demanding training schedule—constantly pushing ourselves to perfection is exhausting while Stacey keeps on badmouthing Priya and me behind our backs. We try to ignore it but it's draining. We trained each day for weeks and there's no such thing as a weekend. I knew it was going to be hard and a busy time, but it's also going to end soon too. It's just about pushing through, making the best out of it. And so far, I met real friends for the first time.

If anything, this is a huge win for the show already.

But it's hard to slow down because, with *Grace on Ice* taking off, our social media is exploding. Luckily, Nina promised to handle all the interview requests coming my way—she's great at filtering out the crap. Speaking of which, she'll be snapping some pics today for us to post later. We have to keep those internet trolls fed, right?

Priya reaches over from the front and offers me some of her veggie chips. I grab a few, crunching on them as I nod at the blue and white fabric draped over her shoulders.

"So where did *you* get Derek's jersey from?" I ask.

She grins mischievously. "He sent it to me when he found out I was coming to the game. Isn't that sweet?"

I arch an eyebrow. "Uh-huh. Real sweet…" Jesus Christ. That guy is so after her panties.

She rolls her eyes, catching my sarcasm.

Priya's still a virgin, waiting for her knight in shining armor, but I hope she's not tossing all her principles for a guy, or rather two. Because as far as I know, Mason's still in the picture, though she goes silent each time I ask about him. Priya's a hopeless romantic, and that jersey stunt likely scored Derek major points. She's the sweetest girl, but her taste in men is earth-shattering bad.

I can't understand why she would choose to flirt with Derek instead of, for example, Jayce? After all, he seems like a decent guy. And if he's not her type, then maybe one of the other twelve hot guys on the Falcons?

Anyone but Derek. Or Mason.

"Speaking of jerseys, how come you're not sporting Riley's?" Aiden asks casually.

My stomach twists.

Shit. I can't exactly tell him that wearing his name feels too real right now.

"Oh, you know, jerseys don't really flatter me," I say with a forced laugh, waving it off. "Too bulky." Wow. I'm a *bad* liar.

I know it's a stupid excuse, and Aiden's not convinced. Truth is, I don't want Riley reading too much into it. He invited me to his game, to support him, but wearing his name feels like crossing a line. Like I'm just another fangirl craving his attention. Overthinking, as usual. Classic. But I can't shake the fear that one wrong move could mess up what we've got. So I left the jersey at home, neatly folded away. Out of sight. Out of mind.

Priya leans over again, eyes sparkling. "You won't believe this." She practically shoves her phone in my face, showing her Insta feed.

I snatch the phone. "Wait. Is that you kissing out in the wild?"

Priya sighs like a princess who got the wrong pearls. "He kissed me after the show yesterday."

"He chose to kiss you in front of the studio rather than backstage?" I say, my eyebrows arched.

Nina leans in, squinting at the screen. "And it's already out there?" She frowns at me, like she smells something fishy too. "Awfully convenient to kiss you once and already have 'paparazzi' ready to take a photo." She forms air quotes with her fingers. Mason's on the bottom of his acting career, basically a one-hit wonder. There's no way the paparazzi would be interested in him on his first show.

"Priya, he's using you," I say.

I love her too much to not be brutally honest with her about this. Friends aren't here to sugarcoat the truth. We need to look out for each other, because let's face it, love can make us blind as bats in broad daylight.

"Why would he?" She's not amused, but she needs to know, even if her heart's got her head in a spin. I've got a bad feeling about him. "If he wants to do this for PR only, he could have asked. I mean, it's nothing people haven't done before to get those votes up."

"Did he ever say he actually likes you?" I ask, while Nina checks his profile next to me.

Priya hesitates. "No."

"Does he ask about your private life, outside the show?"

"No."

"There. He's using you for clicks."

Nina nods. "Yep. Hate to say it, but Mason's playing the PR game without you, honey. Rumors can be as good as a real relationship. His Insta? Total self-love fest. Mirror selfies for days, and he captions one as 'your daily mood pill.'" Nina pretends to gag. "He's full of himself."

Priya snatches her phone back. "But I like him."

Nina and I snort. "You like his face," I add.

And I wonder if that's my hang-up with Riley, but then I see him curled up with a book, worrying about me, buying tampons as if he wanted to open a black market shop, always checking in, always making me laugh when I need it. No. Riley's a catch. More than just a pretty face. Only problem is, I don't think he knows it.

"You could use him too," Nina says coolly, her PR instincts kicking in. "But don't fall for him. He's not who he seems. That man is just out for likes and views."

"Nina's right," I say. "Just be careful with him, okay? Don't let him play games with your heart."

"Okay. Maybe I should focus on Derek then."

"No!" All of us, including Aiden, say at the same time.

AIDEN WHIPS into the stadium lot, and we can't help but chat about our go-to game snacks as we make our way inside. I nearly choke on the overpriced parking fee—twenty bucks? Seriously? But Aiden barely bats an eye, no hesitation in pulling out his wallet. I suggest crowdfunding with our group, but he just shrugs it off. As we enter through the doors, the metal detectors and massive crowd engulf us like a tidal wave.

We have to push and weave through the migration of fans heading toward the arena entrance.

But Nina leads us straight to the players' section, and we walk past walls decked out with memorabilia from Boston's rich hockey history—jerseys of Bobby Orr and Ray Bourque, and framed photos of iconic victories. I just know Riley's gonna have his spot in New York someday too. He's incredible.

Nina flashes her credentials. She's making security a breeze, and soon we're in the player section. The heavy door swings open to a quieter, more exclusive area. The soft lighting leads us to plush, cushioned seats near the player benches and penalty boxes.

Aiden looks around the bustling arena with wide green eyes. "This is my first hockey game," he says.

Priya opens her mouth in mock shock.

"Can you believe it? I've really never been to one before."

Memories of my own hockey days come flooding back as I watch the lights dance on the ice in front of us. "I've been to a few," I say, trying to downplay my experience but unable to hide the sadness in my tone. My coach used to take me to some college league games when we had off days from training. The memory churns in my stomach, causing me to ball my fingers into fists until my knuckles turn white. The familiar hurt in my palms as my nails ram into my flesh gives me a short release. But no. Don't think of him. Just don't. It's not worth it. I'm here to enjoy my weekend.

But my heart starts to race anyway and I try to breathe past the lump rising in my throat.

Aiden shrugs. "Growing up on the farm, there wasn't much time for anything besides tending to the strawberries and cows."

Nina lets out a dreamy sigh as she enters the corridor, expertly balancing a tray piled high with popcorn and beers.

My eyes widen at the sight of it all—this must have cost a fortune. In passing, I saw one beer cost over nine dollars.

"Farm life sounds so charming," she muses as everyone takes their snacks. "But let's be real, I'm way too lazy for all that. Wrangling athletes is more my speed."

"You do have a way with them," I say, and since I'm still hesitating on taking the snacks from Nina because they are expensive as hell, she holds the tray out to me with a grimace on her face that could freeze hell over. "Take it."

I sigh. "Thank you," I say and take the popcorn and beer.

"No problem, girl."

For me, it would be a problem. Sometimes I just feel like the odd one out.

Everyone always seems to have endless funds for their weekend plans, while I'm struggling just to afford the bus. If it weren't for these free tickets or Aiden driving, I wouldn't even be able to join them. But I'm working to change it. Change it all.

Then, the players hit the ice. I sit up straight, watching their powerful strides send sprays of frost into the air as they start with their pregame warm-up.

"Is it wrong that I want to call each one of them daddy?" Priya sighs next to me, munching away on some popcorn.

"Yes. I think this is your first and last Falcons game," I say, shooting her a wink.

But despite what I say, my eyes immediately find Riley, his tall frame and broad shoulders impossible to miss. He's tall without his hockey gear but now, he seems massive. Damn it. I want to call him daddy too.

I've watched his past games on my phone during breaks on set, but seeing him in person, all rippling muscle and that deadly focus, sends a jolt through my body. He's easily the most stunning man I've ever seen, and the mere sight of him has me shifting in my seat. I take a long sip of my beer, trying to stifle the flames licking at my core, but it's not that easy since I know how quickly his fingers work.

As if sensing my gaze, Riley's head snaps up, his whiskey eyes locking with mine. For a moment, the rest of the world fades away, and it's just the two of us, caught in a silent exchange of longing. He smiles at me but then his brow furrows as his eyes flit over me. I follow his gaze, my heart sinking as I realize what he must be searching for.

His jersey. The one I'm not wearing. Shoot.

Disappointment flickers across his face, and he vanishes from the ice, leaving me to wonder if I've made a terrible mistake. Yep. I should have worn it. I guess he's thinking about our fake dating rules. A real girlfriend would wear it. But having his name on me feels like I want it there. And I think I do, and that is what scared me. I wanted to wear that damn jersey. I wanted to wear his name. That's why I put it in the drawer. Because I can't wear it. I can't be his real girlfriend. Even if he wants it, too, he wouldn't fit in my life.

"Oh my god, I've always had a thing for goalies." Priya lets out another exaggerated sigh, her eyes lingering on Derek as he stretches, showing off his impossibly flexible body in the corner of the rink. I roll my eyes and let out a snort.

"Since when, Priya? You told me you love centers." I don't think she likes hockey in general though, just the players. She's the exact opposite of me, I only care for the game. I never liked the players since they blocked my rink.

"Since today." Her doe-eyed gaze makes me lightly box her.

"Stop it. You're drooling."

And then her phone buzzes, and I watch her go doe-eyed for a whole other reason. I'm almost begging her to drool over Derek again because Mason texted her, asking her what she's doing. "Look! He *is* interested in me!"

And just seconds after, he asks if she can make sure that he has some moments where he dances alone in their next choreo. Gross.

"You're not considering, right?" I say, frowning at that screen. Aiden and I come up with the dance together. Of course, Mason lets Priya do all the work.

That's when a commotion ripples through the crowd, and I turn to find Riley striding toward me, his jaw set.

Without thinking, I rise to my feet, my body moving on its own accord. I check if he's angry with me, but he's not. Not really. At least he's not looking like it. No, he's smiling, and we both rush into an embrace like we haven't seen each other in years.

I lean in, and my lips find his in a kiss that's meant to be a show for the cameras but feels all too real. I want to think it's meant for show because the kiss happened so naturally. I didn't plan it. I just saw him and *had* to kiss him.

He responds instantly, his strong arms pulling me closer. He kisses me again. Just like one wasn't enough.

Riley breaks the kiss and rests his forehead against mine. "I missed you."

The words send a twisted kick of something through my chest, and I search his eyes, trying to discern if there's any truth behind them. Just as naturally as the kiss felt, I push his hair back from where it's fallen over his green headband.

There's pure honesty in his eyes and I'm stunned. Unable to even form one word.

No hint of a lie.

Did he mean it? Did he really miss me? There's no way. Or is he just playing his part to perfection? Yeah. It must be.

"Why aren't you wearing my jersey?" he asks—a hint of vulnerability in his tone now.

"Maybe I wanted to keep you on your toes."

Riley clutches his chest like he's in a soap opera,

dramatically gasping. "Oh, the betrayal!" Then his gaze turns serious again. "Never do this again."

He lets go of me to reach into his pocket and pulls out a felt pen. With a mischievous grin, he scrawls his full name across my chest, the bold letters standing out against the stark white of my T-shirt. He didn't just—

"There," he says, capping the pen. "Fixed it."

He presses a kiss to my cheek, his stubble grazing my skin. Somewhere in the back, I catch Priya squealing.

"Great. Now I look like I can't afford your jersey. Thanks."

He smiles. Oh, that stupid smirk of his. I hate it with all that I've got.

"You know what? I'm always here to help a damsel in distress." And then, Riley fucking Huntington pulls his jersey over his head. Right there. In front of everyone. With a million phones aimed at us.

He stands there in only his white shoulder pads, the godforsaken shape God and the gym gave him peeking out from underneath it. I gulp, my fingers itching to touch him, but I manage to frown at him instead. How? I don't know.

He hands me his jersey, his hair even more ruffled than before. "Here, baby."

I watch as people take photos of us, making videos. I want to throw that damn jersey in his face, but from that look on his face, he knows I can't turn the offer down. His gaze basically screams *We have an audience.*

I bite my lip, planning to take it, but not before I, too, undress and give him the white shirt I wore. The grin dies and there's this tic in his jaw again. It's just one fucking second, but his eyes fly to my chest.

To the bra I'm wearing.

It's not a lacy one. I don't know if I could have pulled that off. I'm wearing a comfy white longline bra, but it's enough for him to swallow hard, and I'm pleased with the look he gives my boobs. Just when I want to retort something funny, he pulls his jersey over me. Not gently at all. It's like he's doing everything he can to quickly cover me, and I feel like a child getting dressed after a tantrum.

Once I'm covered, he gives me a very angry peck on the cheek. "You're here to bring me luck. Not a headache, babygirl."

Then he's gone, striding back toward the ice with a newfound spring in his step.

I sink back into my seat, my fingers tracing his number on my chest, a giddy smile tugging at my lips. But beneath the elation, a nagging realization lurks in the back of my mind, threatening to shatter my emotions from within.

Even though I did everything I could to avoid it, it's time to admit it.

I have a crush on Riley Huntington.

Priya shoots me a giggly glance. "That. Was. So. Cute!"

I shove some popcorn in her mouth.

Twenty-five

LIORA

"Ladies and gentlemen, welcome to tonight's matchup between your hometown heroes, the Boston Bears, and the visiting team, the New York Falcons!" The announcer's voice booms over the loudspeakers as the Bears burst out of the tunnel, one by one, each greeted with thunderous applause.

My heart goes cannonballing as I watch the Falcons rush to the ice next. They are met with a mix of polite applause and boos from the home crowd, and I want to strangle each one of these idiots who booed at them. We stand up and howl like the wolves to support them.

When the lights dim once again, a spotlight shines on a lone singer on skates standing at center ice.

The crowd falls silent, a collective breath held in anticipation as she performs the national anthem. On the ice, the players from both teams line up along their respective blue lines, standing shoulder to shoulder. Helmets off, they hold them under their left arms, their heads bowed slightly.

The Falcons wear their dark blue and white jerseys and stand on the left side of the ice. Riley's stance is so solid and confident. His eyes search mine. I smile at him and he smiles back. Next to him, his teammates stand tall, their eyes fixed on the flag hanging above the scoreboard.

As the final notes of the anthem ring out, the arena erupts in applause and cheers, and all the players replace their helmets and skate to their positions, ready for the face-off that will signal the start of the game.

The puck drops, and the game is on.

I lean forward in my seat, eyes glued to the ice as the Falcons and Bears swarm like bees around a hive. But where is he?

My gaze darts from jersey to jersey until finally I spot eighty-seven. He's on the bench, his leg bouncing with pent-up energy as he watches his teammates battle for control.

Come on, Coach, put him in, I mentally will, my fingers tapping an impatient rhythm against my thigh.

The first period is a flurry, with both teams testing each other's defenses. The home team strikes first, a wrist shot from the blue line finding the back of the net. Derek looks furious. The crowd erupts and the goal horn blares as fans leap to their feet. Priya and I make a face.

After what feels like an eternity, the line changes and Riley hops over the boards. He charges into the fray, his powerful strides practically eating up the ice. And you can say what you want, but the minute he touched down on the ice, the crowd turned electric.

Everyone knows it's a whole different game when Riley's out there.

Within seconds, Riley and Houston clash like gladiators. My stomach drops. *Don't blow it, Riley. Don't blow it.* They smash into the boards, jockeying for the puck in the corner. Houston leans in, his mouth moving rapidly as he no doubt tries to get a rise out of Riley.

Don't take the bait, Ri. Don't.

I chew my lip, knowing how important it is for him to keep his cool.

The camera pans to me and I school my concerned expression into one of composed support, even as my heart pangs against my rib cage. This game means everything. I need Riley to stay focused.

Houston cross-checks him and Riley stumbles. I let out a shriek and feel Priya's hand on mine.

"He's fine," she says, and at first I don't know why she would say that, but then I see the picture of me displayed on the TV above. I'm shocked and then I'm shocked at how shocked I am, but I have no time to reflect because there's this cold anger flashing in Riley's whiskey eyes, and for a moment I fear he'll retaliate and cost us a penalty.

He starts skating hard for the tunnel and I spring to my feet.

No, no, no! Slamming my palms against the glass, I catch his gaze, silently begging him to walk away.

And thank the heavens he retaliates with a quick counterattack. I let out a sigh and watch Riley weaving through the defense and beat the goalie with a perfectly placed shot. Before I can even process what just happened, Riley turns to me and mouths what looks a lot like *That was for you.*

I sit down again. I don't know if my heart will survive another live game.

When intermission arrives, I get a text from Riley.

> Puckster: How are you up there?

> Liora: Dying. This tension kills me.

> Puckster: Sweet. You're worrying about me.

> Liora: I am not, just waiting for another goal for me.

> I'M TOTALLY WORRYING ABOUT HIM.
>
> Puckster: Coming right up, baby.

THE SECOND PERIOD sees the physicality ramp up, with big hits and aggressive forechecking. A fight breaks out, but not between Riley and Houston. It's Colton and Houston. The crowd roars as gloves are dropped and punches are thrown. The referees break it up, sending both to the penalty box.

The Bears break away with a smooth tic-tac-toe play, the puck effortlessly passing between their sticks before landing in front of the net for a tap-in goal and I'm screaming my lungs out.

And in the last seconds of the game, I watch Jayce nodding to Riley just before swiftly dodging an opposing player's flying elbow and passing the puck off to him. Riley takes off down the ice and scores his third goal.

Yes! I pump my fist, pride surging through me. "That's my man!"

"I manifested it," I hear Priya say to Nina, but I'm glued to Riley. I don't hear anything. "They even are star aligned. Their signs match perfectly."

The ref's whistle pierces the air.

Riley throws his head back in relief.

The red goal light flashes.

The buzzer sounds.

We won.

Leaping up, I hug Priya as we jump up and down. We fucking won!

Twenty-six

RILEY

The first thing I think about after we win is Liora.

And I see her waiting there for me with the other family members of the players, and we stupidly grin at each other. Oh, I could get used to this.

Behind me, I hear Colton whisper to Jayce. "Do you see how he's looking at her?"

"Yeah," Jayce whispers back.

I'm tempted to ask about how I look, but she's heading my way, and I can't help but feel giddy because I get to kiss her again. I want to take her to every game, spending every day together outside, just to play the perfect fake couple—it's becoming a fun game.

Just as Jayce says, "Yeah, like he's in love," Coach whisks me away to the other side. Away from her. And I can't describe the disappointment that washes over me.

He's babbling away, excited as Christmas Eve about me not acting out. I truly believe it's because of Liora. Because of that friendly face behind the glass that grounds me, makes me believe that I'm worth it to be here. It's not my parents. It's me who brought me here.

"Riley, my boy! That was some game you played out there!" Coach exclaims, slapping me on the back.

I turn my head to search for her, but the crowd is already between us, her eyes on me as I mouth a *Sorry*. "The way you kept your cool, even when Houston was trying to get you fucked again...I'm proud of you, son."

I nod, my eyes still locked on her. Damn. She is so pretty in my jersey. "Thanks, Coach, glad you're happy for once."

Coach follows my gaze and chuckles. "Ah, young love. I remember those days." I want to say it's not love because fuck that word is heavy, but he just barrels on like a freight train. "We need to focus on the media now. They're waiting for you."

I tell him that I need to see her first, but he just shakes his head and pulls me toward the media section. "We need you to discuss that heated moment with Houston and the way you turned that game, boy."

I look at Liora, feeling so disappointed and wave goodbye to her. I know she needs to go because they have to go back to practice. She has an insane schedule. This show needs every second she can give. But damn, it's going to be days until I can see her again. Our team is staying in Boston for another game against the Bears before heading home to prepare for two more matches against them in New York.

But duty calls, and I know I have to put on my game face for the cameras. So, I'm giving interviews to local radio stations and sports journalists. They're all asking about our strategy, how we managed to weave through the opposing team's defenses like the rink was ours. I answer their questions on autopilot.

After the interviews, we have a press conference. It's me, Jayce, Colton, Derek, and Shane, all sitting up there to discuss our plans all over again. The interviewers fire off questions, and I do my best to answer.

"What adjustments did you make from the last game?" one of them asks.

I lean forward, resting my elbows on the table. "We watched a lot of tape," I say. "We studied our opponents, looked for weaknesses in their strategy, and then we adjusted our own game plan accordingly."

Jayce nods beside me. "Coach really drilled us on the importance of adaptability," he adds. "We knew we couldn't just rely on the same old tricks. We had to be ready to change things up at a moment's notice."

As we talk, I can feel the energy in the room shifting. The reporters are hanging on our every word, eager to get a glimpse into the mind of a winning team. But then, the reporters' questions shift, and suddenly, they're asking about that moment—the one where Liora was banging on the glass, crying out my name, trying to pull me back from the brink.

"It seemed like an important moment," one reporter says. "Does it make a difference, knowing there's someone watching who loves you?"

I pause, considering the question.

I've always told them that my family watches from home, that they're too busy with their business to come to the games in person. But the truth is, they don't really care about me. They only care about the numbers, the stats, the wins and losses.

My relationship with my dad is so fucked up that he only communicates with me through Ethan. He updates him on all the opportunities I've missed and what I should be focusing on next.

"It makes all the difference in the world," I say finally, my voice rough.

As the words leave my mouth, I am taken aback by how true they are.

Having someone out there cheering for me feels different.

"Knowing that she's there, that she believes in me…it gives me a strength I never knew I had."

The reporters keep pushing, asking more questions about Liora, about our relationship, asking me if I can describe her a little.

"Well, let's just say, since she's come into my life, I have an unhealthy number of dead plants in my apartment, because she likes to save what others think is rotten." That thought makes my stomach twist. I suddenly feel like something rotten she's ready to heal too.

Although there would be so much to add, like her dancing through my kitchen to silly songs or the moment when I discovered she showers with *PAW Patrol* shampoo. The moment I got addicted to that smell on her. I'm glad when Coach says that we're not here to discuss my horizontal mambos but rather our gameplay, I can't help but laugh out loud.

It's about time to do that mambo. I shit on the consequences. I'm ready to go full in and just hope I'm not about to ruin it. Because if someone was ever worth getting hurt over, it's her.

PLAY-OFFS ARE hella different from the regular season. Unless you get a sweep and end a series early, there definitely isn't time to have a bunch of practices. There is a ton more video review than the regular season as we try to figure out how to counter what the other teams are doing. We're staying in the hotel, having a bit of general calisthenics and massages to keep our muscles activated. Free ice time is important—it's wild what it can do to your head. Coach just emphasized no partying until the play-offs are done. Since we actually have a chance at the Cup, we behave for once.

That and my little blonde monster is why I don't have girls in my hotel room like last year. Instead, I lie in my hotel bed and text Liora because I really miss her.

Hey. I delete that again. What should I text her? Stop acting like a teenager. Just text.

> Riley: What are you doing?

Much to my surprise she immediately texts back with a photo of the dance studio. It shows Aiden with two dance teachers.

> Bladezilla: Aiden is learning how to lift me in this new routine. I'm just watching and texting with Mom until it's safe enough for me to try.

> Riley: How long have you been training?
> Starting to worry you're overdoing it.

> Bladezilla: Five hours.

> Riley: You should take a break.

> Bladezilla: What are you up to? Practicing your victory dance with the Cup?

> Riley: Nah, just had a spa day.

> Bladezilla: Sounds fun.

> Riley: Sitting in a sauna with twelve naked dudes scratching their asses isn't, trust me.

> Bladezilla: A man's gotta do what he's gotta do.

> Riley: I'm bored. Send me something beautiful.

Bladezilla: *Sends photo of the night sky*

Riley: How about you turn that phone around?

Bladezilla: I'm not sending you a photo of me.

Riley: Why not? Not asking for nudes.

Bladezilla: I'm working, Riley.

Riley: Makes it more fun. Here, I'll go first.

Bladezilla: You're not sending nudes!

Riley: *Sends selfie lying back, winking*

Bladezilla: *Sends a photo, looking serious*

Riley: Love that look. Feels like home.

Bladezilla: Gotta go, they're about to lift me up.

Riley: They need three people to lift you? I could do it with one finger.

Bladezilla: They're spotting me. Safety first.

Riley: Good luck. If they break anything, I'm coming after them.

Riley: Will you watch the game tomorrow?

Bladezilla: Only if you win.

Riley: Of course, we'll knock 'em out.

Twenty-seven

LIORA

Life has gotten insane over the last few weeks.

Between Riley's home games, press conferences, and strategy sessions, I've barely seen him in person—just snippets on screen and hurried conversations we managed to squeeze in between my own interviews and training sessions. Nina kept our social media alive, digging up old photos for posts and stories because we were too caught up to take new ones to show the world we're alive. I was so busy, I had barely time to eat or even talk to Mom. We usually spend hours talking on the phone but my schedule is wild.

The Falcons advanced to the second round of the play-offs, and I couldn't be prouder of Riley for handling everything without getting sucked into drama with Houston. There were even rumors of dropping the lawsuit altogether. Meanwhile, Priya and I made it to the next round of the show too. Aiden and I plan a rockabilly dance routine next. But honestly, it was all starting to wear on me. Balancing the demands of the show day after day was exhausting.

And while the jury seems mean on screen, it's nothing compared to how they treat us behind the camera. They often comment on our looks and dictate what we should wear according to our shape. Grace's unsolicited advice about not wearing see-through dresses because they accentuated my ass too much hit a nerve. I've always been sensitive about my figure, especially as a figure skater where physique matters. I thought I left this behind in Beijing. But with the end of May approaching, the pressure only intensified, making me more self-conscious each day.

But hey, the weekend sounds promising.

Aiden flew out to visit his mother, and with Riley's team unexpectedly wrapping up the second round of play-offs faster than anticipated, he, too, finds himself with a few days to spare. We agree to catch up over lunch, so I make my way to the arena where the Falcons train. The minute I step into the arena, the familiar cold hits my face, but I'm so nervous to see him that no matter how cold it gets in here, I'll be burning up inside. I go straight to the locker rooms, but before entering, I stop. I can't just go in there. It's full of guys and they could be naked and—

The door opens and Colton comes out. I step back, already apologizing for clogging the door.

"Hey." That's all he says.

"Hey, um, where's Ri?" I could already slap my own face for asking such a stupid question, but it's out. I let it go.

He raises an eyebrow and points behind him.

Wow, so much for a conversation. "Could you maybe—"

"Go in," he says and turns around to leave.

I yell after him, "Do you really think it's okay for me, though?"

He's already at the end of the corridor when he gives me a thumbs-up without even turning around to look at me. I huff out a grunt and decide to just do it. What will happen? I'll see naked guys? Well, I'll survive it.

I burst into the locker room and the first thing I see is

hockey gear strewn about and that scent of sweat and ice hits my face like a slap. Instantly, towels are snatched up and hands scramble to cover body parts. The room turns into a view of asses. Lots of asses. I cover my face and want to bust out again before I hear his unmistakable voice.

"Hey, there she is," Riley calls out.

Without really thinking, I find myself standing on my toes and giving him a soft kiss. But then, I'm taken aback by how easily I kiss him, like it's meant to be, and my stomach drops. Oh no. It shouldn't be like this. We're supposed to have a fake relationship. Sure, we had a moment where things got out of hand and he fingered me, but I really need to get my head straight. "Sorry," I whisper, trying to pull away, but he gently pulls me back, deepening the kiss.

"Don't apologize," he murmurs. "I've been waiting for that kiss."

My cheeks turn pink.

He winks at me. "To be honest, I thought you'd wait for me outside, but I like how you go to full lengths to find me."

He only has a towel around his waist and his hair is wet, fresh out of the shower, giving him this scent of something musky and lemon. I just stare at his chest, his stomach, his tattoos. *Help. He's close.*

But from one ogling moment to the drooling next, all I hear is, "Hey, are you coming to the party tonight?"

I blink and blink again, spotting Derek leaning against the locker to my right.

Trying to banish the image of Riley's abs from my mind, I focus on forming a coherent sentence. To manage a normal conversation, I grip Riley by the hips and move him to the right, putting Derek in front of me.

Sweet Jesus, Riley feels so damn good.

"What party?" I ask, blocking that naked guy on my right

out, but he moves into my vision again, his expression turning serious as he shakes his head at Derek.

"No," Riley says. "Don't you dare—"

Derek jumps in to speak. "Ah, it's a little tradition," he starts and leans against his locker casually. "It's a secret party that only happens when we make it to the semis."

"Yes, exactly. Secret, Der," Riley grunts out.

"A secret party? That sounds fun," I say and notice Riley rolling his eyes.

"No, it's not, trust me."

Derek leans into my space, his hand cupping my ear as he whispers, "It's legendary. Trust me, you don't want to miss it."

Riley shoots Derek a stern look. "We're. Not. Going."

I look up at Riley. "Why not?"

Riley hesitates for a moment, his gaze locking with mine. "It's just...I mean, we talked about taking it easy this weekend," he began, his voice trailing off slightly. "This isn't just like any party it's—we could just chill at home?"

"And how often does a secret party like this come around?" I counter, already knowing the answer. "I like parties."

"Not parties like this," he says through clenched teeth as he tries to tell me something. But I don't get it. It would be a nice distraction.

Derek chimes in. "Come on, Riley. It's tradition." Derek's grin widens.

Riley glances around at his teammates, who watch our conversation with amused interest. He lets out a sigh, conceding defeat with a lopsided grin.

"Come on," I say. I think a party would be perfect to forget all the stress.

"Fine. But we're making it an early night."

"Deal," I agree. "Can I bring Priya?"

"You don't want to. Trust me," Riley says. "It's nothing she'd like. Now let's get some food."

He vanishes to get dressed and I try to get some answers about the party from Derek, but he says he's not allowed to talk about it. What happens there, stays there.

When Riley comes back, I try my luck with him, but all he says is, "You wanted to go. So, I'll treat you just like any other guest. But you can still back out, of course."

"I won't."

"Well then, smarty pants, I'm here for the moment you say I was right, and you regret it."

He takes my hand like it's the most natural thing in the world and walks out with me, never letting go even when we're in a deserted corridor where no one can see us. That's when my phone buzzes, and seeing the name makes my heart race with excitement.

"Um, just a second, okay?" I hide the phone screen from him, noticing his curious glance. "I need to take this call."

"Everything okay?" he asks as I step away, trying to keep my smile under control.

"Yeah, just family."

As soon as I'm out of earshot, my heart leaps with joy as I answer the call.

RILEY'S GAZE bores into me from across the table, his brow furrowed with concern.

"That's all you're having?" he asks, his voice gentle yet probing.

I shrug, poking at a cherry tomato with my fork. "I'm not that hungry."

"Lia, you need to eat more than just a salad. You've been training hard, you need the energy."

"I'm fine, really." I force a smile, but it feels strained on my lips.

Riley leans forward, his whiskey eyes searching mine. "Is everything okay? You seem…off a little."

I avert my gaze, focusing on spearing a piece of lettuce.

How could I tell him that Grace's words had burrowed under my skin like parasites, feeding on my insecurities? That every bite feels like a step closer to losing everything I've worked so hard for? What are some shitty days when I can live a happy life after, right? I've been cutting the calories for two weeks now and I'm glad it shows. It's just for now. I'll be fine. No one said media business is easy.

"I'm just stressed about the competition, that's all," I say, shoving the lettuce into my mouth. It tastes like cardboard on my tongue.

Riley doesn't look convinced, but he lets the subject drop as the waiter returns with his steak. The savory aroma wafts across the table, making my stomach grumble traitorously. I sip my water, trying to ignore the gnawing hunger. The rest of the meal passes in a blur of conversation and barely touched food. As we walk to Riley's car, the cool night air nips at my exposed skin, making me shiver. Riley drapes his jacket over my shoulders without a word.

Once we were on the road, Riley clears his throat. "Lia, be honest with me. Have you lost weight?"

My heart stutters in my chest. "Yeah…I've been cutting back a bit."

Riley's hands tighten on the steering wheel. "Why?"

I swallow hard. Why does he wanna know?

"Why? Tell me, Lia, please, I beg you, tell me why you would treat your perfect body like this."

"Grace said…she said if I don't slim down, I'll get voted off. That I'm too sexy for the show." It's hard to tell him, and even harder that I have to repeat what she said.

The car jerks to a sudden stop.

Tires screech against the pavement.

I grab the dashboard to steady myself, my heart racing.

"Riley, what are you doing?" I say.

He doesn't answer, his jaw clenched tight as he throws the car into drive again. "Taking care of this," he grounds out. His eyes flash with barely contained fury as he speeds toward... toward the studio?

"Ri. There's a speed limit."

"I'm aware." He doesn't slow down.

"Ri. Stop it. Let's get home and get dressed for the party. I'm fine. Really."

He doesn't answer and his jaw tics.

Fear coils in my gut like a snake.

What is he going to do? Confront Grace? The producers? No. Please no.

They'll fire me.

Terror seizes me at the thought of losing my spot on the show, my chance to make everything right again.

I want to scream at him, do something, but I'm too stunned to move. I can't tell if I've been sitting here in silence for too long or if the restaurant was actually this close to the studio, but suddenly, the car screeches to a halt. He parks right at the entrance and storms out before I can even unbuckle my seat belt.

Shaking, I slam the door shut and scramble to follow, my heels clicking rapidly against the pavement as I try to keep up with his long strides.

"Riley, wait!" I call out. He can't be serious. I just lost a few pounds, nothing much. I'm eating enough, just less fat and carbs for a bit.

Why would he be this angry? I just don't understand.

But he doesn't slow down, his broad shoulders taut with tension as he bursts through the corridors and the open-space office. The black carpet floor and the white walls blur in my vision as I try to catch up. Hold him back. But I'm too slow and he barges into the producer's office, the door banging against the wall with a resounding crack.

I don't know what he says to them, but as I run up behind him, he's just standing there, rigid. I can't tell if my mind is playing tricks on me or not, but I swear I can see his pulse pounding in the center of his neck.

I find Grace and the other judges gathered with our producers and directors around a gray round table cluttered with papers. Behind them, a paused video of yesterday's show fills the screen. They all look up in surprise, eyes widening at Riley's furious gaze. Grace's eyes flicker with a strange emotion when she spots me standing behind him, utterly shocked.

"If I hear one more comment about Liora needing to lose weight, I'm going public with everything that's happened behind the scenes of this show," Riley snarls, his hands clenched into fists at his sides. "I can make our text messages go viral in seconds. You have contestants and judges that are toxic, and requirements that are from the eighties. Liora's perfect. She's your best skater, and you're going to lose her if you keep up this bullshit. It's the first season. Be wise and make it to a second."

Grace opens her mouth to protest, but Riley cuts her off with a sharp gesture. "No. I want you to apologize. Liora is perfect the way she is, and if you can't see that, then you're the ones with the problem. Not her."

Silence falls over the room, heavy and thick with tension.

I stand frozen in the doorway, my heart racing as I watch Grace open and close her mouth like a guppy.

"You told her to lose weight?" a producer turns to Grace, and I see her shift in her seat, swallowing her red lips.

"I didn't call her overweight. She isn't. Her curves are just gathering an audience we don't want."

"Says who?" Riley barks out.

"The comments on each of her videos," Grace says, but the way she looks makes me believe she actually regrets what she's said to me.

"Well, then be happy someone is interested in your show. That could change. Especially once they hear how toxic the work environment is," Riley says.

Grace stays silent.

"This isn't acceptable," the director says. "We're sorry about this, Miss James."

Riley nods to Grace. "Go on, apologize, or we're out of here."

My stomach drops. He can't say this to her. No.

Finally, Grace nods stiffly. "Understood, Mr. Huntington." She then looks to me. "I'm sorry, Miss James. It won't happen again."

Riley gives a curt nod, his eyes still blazing. "Good. See that it doesn't."

He then turns on his heel and stalks out of the office, leaving me to hurry after him once more, but hell, I'm fuming. Tears sting at my eyes, and I don't know what to say, but I'm ready to kill this man.

He had no right to do this.

I can feel Grace's wrath brewing. She's going to make sure I regret this at the next show. I just know it.

Riley gets in the car, but I keep walking on the sidewalk, determined to take the subway. There's no way I'm getting in that car. He crossed a line—no, he jumped over it and soared far beyond. Grace is going to hate me for this, and she'll never forget it. I'm only three shows in. The money I've earned so far isn't nearly enough.

I just can't believe he did that.

Riley drives alongside me, the window rolling down. "Get in," he barks out.

"No."

"I said get in."

"I said no." Idiot.

I keep walking, straight ahead.

"Liora, I don't even know why you think you should be angry with me, but I beg you to get in my car."

Okay, fine. He asked for it. I can't hold back any longer. "You shouldn't have done that," I burst out, my voice shaking. "What if they fire me now? You had no right to interfere like that, Riley!"

His whiskey eyes are molten with intensity. "They'd be idiots to fire you. You're their star. And I'm not going to sit back and watch them tear you down. Not now, not ever."

I shake my head, tears pricking at the corners of my eyes. "It wasn't your fucking place. As if they're going to drop this! They are probably writing me out right now! Planning on getting rid of me!"

"It's a live show. They can't."

"Oh, you have no idea what they can do. Of course there are scripted parts."

"Get in."

"No!"

"If they fire you, I'll kill them."

"Great! And what do I do then? Huh?" I scream, leaning into the open window. "I don't have a trust fund! I don't have any money! I have what I came here with! That's all! I need this show, Riley!"

He blinks. "I will give you the money."

I throw my head back, laughing bitterly. "Oh, of course you will. The man with all the money in the world will just give me a million dollars. How generous of you. What am I to you, Riley? Your whore? I won't take a cent from you."

"Stop being so fucking stubborn!"

"Stop getting your nose in things you shouldn't! You're my

FAKE boyfriend, not my real one. You have no right to act like this. Are you out of your mind?"

A heavy silence stretches between us. I think I see hurt in his eyes, but it's quickly replaced by an angry frown.

"Fine," he says, driving off.

I stomp my way to the subway.

AFTER A LONG FACETIME SESSION, I stand in front of the mirror in my bedroom, turning from side to side as I examine my reflection. The lingerie I'd bought on a whim some years ago hugs my curves, the cheap lace barely concealing my skin. It looks good. And that's what I need for tonight. To feel good. The party is just perfect for this.

On my angry stomp home, Nina called and sent over a contract, stating that Riley would cover all my expenses if his interference got me fired.

I combed through the fine print, and it wasn't a trap—no strings attached. Just a legal apology.

Nina managed to calm me down a bit, but I still believe Riley overstepped. I overstepped, too, when I talked to his coach, but Riley has a contract. His coach can't fire him like that, and he knows it wasn't Riley shouting but me. Grace will think I didn't have the guts and sent Riley instead, like he's my bulldog. That's a huge difference. Or maybe it's not. Shit. I don't know anymore. I think Riley and I have lost track of where we stand. What we are. Maybe we need to cut it. Maybe we shouldn't go to this party after all, even though I desperately need a distraction.

But I want to go to this party. I want to talk to other people. Talk about something other than Riley, the show, my past.

I just want to have fun for a couple of hours.

I bite my lip, suddenly unsure.

Is the lace too much? Does it look cheap?

I snap a photo, and it looks good, but it's not like anyone's going to see it tonight anyway. I put my outfit on, and I'm glad my bra doesn't show, but I still have a weird feeling. I want to look good tonight.

I need a second opinion.

Before I can second-guess myself, I snap another quick photo and send it to Priya.

> Liora: Is this okay?

I hit Send before I can change my mind. But as I stare down at my phone, my heart stops. The message didn't go to Priya. It went to Riley. And I didn't send the pic with the dress. It's the pic of me in my lingerie.

Oh God. Oh God, oh God, oh God.

I frantically try to delete it, but my fingers are suddenly shaking as I tap at the screen. And it's too late. He saw it.

My phone buzzes in my hand, startling me so badly I almost drop it.

With a sense of impending doom, I read the text.

> Puckster: Lia.

That was all it said. Just my name. But somehow, I can feel the weight of unspoken words behind it.

Before I can respond, another message pops up.

> Puckster: You're trying to kill me, aren't you? Because it's working.

A surprised laugh bubbles up in my throat, a blush heating my cheeks. I can picture the look on Riley's face, the heat in his eyes as he stares down at the photo. My thumbs hover over the screen, my heart racing as I try to decide how to respond. This is dangerous territory. And I'm still mad at him.

Maybe I am. What are you going to do about it? I hit Send before I can lose my nerve.

> Puckster: Why are you wearing such nice lingerie anyway?

OKAY, HE THINKS IT'S NICE. IMMA WEAR IT.

Liora: For the party.

> Puckster: You still want to go?

Liora: Sure. I promised to meet Derek.

IT TAKES SEVERAL MINUTES AND BLINKING DOTS UNTIL HE FINALLY ANSWERS.

> Puckster: No.

Liora: What no?

I FEIGN IGNORANCE, STILL GRINNING LIKE AN IDIOT.

> Puckster: Sorry, but there's no chance anyone is seeing you in that tonight.

Liora: Don't be so sure of it. I'm out for blood.

> Puckster: I'm your fake boyfriend and we have rules. We stick to the rules.

Liora: Bossy. Meet you in five.

I dress to kill: knee-high boots, a black miniskirt, and a white blouse that shows off my cleavage.

I'm not exactly proud of it, but when I stomped back home, I couldn't resist stopping at a tiny dress shop after catching a glimpse of it in the window. I haven't bought much for myself over the years, but I just had to have this outfit.

My hair falls sleek over my shoulders as I head out. But when I see him, the joke is on me because he looks so hot that I have to swallow—hard. The way I want this man. It's not healthy anymore.

He leans against the wall in black jeans and a fitted black shirt, showing off all his muscles as he adjusts his watch. Shit. Black suits him so well.

There's a cocky smirk on his lips, so I brace myself.

"I texted Derek," he says as I approach.

"Oh?" I reply, striding to the door and making sure I swing my hips more than enough. And I'm pleased with the way he looks at me. Like he wants to devour me.

"He never said he'd meet you there."

"Oh, about that." I grin, swaying toward the elevator. "I just wanted to see how you'd react. Also, I still hate you, so don't think your good looks will charm me—it's not working."

He winks. "It is."

"In your dreams."

He steps closer, lowering his voice. "Well, you are in them."

"Careful, you're sounding like you care," I retort, giving him a once-over. Why does he smell so good? This isn't fair. I planned on giving him the cold shoulder, but all I want to do is take that stupid hair and pull him in and kiss him. "But I have to give it to you, you clean up nice. Almost like you're trying to impress someone."

He presses the elevator button. "You know, for someone who hates me, you're awfully invested in my wardrobe."

"Just making sure you don't embarrass me. Let's go, pretty boy."

Twenty-eight

RILEY

That woman is going to be the death of me.

I snapped at Grace because she doesn't understand just how much I crave that sweet ass of hers. It's a fucking work of art. And Grace messed with it. My everything.

Anyone trying to keep her from flaunting it is my mortal enemy.

I swear, if she hadn't apologized to Liora, I would have torn apart that office in a rage. I can't help but get protective when it comes to her. I know it was a step too far, but I just can't wrap my head around why she's so easily talked down. Can't she see how fucking beautiful she is? She's indeed killing me with that dress today. It barely covers anything, leaving those holy cheeks just begging for my hands to grab onto them. And that blouse…the fabric outlines every curve of her chest. That neckline is practically daring me to dive in and suck on her pointy nipples. The way her tits bounce with every step she takes. She's driving me wild.

Good thing I can fight, because I'm certain everyone will

be drooling over her when they see her tonight. But she's mine, and I'm not sharing.

I'm only taking her to this party tonight against all odds because she insisted and I can't say no to her.

The party location changes each time to keep things exclusive. This time, we're in Brooklyn, and when we sneak in through the back entrance, Liora has to sign a contract promising never to speak a word about what goes on here tonight.

I hoped this might scare her off, but she signs without hesitation.

Maybe she's trying to prove how brave she is, or maybe she just wants to give me a thrill, and it works. Because damn, with all these hockey players eyeing her up and down like hungry wolves, I don't trust myself around her. I doubt my frown will disappear anytime soon.

I have my hand on Liora's back as we make our way into the main room. Liora's eyes widen as she takes in the plush red couches, the glossy black walls, and the shimmering chandeliers hanging from the ceiling. She throws me a questioning look, but I just shrug, trying to play it cool. I know it's like a scene out of the movie *Eyes Wide Shut*. It's an old secret tradition. A way to keep it interesting for us players. It was everything for me back then when I was a rookie. Now, it's just a pain in the ass, knowing that I will hate every second of it soon.

"Still sure you want to stay?" I ask, leaning in close so she can hear me over the pulsing music. *Please say no.*

"Yep. I'm not going anywhere."

"Of course." This woman.

Across the room, I spot Colton and Jayce huddled around Shane, probably trying to keep the poor kid from having a nervous breakdown. Derek's already chatting up some girl in a skintight dress, and I can't help but feel a twinge of satisfaction that Liora's not talking to him. She nearly gave me a heart attack with that text earlier.

After a few more drinks and mingling with people, it's clear that Liora is on a mission to make me pay for today. She's all smiles with everyone else but icy with me. Every time I lean in for a kiss, she shuts me down. No matter how many times I remind her that we need to keep up the charade, she just says, "Couples fight. We're having one."

And just when I'm about to beg her to stop with the cold shoulder, the music cuts off, and Derek steps onto a raised platform, holding a glass bowl. Normally, the captain organizes this party, but Jayce despises it, so Derek took over. Maybe we're just getting too old for this.

"Listen up, everyone!" he calls out, his voice echoing through the room. Everyone stops chatting and stares at him. All ears. "It's time for a little game. All the guys who want to participate, drop your watches in this bowl. Ladies, if you're feeling adventurous, you'll draw a watch and head into the closet." He points to two big black double doors behind him. "The guy whose watch you pick will join you for a little adult version of seven minutes in heaven." He winks and the crowd claps and howls.

My heart hammers in my chest as I watch Liora's reaction, trying to gauge her interest. She doesn't even flinch. In fact, she looks...excited? What a little brat.

I lean in close to her, my lips brushing against her ear. "Lia, we can go home if you want. You don't have to do this."

"Oh, I want to do it." With that she goes off and keeps on talking with others. As if showing me that I'm not the only one she's interested in.

Jealousy surges through me, hot and bitter.

The thought of her in that closet with another guy, their hands all over her, their lips on her skin...it's enough to make my blood boil. I watch her, clenching my jaw and trying to contain the rage bubbling up inside me. Before I can stop myself, I march over to the bowl and throw my watch in, the metal clinking against the glass. Liora's eyes widen in surprise, but there's something else there too—a flicker of heat, of challenge.

Two can play at this game, Lia.

I step back, crossing my arms over my chest as I lean against the wall and watch her flirting. My heart is pounding, my palms slick with sweat, and I'm happy as the waiter comes by and I grab another drink from his tray.

Liora takes another cocktail as well, saluting me from afar, all the while she grins at a man I don't know. To heighten the thrill, we allowed the team to bring some close friends. The guy Liora's talking to is one of them. She smiles at me. Oh, she thinks she's got me all figured out, but she has no idea what she's in for.

Twenty-nine

LIORA

Riley's eyes burn into me from across the room, his brows knitted together in a deep scowl. It's like he's trying to send a message, but I'm too angry to decode it.

I tear my gaze away, pretending to focus on the guy in front of me, who's babbling on about his…ducks? Who gives a shit. All I can think about is how badly I want to make Riley squirm after the stunt he pulled today. Childish? Maybe. Worth it? Absolutely.

And really, what's the worst that could happen in seven minutes? I glance around at the other hockey guys I've been chatting up all night. They seem harmless enough. Riley's teammates would never try anything sketchy. But I down another drink, nerves fraying.

My stomach twists into knots as the first girl reaches into the bowl and draws out a watch. I hold my breath, watching intently to see which guy she picked. *Not Riley. Please not Riley.* It's Colton. Thank God.

The lucky couple disappears into the closet and emerges exactly seven minutes later, faces flushed. This goes on for several rounds. Some couples make a beeline for the door once they get out, clearly eager to take things further. Others head upstairs—apparently this party house has plenty of rooms for exactly that purpose. But there are some who quickly chat up with others.

Derek thrusts the bowl toward me, and I hesitate, my hand hovering over the tangle of watches. Shit. Riley's penetrating gaze bores into me, silently warning me not to do it.

But screw him.

I'm so sick of his head games.

My pulse races as I snatch a watch and drop it into Derek's open palm, my heart thudding wildly in my chest. "Great choice."

"Whose is it?" I know it's not Riley's. He's got a red rim around the clock face. I can't lie that I'm disappointed. But it's the game. A kiss won't hurt, right?

Maybe kissing someone else will help us. Maybe that's what we need to fix whatever wires got crossed between us.

Derek puts his hand on the small of my back. I turn to see Riley, and he's either trying to kill the person whose hand is on my back with his gaze alone or me. I suddenly can't lie to myself anymore. I want to kiss *him*. No one else. But Derek leads me to the closet anyway, and doubts flood my mind even more. What the hell am I doing? This is my first swinger party, and I'm about to take part in a game that could go horribly wrong. I should back out now before it's too late.

But then I think of Riley's face if I bail. I don't want him to be right. No. I'd rather kiss another guy than admit I was wrong. The only intelligent choice here, am I right?

Shoot. I'm an idiot.

Derek shuts the door behind me, leaving only a faint red glow to illuminate the room.

It's empty—just me and my pounding heart.

My thoughts spiral into a frenzy. What if Riley never looks

at me the same way again? What if this ruins everything? But then I recall his infuriating smirk, that knowing look that makes it clear my heart beats only for him these days. My resolve stiffens.

I'm going through with this.

BUT INSTEAD OF a stranger's face, it's Riley who steps in, his expression rugged.

A sigh of relief escapes my lips and I realize how much I desire him. Despite everything inside of me screaming that he is off limits, I can't help but want him more than anything else.

He slams the door shut. "Surprised to see me?" There's nothing nice in his voice, not a hint of that joking side of his.

"Disappointed, actually. I was hoping for someone else." Oh, what a lie.

He laughs, but there's no humor in it. "Well, too bad. I'm the only one for you. And I'll make you pay for putting me through this."

I stumble backward until my spine hits the unforgiving wall.

The look on his face—pure hate and bliss—makes my heart expand and my skin prickle.

Riley's presence fills every inch of the room, shrinking its already small space.

He strides toward me with hungry eyes and slams me against the wall. He grabs my wrists, yanking them above my head in a vise-like grip while his strong body holds me captive, not giving an inch of mercy.

And then his mouth crashes onto mine in a bruising kiss that takes all the air in my lunge.

I try to resist, but my body melts against his strong touch, unable to fight the firestorms that race through my veins. I can't move anymore, feeling nothing but all of him against all of me. I'm just standing there, letting him fight with my mouth until I manage to bite his lips.

He pauses, and we both take deep breaths as if we've just finished a marathon.

"I hate you," I growl against his mouth, but he stops me from speaking with his.

"Oh yeah?" he breathes. "Then say it again. Lie to my face once more." His hands roam over my boobs. He squeezes them so hard it hurts, but it also feels so good. I hate it, but a sigh escapes me, and he knows just how much I want this.

"Say it again."

"I hate you."

He grips both of my hands with one, the other impatiently fumbles at my skirt. With a mischievous smile, he swiftly rips off my panties.

I gasp. "It's the only lacy one I own."

"I don't fucking care," he growls, and I should hate the way he says it. This angry bark. The way he pins me down like I have nothing to say, that I should know he weighs way more than me. That he can do anything he wants, and I have no chance against him, but I don't hate it. I love it.

His fingers bore into my pussy. "If you hate me, why is your pussy so wet for me?"

I don't say anything and try with all I've got to stare back at him with the hate in my eyes I always tell him I have for him. He keeps one hand clasped above my head and moves the other down to grip my chin.

His hips press so hard against me that I cry out. "If you hate me, why do your eyes plead with me to kiss you? Why is your body arching against mine? Why is your pussy pressing into my hand, huh?"

I have no answer. None I could say out loud.

"You like me." His lip crashes against mine again. Hard.

I bite his lip again. "You wish."

His words ignite something deep inside me, and suddenly I'm kissing him back with equal fervor. Our tongues battle for dominance as he pushes me against the wall again and again. Moans and gasps fill the air around us as thighs grind against thighs, skin slides against skin. I reach down and touch him through the denim, eliciting a low groan from his throat.

I could feel his throbbing erection straining against his tight jeans, pulsating with need. I couldn't resist teasing him, rubbing my hand over the bulge and feeling it grow harder under my touch. He leans in close, scraping his teeth along my neck. My desire is building as I eagerly unbutton his jeans. Suddenly, he pushes me back and I fall to my knees.

As I gaze up at him, his hands splayed against the wall above me, I can see the lust in his eyes as he whispers, "Don't forget your promise." He presses his rock-hard dick against my parted lips. "Next time you see it," he breathes, "you'd kiss it."

There's a wetness between my legs, an otherworldly ache in my core growing with every passing second and I can't wait anymore. My breath catches in my throat as I free his hard cock.

It springs forth, long and thick, and veined and pulsing with need.

The skin is a deep shade of rose, and when I fist it, I draw a finger over its head—a smooth, glistening dome. He throws his head back, moaning, and my finger gets draped in precum. The scent of his arousal fills my nose—musky and masculine, combining with the faint tang of soap from his shower earlier. It's a heady aroma that makes me flush with desire. And shit. I can't help but stare for a moment before leaning in. I press a long kiss on it, make sure I envelope it with my plush lips, and when he presses against it even harder, I gasp.

I raise my eyes to meet his intense stare. He looks at me as if he wants to consume me entirely. "Fuck, you look gorgeous," he whispers.

I wrap my hand around his erection, never breaking our eye contact.

He grasps onto my hair with enough force to make me feel a slight twinge of pain. "Take it," he commands, pulling my head toward his groin again.

"I only promised to kiss it," I whisper, but I have to hold myself back to not kiss it again, to not swallow it whole.

That look on his face is killing me.

"Take. It. I. Said," he says, frantic.

"Make me."

"Fine but I'm going to be honest with you," he says. "I'm not going to be gentle, so if you can't handle rough, speak up and I'll go."

"I love it rough. Bring it on," I say.

He grips my hair even harder and shoves his penis against my mouth until it breaks through my lips and down my throat. He pushes my head against his groin until we slam against the wall together. Tears sting my eyes, and I place my hands at his thighs, steadying myself. I take him fully into my mouth, swirling my tongue around his shaft as I bob forth and back.

"Fuck, just like that," he says, guiding my head with his hands.

I hollow my cheeks and suck harder, spurred on by his praise.

I want to make him feel good.

I take him deeper into my mouth, my lips sliding down his shaft as my tongue swirls around the base. He groans and his hips buck. I can hear the wet sounds of my mouth on his cock, the sloppy, messy noises that are so fucking hot. I know he loves it, I can feel the way his breath hitches every time I take him deeper, my throat constricting around him. I gag, but I don't care.

My hands roam his body and trace the contours of his abs. I can feel the tension in his muscles, the way they tighten and flex as he nears the edge of release. And when he finally comes, it's with a roar, his cum hot and thick. It fills my mouth and I swallow it down.

"Fuck," he says, tremors still shooting through him. "Fuck, Liora. What the fuck."

I pull back, licking my lips, and I look up at him once more, my eyes still oh so heavy with desire. He pulls me to my feet, crushing his lips to mine as he tastes himself on my tongue. It's dirty and filthy and so hot. "I'm gonna make you cum so hard, this was the best blow job I ever got," he says, but the door swings open.

"Hate to say it, champ, but your time is up."

If looks could kill, Derek would be a dead man now.

THE MINUTE WE'RE OUT, Riley says, "We're leaving. Now."

"I need to grab my jacket," I protest.

"Leave it here." He tugs me toward the door, but I resist. "Riley, I honestly thought you'd never ask, and I can't wait to go home with you, but I need this jacket."

Not only did he tear my panties, but now this. Doesn't he realize these are the only clothes I have?

He sighs but nods toward the coat check. "Quick. I'm bursting."

I laugh and dash over to get my jacket as he pulls out his phone to get us an Uber.

The attendant is busy sorting tickets, and it takes a minute to get his attention.

Finally, I snag my jacket and hurry back, only to find some sneaky girl trying to flirt her way into Riley's heart. He doesn't look interested, but I just swallowed his cum. There's no girl talking to him tonight but me.

I stride toward him, grab him by the collar, and yank him away from her, crashing my lips into his with enough intensity to make the girl sigh in annoyance.

I break the kiss and glance at her.

"Sorry, licked it, it's mine."

Then I wink at her, grab my man's hand, and get him out. ASAP.

Thirty

RILEY

I have no idea how I made it out of the Uber without fucking her right there, but we made it into the apartment complex.

Liora yanks me into the elevator and presses me against the frigid metal wall, her hands gripping my shirt collar. I return her intense kiss as she begins to unbutton my shirt. "Damn, Liora. I need you so badly."

She lets out a low moan as she pushes my shirt off my shoulders, her fingers tracing the lines of my chest. I reach down and grab her ass, pulling her tight against me. I can feel the heat radiating off her, and I know she's just as turned on as I am.

I slide my hand up her thigh and her breath catches in her throat as my fingers slide under her skirt again, feeling her still wet and eager for my touch. I caress her clit, gently moving my fingers in circular motions over that sensitive spot as she squirms against me.

The elevator bell chimes, and without breaking our heated kiss, we stumble out and into my apartment. We barely manage to open the door before shedding our clothes. Her skirt drops to the floor, followed by my shirt. In our haste, a shoe lands on the lampshade, leaving a trail of chaos behind.

We crash into the kitchen corner and our groans fill the air as her hands roam wildly over my hair, chest, hips, pecs, abs—fuck, everywhere. I try to touch every part of her at once and declare that two hands are not enough. Our movements are frantic and feverish, and we stagger toward my room.

"Fuck, I need you," I pant, and we collide with the couch, the wall, and her door along the way. With one swift motion, I unclasp her bra and let it fall wherever it may. I eagerly kiss her lips and almost stumble over my own pants bunched around my ankles.

She yanks on my hair, and I dig my nails into her back, both of us consumed by raw, primal need. It's like we're two wild animals, clawing and tearing at each other, desperate for more. The heat between us is intense, uncontrollable, and I can't get enough of her. I feel starved. And it just doesn't get better. We kiss like warriors, and she fights back just perfectly.

By the time I fling her onto the bed, we are both naked. I take a moment to admire her, her creamy skin flushed with arousal, her blonde hair splayed out on my pillow, her chest heaving with ragged breaths, as those blue eyes roam over my tattoos, my abs—just every part of me.

She's a goddess, and I'm a man on the edge.

I kneel at the foot of the bed, just looking at her.

She is a vision, laid out before me with her legs spread.

Her skin is flushed pink with arousal, and her wetness glistens in the dim light of the room. I can see every curve and contour of her body, the way her breasts rise and fall with each breath, the way her hips tilt up toward me. And in the center of it all, her swollen clit beckons me closer, aching to be touched.

"Fuck, Liora, you're so wet, it drips down your thighs."

"All for you."

I sigh. No dream I've ever had about her could top this. I've imagined this moment over and over again, and no dream could be this perfect.

I open the condom, sliding it over my hard dick and stroking it. Her eyes fall on my length.

"Touch yourself," I rasp.

She slowly massages her breasts. There's a dare in her gaze. She's so sweet but oh so sinister it drives me crazy, and I pump even harder. She pulls on her nipples until they are hard and pink. I can't tear my gaze away. Liora's killing me.

She moves her right hand down between her legs, her fingers slipping easily into her pussy, and I just stare. Watch her. Sighing, my own hand wraps tightly around my throbbing cock. I take in every stroke, watch her, learn how she likes it, where she needs that touch. I can see the muscles in her thighs tensing as she works her fingers in and out, her thumb circling her clit all the while. Oh, I can see it swelling even more, and I just know I have to taste her.

Leaning forward, I bury my face between her legs, my tongue lapping at her clit as I slide two fingers inside her. I press my dick against the mattress because, shit, I can't take it anymore. I need friction. Any friction, and she tastes so fucking good.

Her hips buck against my face as I fuck her with my tongue. Her muscles clench around it, her orgasm building as I work her clit with wet strokes.

I insert my fingers inside her once more, watching as she throws her head back against the pillow and grips the mattress tightly, each thrust pushing deeper and deeper.

"Shit, Riley," she says, and my balls tighten.

I press my dick harder against the mattress, dying to finally get inside of her.

But I'm not done with her yet.

Pulling my fingers out of her, I lick them clean, savoring the taste of her sweetness. "You taste amazing," I say and smile at the way she looks at me. The way she's so turned on.

I climb up to her mouth, my cock pressing against her entrance. I kiss her and she spreads those thighs for me.

Her lips are so swollen and glistening—fuck, it's everything I've ever wanted.

I tease her entrance with the tip of my cock, savoring the feeling of her against me.

I need to fuck her.

But first, I want to taste her again. I slide my fingers back inside of her, her slickness coating them as I pull them out. I bring my fingers to my mouth once more, sucking them clean, the taste of her sweetness sending a jolt of pleasure through my body as she shivers just from watching me.

My cock twitches with need. "Please let me fuck you."

"Shut up and fuck me already," she says.

Laughing, I say, "Look who's so needy."

I reach down, my hand wrapping around my cock, and rub the head against her, teasing her with its size. She gasps, her hips bucking up to meet me. I can feel her tightening around me, her body begging for me to fill her up.

"Please," she begs, her voice hoarse with need. "Fuck me. Please, Ri."

She grabs my ass, pulling me closer.

With one swift move, I drive inside of her, my cock filling her up completely.

She cries out, her body arching off the bed as she takes every inch of me.

"Good girl. You take it so well," I say, the feeling of her tight, wet heat around me almost too much to bear.

My hips thrust in and out of her in a steady rhythm. The wetness of her envelops my shaft, her warmth inviting me deeper.

She wraps her legs around my back, pulling me closer as

she meets me thrust for thrust. Our bodies move in sync, the friction building between us. Her breath hitches as I hit that sweet spot inside of her, and I feel myself getting closer and closer to the edge.

But then, there's a shift.

I notice her crying out, but there's no corresponding throb inside of her.

Her walls don't tighten enough, and my dick almost immediately loses all its blood. No, for fuck's sake. She's faking it. No.

"Stop," I command.

Her eyes grow wide.

I wrap a hand around her neck and thrust my dick even deeper inside until she gasps in pain this time. "You think I can't spot an orgasm? I know how an orgasm feels, baby." This alone tells me she's only ever been with fuckboys who don't know how to please her. "Don't you ever try this on me again," I say, and it transforms into a curse as I thrust again.

I press her gently into the bed, my hand firm but tender around her delicate neck. My grip tightens with a surge of need, then softens as I stroke her neck and whisper, "Don't worry. I'm going to show you how to come properly on my cock."

I pull my cock out of her, grab her by the waist, and turn her around in one swift move. "But first, you're gonna pay for the faking."

"Riley, I'm—"

I slap her ass, not too much but enough to make her yelp a little. She turns to face me and there's a wicked glint in her eyes.

"That wasn't all you got, right?"

I slap her again, and she cries out. Real and raw and I revel in the way she cries out and sinks down before me.

I press her back down with my hand, positioning her ass

just how I like it. Seeing this ass like this will ruin me for every other girl. Because this is perfection.

"Now go, apologize, babygirl," I say, cupping her cheeks and squeezing them. Fuck, it feels even better than I thought. Her ass is so round and soft.

"I'm sorry," she whispers, her voice trembling while I fuck her.

"It's okay, baby. I'm gonna make you feel so good that you don't have to fake it anymore."

I keep on gripping her ass, and she gives me those little pathetic moans I love so much while I push inside of her from behind, the sensation of her tightness around me sending waves of pleasure through my body. As I fuck her, I reach down, my fingers finding her clit, and start to rub it in slow circles in time with my thrusts. She cries out again, louder this time. I can feel her walls clenching around me, the pleasure building inside of her. I'm not gentle. No. I fuck her rough. Just like she deserves after this stunt, but she likes it. My fingers rub harder while my others work her nipples, and just when she cries out so loud that I know she's close, I stop.

"What. Riley, I—"

I move us so I'm on my back. "Ride me. I need you to come on my cock, baby."

And with that, she straddles me, her wetness sliding easily onto my cock as she rides me. It's slow and sensual at first, her hips rocking back and forth as she grounds herself against me. But soon, she's bouncing up and down, her tits jiggling as she takes me deeper and deeper.

"Yeah, baby, use me."

Riley, she mouths, but I can feel that she's still somewhere else in her head.

"Stop. Pleasing. Me," I snap, guiding her hips slower, making her grind that clit on my stomach, until she whimpers in a desperate way again. Yeah, that's how she likes it.

"Use me, I said. Don't fucking think about if I like it because I always will."

And that's when she rides me like I'm her tool, and fuck yeah, I love it.

I reach up and grab her breasts, my fingers pinching her nipples. I can feel myself getting closer, my orgasm building as she grinds her clit over my pubic bone over and over again. She doesn't care if her movements do anything for me. She works my dick just like she wants it, and I can't hold it anymore.

She groans and the walls inside of her clench around my cock. I start to push my hips up and down and up and down so fast she's vibrating against my skin. My free hand moves to the back of her neck, pulling her close and pressing my lips against her damp skin.

"Shit, Riley. I'm…I'm so close," she says, and I keep on pushing. Faster and faster. "Fuck. You're like a huge vibrator. This…this is so good."

My orgasm is building and building, my cock swelling inside of her as she rides me harder and faster. I can hear the wet sounds of our bodies slapping together, the dirty, filthy noises driving me wild as I kiss her fucking hot neck.

When she finally comes, she shouts my name, her body shaking as she collapses onto me. As if she's pushed a button, the minute I feel her come, milking my cock, I explode inside her.

Fucking hell.

As we lie there, panting and sweating, I know that this is it. This raw, dirty, and unapologetic need is what I wanted. What I craved.

She ruined me.

Because now I won't ever let her have sex with anyone but me.

"Fuck, that was incredible," I say.

"Yes," she whispers, collapsing onto the bed beside me.

We lie there, both staring at the ceiling, for what feels like seconds or maybe minutes—I'm not sure.

"Just don't ever fake it again, okay?"

"I'm sorry," she murmurs, her voice barely audible. "I was afraid I'd take too long. My ex couldn't stand it when I did, so I guess I just got used to faking it."

I take her hand in mine. I hate the word *ex* on her lips. I also hate that idiot fucker. Worshipping her is everything I need. "I don't care how long it takes. Every moment of having sex with you is pure bliss, baby."

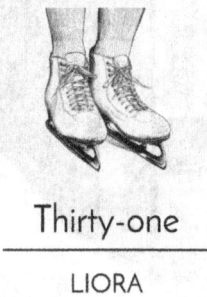

Thirty-one

LIORA

I wake up to an empty bed, missing Riley's warmth already. My heart sinks for a second until I see a steaming mug of coffee on the nightstand with a cream-colored note next to it.

There's a flutter in my sternum and I grab the note with sleepy fingers.

You've made me an addict. The happiest man alive. I can't wait to come home to you tonight. Have the best day.

—Ri

A mix of joy and fear floods me. My heart is completely his now, no question about it. But a pro hockey player and…me? Deep down, I know this can't last forever. He's in his prime, ready to party, travel, and enjoy the single life. I can't cage him, but life with me would mean exactly that. I can't just transform his carefree bachelor lifestyle into something serious overnight.

We talked all night long.

He shared stories about his grandmother and his college years, and I told him about how I started skating, inspired by a Hungarian pro skater who gifted me her old skates.

Something changed between us that night.

When he asked if I truly hated him, I said no. I really don't. There's no denying it anymore.

I have feelings for him. It's too late now, and that night I decided that whatever happens, I want to have fun with him as long as it lasts. Stop the charade. Stop the lying. Yes, he has the power to hurt me, and I know he will. But I'll enjoy it while it lasts. It can be a great memory. Something I once had. I had him. It has to be enough.

I make my way back to the studio, knowing that Grace is most likely still angry after Riley defended me. But I can't avoid her forever. It's time to face it head-on and be brave for once.

THE DANCE STUDIO is oddly quiet when I arrive.

I find Aiden slumped against the mirror, head hanging low, and my stomach lurches.

"Hey, what's wrong?" I ask, dropping my bag.

Aiden looks up, eyes all red. I run to him. My breath hitches. Wordlessly, he holds out his phone. A video is paused on the screen. I press Play and watch as Aiden pulls a man in for a passionate kiss. The mystery man turns slightly, and I gasp.

"Ethan? How the hell did you two even meet?"

"Riley's party. We got to talking and just…clicked." A wry smile tugs at his lips.

My brain pounds with a thousand questions I don't have answers to, but Aiden must have sensed they all boiled down to one: Why? Why him? Ethan's the grumpiest of all grumps I've ever met. And I've seen Riley in the morning. That's no joke.

Aiden is pure sunshine. If he were an egg dish, he'd be sunny side up all the time. It just doesn't make sense.

Aiden lets out a light, amused laugh. "I know he comes across as uptight, but there's more to him. I like peeling back those grumpy layers."

I shake my head in wonder. "Well, to each their own, but… who leaked this? It's clearly a private moment."

Aiden's face hardens. "No idea. We were so careful…"

There's anger boiling up inside of me. I hate he has to be careful. In what world are we living? I thought we were better now, but it's still so fucked up and I think the media world is like a tiny cut out of the worst of human beings. The amount of people who are willing to exploit others is crazy, and I honestly can't wait until this show ends. *Grace on Ice* is fucking toxic, and I hate that you have to look and be a certain way so that people will love you. I hate that you have to hide your love to seem worthy of the love of strangers.

Aiden's eyes dip to my hands and I realize I've fisted them so hard my knuckles have turned white. Just then, Ethan storms into the room, his brow knitted together and his jaw tight. "We have to find out who's responsible for this and why, immediately. I won't let some pervert with a camera ruin everything for you."

As Ethan walks in, Aiden's face lights up with a smile that confirms everything for me. Ethan glances at me with his usual disapproval, but it quickly fades when he meets Aiden's eyes. There is so much passion between them that I can feel it in my own skin. It disappoints me to think that people want to ruin the happiness of others. Why do we have to be so closed-minded? Love comes in all different forms, and we should focus on eliminating hate instead of trying to control and restrict the best aspect of being human.

"Ethan, how did you even get in here?" I ask, totally taken aback. "You can't just walk into the dance studio."

Ethan scoffs. "I've been an agent for years. I know a thing or two about getting where I want to go."

Aiden's phone buzzes and his face falls as he reads the message. "Well, my agent says the movie I was up for just dropped me from consideration. Apparently, I'm too much of a 'risk' now."

Ethan's eyes flash with anger. "I know. That's why I wanted to see you. Enough is enough. We're going to take control of this narrative." He crouches down in front of Aiden, a strong hand resting on his kneecap. "I'm setting up an interview for you. It's time to share your truth, on your terms."

"I don't know. What if this ruins everything for us?" He glances at me.

"This shouldn't even be a question. Why does it matter who we love outside of the rink? It's about our skillset. It might seem romantic for two people to find each other on a TV show, but that was never the case for us, Aiden. Everyone knows I love Riley." The air suddenly leaves my lungs, and I fear it won't return. Love...I don't love him...that word is way too strong. No.

Ethan clears his throat. "What she's trying to say is, people will support you. There might be ignorant comments about all figure skaters being gay and all that nonsense. We just ignore it, okay? There will always be haters because their lives lack any real substance besides spreading hate. We have to speak out on this. Tolerating it means it stays like this."

I nod. "Ethan's right. The world needs more openness. It's time people understand that. Hiding and hurting helps no one. If you want to be true to yourself, let's fight for it. You deserve justice."

Aiden takes a shaky breath. "There's something else. My grandma...she's sick. Dad called me to tell me she might not make it until Monday."

"You should book a flight to see her ASAP. Take all the time you need. We'll handle things here," I say.

Aiden shakes his head. "You know as well as I do, there's

no taking time off. We have a show to run. We can't just take a day off."

I grin, a mischievous idea forming. "If only we had a skilled skater who loves being in the limelight and could step in for you for a week."

Ethan and I exchange knowing glances. He joins my smirk.

"You're right, we do have a bit of a break coming up! Between the third play-off and the Stanley Cup games. You think Riley could step in? Learn a dance routine with you?"

I grin wider. "I think I know a way or two to get him in on this."

Ethan laughs. "Shit, I'd pay to see him dance on ice. The number of times he's joked about it, seeing him struggle would be priceless. And I think *Grace on Ice* would profit from it. Just imagine the hype on social media once they know their favorite hockey babe is taking part in a reality show."

It's clear Ethan is evil. But he's not wrong. "Should I ask him?"

I look to Aiden.

"Let's," he says.

Ethan stands up. There's a newfound enthusiasm sparkling in his eyes and I'm not sure if I should be happy or afraid. Maybe both. "Great. You'll visit your grandma and I'll make sure every tabloid covers your movie roles being dropped. And I'll book a talk show. This needs to be huge."

Thirty-two

RILEY

I don't cuddle.

I don't cling.

I don't wait until I make plans before I ask a girl what she is doing.

But I do it all with Liora.

And it's all me.

She doesn't even want me clinging to her like a damn nettle, but I just can't help it. And she knows it. She even convinced me to join her on the ice, during my one week off when I'm supposed to rest and relax. Am I out of my mind?

I mean, do I want to wear flashy ice-skating outfits?

No.

Do I want to swap hockey skates for ice-skating shoes?

No.

Am I doing it because she asked?

Hell yes.

I can't say no to that face.

Maybe she's cast some kind of witchcraft on me because this isn't how I usually roll. Is it possible that I'm sick? Because no matter what happens, the way she makes me feel won't go away anytime soon. Or ever. I don't think anyone can make me feel this alive.

The rest of the week goes smoothly, and it feels like I'm in a little bubble with Liora. We spend our evenings watching Disney movies, and she can't help but laugh at me when I get emotional over them. While I hate that they make me cry—sometimes, and only briefly, like, one tear at a time—there's just something special about seeing cartoon characters do everything for the ones they love. She mentioned not having a favorite cereal, so I bought a variety of options and had her taste each one until she declared her love for Kellogg's Frosted Flakes. It may not have been my first choice, but now we can enjoy cereal together.

Despite all the cute and sweet moments, there's something else going on with Liora and she won't tell me what it is. I've tried asking about her tattoos and the Olympics, but she always steers the conversation in a different direction. And I'm terrified that if I push too hard, she'll pull away from me for good. It's another new feeling for me—usually I'm the one doing the pushing, not pulling.

I've been busy with games against the Hurricanes, and tomorrow will be our last home game against them before we potentially move on to the finals against the Florida Bay Blazes. If we win, we have two weeks off.

Another dream come true is getting to fuck Liora the minute I come home. And fuck do we have mind-blowing sex. I can never get enough of her. After I'm finished pleasing her today, I make my way up her bare legs and settle on top of her abdomen. It's the first time I've noticed a faint white scar there. It's a horizontal line across the lower abdomen, just above the pubic hairline. I wouldn't have seen it since the scar has already faded to a pale white, but I notice it while I stroke over her stomach; it's lightly raised compared to the surrounding skin.

"Where did you get that scar from?" I ask, caressing it.

She stiffens and I wonder if I've asked the wrong thing.

"It's been a long time. Long story. Oh, and Riley, your sister is calling."

My phone buzzes on the nightstand. What a convenient time for Rosalie to call.

Liora is a pro at avoiding questions.

It's something she's been doing for a while now. She doesn't hesitate to share stories about her mom and how the trailer community has become like family to her, or how she cooks for her eighty-year-old neighbor. But when it comes to certain topics, she shuts down. I brought it up with my therapist, and he advised me not to push her on those sensitive issues. His advice still rings in my ears, sound and clear:

Sometimes, people find it challenging to open up about painful experiences, even with those they care about. It's essential to respect their boundaries and allow them the space they need to process things in their own time.

It's hard to wait but I have to.

It's her story to tell.

"Can you give me my phone?" I say, trying to hide my disappointment.

"Sure." She leans over, and that scar is all I can see.

Questions over questions over questions swarm in my mind.

I just hope no one hurt her. Maybe she's not telling me because she knows I'll kill anyone who did hurt her.

"Riles!" My little sister's high-pitched voice blasts out of my phone.

I put her on Speaker so that Liora can get a taste of what she'll have to handle in a few days. I have never introduced a girl to my parents before. The idea of someone discovering their true nature has always terrified me. Being in their presence was nerve-wracking enough, but just the mere idea of her accompanying me, knowing that there's something worth loving, somehow makes facing my parents less daunting.

I roll my eyes and Liora plays with my hair, the way it soothes me. In this regard, I'm like a dog. Easily pleased.

"Rosalie," I grunt back. "What do you want?"

"Riley Richard Huntington. Are you purposely trying to avoid your favorite sibling? And what kind of question is that? *What do I want?*" She mimics my every word like a cartoon character on steroids. "Is it so hard to believe that I just want to hear your beautiful voice and make sure you're still alive?" she huffs, feigning offense.

"You're my only sibling, and yes, you never call unless you need something."

"Riley, has anyone ever told you that your communication skills are severely lacking? Perhaps next time, try something along the lines of: 'Well, well, well, if it isn't the nicest sister in all the land. How has your dancing been going, dearest Rosalie?'"

Liora stifles a giggle, and I'm on the verge of chucking my phone out the window. What did my therapist say? *In stressful situations, breathe.* So I do. I fucking breathe. And again. Slow and steady until it's the most aggressive breathing I've ever heard. "How's that dancing of yours coming along, Rosalie?"

"Amazing! Thank you so much for asking. I landed the lead role in *Swan Lake* and it's going to be epic. But, ugh, Julliard is so rigid and uptight. Can't wait to be done with it," she complains in typical Rosie fashion. She always finds something to complain about, even when things are going well for her. She can't help it, it's a Huntington problem.

When she got accepted into Julliard, I couldn't believe it. My free-spirited sister, who spent her summers in Europe partying with friends and trying to convert people to veganism and a hippy lifestyle, now spends her days perfecting her ballet moves and rubbing elbows with the elite of New York City.

It just doesn't seem like her.

But then again, Dad has always tried to mold her into a refined Upper East Side girl. She used to like animals, ride horses, and feed every stray we met on holiday, but that's not what Dad wants for her life.

He wants her to become New York's number one ballerina and marry a rich-ass finance guy. She may be Daddy's girl on the surface, but I know there's a wild spirit underneath all that ballet and high society bullshit. The only time I see her truly happy and carefree is when she's on the beach in Malta, with her hair tousled and surrounded by a sea of hippies. I can only hope one day she breaks free from the chains that are holding her back. Just like I did, but it comes with a price.

You're practically excluded from the family once you say no to Dad. And Rosalie is not ready for that just yet.

"But there may be one teeny tiny thingy," she says, and I sigh. Typical.

"What, Rosie? What teeny tiny thingy?"

"Can you take me home when you head to that gala? I have class until late and Dad wants me to show up early, but I can't make it unless you take me." I hear her grinning from ear to ear while she orders a vanilla soy latte somewhere.

A three-hour ride with my sister?

Poor Jay.

He's got to sit with her in the back, and she can be such a pain in the ass.

"Wait a minute."

She keeps on talking, but I put her on Mute, look up to Liora, and ask, "Is it okay if we take my sister to the Hamptons?"

"Sure, why would you even ask?"

"Because I hoped you'd say no."

She rolls her eyes. "Rosie missed something. You also lack some social skills."

I sink my teeth into her thigh, and once she stops hitting me playfully, I put my sister back on Speaker. "So, yeah. We'll take you."

Rosalie squeals and I rub the bridge of my nose, because that was so fucking loud.

"It's three o'clock on Friday then! Can't wait! Bye Ri, don't get riled up until then!"

I hang up. "She likes wordplays."

"Your second name is Dick?"

"Of course, that's the one thing you take from that awful convo." My mouth twitches. "Is it too much dick for you?"

"Never."

She grabs my shoulders and tries to lift me up, but let's be real, my little spitfire isn't able to move me an inch. So I crawl up to her, desperate for a kiss.

She suddenly tenses up.

"Riley," she says, and I wince.

Oh no, I know that tone. What did I do now?

"Is that a picture from one of my commercial shoots hidden in your bookshelf?"

I freeze. Damn it, I forgot about my stash of jack-off material.

"Um, no?" I reply sheepishly.

She smacks my shoulder playfully. "I thought I lost it on the subway and suffered from humiliation for over five months! And you've been hoarding it in your room the whole time? Come on, why would you do that?"

In a desperate attempt to avoid explaining myself, I kiss her passionately. Fucking hell. This is embarrassing.

"Riley," she pushes me away with a cute frown on her face.

"Okay fine, confession time. Yes, I took it because I couldn't stand the thought of someone else ogling your perfect ass."

At first, she looks at me like I've lost my mind, then she bursts out laughing. "Are you serious?"

I sigh and nod reluctantly. "I wish I wasn't."

But I'm not about to tell her what other naughty things I did with that photo. Fuck no.

She continues giggling before her cheeks turn red and I can tell she's getting turned on by the idea of—well, I have no idea of what exactly. I like to think it's because I protect her ass with all my might.

The downside of her being turned on? I have a boner now, too, and we're supposed to be getting ready for practice. But fortunately, I'm skilled in the art of problem-solving. With a mischievous grin, I scoop her up princess style and carry her off toward the bathroom.

Her eyes widen in surprise. "Riley, what are you doing?"

I just wink and say, "Just making sure we're not running late."

She opens her mouth to protest, but my body gives me away and I feel a familiar stirring between my legs. The minute it does, her gaze transforms into one of desire. I carry her toward the shower, turning on the water and letting it cascade over us. I let her down and gently hold her face in my hands while I kiss her. A few seconds later, the room is filled with hot steam while water rains down on us.

My hands glide along her curves, over her wet skin, while hers explore every inch of my body. I'll never get enough of it. I take my time to run my fingers up and down those gorgeous tits and then smooth my hands over her firm ass. I lower my head and kiss her neck, and when she gives me that guttural sound I love so much, I encircle her breasts—kneading them, teasing those nipples with my fingernails all the while my penis presses firmly against her. *Fuck*. I can feel it against her stomach as I rub it against her skin.

I glance at her through my eyelashes, just to take her in. So beautiful. No matter what she thinks. She's mine. All of her is mine.

The water drips from her nose and she looks up at me—as if I'm the best thing that's ever happened to her, and something inside of me wishes it were true.

I want to be the best thing for her.

"I can't believe you still look at me like that," she says.

"Like what?"

"Like—"

"Like you're everything I ever wished for? Like you're the girl I've always wanted but never thought I deserved? Then yes—this is exactly how I look."

Her hands wrap fiercely around my neck as our lips crash together in a wild, uninhibited kiss. Desire surges through me like a tidal wave and I kiss her back with all the pent-up longing I've held for her. She rises onto her tiptoes, swaying unsteadily, and I catch her as we stumble against the tiles. Turning her around, I kiss and nibble at her neck and shoulders. When she grinds her wet ass against my throbbing cock, my self-control starts to crumble. I grasp her tightly while she circles her hips, driving me crazy. Her whimpers shoot directly to my cock, and I slide my fingers between her legs, greedily plunging into her. Our bodies move and move—I can't help but groan from the intense pleasure.

Damn. I need her closer.

And just like that, she turns around.

I slam my hand against the wall behind her and grab her ass roughly, pulling her toward me until our bodies are pressed together. Our mouths crash hungrily, and I devour her with my tongue. My other hand moves to her waist, and I grind against her.

"Oh fuck," she gasps, and I slip a finger inside of her, pumping it in and out at an increasingly faster pace.

I feel every moan and shudder coming from her body, responding to my touch.

"You want me inside you, baby?" I say, watching as water streams down her flushed face.

She nods eagerly and I use my thumb to rub circles over her swollen nub, pushing her closer and closer to the edge. Gasping for air, she reaches for my cock, but I pin her hand with my pelvis, denying her for now.

She jerks her hips toward me. "Riley." Oh, that pathetic, desperate sound. I love it so much.

"What do you want?" I nip at her bottom lip teasingly as I continue to thrust my finger in and out of her. Fuck she's so undone. It's everything I ever wanted.

"Tell me what you need, and I'll give it to you."

Her eyes burn with desire as she stares back at me. "You."

"And where do you want me?" I twist my finger inside of her, hitting a spot that makes her cry out in pleasure.

"Right here."

"Say it." My vision blurs with desire. She's getting wetter and it has nothing to do with the shower.

"Say it, baby." My gaze roams over her face, taking in every detail while my cock strains against her hand—hard and pulsing.

"Your damn cock," she says between moans.

"Where?" I push my finger deeper, hitting that spot again and again. My fingers are so slick with her arousal.

"Oh fuck. I need…"

"Say it." My voice is low and husky as I watch her unravel under my touch.

"I want your cock inside of me," she cries out, lost in the moment.

And with that, I finally give her what she wants.

I hoist her up and plunge into her wetness with a primal intensity that only adds to the heat of the steamy shower.

"You're so wet for me, baby," I whisper against her lips.

With flushed cheeks, she cries out again and I fuck her harder.

She feels so good. So fucking good.

She gasps against my neck, wraps her legs tighter around me as I thrust into her again and again. We set a rhythm that's both harsh and oh so fucking perfect at the same time. When she lowers her head, he licks over my nipple, and I let out a deep sigh. Tendrils of pleasure coil around limbs when her warm, wet mouth envelops them, an almost-pain I wanted more of.

I grasp her breast roughly, my other hand squeezing her tight ass as I circle and twist her nipple. My hips thrust relentlessly, hitting her clit over and over.

"Fucking hell." I let out a slow hiss. "You want more?"

She whimpers in response. But instead of giving her more, I stop—a wicked smile on my face.

"Did I take away your ability to speak? I asked if you want more."

"Yes. Yes. I-I'm coming," she stammers out.

I pause again, relishing in her desperation. "Yes, what?"

She looks up at me with fire in her eyes. "Riley," she snarls, ready to kill me. "I need more."

I push forward, feeling the tight resistance of her entrance before pulling out again. "Say please," I say.

She's on the verge of screaming at me, but instead, she takes my hips with a ferocity that draws blood from my skin. She grinds her body against mine until my throbbing dick is poised at her dripping entrance again, but I refuse to let her take it in. Absolutely no way.

She has to work for it.

"Say. Please."

She bites her lip and I push my hips forward, that wet head of my cock teasing her clit again.

"Please," she chokes out the word and I let my cock glide back into her.

She clings to me and I fuck her against the cold tiles, taking us both to the knife's edge of insanity. Her warrior gaze is locked on me as she rides wave after wave after wave. I increase my speed and then, with one final thrust, we both explode in a frenzy of shivers. White-hot pleasure blazes through me and I basically collapse against the cold tiles with her in my arms.

"Oh shit," she gasps.

"This should be illegal," I pant.

I PULL up in front of Juilliard's main building, a striking, modern structure with shimmering glass walls that gleam amid the artistic pulse of the city. Its design blends sleek contemporary style with subtle nods to classic architecture.

Rosalie's posted up at the entrance, leaning against massive stone columns like she owns the place. Her pink ballet dress flutters in the breeze and those oversized black shades on her nose could hide a small country. She stands nonchalantly, with her black hair pulled back into a neat bun, one hip cocked to the side, Louis Vuitton bags dangling from each hand. It's enough of a show to make you forget she's the same girl who got cuffed for joyriding without a license, partying underage, and running wild with a biker gang for a week last year during spring break. Ladies and gentlemen, my sister.

Jayce, sensing the impending storm, quickly hops out to retrieve her bags. I sigh. That princess always gets what she wants.

"Hey, losers!" she chirps, sliding into the backseat. Sweet perfume mingles with the air and bites at my nose.

Jayce sits down next to Rosalie, and without warning, she throws her feet onto his lap. "Jay, be a darling and give me a foot massage, will you?"

I snarl at her. "Rosie, sit properly."

She sticks her tongue out at me but complies and pulls her feet back. "You're all so prudish," she complains, then turns to Liora with a smile. "Hi, I'm Rosalie, the fun sibling. Sorry about these two, they've got broomsticks up their asses."

Liora chuckles, extending her hand. "I'm Liora, nice to meet you."

Rosalie takes her hand and shakes it.

"What's with the sunglasses?" I glance at Rosalie's shades.

She shrugs. "I've been partying a bit, and my eyes are sensitive to sunlight."

I grunt, hoping that's all there is to it. My sister's always been a handful, and I can only pray she hasn't gotten herself into trouble again. But she's an elite dancer. She wouldn't—couldn't...

As we merge into traffic, Rosalie leans forward, her elbows resting on the front seats. "So, Liora, tell me everything. How did you and my brother meet? I want all the juicy details!"

Liora glances at me, a small smile playing on her lips. "Well, it's a long story..."

I reach over and squeeze her thigh.

"Ew. Can you stop that?" Rosalie interjects, glancing pointedly at Liora. "I mean, I've seen those cringy videos of you two, but I prefer to pretend they don't exist."

From the rearview mirror, Jayce looks like he's been handcuffed. He's stiff and rigid—while my sister invades his space, hogging the entire backseat for herself. I mouth a silent apology to him, and he grins back knowingly. He's seen Rosalie in action before. She's always like this.

Liora launches into our story about meeting at the last gala, and I notice Rosalie tense up this time. I tense up too. Shit.

"Um, the last sports gala Mom hosted. The one in January?" she says.

"Yep," I mutter, suddenly fascinated by the traffic.

It's a quiet street, not exactly demanding my full attention, but I stare nonetheless. Damn, I forgot Rosalie was there. She's been with me all the time. She probably knows better than anyone that I was drunk as a skunk and couldn't have possibly talked to a girl.

"Just to be clear: is this the same night I had to hoist you into the pool house because you were so determined to win that ridiculous rugby game that you nearly broke your leg?"

I swallow hard. "Yep."

She turns to Liora again. "Wow, you've got low standards, huh?"

"Rosalie!" I yell.

"What? You couldn't even string together a coherent sentence because your leg hurt so much. You looked like a child who had fallen. The only thing you managed to say was, 'Where's the booze?' while pointing in random directions until someone finally showed you. I can't believe someone like her would have flirted with you."

To my surprise, Liora bursts out laughing, and I start to relax a bit. "Well, I guess I have a weakness when it comes to taking care of injured men."

Rosalie makes a dramatic gagging noise, and I roll my eyes.

"She had to leave early, we swapped numbers. That's it—everything else is just ancient history," I say with a smirk.

My mom's guest list is always a mixed bag, so we couldn't possibly know everyone. Besides, it's not like my mom meticulously plans these things—she's the worst with paperwork. I had to tread carefully with that lie; my sister is basically a human lie detector, ready to don an FBI cap and interrogate us to death. Sometimes she's too smart for her own good. "Rosie, drop it."

A little crease forms between her eyebrows, and she leans back, wearing that *I've got you now* expression.

I quickly steer the conversation to her, which is usually an easy task. She loves talking about herself and wastes no time filling us in on her hectic schedule, the grueling training, and her disdain for the snobs she encounters.

That's until my damn sister starts squeezing Jayce's bicep. I nearly slam on the brakes. Can't she behave just once?

"Oh my, you got *shredded* since the last time we met," she exclaims, kneading his muscles.

"Haven't I always been?" Jayce says, meeting my angry gaze in the mirror.

"Not like this. Mm-hm," she continues, and all of my hair stands on end.

"Stop annoying my best friend," I say, trying to keep calm.

"But what if I'm genuinely interested in how many more muscles he's got? Maybe he's got an eight-pack now and maybe, just maybe, I should go and investigate," she teases, causing a vein to throb on my temple. She knows exactly how to push my buttons.

Liora turns to Rosalie. "Actually, I'm more curious about how Riley and Jay met. I've heard bits and pieces but never the full story."

I smile at Liora and mouth *Thank you* at her.

Rosalie whistles. "Ooh, that's a good one! Jay, care to share with the class?"

Jayce swallows, his eyes darting between Rosalie and me. He frees his arms from my sister's clutches and says, "It was during summer break in college. I was making some extra cash as a construction worker when I got assigned to build the pool house at the Huntington's mansion."

Rosalie fans herself dramatically. "It was the hottest summer on record, and I had to cool down every so often, if you know what I mean."

"Weren't you like thirteen?" Liora says, and I'm stunned she remembers how old my sister is. I only mentioned it once.

"I always liked older," Rosalie says.

Liora looks at me and I roll my eyes. "I told you; she's a pain in the ass. She always annoys my friends. Jay's known her the longest and Rosie knows my friends are a no-go, but the minute you tell her 'no' she hears 'yes.'"

I shoot her a warning glare.

My sister just winks at me. "Anyway, that's when Riley and Jay became friends. They both attended Cornell University, since Jay moved there in his second year."

I nod, picking up the story. "Jay got a scholarship. He comes from a small town in Suffolk County and had to work his ass off to make it to where he is now. So proud of you, man."

"Please. It's nothing," Jayce says, his cheeks suddenly red. He always plays his achievements down. As if it was pure luck that he got so far. He's older than me, and while my parents had already secured my spot in college, he went to work in construction after high school, hoping to get noticed for his exceptional hockey skills.

"It's not. You're a genius and you know it. We ended up being drafted together because of how well we played as linemates."

"And now you've got your own house in the Hamptons, Jay?" Liora asks.

"Yes. It was the first thing I bought once I had some money to spare. I think it was always a dream to have a summer house there."

"It's just awfully close to my parents," I grunt.

"It's the best coast," Jayce says.

As we pass through the gates and enter my parents' sprawling mansion, a feeling of unease washes over me. My family's always been complicated, and I know that the next few days will be a test of my patience again.

Jayce hops out of the car and grabs his bags from the trunk. "I'll see you guys tomorrow," he says, heading toward his house across the street.

"He's not coming to the dinner?" Liora asks.

I scoff. "Hell no. Everyone who can avoid my parents does, and I'd be right there with them if I could."

My sister heads inside, and I take Liora to the pool house.

It's a cute little house with an open layout, comfy sofas, a fireplace made of stone, and a loft bedroom that looks out onto the pool. Everything is in cream and white. It's nice but nothing against the big house.

"I hope you don't mind staying out here. My parents kind of took over my old room and turned it into a yoga studio the minute I moved out," I say.

"Are you kidding," she says.

I watch her take it all in, turning around and looking at every corner of the pool house like I just brought her to a castle. If she's this amazed by the pool house, I can't wait to show her the main house. Hell, I want to show her the whole world. If this surprises her, imagine her face when she sees France, Spain, Italy, Austria, Japan—anything beyond this small pool house.

"This is beautiful. But why would anyone need their own yoga studio?" She turns, checking out the cozy kitchen on the side and the stylish bathroom.

Suddenly, she calls my name, snapping me out of my thoughts.

She smiles, the prettiest smile of all smiles. "What are you doing, Ri?"

"Honestly?" I walk over to her and wrap her in my arms. "Just looking at you. You're what I think is beautiful."

She blushes, and I lean in to kiss her softly on the mouth.

While I'm in the shower, I overhear her taking another one of those mysterious phone calls. Sometimes she sounds like she's talking to a kid when she answers. I've asked her who it is, but she won't tell me. I'm starting to get worried. I really hope she's okay. Every time I ask my therapist what I should do, he tells me to be patient and show her I'm a safe space so she can open up when she's ready. And that's what I'm doing, even though it's hard for me to be patient when I worry for her.

Thirty-three

LIORA

"Are you ready?" Riley asks, lacing his fingers with mine as we make our way around the opulent fountain at the center of the circular drive. I swallow as I gaze up at the white stone steps leading to the grand wooden double doors of the mansion before me. Those columns seem to reach to the heavens.

"Yes." No. This is insane.

And it's just the house they spend their summers in. *Just.*

My eyes drift to the sprawling stone facade to the gleaming windows that line the upper floors. Ivy creeps up one side, giving the villa an old money charm.

How could I be ready to walk into this castle of a home? I'm a trailer girl.

Even when my life was more stable, we had a one-story house with four rooms—just enough for us. But this...I look up at the towering enormity before me. It's just way too much.

"Then let's go. I should warn you; my parents aren't the friendliest. Or friendly at all."

With a deep breath, Riley leads me up the white stone stairs and rings the bell. A booming chime resonates throughout the entrance. We wait and my heart does its own dance behind my rib cage.

More seconds pass.

I inhale the scent of freshly cut grass.

The fountain splashes away behind us.

"You don't have a key?"

Riley shakes his head. "I'm just tolerated here, Liora. The minute I moved out, that key was gone."

Bending down, he presses a gentle kiss to my forehead, his touch around my waist growing more reassuring. In this moment, it strikes me that what he craves is stability. A reminder that he's not a mere possession. Something his parents own.

The entrance slides open, and a woman, who appears to be in her early sixties, greets us.

From the google search I did before, I know it's his mother, Eleanor.

Her red mouth stretches into a wide grin as she says, "Riley, darling! You're finally here!"

But nothing, except that huge mouth with all those way-too-white teeth, moves on her face. Not one wrinkle. She looks unreal in her shiny white designer dress and that pinned-up brown hair.

I squeeze Riley's hand and we enter the grand foyer that seems to consist of nothing but white marble.

I glance down at my simple red dress, feeling underdressed and out of place.

"You look beautiful," Riley whispers, flashing me a hint of that cocky grin of his.

Heat rises to my cheeks. Shit. Is it that obvious that I don't like it in here?

"It took a long time for you to arrive," Eleanor says, and Riley's smile drops.

"We had to wait for Rosalie's classes to finish," Riley says, and I almost do a double take when I see him.

It's not the Riley I know.

There isn't even a hint of that cockiness in his smile or a twinkle in his eyes anymore. He simply stands there, a mere shadow of his lively self, watching as his mother closes the door behind him.

If it weren't for the way he grips my hand and the racing of his pulse, I might think he had turned into a statue. I don't want him to be like this. It's not him. It's not my Riley.

"Ah yes, this poor girl, always so hard on herself." She sighs and looks at me. And the whole foyer turns colder than it already is.

"Mother, this is Liora James, my girlfriend," Riley says, and at the word *girlfriend* my stomach does something funny again. *His girlfriend.*

Her critical gaze sweeps over me head to toe.

"Lovely to meet you, dear. I'm Eleanor Elise Huntington." She air-kisses both my cheeks and a wall of sweet perfume hits me right in the face. "Shame on you, Riley, for not bringing her around sooner! Let's have a mimosa, shall we?"

She doesn't even wait for an answer and struts off, her high heels *click-clacking* loudly as she goes.

Who introduces herself with her second name?

I just blink and blink again, but Riley saves me and leads me along as I stumble behind him like a toddler learning to walk for the first time.

This woman managed to insult Riley twice in less than five minutes.

This isn't a mother.

I watch her swaying hips and start to feel a twinge of sadness for Riley.

"It's just that these rooms are so much bigger," Riley says, guiding me through spaces easily double or even triple the size of my small trailer. There are pictures of people and places I don't know all over the walls, with shiny frames catching the light of fancy chandeliers. And there are big bunches of flowers everywhere, each larger than my head.

"You don't need to apologize," I say.

"It's just…" He takes a deep breath and restarts. "I know they'll try to make you feel inferior, like you're insignificant compared to their accomplishments. I'm sorry for bringing you here and potentially subjecting you to their belittling ways, but just having you by my side makes me feel…better."

My heart swells and I stand on my toes to give him a kiss. "No matter what they say, they can't change how much I like you, Ri."

Eleanor leads us through a round marble archway, and thank goodness, I didn't know how rich he is earlier. I was already impressed by his penthouse. But this villa—it's like those mansions in movies that make you wonder what rich people do with all those rooms.

Riley grew up like a prince.

I feel like my ten-dollar shoes shouldn't even be walking on this ground!

We enter a formal dining room with a long oak table. At the head sits a distinguished older man in a dark gray suit—Henry Huntington. Picture a man in his sixties with impeccably styled salt-and-pepper hair, the kind that looks effortlessly perfect yet undoubtedly requires regular trips to an exclusive barber.

He's reading the newspaper and doesn't glance up to us until he seemingly finished reading the article, but when he looks at us, I feel like I've time traveled.

Riley is his spitting image.

But where Riley is smug, there he is, contained, where Riley's hair is wild and sexy, there is his, tamed and solid, where Riley's gaze is full of life, there is his father's, deadly.

He stands up, straightening his gray suit jacket, and an icy glare washes over me. Same whiskey eyes.

Riley clears his throat. "Dad, this is—"

"You couldn't be bothered to dress up, son?" he interrupts gruffly, eyeing Riley's jeans and untucked white button-down. I feel Riley tense beside me.

When Henry looks at me, he raises an eyebrow and swiftly goes back to Riley. Not saying a word.

"It's just a family dinner," Riley says.

"You introducing your first girlfriend to us is something special, don't you think?" he says, and finally nods at me, and that's all I get for a greeting. So I nod back. Prick.

"It sure is, but I don't need to dress as posh as you to welcome people into my life," Riley says.

"No, you do it naked and weekly. We know."

His mother laughs in a high-pitched voice, sitting down across from him, and since no one chimes in, I feel awkward. Why would she laugh at a comment like this?

Riley lets out a sigh that seems like he saw it coming, almost like he knew this was bound to happen.

"Why don't we all take a seat?" Eleanor suggests.

Riley walks me over to a wooden chair at the long side of the table. With a gentle gesture, he pulls out the chair for me and I sit down. His father takes his seat at the head of the table once more, his eyes still locked on Riley's every move.

I just can't help but feel sorry for him.

There's no love in either of his parents' eyes.

My own mother loves me with every fiber of her being and I miss her. We may not have much, but I know that I mean more to her than any material possessions ever could. I bet Riley's father would trade him for his wealth any time.

Riley sits down next to me, his hand resting reassuringly on my thigh.

Part of me feels like we should refrain from touching in

front of his parents, especially when they are so rigid and distant, but when I try to remove his hand, he holds onto mine firmly. The look he gives me tells me he doesn't care about what his parents think. And his hand remains because he wants it there.

Just then, Rosalie, in white sweatpants and a crop top, bounds in and I almost gasp.

She kisses both parents on the cheek before plopping into the chair opposite from us. She has her hair up in a messy bun and grins at me, then she looks at her father.

"Daddy? Why the scary face? Loosen up a bit, it's just food." She then touches his hand, and he actually smiles at her. I can't believe it.

It doesn't take a body language expert to know that this man loves his daughter.

Henry touches her hand softly and suddenly, there is another man sitting there. And my heart sinks deeper and deeper. The realization hits me like a ton of bricks. The man I thought was cold and heartless, actually has emotions. It's hard to believe that under his tough exterior lies a beating heart, but it seems like it only beats for one person—his daughter. No one else seems to matter to him.

How can you love one child so much and the other just not at all? My heart breaks for Riley.

I look up to him, but he doesn't even register it. He studies his hand on mine, as if I'm the only thing that matters right now, and when our eyes meet, I know this is normal to him. I think of my mom, how she cuddled me during the night, kisses me even now on the forehead, demands me to call her each day, which I don't do because I don't have the time, but still. I can tell, Riley never had this feeling once.

"How do you feel?" Henry asks, still gazing at his daughter as if she's God reincarnated.

"Fine," she says, and something dims in her smile too. "I got the lead role for *Swan Lake*."

Eleanor claps her hands together. "Oh honey! This is amazing."

"Congratulations," her father says. "You earned it."

Rosalie smiles, but it doesn't reach her eyes.

A suit-clad waiter emerges with a tray of appetizers and mimosas.

"Riley, tell us about your latest game," Rosalie says, already drinking her orange mimosa.

"I heard your performance was...lacking," his father says, swirling bourbon in a tumbler.

Riley's jaw clenches. I squeeze his hand under the table, heart aching at the hurt in his eyes. I can't take this look on his face anymore. I'm fuming.

"I'm sorry, Mr. Huntington, but this is wrong. Riley achieved one hundred and fifty points in only one season, and he didn't even play in every game. He's most likely going to get the Conn Smythe Trophy for the most valuable player. He has exceptional skills and, if he keeps up his game next season, he could even break Gretzky's—"

"No one breaks Gretzky's record ever. And I think he's closer to the most penalty minutes record than Gretzky." He drinks his bourbon, and I can't help but gulp. Didn't he hear me? I look to Riley, but he just smiles at me.

"Thank you," he says and kisses my cheek.

"It's nothing to thank me for, this was all you. You are incredibly skilled, Riley." I say it loud enough for everyone to hear.

I remember how devastated Riley was when Derek hit him and told him he didn't deserve his spot on the team. His dad had planted these thoughts in his head, manipulating him into believing he wasn't good enough. But it's not true. Riley is amazing, and I want to make him see his own worth so badly.

His father scoffs at that, and I am ready to punch that man.

I understand Riley. I wouldn't want to think that this man owns my career for even a second.

The interrogation continues as we start the posh meal, his father's words cutting deeper by the minute. Despite Rosalie's attempts to defuse the situation, it's clear that Riley's father hates him. They don't even know him well enough to remember that he's allergic to celery, which I luckily notice in the salad right away. When Riley doesn't eat, his father insists he stop the nonsense, showing no concern for whether Riley's throat might swell up. I take the salad and hand it to the waiter, glaring at his father as if I could kill him on the spot. He doesn't even so much as blink.

But no, it's not actually hate that drives Riley's relationship with his father. I don't think so. It's more like a twisted sense of control. The man seems to have some sort of all-knowing power over Riley's life—from the minutiae of his meticulously planned diet to the tiniest slipup like indulging in a burger last wee—his dietitian says yes, his father, apparently no. Sure, strict diets are necessary in sports, but even my coach has told me that sometimes we need to loosen up and indulge to avoid stress and releasing cortisol, which can weaken muscles and mess with our mood and immune system. So yeah, occasionally we gotta give our body what it craves—some downtime. It seems Riley's father only shows love, affection, and respect if Riley acts in a way that he approves of. It's almost as if he wants to manipulate his son into behaving a certain way by using love as a weapon.

I'm just glad Riley doesn't care about making his father happy. Screw him and his oppressive ways. I mean, even our minds need a break from the constant pressure of sports. We can't always be perfect robots following every rule. Thank goodness Riley found a way to escape this man's clutches, even though he gives it his all to keep that leash around his son's neck. And in some way, I think he managed just that.

But Riley's gotta cut that last cord and let go of that deadbeat in his heart.

His father is like a parasite, holding him back from being the man he wants to be. And even though he's doing everything right, just a tiny flicker of Daddy's dearest hold is still squeezing him tight, threatening to drag him down with all that toxic shit. I've seen where Riley comes from—nothing but a messed-up childhood with only his sister to rely on. But it's time for him to break free and rise above it all. That's what families are supposed to do, right? Lift you up instead of bringing you down.

Sitting at the lavish dinner table, surrounded by perfect manners and low-fat cuisine, I can't help but notice the tension between Eleanor and Henry. She babbles on about selling houses, trying to fill the awkward silence left by his constant interruptions. And then there's Rosalie, the glue that holds this dysfunctional family together. The only one they all seem to truly love. But as I continue to bite my tongue, feeling like an outsider, I watch how she plays her role. Always vying for attention, deflecting their scrutiny from Riley.

It's like she's been protecting him her entire life. And maybe she has.

The waiter sets down a fancy chia pudding with exotic fruits I can't even pronounce, and Henry clears his throat, turning to me.

"Do you still keep in touch with Sandford Hayes?" he asks, causing my spoon to clatter against my plate.

What did he say?

Eleanor gasps in shock at the noise I caused, while Rosalie stops scrolling through her phone and gives me a concerned look.

But I can't hear their voices or even feel Riley's hand on mine.

All I can focus on is the name that has sent me spiraling into panic, that made my whole body shiver, my throat dry—Sandy.

My body tenses up even more and sweat beads form on my forehead.

Breathe, I remind myself. *Just breathe.*

With trembling hands, I stir the pudding around in an attempt to distract myself. "No, Mr. Huntington," I manage to say in a forced calm tone. "I haven't seen my former coach since I left the Olympics."

Sandy. Don't think of him. Breathe. Breathe!

"Sandford reached out to me," Henry reveals, and I look up at Riley's father with pleading eyes.

Stop saying his name. Please. Stop.

Thirty-four

RILEY

I watch as Liora's body stiffens, fear etched across her face.

I know that look all too well—the feeling of being completely out of place in this house. But now, it's more than just discomfort. It's an overwhelming sense of protectiveness that washes over me. I wrap my arm around her chair, trying to offer some comfort while she absently pushes the pudding around her plate.

My father's gaze is fixed on her. "Did you know I'm friends with him?"

She startles, shaking her head. "No, sir. I didn't."

"Dad, can we please not—"

"He told me you quit because of some petty heartbreak. Is that true?" my father continues, disapproval written all over his face.

I hate this man so much.

My chest tightens at the thought of Liora giving up her dream because of a breakup. It couldn't be true. Before I can say anything, Liora shifts in her seat and speaks up. "I'd rather not talk about it, if that's okay."

I catch Rosalie's concerned glance and she mouths to me, *Get her out.*

Without hesitation, I stand up. "I'm so sorry, Mom, Dad, but it's getting late and Liora and I have a big day tomorrow before the gala. Thank you for dinner, good night!"

I help Liora up and as we make our way out of the dining room, I hear Rosalie launching into a story about receiving a standing ovation from New York's mayor last week.

Once we're alone in the hallway, Liora's breathing becomes frantic and she starts trembling uncontrollably.

I take her face in my hands and try to calm her down. "Hey, shhh, what's going on?"

But Liora doesn't respond, unshed tears glitter in her dull eyes as she struggles to catch her breath. My heart clenches. "Just breathe, Lia. I've got you. I've got you."

Fuck. I need to snap her out of whatever is happening.

I scoop her up with ease, her limp body a telltale sign of her distress. I think her heart goes a mile a minute. Liora always put up a fight whenever I tried to carry her princess style, but not today. I need to get her back.

I walk toward the beach on autopilot, holding onto her tightly as I make our way through the house and out into the night.

My therapist's words echo in my mind. *Channel your emotions, focus on your surroundings.*

That's exactly what we need to do right now.

"Can you smell it? The sea?" The salty tang of the ocean breeze engulfs us as we make our way to the beach just behind my parents' house. It's a familiar path, one I've walked countless times in my childhood. "Listen to the crash of waves," I say, the sound like a soothing metronome in front of us. The soft grains of sand shift under my feet as I walk, Liora's tense shoulders gradually loosening with each step. "Feel the wind," I continue.

She places her hand over my heart, and I can't help but lean down to press a kiss to her hair. "I feel your heartbeat," she says softly.

"It's a mess," I confess.

"It's all I need right now."

My stupid heart gives a happy spin.

I sit down on a weathered piece of driftwood, still holding her close to me. "You know, my grandmother taught me how to swim on this beach," I tell her, just to keep saying anything, but there's a tiny smile tugging at my lips, and I catch myself tracing little hearts on her back with my finger. I've never done this before. Telling a girl so much about myself. About what I truly feel like. "Gran's the only family member besides Rosie that I truly care for. She's an incredible woman, so patient and kind. The opposite of my parents. I used to spend a lot more time with her, but during the season, it's nearly impossible. I'm just glad if I can manage to call her once a month. I can't wait for the off-season when I'll finally have time to visit her more often."

Memories flood back to me like the tide as I think about spending summers here with her. Each time my parents fought, she was there, taking me and Rosalie away. We built sandcastles with shells and stones. It was beautiful.

Her hand remains on my chest, seeking comfort in the chaos of my racing heartbeat. "I can't wait to see her tomorrow," I continue.

The idea of introducing her to my grandmother feels like a daring decision, one I never had the courage to make before. There's nothing fake about it. It's the most real thing I could do. And yet, there's a warm and comforting feeling blossoming in my heart at the thought of them meeting.

I know they'll love each other. And I know I want them to.

"If you asked me as a child, I would have said I wanted to live with gran. She's nothing like those rich-ass people. She comes from one of the wealthiest families around here, but she doesn't flaunt it. She lives modestly, cooks for herself, and even donates her wealth to those in need."

A pang of guilt hits me as I think about my own privileged upbringing. But then again, it's not like I had control over that.

"I guess it's where my Fruit Loops addiction comes from too. I hated eating healthy and she always bought the cereal I wasn't allowed to eat," I say, causing Liora to let out a giggle.

But then her tears resurface, and she attempts to brush them away. "I can't with you and your Fruit Loops," she says with another forced chuckle that quickly turns into a choked sob.

I hold her closer. "If you ever want to stop my tantrums, throw a blue loop my way and I'm a happy man."

"They all taste the same," she says, snorting.

I mock gasp. "Don't you ever say something so cruel again."

"You're silly."

I kiss her hair. "You're better?"

She nods against my shoulder. "Thanks."

"Always."

The moon casts a silvery glow across the dark waters and we both stare at the sea for a few heartbeats.

"Lia…what happened back there?" I ask gently, hoping she will finally open up.

Her body tenses once more, her breaths becoming short and shallow as she seems to search for the right words.

"I'm sorry, Riley," she says with a sigh. "There are just… some things I can't tell."

My heart sinks at her words. "Why not?"

Liora pulls away from my embrace, wrapping her arms around herself. Tears still glisten in her eyes, and I feel a pang of anger toward whoever or whatever is causing her pain like this.

"Because...because I'm afraid," she admits. "Afraid of what people will think. Afraid of what your father might already know." A wave of emotion washes over me as I realize the gravity of her words. When he asked about her coach earlier, it had seemed like an innocent question—but now, it feels like a loaded one. "I-I can't talk about it," Liora chokes out before falling into silence once again.

I can see the fear and vulnerability in her eyes as she looks up at me for reassurance. I want to protect her, to keep her safe from whatever is causing her pain. But how can I do that when I have no idea what's going on? I'm torn between wanting to shield her from everything and needing to step back to let her cope with it at her own pace. I don't want to do the wrong thing, but then it just spills out of me. "Did your coach hurt you?" I brush back some baby hairs that have fallen onto her forehead.

Within seconds, her face is a whirlwind of emotions.

My mind races.

"I know what you're assuming," she finally speaks. "But it wasn't a sexual assault."

The conflicting thoughts in my head only intensify as I try to process her words.

Something lightens in my chest but the knot in my throat just won't loosen up. I want to shake her, scream at her to just tell me, to let me help. But I don't. Instead, I say as calm as I can. "I understand that you don't want the media to know. But I thought we trust each other now, since we are...we are—" Fuck. Something gets stuck in my throat.

Her eyes flicker, a glimmer of hope sparking to life. "Yes, what are we, Riley?" she asks, her voice soft, almost fragile, like she's holding her breath, waiting for me to say the words she's been wanting to hear. But before I can even process what I feel, what I really want, the stupidest word slips out of my mouth. "Friends?"

The hope in her eyes dims instantly, like I just snuffed out a candle.

Her shoulders drop a fraction, and I can see it—she was waiting for more, hoping for more. And I let her down. I let myself down.

My stomach sinks.

And she freezes.

Fuck *friends* is the wrong word. We're more than friends.

Why did I have to ruin it? Why couldn't I just keep my mouth shut?

"Friends," she says, with a forced smile and a nod. "That's what we are. Friends who fake dated."

We both know it's not true.

We've been pretending for so long now. I'm so fucking sick of pretending. But we've never talked about what we want. What do we want? What do I want? Fuck.

She wipes away another tear and gets up to leave.

My heart races as I watch her go, leaving tiny footprints in the sand, her red shoes in her hand.

Seconds turn to minutes.

And a sudden gust of chilly wind snaps me out of my daze, hitting my cheek like a slap that jolts me back to reality.

No.

Wait.

I won't ever let her go.

I've done stupid things in my past, but I will never make this mistake.

I run after her. "Lia, please wait. *Please.*"

She doesn't.

So I sprint. "Liora!"

She turns around, there are several feet between us, but I see that her jaw is so tight. That her eyes flash with anger. The kind I never want to see again. "What, Riley? What?"

"I asked you to wait!"

"Oh, and when you ask, I should do it just like your little dog? Surely not!"

"No, I want to talk to you!"

"Oh, for fuck's sake, what do you want then?"

I scoff. "What I want?"

"Yes! What you want! You started kissing me, started treating me as if there's more to us, as if there's—"

"Real feelings? Even though the contract forbids it?" I take a step closer, my heart pounding.

Her blonde hair whips in the wind as she looks at me as if I have a knife ready to stab her. "Yes, Liora. Because I do have real feelings for you."

She laughs, but it's bitter. "Feelings?" she yells. "You're really going to stand there and say that now? You don't even know what you're getting into!"

"Yes, because you won't let me in," I yell back, my voice cracking. "I didn't mean for it to happen, but it did. And I know it's not part of the plan, not part of the contract we signed, but it's real. And it's ruining me."

"It was fake," she says as if daring me to say the truth.

"It wasn't," I insist. "It was real. Every moment, every touch, every kiss. It was real all along."

She takes a step back, crossing her arms over her chest, as if to shield herself from my words. "But friends don't catch feelings."

I scoff. "I'm sorry I said that, okay? We're not friends. At least I don't want you to be *just* my friend. I fell for you, I fell so hard, and I'm still falling."

There. I said it.

I practically ripped out my heart and gave it to her.

She doesn't say anything and I'm getting anxious.

I add, stepping closer. "I may be an idiot because this is supposed to be fake, but I had feelings the minute you walked into my apartment. I spent all my fucking teenage years obsessing over you, and you turned out to be the most funny, cute, smart, determined, focused, talented, and thoughtful human being I've ever met. I wanted to hate you. And I did, but only because I was terrified—terrified that if I let myself love you, you wouldn't love me back."

A single tear runs down her rosy cheek. "It's not that easy—"

"No," I say, shaking my head. "No, I won't let you push me away. We can figure this out. We can find a way. Because I know it was real for you too. You don't have to say it. I felt it."

She rakes both hands through her long hair, her mouth opens but no sound comes out. I know if I go now, she wouldn't come back to me. She'd leave me. But I say it anyway, "Let me help you."

"No one can help me." Her words are sharp, but her voice cracks and her breath hitches.

I close the distance between us, captivated by the moonlight casting a soft glow on her beautiful face. Her eyes, swollen and rimmed with red, meet mine as tears run down her cheeks. I kneel softly, letting my hands slide from her shoulders to her hips as I lower myself onto the sand, feeling it yield beneath my knees. "I'm not leaving, Liora."

Her voice drops to a whisper. "You say this now." The tiny crack in her voice makes my stomach clench.

"I will always say this."

She shakes her head.

"Try me."

"I'm afraid."

"Of what?"

She sinks down to me, and my hands glide up her thighs to her back until I have her shoulders firmly in my grasp. She leans into me, and I'm on the verge of fucking begging her to finally let me in, just a tiny bit. "Of what, Liora?" I whisper again, gently pushing her blonde locks behind her shoulders to reveal her beautiful face.

"Of you telling me I'm too much. Of you leaving. Of you giving me hope that I can have it all and crush it once you know the truth about me."

I kiss her cheek. "I know words alone won't convince you because I need to show you. But this will take time. No matter how hard you push, I'll keep coming back. I've never felt as stable as I do with you. The way you make me feel, Liora, it's all I need, and I'm dying to give it back to you."

She cries and I hug her tighter. "How about we try baby steps? I want to prove myself to you."

She falls around my neck, and I gently cup the back of her head, my fingers threading through her hair. I'm so glad I'm not the stupid idiot I was years ago. Past Riley wouldn't have run after Liora. His ego was too big for that. But this is about her finding a way out of this dark tunnel she's in.

"My coach," she starts, and I sigh in relief that she's willing to let me in a step, "and I had a relationship."

She looks up at me, as if that's enough for me to judge her but I nod, showing her that I don't care about which men she loved before me. I'm careful to not let any emotions show.

"Sandy was everything to me. He found me in Hungary when I won the championships. He visited Europe that year, scouting here and there, and he saw me and got my family to America, and in no time, I was an American citizen with an American passport, working all day every day to get into the Olympics. When I won gold in South Korea, I was only fifteen and that's when I fell for him. He was twenty-five."

My stomach drops.

"There wasn't anything happening until I turned eighteen, but he did flirt with me. He groomed me. I didn't realize that back then, but I always found him attractive. I had such a crush on him. It's embarrassing just thinking about it now."

She swallows and I can tell it's hard for her to tell me. The shame in her eyes is so visible, and I want nothing more than to ease it for her. But for now, I can only listen closely to whatever she chooses to share. She's started opening up, and that's all I need. Her trust is a crucial step, and I'll cherish every bit she's willing to give.

"I didn't go to school. My only friends were my mother and Sandy. He wouldn't let me have any other friends because our sole focus was winning every championship. I spoke to other skaters, but I always saw them as rivals. Sandy became the center of my world. I never told my mom that I had these daydreams about my coach, how my thoughts would always drift to him in a way that felt more than just a crush for years."

"And your father?"

"There's not much about him. He was an ass. I guess I was looking for some fatherly approval, and I got it from Sandy. I desperately wanted to be his perfect girl and wanted to believe so desperately that his wife wasn't good to him. I painted her as the villain, even though I was trying to steal her man. I still feel so bad, Riley. I was the worst."

There's another tear running down her cheek and I can't forget that sight of her before me. It feels so raw. With the beach behind her, her kneeling in the sand, in this light dress, the moon reflecting on her hair.

"You're not the worst," I say, kissing her cheek. "You were a kid."

Amid her tears, she lets out a hiccupping sob, her breaths coming in uneven, staccato bursts now. This is breaking my heart. "I started to wear makeup even to rehearsals, I got so jealous of his wife, his kids. I did everything that he wanted me to, and I grew up. I wasn't his little girl anymore. I feel so stupid…"

"Don't," I say, "really, don't."

"No. I was stupid." She glances at her fingers, kneading them.

I shake my head. "Lia, you idealized him and probably mistook your own feelings."

"I think I wanted a father, but mine was treating my mom so badly that I dreamed of killing him. I cherished the moments we weren't at home. When Mom, Sandy, and I drove through the states, heading to championships. I loved spending all hours of the day on the rink, trying to be perfect for Sandy. For that smile of his. For a hug, later for a kiss on my cheek, or on my forehead, and then on my mouth."

She avoids my gaze, and though the darkness is thick and only the moonlight illuminates her face, I can still see the flush of shame on her cheeks, and it cuts me deeply. I gently cradle her chin between my thumb and forefinger, guiding her to look at me. When our eyes finally meet, the pain in her eyes shatters me. She gazes at me with the fearful expectation that I might walk away simply because she had an affair with her former coach.

"It's okay," I say.

"I feel so bad," she says, her voice barely a whisper.

"Don't. It's okay, Lia. It's normal for teenagers to fall hard for someone. It happens, even if it shouldn't."

She shakes her head. "Once I turned eighteen, it was the year before Beijing. My second Olympics. I had the best sponsors, everyone was counting on me, and I was head over heels for Sandy. Our affair started some weeks after my birthday. He was the first man who ever touched me, the first man to have sex with me, and I was so in love—or I think I was—but it was one sided, because after training, after he called me his perfect girl on the rink and behind the lockers, he went home to his wife. He never said he'd leave her, never told me he loved me, but I wanted to believe it. I wanted it so bad, Riley."

That's when a tear escapes and trails down her cheek, and I

catch it with my thumb. I press a gentle kiss to her temple and pull her closer, holding her tightly. She nestles against me, her breath warm and soothing against my neck.

"At some point I realized I didn't really love him. I just wanted his approval so badly because my own father was absent when I needed him the most. Eventually, Mom and I got Dad out of our lives, and that made me stronger. I knew I could help myself, and I was planning to leave Sandy after Beijing. I just needed that gold first and that's what I focused on."

There's a pause and she sighs deeply.

"Thank you," I say once I'm sure she's done. "Thank you for sharing that with me. Now I know that whenever my father brings up his so-called friend, I'll do everything I can to stop him. I won't let you get dragged into that again, okay?"

"Okay."

"And just to be clear. We're not fake dating. We're dating now and I'll finally burn that contract."

She huffs out a laugh and nods. "Yes, we're dating."

She nods, and we share a kiss. It's gentle and unhurried, unlike the heated ones we usually have. This kiss is slow and tender, filled with so much emotion that I hope she'll realize I'm not the only one who's fallen in love. But I've already pushed too much, so I take her back to the pool house.

But once I flick on the light, the full weight of her sadness hits me.

The night had hidden her tear-streaked face and puffy eyes, but now they're all too visible. Without saying a word, I help her out of her dress and into her silky pajamas. Once she's settled, I press a tender kiss to her forehead.

She brushes her teeth while I turn on the soft, calming light beside our bed and find the book she brought with her.

It's called *Moonlit Desires*. She'd mentioned Priya lent it to her, and when I skim the blurb about five werewolves falling for the same girl, I can't help but chuckle softly. It's a bit surprising, seeing Priya's taste in books take this turn, but to each their own.

"You're planning to read that?" she asks, a smirk playing on her lips.

"Definitely," I say just to keep that smile a little longer. "But only if you're right here with me."

I hop onto the bed and hold the blanket open, inviting her to snuggle under it.

She flashes a full grin now and snuggles up against me, her body soft and warm as she rests her head on my chest. I wrap the blanket around us both, then hold up the book so we can both read.

"Get ready for the best bedtime story you've ever had," I tease. "I'm the perfect narrator."

"I can't wait for you to read the knotting scene out loud."

"The what?"

"Oh, my sweet summer child."

Thirty-five

LIORA

Riley leads me toward the gala's entrance, and the first thing that catches my eye is a huge poster board with bold white letters that scream: *Hamptons and Huntingtons—A single-day experience that brings together some of the biggest names in sports. This invite-only event for two hundred guests—including VIPs, tastemakers, athletes, and power brokers.*

The gala is held in the Parrish Art Museum, where modern and minimalist design stands in stark contrast to the surrounding countryside. It looks magical though. It's made of gabled sheds, set side by side, so that the profile of the building resembles an upside-down W. It manages to look like a huge white stable and a modern art piece at the same time, while all the rich people in the world are mingling within.

My heart pounds, nearly drowning out the clicks and flashes already erupting around us. I'm not used to this. The glitz, the glamour, the hungry eyes of photographers.

As if he's sensing my discomfort, Riley pulls me close, strong arms snaking around my waist, and whispers in my ear. He's done that a lot since we got here, and I'd be lying if I said I don't enjoy it. The sense of security he provides is comforting.

He makes me feel so safe, as if nothing could ever harm me again while I'm in his arms.

"You look absolutely gorgeous tonight." Riley's whiskey eyes twinkle as they catch the glow of the fairy lights above us.

He had a designer come over to the pool house to show me some dresses. I tried to argue, but he was set on getting me a dress he had in mind. He insisted that for a gala where designers show off their creations, I couldn't just wear any dress. Eventually, I gave in.

I hadn't let anyone spoil me like this since Sandford.

He'd buy me things and then use it to put me down, calling me his little gold digger for accepting his gifts. I swore I'd never let a guy do that to me again. But Riley's excitement about giving me something is different. It's like the joy I feel when I give my mom a present. It's not about the gift or the dress—it's about how happy it makes him to see *me* happy. It's moments like these that make me question how I ever thought he was anything but a genuinely decent guy. I needed Nina to practically drag me into his arms to see it. It taught me that we really shouldn't judge people based on their outward appearances. I should have known better.

The dress is silver with a low-cut back, glittering with tiny stones, and he even got me a matching necklace. Looking at myself now, I've never felt this beautiful before. I'm relieved I got my hair and makeup back in place, because as soon as Riley saw me in that dress, he couldn't keep his hands off me. We ended up having sex right on the floor.

It was so spontaneous—I don't even know how it started. But when I saw him in his tuxedo and the way he undressed me with his eyes, I just had to climb my man. I couldn't help it.

I melt into Riley's hug and my head tilts up to meet his soft lips. He was so cute all day, I showed him the routine I came up with for the show and he spent his free time trying out some lifts. We used the pool to make it easier for him, since even though he's way stronger than Aiden, he's lacking the ice dancing classes he took. But I did my best and so did he and I think we'll rock it next week.

The world fades away as we kiss, deep and sensual, not a care for the dozens of cameras capturing our private moment. It feels...right. Natural.

My mind spins dizzying fantasies of a shared future—a cozy house, a fluffy dog, children skating wobbly circles on a backyard rink.

I want it all, so badly it aches.

But deep down, I know it's just a beautiful dream.

The doubts kick in, fighting against the burgeoning hope in my chest.

Sooner or later, the cracks will show.

The hurt will come.

My tender, naive heart will shatter.

The last time I felt like this when a man looked at me like that was the beginning of my downfall. And this time, my heart beats twice or even thrice as much.

I bury my face in his strong chest, wanting to stay lost in this perfect moment for as long as I can. Because despite every logical part of my brain screaming that it will all fall apart... I've already tumbled headfirst.

I'm dating Riley Huntington.

And I'm in love with Riley Huntington.

But I can't tell him because it makes it true.

He'll act like it's true, but eventually he'll leave because life will be too much for him because he's not ready for it. I believe that he wants to be ready. But he's not.

I only shared the tip of the iceberg with him, but credit where it's due—he never once judged me for my silly *Lolita* love. Still, he has no idea what life has in store for me or how much he'd need to change to be part of it. I like him too much to even ask him to make those changes for me. I'm not that selfish.

Someone clears his throat, snapping us out of our intimate bubble.

Riley and I pull apart and look over to see Jayce's sheepish grin.

"Get a room," he says.

Riley hugs him. "Shut up, man. Good to see you, nice suit."

Jayce is dressed in a sleek black suit, his black bow tie accentuating his mesmerizing blue eyes. Just as we're about to step onto the concrete floor inside, Jayce's eyes widen, and I follow his gaze to see a red car pulling up behind us, swarmed by paparazzi. Out steps Rosalie, a knockout in a tight red dress. Her black hair is elegantly styled in an updo, with loose curls cascading down her back.

A sly smile graces her bright crimson lips as she gazes up to a man right behind her. I don't recognize him at all, but the excited murmur of the photographers tells me he must be somebody. My gaze flits over his artfully tousled bleach-blond hair, the smudged black eyeliner, a half-unbuttoned shirt under a carelessly expensive red suit—he oozes rock star attitude. I wonder what Daddy will say about this.

Riley sighs. "Jett Vaughn, really, Rosie?"

"Since when are they a thing?" Jayce asks, his jaw tight as he watches them approach.

"Who is he anyway?" I say and both of them look at me as if I've lived under a rock and, well, I did.

"Some hot new singer, I fear," Riley says.

"Pop punk shit." Jayce grimaces.

"Hi guys," Rosalie says, halting in front of us, but her man doesn't wait with her, he just winks at Rosalie and goes in. No hello or anything.

Seems like he's learned from Henry Huntington.

Rosalie doesn't appear to mind as she casually loops her arm through Jayce's, causing him to tense up like a soldier ready to fight. What's up with him when she's around?

I asked Riley at some point, but he didn't think he acted any differently. I put it down to a man's brain failure. They usually aren't the greatest empaths. But there is something between them. I just know it. The way both of them act around each other. Riley asks her if she wants to give him a heart attack by dating such idiots, and even though she responds with a cocky answer, she flashes Jayce a flirty grin at the same time that either Riley doesn't want to see or he ignores on purpose. But I think they have a thing for each other.

We go inside, Rosalie and Jayce walk in front of us and I watch how her fingers trail along his arm. Jayce is so stiff though, not one flicker of a grin or anything.

"Did they ever date?"

"Who?" Riley asks as we go inside. We don't have to show any badges, everyone seems to know Rosalie and Riley, since its their mother's gala.

"Jay and Rosie."

Riley tenses up. "Jesus, no. Why would you think that? He grew up like a brother to us. He's known her since she was thirteen."

Well, tell me about young girls falling for older guys…

"It's just…they act strange."

"You've said this before." Riley watches them and shakes his head. "But no, Jay just hates Vaughn as well. He's very protective over Rosie." Okay, he either got one or two too many slap shots against his head or he *really* doesn't want to see it. I get a feeling he would hate seeing them together. "Also, Jay knows my sister is off limits. And he's almost thirty, ready to settle. My sister's not."

The grand hall is dripping with low hanging chandeliers, a

bizarre contrast to the modern barnlike structure. The glimmering lights almost seem out of place in this rustic setting. Yet, they cast a warm and inviting glow over the opulent furnishings. It's like stepping into another world entirely.

Crisp white linens adorn several long tables, topped with silver place settings and decadent floral arrangements in rich hues of white and blue. Famous athletes from every major sport mix and mingle, dressed in designer suits and gowns. They flutter around like peacocks, clutching flutes of champagne, not even thinking about sitting down just yet.

Some years ago, this would have been everything for me.

Now, I can't wait to get home.

"You're almost thirty too. You looking to settle down as well?" I ask, throwing on a cocky grin, trying to keep my words in check, not wanting to get my hopes up too much.

A waiter carrying a tray of champagne passes by, and I take a glass with alcohol, while Riley opts for the nonalcoholic version. Their coach banned them from drinking before the finals.

"In two to three years, maybe, yeah," he says and my stomach sinks. "You're still young, so I wouldn't rush anything."

I don't hear him talking about us as if we'll still be a thing in three years.

I just grin up at him and take a big, big sip of my champagne.

My gaze shifts to the commanding presence of Eleonore, who effortlessly dominates the room, and then to Rosalie, standing with Jay a few feet away. She finishes her drink and sets the glass on a passing waiter's tray before excusing herself.

I watch her saunter to the bathroom.

Jayce and some athletes come over to us. They don't seem to recognize me and I'm glad. I don't always want to answer questions about quitting the Olympics. Maybe disappearing without a word wasn't the smartest move—I should have come up with some white lies to keep them quiet. But then my sponsors might have believed me even less. Who knows where I'd be now?

Riley is chatting with a sports broadcaster when I see Rosalie come out of the restroom again. She's subtly sniffing and dabbing at her nose. It hits me like a lightning bolt when I catch a glimpse of something white glittering under her nose, just before she wipes it away.

Vaughn meets her outside the bathroom and gives her a kiss.

I pull my hand away from Riley and make my way to Jayce. It's clear he noticed too—he can't seem to take his eyes off her.

I lean in close and whisper, "Did…did Rosalie just do coke?"

He sighs heavily, resignation etched on his face. "Probably. She's constantly acting out, seeking her dad's attention. But no matter what she does, she'll always be the good child in his eyes. The perfect daughter she hates to be."

I watch him watching her, leaving for the garden with her hand clasped on Vaughn's, her head thrown back laughing.

"Don't tell Riley," Jayce says.

"What. Why?"

"It's not like he doesn't know she overdoes it, but he'll get angry and they'll have a fight. It won't help anyone. She won't stop with the shit and his night will be ruined. Believe me, we tried everything, but no therapist will work with her until she's ready to work on herself."

"But how can she do drugs as a professional ballerina?"

Jayce shrugs. "She's dancing on her grave."

"Are you citing Gelsey Kirkland?" One of the most famous ballet dancers from the '70s. She used to battle several addictions while being the best performer of her time.

Jayce nods.

"She's using coke at parties, and I think she's trying to get herself expelled from Juilliard. They have strict rules—one strike with drugs or excessive drinking, and they're out."

I look up at him, my eyes big like saucers. "She wants to get kicked out?"

"She hates it there."

"Why not just stop then without ruining her body?"

"She's dramatic."

I don't get it.

Before I can respond, Mrs. Huntington takes the stage, and the room falls silent.

Eleanor starts to speak, her polished veneer firmly in place, and all I can think is that this glittering world of wealth and privilege is far more tarnished beneath the surface than I ever imagined.

"GRAN, I want you to meet someone special," Riley says, guiding his grandma to me after his speech. "This is my girlfriend, Liora. And this is my grandma, Lilli Huntington."

"Oh, my dear, I'm thrilled to finally meet you," she exclaims, clasping my hands in hers. Her touch is gentle, her smile radiant. She's the kind of elderly woman who still looks young despite all the wrinkles she doesn't hide and her white hair that's cut shortly. She's as small as I am and looks so tiny as Riley has his arm wrapped around her. "I've heard so much about you from Riley. He positively lights up when he speaks of you."

"You've heard so much about me?" I blush, glancing at Riley, who grins bashfully.

"He calls me on away periods," she says proudly, and I think that is actually so sweet.

We chat casually, with Granny sharing funny stories about Riley's childhood and beaming with pride over his achievements. I can't help but feel a connection to her warmth and the way she genuinely cares about her grandson, especially compared to his parents' cold indifference.

Just as we all settle at the table, ready to ask Granny about Riley's cereal obsession, Rosalie's laughter cuts through the air. It's loud, grabbing everyone's attention. Oddly, even though her parents are sitting right across from us, they seem to be ignoring their daughter's drunk state.

She sways in her seat, a nearly empty wine glass dangling precariously from her manicured fingers. Jayce's jaw tightens next to me, a muscle ticking in his cheek as he observes her.

"Rosie, I think you've had enough," Riley says, reaching over the table for her glass.

She jerks away, sloshing wine onto the white tablecloth. "Oh, lighten up, big brother," she slurs, her words slightly blurred around the edges. "It's a party, isn't it?"

"You're sure you don't want to come with me, baby?" Vaughn says and, as if we're not sitting across from them, kisses her with tongue. I feel something against my thigh and notice that Jay is balling a fist next to me. Shit, he's so gone for her. "I bet the party in New York is better."

"I can't." Rosalie pouts. "My family needs me, galas are *important*." She stretches out the *important* and rolls her eyes dramatically.

"Fine. See ya." Vaughn kisses her one more time and then leaves without saying goodbye. And no one seems to care. I glance to their father. Not one single move. He's still talking to some men, looking all business.

Rosalie takes the opportunity to whistle for the waiter.

Riley shoots Jayce a pleading look.

With a curt nod, Jayce slides into the seat beside Rosalie, gently prying the glass from her fingers. She pouts again, leaning heavily against him, her hand coming to rest on his thigh.

I watch, uncomfortably transfixed, as Jayce carefully puts her hand away, his gaze darting to Riley. He threw his hands up in front of his chest, palms pressed together like he was saying thanks.

Rosalie lurches to her feet, swaying slightly. "I need the little girl's room," she whisper-shouts at Jayce.

Jayce stands up, holding out his hand. "I'll keep your bag safe," he offers, his tone brooking no argument. For a moment, Rosalie looks like she might protest, but then she shrugs, thrusting her clutch at him before staggering away, Jayce trails behind her like a shadow.

Riley's shoulders slump. "Thank goodness for Jay. He always takes care of her when she's like this. I can't stand it when my sister pulls these stunts."

"Does your dad ever get mad at her?" I ask.

Riley snorts. "Never. She could be lying on the floor and he'd think she was just taking a nap from all the ballet training."

"That is insane…"

"I don't know what's wrong with my parents, but they always make me out to be the villain and put Rosalie on a pedestal she doesn't want to be on. It hurts more than they realize."

I reach under the table and grab Riley's hand, intertwining our fingers.

We focus back on chatting with his grandmother, the aroma of truffle and caviar filling the air as the waiters swirl around us like bees.

"YOU COULD BE captain of the team by now, if you had your act together," Riley's father hisses in between the main course, drawing the attention of the whole table.

Rosalie's halfway sober now and actually sitting next to Jayce, behaving like a decent human being. I don't know how he did it, but he worked some kind of magic. She's barely touching him anymore, and whatever he's saying must be working, because she seems to be calming down. It's like he's got a PhD in handling drunk drama queens.

"Your temper, your lack of control—it's holding you back. It's your own damn fault," Henry says.

When Riley tenses up, I feel a surge of anger climbing up my chest. Not again. Can this man not stop?

His mother chimes in, her tone dripping with false concern. "I do hope you'll sort yourself out soon, darling. All these women you're seen with…it's not a good look."

I frown at her. I'm not a good look? Have you seen your daughter's boyfriend? Thank you, bitch.

"I'm in a serious relationship with Liora," Riley says. "And I'd appreciate it if you'd talk about her with respect."

Eleanor purses her lips, and I notice Riley's dad shooting a look at the man across the table—Steve, Howie, or whoever he is. It's like he's silently confirming all the doubts and criticisms he's shared about his "failure of a son" seconds before.

"They were gonna give him a second chance, but then he went and got himself locked up. Can you believe it?" his father says, as if Riley wasn't actually sitting next to him.

"What a waste of talent," the man remarks to no one in particular.

I look at Riley, waiting for him to do something, anything.

Why is he always ready to defend me but never stands up for himself when it comes to his parents? He can hold his ground against Ethan, Nina, his coach, and Houston's agent, but when it comes to his parents, he just lets them steamroll him. And I realize he gave up on them years ago.

"But what's your plan if hockey doesn't work out?" some lady from the other end of the table pipes up.

"Oh no, not Aunt Suzie," Granny mutters under her breath.

"Kid's got nothing going for him. Failed all his classes in college," his dad says, shaking his head.

My jaw clenches as I try to contain the bubbling anger inside me. How dare they say such things about him? Do they even watch his games? He's amazing and so are his stats.

"That's not true," Granny grumbles before breaking into a fit of coughs, her voice no longer as strong as it once was.

My anger simmers and grows and boils over, like a raging inferno inside me. I just can't believe them. His family. The people at this table.

"Well, he definitely didn't inherit my smarts." His dad laughs, and everyone else joins in, including Eleanor, who's laughing the hardest. "Always needs a calculator because he can't do math in his head." My hands ball to fists. More laughter erupts around the table. "I guess that explains why some of his passes are so off."

Okay. I can't take it anymore.

I shoot up from my seat, scraping my chair against the floor loudly, causing everyone to turn their attention to me with open mouths.

My hands tremble with barely contained anger as I glare at Riley's creators. They don't deserve to be called parents.

"Enough," I grit out through clenched teeth. "You don't deserve him. None of you do, except for his grandmother—sorry, Lilli."

Granny raises her hands in surrender, a wide grin on her face. "No offense taken, honey."

I pull Riley up by his arm and turn to face his parents again, my voice loud enough for everyone to hear. "We're leaving, but first I need to make something clear. Riley is the best player in his league, he has the most scores, and one day he will beat Gretzky's records. And do you know what will happen when he does?" I point accusingly at all of them. "None of you will be invited, except for Lilli."

I hear a hoarse cheer from Granny.

"You don't know anything about your own son. Riley is the kindest person I've ever met—always giving back to the community with free skate courses and camps for kids whose parents can't afford them, even during his own season. And yet you sit here and claim he doesn't have control over his career, his scores, or his own records? That's complete nonsense."

I lock eyes with his father then, my tone dripping with venom. "And as for you. You never made it far in hockey because you weren't good enough. All the hate you feel toward your own son should be aimed at yourself. Go get some help with those wires in your brain that are clearly malfunctioning, because you are missing out on an amazing son." I almost shout the last part because, fuck it, it's true. "Maybe one day you'll come crawling back and give this man the love he deserves, but until then, let me fill you in on some vital things about him that you missed out on. His favorite color is blue, he loves thrillers, hates caviar, and oh, he's allergic to celery, so why the heck is it on the menu? And most importantly, he loves—"

"You," Riley says, causing me to freeze mid-rant.

Suddenly, all the thousands of words I was ready to unleash dissipate into thin air.

What? He said what?

I turn to look at him with surprise and my heart swells as he pulls me into a kiss. "What did you say?" I whisper.

"I love you," Riley says and pulls me in for another kiss. "You crazy little bulldog of mine. I love you." He kisses me again, and I hear clapping and cheering from the tables around us, including from his granny, who is whistling and coughing with mirth in between.

"Come on," he whispers and tugs on my hand. "Let's go."

We say goodbye to Lilli and basically run out of the door.

Everyone quickly goes back to their conversations, as if nothing had happened. I'm not delusional enough to think my little speech will change their behavior. Honestly, these people are so stuck up, they probably wouldn't even notice if the sky turned purple.

But I had to take a stand.

As we make our way through the crowded room, ignoring the curious stares and whispered speculations, Riley lets out a relieved sigh next to me. It feels like he just shed all the unwanted thoughts he ever had.

"Fuck. You're. Fuck," he says, smiling from ear to ear. "You're incredible."

I can't help but grin at his flustered words, feeling my cheeks heat up as well. "I just couldn't sit there; I hate your parents. I'm sorry."

"Praise the universe. I hate them too," he mutters.

I want to grab his face again and pull him down for another round of kisses, but then suddenly a familiar figure steps into our path and my heart stops.

No, this can't be.

It's Sandford, looking just as handsome as I remember, but with a few more lines on his face. His blue eyes widen as they land on me, and I can't help but feel a flutter of nervous excitement in my stomach.

It's been years since our explosive fight in Beijing.

I could still feel the sting in my heart, but here he is, standing in front of me. His hair is still a mane of wavy blond, his square jaw cleanly shaven.

"Hey," he says, his voice oozing with false sincerity.

Riley's grip tightens around my waist as we turn to face him. Sandford's eyes rake over me, lingering on the hand that Riley has placed possessively on my waist.

"What do you want?" I snap.

He leans forward, a move that used to make my heart flutter but now only sends chills creeping down my spine.

Riley is quick to react, pushing Sandford away before he can get too close. "Don't even think about it," Riley growls, his protective instincts kicking into high gear.

Sandford laughs, brushing off Riley's warning like it's nothing.

But we all know Riley could take him down without breaking a sweat.

"Sweety," Sandford says with a sly smirk, using the same endearment he always did when he wanted something from me. But I am not that naive girl anymore. I have changed and I owe it all to him. He made me grow up fast.

"I'm not your sweety anymore," I sneer, emphasizing each word. "I told you once and I'm only telling you this twice, don't play me, I don't want anything to do with you. Get out of my way."

But Sandford doesn't listen. He never did listen to anyone. "Why didn't you call me back?" he demands, completely disregarding my previous statement. "I just want to talk."

I swallow hard, trying to keep my composure in front of everyone watching us. "You talked enough on TV," I retort, remembering how he tried to twist the truth to make himself look like the victim.

That poor man.

His young, teenage protégé, all wild and naive, running

away from the Olympics. The hate I got on social media made me cry myself to sleep, even though there was so much more I had to cry about.

"I never want to see you again. I mean it, I'll get a restraining order if I have to."

Sandford laughs, probably thinking about how broke I am and that I can't afford to come after him. But he has no idea how much I've earned from the show. If I win, I'll finally have the means to track him down. And I will.

He reaches out to grab my arm in a desperate attempt to stop me from leaving. Before I can react, Riley is there, standing between us, his eyes shooting daggers at Sandford. It's then when I realize he's half a head taller than him. "If you touch her again, I will knock you out," he warns.

Sandford looks up at him with a steely gaze, showing no signs of fear. "Another sports career ruined over trifles? How pathetic."

Trifles? He can't be serious.

The anger inside me boils over as I look at him and all the hurt he's caused me.

"Trifles?" I say.

Riley doesn't throw a punch.

I do.

My fist connects with Sandford's jaw, but the pain shooting through my hand is nothing compared to the satisfaction rushing through me now.

"Leave me alone," I spit, cradling my throbbing fingers. "I never want to see you again."

Riley pulls me away before anything else can happen, leading me outside into the cool night air.

As we walk toward our waiting car, I lean against him for support, tears prickling at the corners of my eyes.

I let out a groan of pain as Riley quickly inspects my hand.

"Oh no," I mumble, realizing what I've just done. My hand. I need it.

I have never hit anyone before and I didn't even do it right. But it was never just trifles and Sandford knows it.

"Fuck. Hospital. Now. I think you broke your thumb," Riley says.

Thirty-six

RILEY

"You're crazy," I grunt out as I tape up Liora's blue thumb again. "Most people would rest an injury like this."

She just smiles, flexing her fingers gingerly. She was incredibly brave facing Sandford again, and while we waited at the hospital, she shared her plan to finish law school and come back to finish him. I absolutely love the idea. But the best part was when she told me she wasn't afraid to see him again because I was by her side. Hearing that made my heart swell.

"Good thing I'm not most people then. A little tape and some painkillers, and I'll be fine. I've skated through worse," she says.

That competitive fire in her eyes—it's the same look that drew me to her in the first place. That relentless drive to be the best. I shake my head but can't shake my smile. That's so hot. "All right, ice queen. Let's go warm up then."

We kick off the session with some dynamic stretching, and Liora insists on pushing through, even though she winces when putting weight on her taped hand. I promised her I'd stay professional, but it's a tough promise to keep with her perfect ass constantly tempting me. The way it flexes? It's a death sentence. My thoughts are getting as intrusive as those annoying pop-up ads online—which, let's be honest, is saying a lot.

When we lace up our skates and hit the rink, I find it hard to keep up with her fluid movements, feeling like a hockey oaf next to her graceful glides.

"Bend your knees more on the mohawks," she instructs as she demonstrates a flawless three turn. "And keep your free leg straight."

"Yes, ma'am," I say and mimic her motions clumsily, almost eating it on the slick ice. Her musical laughter echoes through the empty rink. God, what I wouldn't do to bottle up that beautiful sound. Maybe, just maybe I played a little extra clumsy to see her smile more. Just maybe. I'm an addict. Sue me.

We run basic drills for thirty minutes until a sheen of sweat glazes both our brows. When she wants to start on the choreo she came up with Aiden, I hold up a hand to stop her. "Actually, I had another idea."

Her delicate brows shoot up in surprise as I pull out my phone and sync it to the rink's sound system. When the lyrics of "The Bad Touch" by the Bloodhound Gang blast through the speakers, Liora's jaw drops. I give her an eyebrow waggle and start gyrating my hips to the provocative beat.

"What. The. Heck. Are. You. Doing?" Her eyes go wide as I shake my booty. To top it off, I even put on my shades. Yes, baby.

"Improving your choreography!" I shout over the music, launching into an absolutely ridiculous dance involving pelvic thrusts and jazz hands. I look like the world's worst male stripper, but I just don't care.

It works—Liora bursts into another fit of giggles, her eyes crinkling at the corners as she doubles over with laughter. No sound in the world could ever top that. I'd make a complete fool of myself every day if it means keeping that smile on her face.

Especially after that weekend. She was so down that I just needed to make her laugh and have fun with me.

When I told my coach I was dedicating four hours a day to training with Liora, he thought I'd lost my mind. But watching her twirl on the ice, blonde ponytail whipping behind her and blue eyes sparkling with joy, I knew I'd made the right call. I'd put in double shifts, triple shifts, whatever it took to make this work.

Because that girl? She is worth it.

I'd do anything to make her dreams come true. I'd hand over a million dollars in a heartbeat, but I know she wants to achieve it on her own. If I can't help with money, at least I can support her with my exceptional ice dancing skills—even if that means air-humping in the middle of the rink to a song about "getting it on" like animals on the Discovery Channel.

Liora snorts and skates over to swat my arm. "You're ridiculous, you know that?"

"Ridiculously charming and talented? I agree."

"More like a ridiculously bad dancer."

I clutch my chest in mock pain. "You wound me! I thought that choreo was pure gold."

"In your dreams, hotshot." She rolls her eyes, but her smile stays firmly in place. "Now let's run it again from the top, and this time, leave your disco moves in the nineties where they belong."

She rolls her eyes again, clapping her hands like I'm a cattle to move, and we launch into practicing her real choreography, my muscles still aching from our session back at the pool house the other day. But no way in hell am I going to mention that to Liora. Ever. She has enough on her mind with the competition looming just days away, so it's the least I can do not to make her worry about my extremely manly muscles, right?

Our pairing seems to have the whole country buzzing.

Especially after those kissing pics of us from the gala "leaked" online. I'm pretty sure Grace is cackling with glee at all the free publicity. Even the network execs are banking on our star power, hyping up our dance as a must-see moment. Ethan texts me that they expect it to be one of the most watched episodes ever. No pressure or anything.

I glance over at Liora, at the determined set of her delicate jaw as she marks out her steps. Most people look at her and see a pretty blonde ice princess.

But I see the fighter beneath, the girl who claws her way to the top and keeps getting back up no matter how many times life knocks her down. They call me crazy for doing this. A hockey player trying to figure skate on live TV? But they don't know Liora James like I do. And if she thinks I can do this, well then...I sure as hell am going to prove my babygirl right.

"OKAY, let's run it again from the top," Liora calls out after reviewing the video she made of our performance. "And this time, really lift through your core on that overhead press. I should look weightless."

I flash her a cocky grin. "Babe, you're always like a feather in these arms. I am bench-pressing two of you on a regular gym day."

"Less talking, more lifting, Huntington."

"Yes, Coach." I mock salute before skating over to our starting position.

The music starts and we're off, gliding and spinning across the ice in perfect sync.

I hoist her effortlessly overhead, reveling in the feel of her lithe frame in my hands.

We move through the choreography seamlessly, like we've been doing this for years instead of mere days. I've never felt so in tune with another person before, so completely in the moment. And as the final notes fade away, I lower her gently to her feet, our faces mere inches apart.

Her blue eyes sparkle up at me, alive with exhilaration and something else I can't quite name. "That is…"

"Amazing," she finishes breathlessly.

"Riley, I think we might actually pull this off." I tighten my grip on her waist, drawing her closer. "Told you, Lia. You and me? We can do anything."

She bites her lip, suddenly shy. She looks so cute with these red cheeks. "I want to try something. It may go wrong but don't freak out, okay?"

Before I can respond, she is off again, building speed with each powerful stroke. I watch, heart in my throat, as she launches herself into the air, spinning so fast she is a blur of blonde hair, black training clothes, and flashing blades.

One rotation, two, three…holy shit.

She does it—a flawless triple axel.

I let out a whoop as she lands, knees bending to absorb the impact. She glides over to me, flushed and triumphant.

"Fucking shit. Liora, that is incredible!"

She shakes her head, ponytail bouncing. "I pre-rotated on the entry. It was sloppy."

"Looked damn near perfect to me." I take her hand, tugging her closer. "You should throw it in the routine. Give people something to really talk about."

"I don't know…haven't landed it cleanly in years. Not since…" she trails off, eyes darkening with old ghosts.

"Hey." I tilt her chin up, forcing her to meet my gaze. "This isn't Beijing. This is here and now. And you, Liora James, are the most talented skater I have ever seen. You are going to nail that triple axel and blow everyone away. I feel it."

A slow smile spreads across her face, chasing away those damn shadows I hate so much. We grin at each other, lost in our own little bubble, until the shrill beep of my smart watch bursts it. "Shit," I glare at my watch as if I'm ready to kill it. "I'm supposed to meet with the team in like twenty minutes."

Liora gives me a light shove. "Go. Be the hockey star you are. I'll work on polishing the ending."

I hesitate, hating to leave. These stolen hours on the ice with her have quickly become the best part of my day. "Can't wait for tomorrow. Prepare to have your socks knocked off by my dizzying spins."

"Can't wait."

She stretches up on her tiptoes to press a sweet kiss to my lips. But a peck is never enough for me—not when it comes to her—so I gently pull her closer, dipping her slightly as I kiss her deeply and fully, savoring the moment.

Once I've managed to say goodbye, her laughter follows me out the door, and I can't keep the dopey smile off my face the whole drive to the arena.

Damn, I have it bad.

She didn't say she loves me, too, but I don't need her words. Her actions tell me she does too.

We will hunt those demons she has.

I want to see that smile on her face daily.

BUT I DON'T, because with May 28 approaching, her smiles seem to be fading day by day.

I know she's nervous, since there are only eighteen hours left until the show. But the way she constantly touches that tattoo on her wrist makes me worry.

Is she trying to rub it off?

I don't ask, but I watch closely, ready to catch her if she falls.

She tries to hide it, putting on a brave face in public, but I see the hurt in her eyes in the quiet moments. When we eat, when she gets dressed or when we lie in bed reading, when she stares at her wrist instead of the words on the page.

Sometimes I'll take her hand and hold onto that tattoo for her, hoping it brings some comfort.

I even bought her a necklace as a gift, foolishly thinking it would bring back that smile I crave, only to be scolded for spending money on her. I just want to treat my princess like she deserves, but she's so stubborn and insists on earning everything herself.

I had to practically beg her to keep that necklace. When she asked how much it cost, I said three. She assumed three hundred and scolded me even more.

Little does she know, it was actually three thousand. She would kill me if she knew. Can't a man spoil his woman once in a while? Unbelievable.

Thirty-seven

LIORA

Nerves are one thing, but this is another.

"How are you holding up?" Priya asks from the makeup chair beside me, her knee bouncing up and down.

"Ughh, I swear I might puke right here," I say, gripping the armrests. "Three more shows, that's it. I just need to make it through three more."

"You've got this." Priya smiles reassuringly at me in the mirror. "Your routine is amazing. They're kicking me out tonight. I know it."

I box her slightly, she still winces.

"Stop saying such nonsense. So is yours. No way they're kicking you out today, you're incredible." I watch as her makeup artist dusts shimmery shadow over Priya's lids.

Priya's voice trembles as she speaks, "I don't know…it just seems to get harder every week. The pressure, the constant training—" Her sentence is cut short as the artist applies a vibrant orange-red lipstick onto her lips. It looks amazing with her russet skin. The reddish brown paired with the orange dress of hers and that lipstick? She's such a pretty babe and she doesn't even know it.

"Derek is coming to watch today. And Mason has been acting really strange about it."

"Sounds like someone's jealous," I tease. "Has he asked you out yet?"

"Who?" she asks.

I chuckle. "That's part of what I'm wondering." I secretly hope Derek does ask her out, though.

"Well, Derek keeps texting, but…I don't know. What if we go on a date and I have to tell him—you know." Her cheeks flush pink.

"If he's that much of a jerk and he rejects you just because you're a virgin, then—"

"Sweeties, trust me," Nora, my stylist, pipes up from behind me, "that will only make him want you more. Men love the challenge."

"But I'm not ready to sleep with just anyone," Priya protests.

"Preach," Nora agrees solemnly. We share an empathetic hum of understanding.

"Then don't," I say. "Tell him and watch his reaction." I'm not a fan of Derek, but I have to admit, he's at least better than Mason.

Just then, Riley bursts in wearing only his studded black jeans, no shirt.

My jaw drops. Holy hell, has he been doing extra training? Or is it the studio light? Those abs are—

"I can't find my top anywhere!" he exclaims, eyes wide with panic.

I know those abs all too well. But those jeans. The way they've styled him. Are his lips even more—

"Liora. The shirt for our number."

I snap out of my hormone-addled daze. Right. Focus. Shirt. "It has to be with the fitting team. Did you check there?"

"They don't have it! I'm freaking out, we go on in like ten minutes!" He runs a hand through his styled hair and I let out a shriek.

"Don't!" I and the stylist scream at the same time.

A wide smile stretches across my face as I glance at the stylist in the mirror. "Just don't destroy your hair and stay calm. We'll find it."

The makeup application is a breeze, and I eagerly hop off the stool to check myself out in the full-length mirror. My skintight scarlet dress is a perfect match to my bold red lipstick. These stylists really deserve more recognition for their talents.

"Thank you, Nora. You're always incredible," I say.

"Thanks, darlin'," Nora says. "You're an easy canvas."

Riley's gaze rakes over me appreciatively before he remembers the crisis at hand. "You look...wow. Okay, wardrobe. I need a shirt. Like, now."

Priya, Nora, and I exchange a glance before jumping into action, riffling through racks of costumes. I pray to the skating gods that we find something, and fast. This routine has to be flawless. Everything rides on it. But as the clock ticks down, my stomach only coils tighter. Where the hell is Riley's shirt? I notice the stylists searching for it, too, and hell breaks loose.

The jittery dread surges up my throat again.

Don't puke.

You cannot puke. You have makeup on.

Pull it together. Prove that you deserve to be here.

If only this didn't hold so much weight.

I'm so close to success .

"Stage call, five minutes!" the director's voice booms across backstage.

Crap.

I abandon the fruitless search and run to Riley.

Just as I reach him, a stylist I don't recognize runs up to us with his shirt in her hands, pointing out a large rip in the back of it. We exchange worried glances. Someone sabotaged us.

"Who," Riley starts, but then the director calls for the last two minutes.

"Go shirtless," I pant. "You're drop-dead gorgeous anyway."

I basically leap into my skates.

Shit. Shit. Shit.

My fingers fumble with the laces as I yank my skates on.

"Three minutes!" someone yells.

In my haste, I notice something sharp jabbing into my heel. Then the ball of my foot. I wince but ignore it. No time. The other skate goes on, and I tug the laces tight.

"Lia!" Riley screams.

Wobbling to my feet, I barely register his words because a searing pain lances through my foot and up my leg. I suck in a breath. What the— It's fine. Mind over matter. I just need to—

Holy shit. The moment I put all my weight on my shoes, agony explodes through my feet. Tears spring to my eyes immediately.

This cannot be happening. Not now. No.

"Hey, you okay?" Riley's brows furrow in concern.

"Fine," I grit out. "Go."

I limp forward, determined to push through. I'm a pro. The show must go on.

He takes my trembling hand in his.

Hand in hand, we glide out.

Breathe. Smile. Dazzle them.

Even if it kills me.

Thirty-eight

RILEY

The roar of the crowd reverberates through the arena as Liora and I hit our opening pose, bathed in that hot spotlight. The music starts and we glide across the surface, each step perfectly synchronized with the song she chose. It's "I Was Made for Loving You," but not the version by Kiss. It's a modern and raw version by Yungblud.

I lift Liora into a triple twist and her muscles tense up. This has never happened before. Something's wrong. We manage the lift, but once I put her on the ice again, I notice a little wince. It's barely there, but the flare in her eyes…she's in pain.

I try to focus on our program, but my mind is racing.

Is she injured?

There's simply no time to think as we move on to our next element.

We spin and leap across the ice. I just know there's something wrong. Her movements are slightly off balance, her jumps not as high as they should be.

But she soldiers on, and the audience doesn't seem to notice.

Until the triple axel.

I watch in horror as she fails to complete the rotation and lands awkwardly on one foot. My heart clenches but the crowd erupts into applause anyway. They have no idea that Liora just performed injured.

But I know.

And it breaks my heart to see her pushing through the pain for the sake of it.

Tears glisten in her eyes, and I know I need to do something. She can't start crying in front of the camera.

But at what cost?

Instead of the planned ending pose, I pull Liora close and we share a passionate kiss, playing our roles for the audience one last time. I use it to shield her face, making her cling to me as the crowd erupts in a standing ovation. Without a second thought, I scoop her up in my arms, cradling her against my chest while we listen to the judges. They are clapping away and giving us twenty-eight points. I don't know how, but Liora manages to thank them with a last forced smile before she pleads me to skate back. My showman's grin hides the fear gripping my heart. In truth, all I can focus on is the way her body trembles in my arms.

"You're hurt," I whisper, waving and skating to backstage.

She barely nods, burying her face in the crook of my neck, and I feel her tears wetting my skin. I spin with her, trying to maintain the illusion that this is all part of the performance until we're out of the spotlight.

Backstage is chaos, but I block it all out, zeroing in on an empty table in the back.

I set Liora down gently, my hands lingering on her waist. "What is it, Lia? Talk to me. Please."

She opens her mouth to reply but a scream of agony comes out instead, her face contorting in pain. Priya comes running over.

"Shit. What happened?" she pants.

"My feet," Liora gasps out between sobs, gesturing frantically at her skates. "My feet!"

Priya and I work quickly to unlace the skates, easing them off as carefully as possible. My hands tremble so hard.

But nothing could have prepared me for the sight that greets us.

Liora's socks, once pristine white, are now drenched with blood.

Razor-sharp shards of glass glitter in the harsh light, embedded deep in the soles of her feet. My stomach sinks. Shock courses through every part of me.

Fucking shit.

My mind reels, trying to process.

I've endured grueling practices and brutal hits on the ice, but this? This is unthinkable. Deliberate. Cruel. Rage builds in my chest as I imagine someone purposely placing those shards in Liora's skates, knowing the damage they would do. Knowing the agony she would have to skate through. Who'd do something like this?

"I…I don't understand," I hear myself say, but Liora is in no state to explain. She's lost to the pain, crying and crying, and fuck. I don't think I can ever forget these heartbreaking sobs. My chest tightens, feeling like it might burst from sheer anger. Fortunately, Priya steps in, documenting the injuries with her phone while giving me directions to the medics. Her calm, methodical voice cuts through my numbness, grounding me just enough to act.

I cradle Liora against my chest again. She weeps into my neck and each sob is like a knife to my heart. Someone did this to her. Someone wanted to hurt my Lia.

"I swear to God," I snarl to the room at large, my vision blurring red with fury as I scoop her up. "Whoever is responsible for this is going to pay. I will sue them for everything they have. I will destroy them." The words feel good, powerful. A promise.

It's what I need to get me going. To get Liora to the meds.

And once she lies on that medical bed, her hand clutching mine like a lifeline, vengeance is the furthest thing from my mind. All I can think of is the way she screams while they take out every fucking single shard.

Thirty-nine

RILEY

"We need to talk. Now." I storm into Grace's office without knocking.

My voice comes out in a low growl, and I know I look like shit from the sleepless night I had.

Last night, I carried Liora into our apartment, practically begging her to take action against these assholes. But no, she just wanted to keep pushing forward, ignoring the threats against her safety. Aiden was outed without his permission, followed by instances of costume destruction and even a physical attack.

This is too much.

I didn't sleep at all, my eyes fixed on her chest rising and falling, making sure she was still breathing. Seeing her scream like that was the worst experience of my life and I refuse to let it happen again. These freaks can't assure me she's safe? Fine, I already hired her a damn bodyguard. A giant orc, one that she can't shoo away with her stubbornness. Because protecting her is my top priority now, and I won't take no for an answer.

That's why I slipped out of bed, careful not to wake her, as soon as weak light finally peeked through the blinds. She was sleeping soundly when I left for the production office, probably knocked out from the heavy pain meds. While I respect and accept her wishes and boundaries, I won't simply stand by if someone is hurting her.

Grace looks up from her computer. "Mr. Huntington, what—"

"Someone put broken glass in Liora's skates. She could have been permanently disabled and I'm not going to sit around now. We need to find out who did this, immediately."

Grace's eyes widened. "Is she all right? Why didn't you tell me last night at the show?"

"Because Lia didn't want me to. And no, she's not all right. She's insisting on competing in the finals, injuries be damned." I start pacing. "This is unacceptable, Grace. I want a full investigation. Interviews, security footage, the works. And I want them prosecuted for assault."

"Of course, you're absolutely right," Grace says, there's genuine shock on her face and I relax a little. At least she's ready to cooperate. "I'll get my team on it right away. Thank you for not blowing this up in the media. The scandal could have ruined our ratings."

I whirl on her, jaw clenched. Oh sure, the ratings are what she cares about. "I don't give a shit about your fucking ratings. I care about Lia's safety and well-being. You better implement rock-solid security protocols going forward, or I'll pull her out of this circus myself, contract be damned. Are we clear?" I won't let her be killed on that show, even if she holds a grudge against me for the rest of her life.

Grace swallows and nods. "Crystal. I promise you, we'll get to the bottom of this. Liora is our top priority."

"She's got a bodyguard now. His name is Ivan. Be nice to Ivan," I say and leave this goddamn place.

THE APARTMENT STANDS in eerie silence as I return; Liora's nowhere to be seen.

Panic grips my chest, and I call out her name, only to be met with a void of sound. With trembling hands, I dial her number, pacing anxiously as it rings once, twice, three times.

Just as I'm on the verge of losing it, she answers, breathless.

"Hey, what's up?"

What's up? Her casual tone hits me like a slap.

"Where are you?" I demand.

"At the rink, training. I told you, I have to be ready for the finals."

I nearly crush the phone in my grip. "You're out of your fucking mind, woman! You can barely walk! Your finger is still swollen, and you need to come home and rest, for fuck's sake."

She sighs.

She dares to fucking sigh.

I'm losing my mind.

"I can't, Riley. I have to push through. It's just two more performances. I can rest later."

"Push through? Lia, you could permanently damage your feet! No competition is worth that!"

"You don't understand." Her voice wavers. "I have to do this. I don't care if I don't ever skate again after this. I need to win. I'm sorry but I'll be home later, okay? I need to hang up. Sorry, Riley. I'm sorry, okay?"

The line goes dead.

My hands tremble as I glare at the phone.

The sheer audacity of her decision leaves me dumbfounded—how could she willingly subject herself to such torment? Why would anyone do that? For what? For money?

What threat is she lying under that she shits on her health? Her life? She could get an infection, nerves could have gotten damaged, she—

A vivid memory invades my mind, replaying the image of Liora's slender figure, marked by a thin and silvery scar stretching across her lower abdomen. I always assumed it was from an old skating accident, but now a darker suspicion creeps in.

What if…

With a pounding heart, I open Google.

TWO EXCRUCIATING HOURS LATER, her key turns in the lock.

Sitting on the couch, I watch as she limps inside and drops her bag heavily on the floor, exhaustion etched on her face, pain evident as she reaches for the painkillers on the kitchen counter with shaking hands.

"Hey," she says softly when she finally notices me.

"Hey." My voice is strained. My emotions barely contained, making her look at me with eyes wide like saucers.

"Ri, what's—"

"I'm not beating around the bush anymore, Lia. I know why you're pushing yourself so hard out there."

The water glass freezes midway to her lips.

"That scar on your belly," I press on gently, "it's…it's from a c-section…right? You had a baby."

The glass slips from her fingers, shattering on impact with the kitchen counter.

I don't care about the glass, but I soften my tone and walk up to her. "If you're afraid, I'll run because you had a kid, I want to make one thing clear: I won't ever run." The closer I get, the more she backs up, until I'm only a foot away from her and she crashes into the fridge behind her.

"Have," she whispers, the words slipping out of her like the creak of a carefully opened door. "I have a kid."

Forty

LIORA

I stare at Riley and my heart jumps in my throat.
The words hang in the air between us.
I have a kid.
I'm a mom.
Saying it out loud makes it suddenly feel so real.

I search Riley's whiskey-colored eyes, trying to read his reaction. Waiting for his expression to change, for him to look at me differently. I'm not just some young twenty-something anymore. I'm a mom. I was a teen mom.

What's that look on his face? Shock? Disgust? Is he judging me or resenting me for having another man's kid?

My stomach twists into knots as I brace myself.

But as I gaze into Riley's eyes, I see none of that.

Just a flicker of surprise, quickly replaced by something that looks a lot like understanding. Or at least that's what I want to see in there. He sighs gently and rests his forehead against mine, the gesture so tender it makes me shiver. I've never seen this vulnerable side of him before.

"Lia," he murmurs, his breath warm on my skin before he

presses a kiss on my forehead. "I told you before, you can't say anything that would make me love you less."

Tears prick at the corners of my eyes and I shake my head in disbelief. There it is. He said it again, even though he knows. "But my life is so messed up, Ri. It's all so complicated…" My voice breaks. I can't turn him into a father from one second to the other.

He pulls back slightly to look at me, tucking a strand of hair behind my ear. "I don't care about that. I care about you and how you feel. If something is upsetting you, I want to know why. I want to help."

I hesitate, unsure if I can handle exposing all my painful scars. I never have. Only my mom knows all of it.

He takes my hands in his, giving them a reassuring squeeze. "I'm here to listen, for as long as it takes. Just let me in. Please. Let me be there for you."

Hot tears spill down my cheeks at his words.

Talking. I should talk. I know but there's this lump in my throat. I take a deep breath, evading his gaze, but he puts his thumb under my chin, refocusing me, looking at me as another tear slowly creeps down my cheek. Slowly. Silently. Like they have for the last five years.

"When I got to Beijing," I start, breathing past that damn constricting lump. "I was focused on one thing only—I wanted to win gold again. I trained day and night, perfecting my routine. But I was exhausted, both physically and emotionally." I swallow. All these pictures come back. Me, looking like a skeleton. So thin, purple rings under my eyes, with Sandford watching my every step. "Sandy…he was so demanding, especially since we were away from his wife. I thought my fatigue was just from the intense training and his constant sexual needs. But then the nausea started, and my breasts became tender. I tried to ignore it, convinced it was just stress."

My voice wavers as I recall the moment everything changed.

Riley grips my hip, gently stroking me with his thumb as I need to take another deep breath. This is so hard. I chained it all up for years. Opening up like this makes me fragile. I lay my life bare in Riley hands now and I am so afraid. Of him telling me that he understands but doesn't want to have a family. Because that's what he gets with me. A mom and a kid. There's no such thing as just me. There will never be and I'm happy about it.

"It's okay. I'm here, I've got you," he whispers, and despite all the racing thoughts in my mind, the urge to run, to vomit, to quit—I keep on talking.

"One day during practice, I got dizzy and blacked out on the ice. When I woke up, a doctor was there, telling me I was pregnant. I couldn't believe it. I was on the pill. But apparently, something went wrong. Maybe I got sick and it messed with the effectiveness, I still don't know how it happened."

Riley listens intently, his brows furrowed with concern.

I forge ahead, determined to get it all out now. "The doctor said if I wanted to keep the baby, I had to stop skating immediately. My body couldn't handle it. So I told my mom, and we cried together for hours. The Olympics were my life, and overnight, everything had changed. But in the end, we decided I would have the baby and move back to the States. When I told Sandford though—" A shudder runs through me at the memory. His face. The rage. The fear I had for my life and my baby.

My eyes feel hot again, the following coming out in horse, clipped sentences. "He was so furious. He said I was ruining his career, and he—he nearly pushed me down the stairs. He threatened me and my mom, forced me to go to some...go to some shady doctor for an abortion."

I feel Riley tense up, there's a tic in his jaw.

I can barely breathe.

I was so afraid. So afraid.

Something constricts my throat, and again, a hot tear falls down my cheek, and I wonder if there's a day in my life when I won't cry.

"My mother tried to get Sandy to his senses, tried to get me away from him without hurting me or the baby, but he brought me to the doctor, forcing him to do it, but the doctor refused. He wouldn't abort without the woman's consent—and he saw my pain, the danger I was in. So he lied to Sandford, said he did it, and gave me the money instead. My mom and I used it to fly back to the US that same night."

I cry so hard now that Riley takes me in his arms, his head resting on mine. His heart beats so fast.

And I cry and cry.

"I was terrified, Riley," I say, shuttering from tears as they ripple out of me.

Each heave, each wince a knife that Sandford pressed into me.

The way he threatened to kill me and the baby for ruining his career.

The way he threatened my mom.

The way he looked at me. A death promise in his eyes.

Riley draws me closer, his warmth enveloping me like a shield, and I cry harder. I've never felt so safe in my life.

I lean into him, praying he won't turn away when he learns just how broken I really am.

"I am so sorry," Riley whispers against my hair, shaking as well. "I am so sorry you had to live through that."

Once I'm able to speak again, I say, "We were so scared of what Sandford might do if he found out. We sold our house, moved to Orlando, and took jobs waitressing and cleaning to get by. But it wasn't enough."

The words catch in my throat as I think of all the hardships we endured. All the times we thought we wouldn't make it, but each time the day ended, the sun went up again, and we tried anew.

"I shut down all my social media, switched to a prepaid phone, even opened a new bank account, terrified Sandford would track us down. Somehow, we managed to stay hidden, even when the sponsors I had for the Olympics sued the shit out of me, leaving me deep in debt. And then—" A ghost of a smile touches my lips. "I had my beautiful baby boy on May twenty-eighth."

That picture. Even now it fills me with such warmth.

The little baby in my arms. Blond hair, the bluest eyes, and cutest little nose I could think of. His tiny hand was so little, it could wrap around my thumb and that was it.

Riley takes my hand and kisses it. "Can you tell me his name? Please?"

"Rory."

Riley's eyes light up and I almost bawl at it again. "Boys with R names are the best."

I don't know how he does it, but he manages to make me laugh. Even now.

I let my head fall against his chest again.

"Mom and I, we were the happiest we'd ever been, even living in that cramped trailer. His little laughs, his tiny hands reaching for us—he made every struggle worth it."

Riley's arms tighten around me, his heartbeat steady against my cheek now.

I draw in a shuddering breath, steeling myself for the hardest part.

"But when he was a year old, everything changed. He got sick, so sick. The doctors diagnosed him with type one diabetes. He needed medication, but the costs…" I shake my head, a bitter laugh escaping me. "We tried everything. I worked myself to the bone, but the debt just kept piling up.

And one day, I couldn't afford his insulin." I look up at Riley, and at the shock in his eyes, the tears come rolling again.

What kind of mother can't buy medication for her child?

Me.

I couldn't.

My voice drops to a horse whisper. "Riley, I couldn't buy him his meds. I couldn't give him the care he needed. I realized—" A sob wrenches from my throat again. "I realized...I...had to let him go."

All the hurt comes back and I almost shatter just thinking about it. I notice my feet give way, but Riley catches me. He cradles my face, his thumb brushing away the tears.

"Lia, you did what you could." His voice is a faint whisper and I realize he has tears in his eyes too.

So I nod, just looking at him and letting it all out. I have no idea how I still have tears left.

That choice. That moment, I knew I had to let go of the one person in my life I loved more than anyone or anything. It killed me and the person I was before.

"Where is he now?" Riley says, still brushing away tears with his thumbs.

My face feels so hot. My nose is so full. I can't even breathe through it anymore without sniffing. Shit. I knew I'd be a mess the minute I started talking about Rory.

"Some friends," I say through tears and bite them back again, and start anew, "Some friends told us about a family in Pennsylvania, a couple in their fifties who always wanted a child but couldn't have them themselves. I made an agreement with them—they would be his grandparents, and they agreed to take him until I could afford to take care of him and myself. They've even paid for flights so I could visit, let us FaceTime whenever we wanted, visited Mom and me. But every time I had to say goodbye—"

The sobs take over again, it's out of my control, each one

rippling through me like a tsunami. Everything I bottled up for so long—the pain, the isolation, the agony of leaving my son behind—breaks free, swallowing me whole. But no matter what, Riley holds me through it all, whispering words of comfort against my hair.

In the depths of my sorrow, one truth keeps me afloat.

Riley is still here. Still holding me. He hasn't turned away.

For the first time in forever, I don't feel alone.

"All the moments I lost," I whisper, pulling back just enough to meet Riley's gaze again. "I missed his first steps, Riley. I missed his first words. I missed his first day of kindergarten, and now he's already four, and I missed his birthday on May twenty-eighth. I have a four-year-old son who barely knows me."

There's a sinking sensation in my gut. When his birthday came around last week, I really wanted to visit him, but I had the show, and it just wasn't possible. I constantly feel like the worst mom, and missing his birthday only makes it worse.

"Shit, Lia…" Riley whispers.

"Mom and I worked ourselves to the bone, saving every penny we could to move closer to my baby. We were so close, Ri. So damn close. But the renting costs always got higher and higher and it felt like we worked for nothing, but then I heard about Grace's show, about the million-dollar prize, and I knew it was my best shot. The fastest way to stop missing moments with my boy.

"I took the money we saved and put it toward rink fees, a new costume since I sold anything but my old skates. I even reactivated my Instagram after five years. I asked if anyone knew of an affordable apartment, since the prices were way too much for me. And then Nina messaged about a cheap apartment…"

"I'm so glad she did," Riley says. "I'm so glad I met you, Liora."

Trailing off, I shake my head. "I have to win this, Riley. It's the only way I can get my son back."

"That's why you did it," Riley says, and I can't quite understand the look he gives me. Admiration? Is it that? "Only a mother would fight like this. Only a mother who loves with her whole heart would put herself at last."

I nod. "I have to stop losing moments, Ri." It's why I can't believe Riley's parents willingly gave away all these moments they could have shared with their son. I never would.

He nods. "We can leave now. Let's go get him."

I shake my head. "No, I need to do this myself, I know you would help me, but I am a week away from finally solving it. I'm not the girl that looks for a rich man to do it all for her."

"You don't have to—"

I put a hand on his chest, so grateful that he wants to help. "I've come so far. I can fix it now. I can't be in anyone's debt anymore. Mom and I worked our asses off to pay the sponsors back. I'm so close to fixing it. Let me fix it, Ri."

He waits, unspoken works hanging between us.

"But…but I understand if it's too much for you, if you don't want to be tied down by all my baggage. I love you, but I love you enough to let you go if that's what you need."

Riley's brow furrows, his whiskey eyes swirling with an emotion I can't quite name. Fear claws at my throat. This is it. The moment he realizes I'm too broken, too complicated. That I've come with a family.

"Lia, I don't know how many times I need to say this, but I'm not going anywhere. There's nothing about you I can't love. Rory is a part of you. How couldn't I love him?"

I gasp for air. Is this real? Is he really saying these things?

"You love me too," he adds. "There's nothing that holds us back now."

"There is. I have a son."

"And I can't wait to meet him."

I rake a hand through my hair. He doesn't understand. "My boy didn't have a mother for three years of his life. I can't just introduce him to a man who might leave us."

He winces. "Why would I leave?"

A desperate laugh bubbles up in my throat. "Because—because you're on the top of your life, Riley! Look at you! You have it all."

Now it's him giving me a desperate laugh. He steps away from me. "I have it all? I was dying inside, Liora. Maybe it's pathetic compared to your story, and I'm weak because, hell, you're the strongest person I know. But, I didn't have it all." He touches me. "Now I have it all. With you. You saved me in ways you have no idea. I was a mess before you. You make me so full, feel worthy for once. That my life isn't just for clicks and other people—for my damn father. You stood up for me and I stand up for you. Let me love you, Lia."

There's a knock on the door and we both jerk up. But Riley's head whips back to me quickly. "I don't want to live without you again. I meant what I said—"

Another knock. Followed by another.

"What is it?" Riley yells.

"Riley!" It's Jayce.

Riley looks at me. Shocked. Then we both check the clock. It's already past eleven. He should have left at ten.

"Shit," Riley says, but he doesn't move, his hands are still on my hips.

"Riley, the bus is waiting right outside your door. We're going to miss our flight!"

"One minute." He turns to me again.

"No!" Jayce bangs at the door again and again. "It's the fucking Stanley Cup, you idiot!"

Riley closes his eyes, battling with all kinds of thoughts, and I sigh deeply. "Ri. Please. Go."

He shakes his head, slowly opening his eyes. "No."

"Riley!" Jayce screams. "I'll break in. I swear."

I narrow my eyes at him. Is he insane? "No what?"

"I don't care about that thing anymore. It's you I care about. I'll help you get this sorted. Now. You're not safe on set and—"

"I am safe," I say. "It's only one show. And you worked all your life for that cup. I am not the one who ruins this for you. I'm not ready for everyone to frame me like they did with Yoko Ono."

"Now you're being dramatic."

"Okay, I break in in one—two—three." Jayce bums against the door.

"Go," I say.

"This isn't me running," Riley says.

"I know."

Another bump on the door. I hear something cracking. "Go!"

"Don't do anything stupid. I'll win that fucking away game, come back, and win that Stanley shit, and—"

I grab him by the waist, pushing him to the door. "He's coming!" I yell, and Jayce stops whatever he is doing out there.

Once I get that huge hunk to the door, he bends down, kissing me, and I kiss him back. "We're sorting this. I am in. I am not running."

I nod and shove him out of the door, where Jayce grabs him by the collar.

Once he's gone, I lean against the door, eyes shut tight from fatigue and the throbbing pain in my feet. How can I make him understand? Right now, he wants me because we're in the honeymoon phase of whatever this is—we haven't even called it a relationship yet. Once the initial excitement fades, he'll realize it's too much to become a dad overnight. And that's what I need if I ever get into a serious relationship again—I want a father for my boy, not men who come and go, leaving him more traumatized than before.

Rory needs stability.

And so do I.

I love Riley, but I can't force him into this life. He's a hockey star and deserves to live like it.

I hear my phone buzzing from the kitchen counter. I make my way over to it, still limping from my injury, and see that Riley has already sent me a text.

> Puckster: I forgot to tell you something. Be nice to Ivan.

> Liora: Who is Ivan?

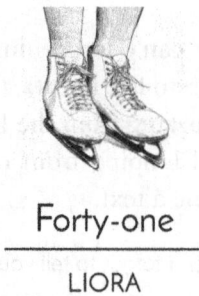

Forty-one

LIORA

Turns out Ivan is a towering six-foot-six behemoth. That Hulk of a man barely fits through doors and apparently is my bodyguard.

A grumpy giant who speaks minimal English and follows me everywhere. He's sleeping in his car outside Riley's apartment and refuses to leave my side. I have no clue where Riley found this man, but it's ridiculous. I tried to get rid of him, but he didn't understand me. I even tried in Hungarian. Not a chance. He blinked and that's it.

I just hope Riley didn't spend too much on this, but knowing him, he probably did, and it makes my stomach clench every time I think of it. Or every time I hear Ivan breathe behind me.

And Grace has taken the training sessions to a whole new level of friendly, even making Aiden suspicious as well. Turns out Riley had threatened Grace with a lawsuit if they didn't find out who was responsible. Great. So much to solving my problems alone.

But they soon uncovered that Stacey was the one sabotaging us all along.

They caught her on camera stealing Riley's shirt, then breaking a small mirror she had in her purse and scattering the pieces in my shoes. And she was the one who took the photo of Aiden and Ethan and sent it to tabloid magazines. On top of that, she stole Priya's makeup and ruined the dresses of other skaters. That bitch.

They dropped her from the show immediately, and the media uproar was intense, leading to another round of interviews where I had to talk about toxic TV environments. I wanted to point out that the judges aren't much better, but I need the money, so I channeled all my frustration into railing against Stacey. But the drama caused a huge uproar on the show, too, leaving only Priya, myself, and one other couple for the finals. I feel sorry for Stacey's skating partner, Russell. He was nice but unlucky to be paired with her, so it's over for him too. I knew it was Stacey all along, but I never thought I could prove it. I don't feel guilty at all about her facing the consequences. She deserves it for every bit of pain she caused me and Aiden. It turns out she also leaked his relationship with Ethan, but we're so ready for it. Ethan booked a ton of shows where we can talk about what happened on set after the finals. It's going to be huge.

Every morning, Riley texts me and calls just to hear my voice. It's actually sweet. I never would have thought he'd be this cute, especially not when he's all macho out on the ice. I'm so gone for him it's actually not even funny anymore.

But damn, watching his final game before the Cup with Priya at his apartment was absolutely exhilarating. Of course Ivan was there, too, watching while standing, but we pretty much ignored him because he doesn't speak a lick of English anyway. When they won, Priya and I did this ridiculous victory dance in front of Ivan, who didn't even bat an eye. Seriously, that man has the poker face of a champ. I can never tell what he's thinking or feeling, if he even has emotions.

There's just one game left before the Stanley Cup.

I couldn't be prouder—or louder. I'm also thrilled that the final will be in New York because I've been missing him like crazy.

That night, Riley texts me from the hotel.

> **Puckster:** What are you doing? I can't sleep.

I snap him a pic of me in nothing but panties in bed.

He's offline soon after, and I can't help but worry. Did I go too far with sending that sexual photo? Maybe he just wanted to talk and not engage in anything physical. Maybe something happened.

> **Liora:** Ri? Are you still here? What are you doing?

> **Puckster:** You really wanna know?

> **Liora:** Yes.

Stupid question.

As soon as I see the voice note, my heart skips a beat. I tap on it and hit Play, a rush of tingles spreading through me.

The sound of wet noises fills my ears—he's pleasuring himself.

A sigh escapes his lips and I feel my panties grow damp.

Fuck, that sound was sexy.

I imagine his hand moving up and down his cock and a streak of electricity flares through me.

> **Puckster:** This is what you do to me.

I don't respond, instead, I'm listening to the rasp in his voice again and the wet flapping in the background again.

Every part of me tingles when he moans for me, and I can't resist slipping my hand into my panties, fingers working quickly over my clit as I crave that friction. Shit. This feels so good.

My phone buzzes again.

> Puckster: Tell me, baby, are you touching yourself and thinking about me? That picture was so sexy, I'm so turned on right now.

I bite my lip, feeling a surge of pure thrill at his words. With one hand still pleasuring myself, I quickly type back a response with the other. "I'm touching myself while listening to those hot sounds you make. I'm so ready for you."

But then my phone rings.

My heart races with nerves as I pick up, not sure if I'm ready for this but also unable to resist his deep voice begging for more. I've never had phone sex before. "Lia," he growls, and I press my fingers harder against my clit. "Tell me what you're doing."

As he speaks, I hear that familiar sound again—the sound of him working himself over the phone. The intensity of it almost pushes me over the edge just from imagining it alone. I run my hand over my thigh, picturing it's him, and then I go back to my clit. I wish he could be here and watch me. I wish he could see how much I'm loving this.

"I have my fingers on my pussy. I'm so warm, and soaking wet, Ri."

"Are you petting it?" he croaks, his voice rough and strained.

"Yes," I breathe.

A groan rumbles through my phone, it sounds like it came deep from his chest.

"I want to taste you. You taste so fucking good. I can't stop thinking about my tongue on your pussy." I can't stop thinking about it too.

He moans again and my fingertips graze over my clit, swollen and throbbing. I can't resist the urge to move my hips, grinding against my hand as I trace tight circles over my sensitive nub. I slid a finger into my pussy, gasping as I feel the warm, slick walls clench around me. In and out, in and out, matching the rhythm of his raspy voice in my head. My eyes flutter shut as I lose myself.

His breath hitches on the other end of the line. "Fuck, Lia. Tell me how wet you are for me."

A flush creeps up my cheeks but I whisper, "So wet, Ri. I wish you were here to feel how wet you make me."

He groans loudly at that, the sound sending a new wave through me. My fingers move faster now, rubbing tight. I imagine it's Riley touching me, his strong hands knowing just how to play my body.

"I'm close," I say.

"I'm there with you, baby," he says, and I hear him pleasuring himself. I imagine his muscles tightening, how his hand moves fast over his pulsating cock, how he spills his cum. Oh my god. "I want to feel your mouth on my cock so bad."

"I'd love to swallow your dick, Ri," I say. "I can't wait to kiss that cock of yours."

"Say my name again."

"Riley," I say, and our heated moans mingle through the phone line as we both come so fucking hard.

I can't wait for him to come home. Even though we won't have much time together with the Stanley Cup game and my show coming up in three days, I really miss him.

I CAN'T BELIEVE the finals are starting in three hours. I'm a nervous wreck. I don't want to bother Riley because he has the Stanley Cup final tonight, of course it has to be the same night as my show's final. I wanted to see it so badly, and knowing we can't be there to support each other just makes my nerves even more on edge. So I FaceTimed Rory.

He and Mom always manage to calm me down, and I know my little guy is watching every show. We FaceTime regularly, but since he's only five, Trish, his Gran, told me he gets so upset every time we hang up that we agreed to limit calls to once a week. But we'll finally get to live our lives together. It hurts like crazy that I can't just hug him every other minute like I want to. I know Rory is hurting even more, especially since I understand how much mothers mean to their kids. That's why I call my mom next.

She's my best friend, and I need her right now—not just to ease my nerves before the show, but for some advice on the Riley situation.

I sit on a couch, chatting with her in Hungarian as Ivan stands guard nearby, keeping everyone at a distance. I take a deep breath, my fingers absently playing with the frayed edge of the cushion.

"I don't know what to do, Mom. What if, in a few months, Riley thinks that I was his greatest mistake?"

It will crush me.

My mother's gentle voice crackles through the speaker. "Sweetheart, you can't let fear control your life. Sometimes, you have to take a chance on love. From what you've told me, Riley seems like a wonderful young man who genuinely cares for you. He wouldn't have done all of that otherwise."

I sigh, my eyes drifting to the bustling activity backstage. Everyone's nervous for the big final. "But what about Rory? I can't just bring someone new into his life without being sure."

"Yes, just take it slow," Mom suggests, her tone reassuring.

"Get to know Riley better first. You don't have to rush into introducing him to Rory. Not as a father figure, at least. Maybe just as a friend first? When the time feels right, you'll know. You're a smart girl."

I nod, even though she can't see me, so I quickly add, "I guess I'm just afraid of opening up again. To trust a man again."

"That's understandable, but remember, everyone deserves a chance at happiness. Don't let your past experiences rob you of a potentially beautiful future. Maybe Riley is the one you've been searching for all along. If not, he's not. Let him go. Get up on your feet again. I'm always here, honey."

"Thanks, Mom. I needed to hear that. I love you."

"I love you too. Now, go out there and shine. I'll be cheering for you on our crappy couch."

I laugh. "Can't wait to see you and watch shows on a new couch."

"I'll cuddle the crap out of you and Rory soon, but for now, come on. Mingle. Have fun. Enjoy this last show as much as you can."

"Bye, Mom."

As I end the call, I lean back against the couch, my mind swirling with possibilities. Ivan catches my eye, and I offer him a small smile. He doesn't move one fucking muscle. Maybe, just maybe, it really is time to take a leap of faith and see where this journey with Riley leads us.

Back in the dressing room, I prop my phone up on the vanity, determined to catch glimpses of the game. It starts an hour prior to our show. The screen flickers to life, and I see the ice, the players, and the roaring crowd. My heart swells with yearning as I watch Riley glide across the rink, his movements so strong and sexy.

Priya and Aiden join me, their arms laden with plates from the catering table. We huddle together, munching on an assortment of snacks, our eyes glued to the phone screen. Mason struts by, pausing in front of a mirror to admire his own reflection. He flexes his muscles, a smug grin plastered on his face, and we all exchange knowing glances, stifling our laughter.

He walks past us, frowning at the snacks in our hands. I roll my eyes and I realize that Riley helped me with another thing. He made me feel so comfortable in my own skin. I don't give a damn about anyone thinking I should stick to the veggie sticks. I love my body and my man does too. I blink. My man? Holy—

"I can't believe I ever found him attractive," Priya says, snapping me out of my thoughts, cringing. We watch him stride out, winking at a makeup artist as if she should faint just because he acknowledged her. "He's become such a jerk lately, especially with the finals approaching. And get this, I caught him texting *seven* different girls at the same time!"

Aiden and I share a look of disbelief before turning to Priya with sympathetic smiles. "Well, thank you for finally coming to your senses. We should find a self-help group for those other seven girls."

"For sure," Aiden says, munching away on a muffin, "you deserve so much better."

"Did Derek text you again?" I ask.

"I thought you'd never ask," she grins widely. "He did but you know with our schedule it's not easy to find time to chat. We'll see, I wanna focus on my school anyway."

"You better," I say.

I still remember her face vividly the moment I told her Riley and I were officially dating. She screamed so loud, I thought my ears might burst. Then she said she already knew because she'd read my horoscope. I just love her.

It's hard to believe that this show turned out to be the best thing that could have happened to me.

I earned enough to pay off my debts, build a future for my

child, find real best friends, and meet a man I love. What more could I ask for? There's nothing else I could possibly want.

As we continue to talk, the conversation shifts to our plans for the future, now that the competition is drawing to a close. Aiden mentions his desire to invest in his career, revealing that all the interviews he gave about coming out as an actor, lined up some promising casting opportunities for him. So many people are reaching out to him. It's making me believe that our world truly has the potential to be a good place.

Priya's eyes sparkle with excitement as she shares her dream of opening her own skating school.

"You know, you guys are always welcome to teach at my school whenever you want," she offers, her voice filled with genuine warmth. "It would be an honor to have you both there."

I smile. "That sounds wonderful, Priya. Pennsylvania is only two hours away from New York, so I'll definitely consider it." I pause, my thoughts turning to the future. "But if I win tonight, I think I'll take several weeks off to spend time with my mom." *And Rory.* "I found a beautiful house in a great neighborhood. Mom and I are going to check it out after the finals. If it's the right fit, we'll buy it with the money I earned. Then I just want to make the most of our time together—collecting moments and enjoying life."

I glance at the phone once more, catching a glimpse of Riley skating toward the net. I hold my breath. *Shit. Riley. Go!* And then—he scores. "Fuck yes!" I scream, people turn to look as all three of us scream and jump, cheering. I just hope he wins. He'll be soaring.

The thunderous applause of the audience snaps me back. "The show is starting," I say, and we turn to the TV behind us that shows us exactly what people see on TV.

The hosts take the stage, and Priya takes my hand. She's

shivering slightly and I gently squeeze her. "We can do this," I say, and she nods.

They welcome everyone to the grand finale of the show.

The stage lights flood the arena, and the crowd goes wild.

I catch glimpses of banners with our names held high. My heart skips a beat when I see one with *Liora and Riley* on it. We definitely won over some hearts last week. I have no idea how we did it, because all I could think of was that freaking pain in my legs, but I watched all the videos after. I spot countless videos on social media platforms, capturing snippets of our performance. Apparently, no one could tell that I was slightly off my game that night. With every move we made together, Riley and I were mesmerizing to watch. Don't get me wrong, Aiden and I have great chemistry, too, but there is just something special between me and Riley that everyone can sense. And that ending lift? It's always being clipped and shared online. Especially when Riley kissed my forehead. So tender. So much love in that little move. All I see is wild concern in his eyes. But the fans see wild love and aren't that wrong.

Shayleen and Tim crack some silly jokes while snippets of our journey flash across the massive screen behind them. I watch, transfixed, as clips of our training sessions and all those interviews play out before the entire arena.

And then, there we are—Riley and me, our chemistry undeniable even through the lens of a camera.

We gave an interview where he made a little joke about me being impressed by his skills. I playfully hit him, and he winked at me in response. We then spent a few seconds just staring at each other. Although I hadn't realized we held the gaze that long, but I remember exactly what I was thinking: how much I wanted to kiss him and how I hated that the camera was filming us. Oh, we kissed after that interview.

Backstage, the energy is electric. Aiden paces back and forth, his eyes closed as he mentally rehearses our routine. I take a deep breath, trying to calm my nerves, too, but it's impossible to ignore the gravity of this moment. One million. I could own one fucking million.

"Hey," Aiden says softly, placing a hand on my shoulder. "We've got this. You and me, okay?"

I nod. "Let's show them what we're made of," I reply, my voice steady despite the butterflies in my stomach.

As we wait for our cue, I glance down at my phone one last time.

Let's win this shit.

Forty-two

RILEY

I'm a man possessed, flying across the ice, battling along the boards, setting up plays. My teammates match my fervor. They block shots and back-check like hell.

With two minutes left, we're up by one. The Florida Bay Blazes pull their goalie for an extra attacker.

I dive to break up a pass and send the puck sailing down the ice…right into the empty net.

The buzzer sounds and pandemonium erupts.

Fucking shit. We did it.

Jayce and Colton crash into me and the audience fucking roars. Hats rain down. Beer is spilled. Shane sprints to the bench and grabs a bottle of champagne, shaking it wildly before popping the top and spraying everyone in reach. We scream at each other as silver glitter confetti falls on our heads like snow.

"Fuck yeah! We did it!"

Laughing, my teammates hoist me up onto their shoulders as I pump my fist in the air, lost in complete elation.

"Stellar season, Huntington." My coach grins, clapping me

on the shoulder as they set me back down. "Don't think you're going anywhere anytime soon. We've got plans for you."

The NHL commissioner skates out to center ice for the trophy presentation. He hands the Stanley Cup to Jayce. Since he's our captain, he's got the rights to lift that damn thing first, and he raises it high above his head with a triumphant yell.

As the silver gleams under the arena lights and the crowd chants our names, I can't wipe the smile off my face. Everything we fought for, all the blood, sweat, and tears—it led to this perfect, shining moment. My heart feels like it's about to burst as we head to the locker room to start celebrating.

Inside, all my teammates are bouncing around with their loved ones while Colton pours champagne into the Cup. It's hilarious how superstitious hockey players are—no one would touch the Cup before we won it, believing it would jinx us. But now, drinking from it after the win is supposed to bring good luck.

We howl and chant just like the fools we are, and I feel like I'm on top of the world. But something is missing.

Handing the Cup off to Malcolm, I turn to Mercer. "Hey, I know I said I'd be at the after-party, but there's somewhere I gotta be first."

Mercer raises an eyebrow and slips an arm around my neck, steering me to the far end of the locker room for a more private chat. "More important than celebrating with your team? You know we just won the fucking Stanley Cup, right?"

I wink at him. "We'll celebrate all summer, coach. Give the others some camera time in the interviews. I'll make up for it."

Mercer laughs, a deep rumble as he holds his belly. "Young love, huh?"

"She's the best thing that happened to me. I need to go get my girl."

"That PR coupe worked quite well, then." He wiggles his eyebrows.

"It did. But you know what they say, sometimes you need to fake it until you make it."

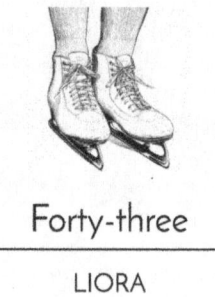

Forty-three

LIORA

My blades slice the ice, heart pounding as Aiden and I glide into our starting positions. We made it to the second round of the finals, but at the cost of saying goodbye to Priya. Tears streamed down our faces as we hugged her tight before she left to go sit with her parents and family in the audience.

The music begins and we launch into our routine. Pain shoots through my ankle on the landings, but I grit my teeth, determined to prove I deserve to be here. As I approach the triple axel, my pulse races.

One, two, three rotations and I land, not perfect but standing. A wave of thunderous applause rises from the audience, a chorus of cheers and clapping hands blending together. We strike our final pose and grin out at the sea of faces—and my heart stops. Riley is there in the front row, holding up a sign: I LOVE LIORA JAMES.

Our eyes lock as the cameras find Riley and I notice Ethan and Nina cheering next to him.

"Three perfect tens!" the judges boom.

Aiden and I hug, but as soon as we're cued to leave the ice,

I skate to the edge of the rink and Riley sweeps me up, twirling me around as his lips meet mine.

"You were amazing," he whispers between kisses.

"I can't believe you actually came," I say, still stunned. "Did you win?"

"No," he admits and my stomach drops. "But it's okay. You're my real trophy."

My smile falters for a moment, but then I realize he's messing with me. I give him a playful smack. "Don't you dare lie about winning the Stanley Cup ever again!"

He laughs, spinning me around once more with a grin. "We fucking won, baby!"

I kick my feet in excitement. "I just can't believe you came." He's just won the Stanley Cup, and yet he came straight to *me*.

I turn to Nina. "You were right. Deep down he really is sweet." The sweetest actually.

"Well, you two, be prepared to celebrate big time tonight once Lia snags her trophy," he says, winking at me.

The break flies by in a blur of nerves before they call us onstage for the audience vote. Clinging to Aiden's hand, I stare up at the screen, hardly breathing. The countdown begins.

Ten.

Nine.

Eight.

I hold my breath.

Seven.

Six.

Five.

Four.

Three.

Two.

One.

Suddenly, Aiden's and my face appears on the screen and

the scream stifles in my throat. We won. We won! Within seconds, Riley hoists me into the air, tears of joy streaming down my face as he whirls me around. I did it. I really did it. Five years ago, I thought I'd lost everything…but now, I have the money for the house and law school.

As the celebration on stage winds down, Riley leans close to my ear. "Hey, I'm inviting the whole crew and production team to the Falcons' victory after-party. You ready to go?"

I nod eagerly, my heart still pounding from the excitement as I look up at him. Gently, I touch his cheek, relishing the pure joy in his eyes. "I love you," I whisper.

He kisses me softly. "I love you too."

Being part of this show turned out to be the best thing that could have happened to me. Yes, it was tough and painful, but it saved my life. Things won't be perfect right away, but Riley has promised to support every decision I make and to stand by my side. I still want to take things slow and spend time alone with Rory first, as he needs his mom right now and I need my kid. Once we're settled and healing, I've agreed to let Riley into our lives more. I'm ready to give happiness a chance, even if it means taking baby steps.

I deserve to be happy.

We make our way offstage when a familiar voice stops me. "Liora, wait!"

Grace approaches, a genuine smile on her usually stoic face. "Congratulations, truly. You know, you've always been too good for this show." She pauses, as if considering her next words carefully. "Listen, I'd love for you to come back next year as a judge. Help us make some real improvements around here."

Stunned, I glance at Riley, who gives me an encouraging nod.

"I…Wow, Grace. That's quite an offer. Can I have some time to think about it?"

"Of course," Grace replies smoothly. "Enjoy your celebrations tonight. You've earned it and I'm sorry. I hope we can talk about everything that went down soon."

Her hand lands gently on my shoulder, offering a congratulatory squeeze right before she makes her way to Aiden and Ethan.

As she walks away, Riley tugs at my hand. "Look at you, already moving up in the world."

I laugh, leaning into his strong frame. "I can hardly believe my life. But right now, all I want to do is party the shit out of this night with you and all our friends."

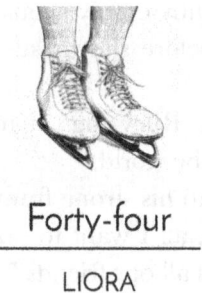

Forty-four

LIORA

My knuckles rap against the red wooden door, my heart pounding in time with each knock. I draw in a shaky breath. The Pennsylvania air feels thick in my lungs. I can't believe this moment is real. That I made it.

The door swings open and there he stands—my little Rory, my baby boy with his mop of blond hair and those piercing blue eyes that could melt even the coldest of hearts. His cherubic face splits into a toothy grin and I notice his little skates are already slung around his neck, his *PAW Patrol* suitcase waiting eagerly by his side.

My knees buckle beneath me, and I slump to the floor. "Bud," I whisper as I reach for him.

He launches himself into my arms with a delighted squeal. "Mommy, Mommy!"

I bury my face in his hair, breathing him in—that familiar scent of him. The same PAW Patrol shampoo I have. Is this really happening? After all this time, all the fighting and sacrificing, do I really get to bring him home?

Rory pulls back, his little hands cupping my face. "I'm gonna live with you, right, Mommy?"

I can only nod, not trusting myself to speak. Because if I open my mouth, I know the floodgates will burst open and I'll be a weeping mess, and I want this moment to be happy. So I just hold him tighter, my heart so full it could burst. My Rory. My reason for everything. Back in my arms where he belongs.

"Yes, bud," I manage, nuzzling into his neck and breathing him in again and again and again. "Yes. Yes. Yes. We made it."

The words feel surreal on my tongue, it's the dream I never dared to voice aloud lest it shatter. But it's real. The solid, squirming weight of Rory in my arms is real. The wetness on my cheeks, the swelling of my heart—it's all real.

We made it.

"Look who I brought with me!" I say, grabbing my bag.

Rory's eyes light up the moment he sees his blue teddy bear. It was his first and only stuffed animal, a simple blue bear I bought from the hospital gift shop, but he loved it so much. He carried it everywhere until he gave it to me on his third birthday. Even then, he barely spoke in full sentences, but he knew I didn't want to leave him and that I'd be there if I could manage the flights to Pennsylvania. I still tear up thinking about it—but my little boy gave me his favorite toy so I'd have a piece of him with me. I promised I'd return it when I was able to get him back.

"Blerry!" he exclaims, and I laugh, remembering how he tried to name his bear Blueberry but ended up with Blerry instead.

Rory hugs his bear tightly and then wraps his arms around me, and my heart swells again and again.

He pulls back after a couple of heartbeats, his face alight as he looks me over. "You were so pretty, Mommy. You won the show! I saw with Gran and Grandpa!"

A watery laugh bubbles out of me. "Thanks, bud," I whisper, tucking an errant curl behind his ear. My baby. My reason for everything.

I never want to let him go. Never want this moment to end. I want to freeze time right here, with Rory safe and happy in my arms, his little hands clutching at my shoulders. I want to memorize every detail—the exact shade of his eyes, cornflower blue with flecks of periwinkle. The constellation of freckles dusting his nose. My nose.

I want to absorb him into my very being, so I'll never be without him again, never have to endure another day, another hour, another second of the bone-deep ache of missing him.

"Where's the hockey player?" Rory asks suddenly, his voice cutting through my spiraling thoughts.

I blink, drawing back to look at him in confusion. "What?"

Rory squirms in my arms, his eyes darting around as if searching for someone. "The hockey player," he repeats impatiently. "The one on TV with you. He is really good! He won the Cup!"

My heart stutters, then kicks into overdrive. "Riley? Yes. His team won the Stanley Cup! He's the best player I know."

"I just love hockey, Mommy," Rory declares, his voice ringing with the absolute certainty only a child can possess, and something tugs around my heart. "I wanna play just like him when I grow up!"

My throat tightens.

"That's great, bud," I manage to choke out, forcing a smile that feels more like a grimace. "But you know, hockey players have to practice really hard. It's a lot of work."

Rory nods solemnly, his little face scrunched up in determination. "I can do it," he insists. "I'll practice every day, I promise! And then…" He lowers his voice to a conspiratorial whisper. "Maybe the hockey player can come visit us and teach me some tricks!"

I laugh. Oh, Riley would love this. "You know what?" I wink at him. "I'll ask him."

Behind Rory, Trish and Spencer, his grandparents,

exchange a meaningful glance, their eyes brimming with unshed tears. Trish clasps her hands together, her smile wavering as she watches us, and I look up at her, my face full with the biggest smile I've ever had. *Yes*, my eyes tell them, *yes, we really made it*. I bought a house. On my own. For me and my baby and a certain hockey player who can't wait to visit us.

Epilogue

FIVE YEARS LATER–RILEY

"So, Dad, I've been thinking about hockey camps for this summer." Rory plops down beside me, his lanky frame folding into the chair. We're sitting in the waiting area of the tattoo parlor. My wife's finally getting the tattoo she's been talking about since our wedding day two years ago. Rory's nearly ten now and growing so quickly. I've started teasing Liora that she will soon be the shortest one in our household.

The word *dad* still fills me with happiness every time he says it. This kid, with his mom's stubborn streak and quick wit, has become such an important part of my life. Before Rory, the word *dad* made me feel uneasy, drenched with so much hate. Even though my relationship with my parents never really improved, we do talk on the phone occasionally, and thanks to therapy, I'm able to visit them without feeling like a complete failure.

My father apologized at one point, and we're making an effort to mend things. It's still challenging, but having my own family has made it so much easier. Finding the love I'd always craved made my anger issues disappear like they were never even there. And whenever my dad slips back into his old patterns and makes me feel down, I look at my son and focus on being the kind of dad I always wished I had.

"Yeah? Which ones are you considering, bud?"

He lists off a few top-tier camps, his eyes bright with excitement. I'm bursting with pride. He's amazing at hockey and school. Anytime someone gives me the slightest opportunity to talk about him, I whip out hundreds of photos because I'm just so damn proud.

"I want to work on my slap shot and defensive skills."

"Solid plan." I ruffle his blond hair, remembering the countless hours we've spent on the ice together, him, me, and Liora. Every home game, they're there in the stands, cheering me on. It's all I need. "You know, with your mom's and auntie Priya's skating school taking off like it is, we might be able to squeeze in some extra ice time too."

Rory grins. "Amazing!"

Liora and Priya are absolutely shining with their skating school, and since my wife became a judge on *Grace on Ice*, the show has transformed into something truly magical. She's managed to rid the show of all its toxic elements, creating a warm and welcoming space for everyone who loves to skate. She's used her platform to raise awareness for mental health and support women in need.

Sometimes, though, she amazes me so much that I half wonder if she might be an alien because there's no way one person could do so much. That woman scares the shit out of me. She even tackled law school and finished in three years, all while giving her all to Rory and me.

She earned her Juris Doctor degree and is dedicated to ensuring that the students at Priya's school never face the same challenges she did. And watching her take down Sandford was incredible. My wife standing up for herself and our son was breathtaking. I wanted to jump in and defend her myself, but seeing her reclaim the narrative and show the world that even when you feel hopeless and overshadowed, you can still fight back—that was awe-inspiring. She's a remarkable role model, and her commitment to helping more girls and women in abusive relationships through pro bono cases is nothing short of extraordinary.

As for me, I'm gearing up for my final years in the NHL. Ever since I broke Gretzky's record, my body's not as quick to bounce back from the grueling games as it used to be, but the fire still burns bright. Each time I lace up my skates, I'm playing for my family. I'm still an idiot but one who's loved.

A piercing cry fills the air, and I turn to see Liora's mom stepping out from the back, cradling Mavie, our baby girl, in her arms. Eszter stands at the same height as my wife. Her gray-ish blonde hair falls in easy, natural waves around her face, and her bright blue eyes have a way of pulling you in. Even with the gentle signs of age, there's a classic elegance about her.

Mavie rases her hands, clearly crying for me.

"What did Granny do this time?" I tease, reaching out to take Mavie into my arms. She settles against my chest, her cries subsiding as I gently bounce her.

I look at her flushed chubby cheeks, those black curls that peek out from beneath a tiny blue hat that matches her adorable dress.

Eszter rolls her eyes, a playful smile on her lips. "Oh please. You know she loves me."

I chuckle, she does. "We all do."

Who couldn't love Eszter? She quickly became like a mother to me too. Her kindness and empathy are so genuine that she even manages to break through Rosalie's tough exterior. And she saved me from all of Oscar's babies. Liora transformed our home into a lush haven, and since Oscar has thrived into the largest plant I've ever seen, she's cultivated even more plants from him. Ezter collected all the new plants and gave them to her friends and colleagues as gifts. Thank fuck.

I press a soft kiss to Mavie's forehead. At a year old, she's already got us all wrapped around her tiny finger. Rory sidles up beside me, his gaze fixed on his baby sister.

"She's hungry," he says, a hint of concern in his voice.

"I got this, bud," I say. He's been nothing but protective since she got here. I never thought I'd be good at this, but hey, I've never dropped the baby!

The curtain rustles, and Liora emerges, a smile on her face. She looks breathtaking, the glow of a woman who knows she's exactly where she's meant to be. She makes her way over to us, pressing a tender kiss to Rory's forehead, then Mavie's, before finally meeting my lips with her own.

"Show me that tattoo," I murmur in between dodging Mavie's playful little punches. She's a daddy's girl through and through and doesn't like it when I kiss Mommy. But I'm a man obsessed. I could never stop.

Liora extends her wrist, revealing the freshly inked dates—our wedding day and Mavie's birthday—etched in delicate script alongside the other milestones that have shaped her life. They managed to make it look like a heart and it's lovely. Complete. I trace my finger over the raised skin, marveling at the incredible woman I get to call my wife.

"It's amazing. I love you," I whisper.

"I love you too. More than you could ever know."

I kiss her again. And as if on cue, Mavie cries and Rory cringes, saying, "Ew. You guys are gross."

Liora smiles up at me and I couldn't be a happier man.

Free Short Story

Want to know what it was like when Rory and Riley first met?

Download you FREE bonus story here!

Pre-order book two

Pre-order Playmates for a discount now! Don't miss out on those free bonus chapters and other pre-order goodies <3

get it here

get it here

Reviews are crucial for indie authors

Thank you so much for reading and taking a chance on this series. Reviews are crucial for indie authors. If you could take a moment to share your thoughts on Amazon and/or Goodreads, or just leave a rating, it would mean the world to me! Thank you immensely!

Love,
   Nova

About Nova Banks

Nova writes romance novels that delve into the lives of imperfect characters. Her stories offer a blend of swoon-worthy moments and a balance of hurt and comfort, but they all lead to a well-earned happily ever after!

Since childhood, she's been spinning tales in my imagination, and now, they're finally making their way onto the page. When she's not writing, you'll find her brewing yet another cup of coffee, drawing or tackling my never-ending TBR list. She loves anything romance and romantasy, particularly novels like "Fourth Wing" by Rebecca Yarros or anything with a hot book-boyfriend!

You can find here here: www.authornovabanks.com

Or connect with her on social media using the links below! She loves hearing from her readers.

Acknowledgments

Rinkmates means so much to me.

Drawing all these characters and bringing my imagination to life has been such a joy. I love writing, but I also have a passion for drawing, and self-publishing allows me to blend both of my favorite things. Thank you for reading and giving me the opportunity to live my dream.

Writing a novel is a journey that takes time, and I couldn't have done it without the incredible support of so many people. Thank you all from the bottom of my heart! A special shout-out to the readers—you're the ones who make this all possible. Thanks a million!

First and foremost, my deepest gratitude goes to my editor, Paisley McNab. This book wouldn't exist without you. English is my second language, and while I read and speak it often, I rely heavily on your proofreading expertise. Thank you SO much, Paisley, for helping me polish my baby! It was such a joy working with you on this project.

I also want to thank my best friend, Sarah, who is always my first reader and loves my books as if she wrote them herself. I couldn't have done this without you. To my sweet daughter, who patiently waited while I jotted down ideas or did a quick read-through—thank you for your understanding and the way you always love my drawings. And to Granny and Mom, who believed in me from the very start, your support means the world to me.

A huge thank you to Karen, my earliest writing collaborator and my personal bookipedia! You know everything about publishing, and I'm so grateful I can ask you thousands of questions every day and plot with you. You're the reason I started this self-publishing journey!

And finally, a special thanks to my amazing beta readers: Ida, Tabitha, Christana, Karen, Cri, Amelie, Megan, Natalie, and Jules! Your feedback made this book the way it is now! You shaped it and helped me with your feedback, your cheers, your kind words.

THANK you all!

With love,
    Nova

Copyright © 2024 by Nova Banks.

All rights reserved.

No part of this book may be reproduced in any form or by any electronic or mechanical means, including information storage and retrieval systems, without written permission from the author, except for the use of brief quotations in a book review.

This book is a work of fiction. Any resemblance to actual persons, living or dead, business establishments, events or locales, is entirely coincidental.

Cover Design by Nova Banks.

Character Art done by Nova Banks.

Internal typesetting done by Nova Banks, legal name Jennifer Tillmann.

Edits done by Paisley McNab (Perfectly Write)

Ebook ASIN: B0CW1792JT

Paperback: ISBN 9783950534641

Nova Banks, first printing 2024